7   210-232 Masons w
betw Mason & . John? C
Cutty ? No _ Knocks Mason
Frankie to take him to hosp, gives Cutty
$500 (killed). Taxi ⇒ Thornbanks

8 233-256
    Living with fear – but has advr
    B & D pension D to pubs in case Mason
all on his side.
        Ends laffing

147-8

The Big Man

Even M?t in G/N as I recall dies
(suffer +) will a minimum of prose
pages — + all-over conclus

The Big Man

William McIlvanney

HODDER AND STOUGHTON
LONDON SYDNEY AUCKLAND TORONTO

I can't accept home ownership 10 ref SL

British Library Cataloguing in Publication Data

McIlvanney, William
   The Big Man.
   I. Title
   823'.914[F]   PR6063.A237

   ISBN 0-340-36689-3

For Siobhàn

What is a rebel? A man who
says no: but whose refusal
does not imply a renunciation.
ALBERT CAMUS

1

'Look,' one of the three boys in a field said as the white Mercedes slid, silenced by distance, in and out of view along the road. The boy had bright red hair which the teachers at his school had learned to dread appearing in their classrooms for it meant mischief, a spark of social arson.

'A shark. A great white.'

His two companions looked where his finger pointed and caught the melodrama of the gesture. The one who was holding the greyhound said, 'Kill, Craigie Boy, kill,' and the big, brindled dog barked and lolloped on the leash. The red-haired boy started imitating the theme music from the film *Jaws* and the other two joined in. Their voices hurried to crescendo as they saw the car disappearing over the top of a hill.

The car moved on under a sky where some cloud-racks looked like canyons leading to infinity and others were dissolving islands. There, floating in the air, were the dreams of some mad architect, wild, fantasticated structures that darkness would soon demolish. They were of a variousness you couldn't number.

'Five,' the biggest man in the car said. He was called Billy Fleming. He spoke without expression. His face looked mean enough to grudge giving away a reaction.

There was no immediate response from the other two. A boring journey had made reactions in the car sluggish. Each was in his own thoughts like a sleeping-bag.

'Five what?' the driver said after a time, thinking it wouldn't be long until he needed the lights. His name was Eddie Foley.

'Dead crows. That's five Ah've counted. Two on the road. Three at the side of it. They should take out insurance. What are they? Deaf or daft? Always pickin' on passin' cars.'

They came to a village called Blackbrae. The council houses at the edge of it, badly weathered but with well-kept gardens, led on to private houses lined briefly along each side of the street. These sat slightly further off the road, solidly and unelaborately built. Designed less to please the eye than persuade it to look elsewhere, they were squat fortresses of privacy. It was hard to imagine much vanity in possessing them. Yet the meticulous paintwork or the hanging plant in a doorway or the coach-lamp on the wall beside a recently added porch suggested a pleased possessiveness. The names, too, had a cosy complacency. There was Niaroo and Dunromin and, incredibly enough, Nirvana. A passer-by might have wondered at how modest the dreams had been that had found their fulfilment here.

The street turned left towards a hill that climbed back into the countryside. Changing gears, Eddie Foley hesitated in neutral and gently braked.

'I think we're lost,' he said. 'Did Fast Frankie mention this place?'

'Has anybody ever?' Billy Fleming asked from the back seat.

'Ask,' the third man in the car said.

At the top of the hill a small obelisk with a railing round it was outlined against the sky. On a bench beside it two men sat and a third stood with his foot on the bench, nodding towards the others. In the hollow of the hill, where the car was, there were mainly closed shops. A building that claimed to have been a garage was empty and derelict. Asphalt patches in front of it might have been where the pumps were. The owner's name was a conundrum of missing letters – Macsomething. The only indication of life between them and the men at the top of the hill was outside the Mayfair Café. The name was carried on a white electric sign, not yet lit, projecting from the wall. The letters declaring the name were slightly smaller than those beneath, which announced a brand of cigarettes, so that it was as if the identity of this place, obviously a focal point of the village, was dependent on a company that had no connections here.

Five teenagers were standing outside the café, two boys and three girls. One of the boys, the smaller one, was doing an intricate but very contained soft-shoe shuffle with his hands out, palms towards his friends. He was wearing jeans and a black tee-shirt, sleeves rolled up to show his biceps. The others were laughing. Eddie Foley put the car in gear, eased along the kerb towards them and stopped. He loosened his seat-belt, leaned across the empty passenger seat and pressed a button. The window hummed down slowly enough for the group on the pavement to become aware of it. The dancer gave his friends a theatrical display of amazement and leaned down towards the open window.

'That was terrific, mister,' he said. 'Could ye do it again?'

'Thornbank?' Eddie Foley said.

'Naw,' the dancer said. 'My name's Wilson.'

'I'm looking for Thornbank.'

'If ye give us a lift, we'll take ye.'

'It's either right or left or straight on,' one of the girls said.

The wit of it crippled the others with laughter. They leaned helplessly on one another and the girl herself had to admit how good it was, her pink hair coming to rest on the shoulder of the taller boy. Eddie Foley pressed the button and the window went up as the car moved off.

'The natives don't seem very friendly,' he said.

'Maybe we shoulda brought some coloured beads,' Billy Fleming said.

'Children,' the third man said, 'grow up into shites quicker every year.'

He was a small man with thinning hair. He wore nice rings and he had grey eyes that were so cold the flecks in them could have been crushed ice. He was Matt Mason.

Eddie Foley took the car up the hill and stopped across the road from the three men at the bench. He got out of the car and went over to them. Two of them looked about forty. The one with his foot on the bench must have been over sixty. He was the one who spoke.

'Yes, sir. Can we help ye?'

'I'm looking for Thornbank.'

'Ye're well out yer way here,' one of the men on the bench said. 'Where ye comin' from?'

'Glasgow.'

'Ye woulda been better holding the dual carriageway tae outside Ayr,' the third man said.

'Ye're wrong, Rab,' the older man said.

In the car Matt Mason and Billy Fleming watched but couldn't hear what was being said. They saw the conspiratorial noddings of the three men before they formed into an advisory committee for Eddie. They saw the pointing gestures, one of the seated men standing up and doing an elaborate mime of directions. They saw Eddie nodding towards the obelisk. In the soft light of late evening the scene had a simple dignity, four men silhouetted against the vastness of the sky in a mime of small preoccupations.

'What's he doing?' Matt Mason said. 'Getting a history of the place?'

Eddie came back across and got in the car. He waved as he drove away and the three men waved back.

'Ah know where we're goin' now,' he said. 'They were nice men.'

'We're not here to socialise,' Matt Mason said.

'That was a monument they were sittin' beside. To the men from the village. Died in the First and Second World Wars. One of them was holdin' somethin'. Some kinda tool. Ah hadny a clue what it was for. Imagine that. Ye would think ye would know what it was for. Ah mean, this isny Mars.'

'Is it not?' Billy Fleming said and glanced across at Matt Mason for confirmation of his sneer.

Matt Mason looked back at him and then looked down at Billy Fleming's trainer shoe resting on the back of the driving seat. The foot came off the seat and rested on the floor. Billy Fleming checked that the fawn upholstery wasn't marked.

The black and white trainer shoes were part of a strange ensemble. They were topped by jeans and then a black polo-neck cashmere sweater, over which he wore an expensive-looking grey mohair jacket. It gave him an appearance as dual as a centaur. Above, he was a kind of sophistication; below, he was all roughness and readiness to scuffle. The face linked the two: a bland superciliousness overlaid features that bore the traces of impromptu readjustment.

'Ah was goin' to ask what it was,' Eddie said. 'That tool thing. But Ah felt such a mug, Ah didn't bother.'

Neither of the other two responded, and Eddie pursued the subject in his mind. The strange object the man had held and the solemnity in the darkening air of those names carved on the obelisk – names he imagined would mean much to most people in the village – had combined to make him feel what strangers they were here, the carelessness of their coming, rough and sudden as a raiding-party. He had sensed in the talk with them a formed and complicated life about the place, a strong awareness among them of who they were, mysterious yet coherent with a coherence he couldn't understand. It was an uncomfortable feeling, as if he were a hick from the city.

The atmosphere in the car intensified the feeling. They seemed to be travelling within where they had come from. The plush upholstery appeared foreign to the places they were passing through. With the exception of Billy's jeans and trainers, their city clothes would have looked out of place outside, as if they had come dressed for the wrong event. The smoke from Matt Mason's cigar surrounded them, cocooning them in themselves.

Negotiating the winding ways, Eddie felt himself subject to the unexpected nature of events, the way an outcrop of land suddenly threw the road to the left, the recalcitrance of a hill. These roads were less invention than discovery. They weren't merely asphalt conveyor belts along which sealed capsules fired people from one identity to the next as if they had dematerialised in the one place and rematerialised in the other. These roads made you notice them, rushed trees towards you, flung them over your shoulder, laid out a valley, flicked a flight of birds into your vision. They made Eddie aware of a countryside his ignorance of which was beginning to oppress him with questions that baffled him. What kind of people would live in that isolated farm on the hill? What kind of trees were they?

'Flowers,' he said suddenly. 'The names of flowers. Ah always wanted to know a bit about that. Ah canny tell one from another. That's true. Ah've got bother tellin' a daisy from a dandelion.'

'Six,' Billy Fleming said. 'That was a cracker. Only thing that wasn't mashed tae a pulp was its beak. Definately the prize-winner.'

Eddie became aware of Matt Mason's silence. He had learned to be wary of that silence. He decided to push his misgivings aside. He was here on a job for Matt Mason. It wouldn't do to confuse his loyalties.

'Fast Frankie's not too hot on the directions,' he said, re-identifying himself with the other two and their purposes. 'Ah hope his information's more reliable. Ye think the big man's what he says he is?'

'Frankie thinks he is,' Matt Mason said, and remembered the time in the Old Scotia with Frankie talking.

Fast Frankie White was a handsome quick-eyed man with a smile as selective as a roller-towel. He had been born in Thornbank – so he should know what he was talking about – and had left it by way of petty theft. He still went back there from time to time, usually when he was in trouble, to wrap his widowed mother's house round him like a bandage. He often said more than it was wise to believe but in the Old Scotia he had sounded convincing.

'Okay. Ye've got a decision to make. Fast. Ah know. But Ah'm tellin' ye. He's yer man. No question. Ah've known him for years. He's the man ye're lookin' for. And easily worked. A big, straight man. Straight as a die. That's what ye need, isn't it? Honesty's the best raw material in the world. Especially the poor kind. He's gold for you, Matt. A rough nugget, certainly. But you could shape him into anything ye want. What's he got in Thornbank? What's anybody got in Thornbank? He's on his uppers. Been idle for months. Used to work in the pits. How many pits are there now? Was working up at Sullom Voe for a while. But the wife didn't fancy the separation. See, that's the secret. That's how you're goin' to get him. He's a great family man. An' what's he providin' for his wife and weans? You can offer him a way to do that. He'll bite, Matt. Ah'm tellin' ye, he'll bite. And once he's got a taste, ye'll have him for good. An' all they're goin' to be able to do . . . With this man? Come on!'

Matt Mason remembered the image of Frankie with his arms crossed in front of him. He had swung his arms apart, hands up, with the brightness and activity of the pub behind him. It was the gesture of surrender we're supposed to make when faced with a gun.

'Different class,' Frankie White had said.

In the almost dark a pit-bing loomed on their right. It was overgrown with rough grass, a man-made parody of a hill. The despoliation of the countryside around them made them feel more at home. Inside the car they enlivened into a conversation.

'Not long now,' Eddie said. 'If he's that good, what's he doin' living in a place like this?'

Matt Mason smiled to himself.

'Maybe he likes the quiet life.'

'He better learn not to like it then,' Billy Fleming said.

'We'll find out how good he is,' Matt Mason said.

Eddie put the lights on.

'He'll maybe not come,' he said.

'Same time every Sunday, Frankie says,' Matt Mason said.

'The Red Lion,' Eddie said.

'Funny name for a hotel,' Billy Fleming said. 'Ye wonder who thinks them up.'

The arrival of darkness had welded them into a group with a unified purpose. The variousness of the countryside was obliterated. It could have been anywhere. There was only the familiar interior of the car and the headlights blow-torching their own path through the night. Matt Mason looked at his watch.

'We'll be in good time,' he said. He looked across at Billy Fleming. 'You ready?'

'Born ready.'

In the dim light he looked as if he might be telling the truth. The big shoulders seemed to be filling most of the back seat of the car. The face, planing intermittently out of obscurity, looked relentless as a statue. He carefully took off his wrist-watch and wrapped it in a handkerchief and put it in his jacket pocket.

Everybody knows and doesn't know a Thornbank. It's one of those places you've driven through and never been there. It occurs in conversations like parentheses. 'It took us four hours to get there,' someone says, 'and the kids were fractious after two miles. We went the Thornbank road.' Hearing it mentioned, outsiders who know of it may still have to think briefly to relocate it. It's the kind of place people get a fix on by association with the nearest big town, knowing it as a lost suburb of somewhere else.

In Thornbank's case the big town is Graithnock, the industrial hardness of which dominates the soft farmland of the Ayrshire countryside around it. Graithnock is a town friendly and rough, like a brickie's handshake. It is built above rich coalfields which have long since run out, ominously.

By the time the coal was gone, Graithnock hardly noticed because it had other things to do: there was whisky-distilling and heavy engineering and the shoe factory and later the making of farm machinery. But the shoe factory closed and the world-famous engineering plant was bought by Americans and mysteriously run down and the making of farm machinery was transferred to France and the distillery didn't seem to be doing so well.

Not much in the way of coherent explanation filtered as far as the streets. At meetings and on television men who looked as if they had taken lessons in sincerity read from the book of economic verbiage, the way priests used to dispense the Bible in Latin to the illiterate. All the workers understood was that there were dark and uncontrollable forces to which everyone was subject, and some were more subject than others. When the haphazardly organised industrial action failed, they took their redundancy money and some went on holiday to Spain and some drank too much for a while and they all felt the town turn sour on itself around them.

For, like John Henry, Graithnock had been born to work. It was what it knew how to do. It was the achievement it threw back into the face of its own bleakness. It liked its pleasures, and some of them were rough, but the joy of them was that they had been earned. The men who had thronged its pubs in its heyday were noisy and sometimes crude and sometimes violent, but they knew they were stealing from nobody. Every laugh had been paid in sweat. The man who had embarrassed himself in drink the night before would turn up next morning where the job was and work like a gang of piece-work navvies.

When there was nowhere for him to turn up, what could he do? Like so many of the towns of the industrial West of Scotland, Graithnock had offered little but the means to work. It had exemplified the assumption that working men are workers. Let them work. In the meantime, other people could get on with the higher things, what they liked to call 'culture'. At the same time, the workers had made a culture of their own. It was raw. It was sentimental songs at spontaneous parties, half-remembered poems that were admitted into no

16

academic canon of excellence, anecdotes of doubtful social taste, wild and surrealistic turns of phrase, bizarre imaginings that made Don Quixote look like a bank clerk, a love of whatever happened without hypocrisy. In Graithnock that secondary culture had been predominant. While in the local theatre successive drama companies died in ways that J. B. Priestley and Agatha Christie and Emlyn Williams never intended, the pub-talk flourished, the stories were oral novels and the songs would have burst Beethoven's eardrums if he hadn't already been deaf. But it was all dependent on money. Even pitch-and-toss requires two pennies.

When the money went, Graithnock turned funny but not so you would laugh. It had always had a talent for violence and that violence had always had its mean and uglier manifestations. Besides the stand-up fights between disgruntled men, there had been the knives and the bottles and the beatings of women. The difference now was that contempt for such behaviour was less virulent and less widespread. Something like honour, something as difficult to define and as difficult to live decently without, had gone from a lot of people's sense of themselves. Sudden treachery in fights had assumed the status of a modern martial art, rendering bravery and strength and speed and endurance as outmoded as a crossbow. An old woman could be mugged in a park, an old man tied and tortured in his home for the sake of a few pounds, five boys could beat up a sixth, a girl be raped because she was alone, the houses of the poor be broken into as if they had been mansions. This was not an epidemic. Few people were capable of these actions but those who weren't were also significantly less capable of a justly held condemnation. That instinctive moral strength that had for so long kept the financial instability of working-class life still humanly habitable, like a tent pitched on a clifftop but with guy-ropes of high-tensile steel, had surely weakened.

Theorists rode in from time to time from their outposts of specialisation, bearing news that was supposed to make all clear. Television was setting bad examples. Society had become materialistic. Schools had abdicated authority. The hydrogen bomb was everyone's neurosis. What was certain was that Graithnock didn't know itself as clearly any more.

Even physically, the town had been not so much changed

as disfigured. Never a handsome place, it had had at its centre some fine old buildings that had some history. They were demolished and where they had been rose a kind of monumental slum they called a shopping precinct. As a facelift that has failed leaves someone looking out from nobody's face in particular so Graithnock had become a kind of nowhere fixed in stone. The most characteristic denizens of its new precinct, like the ghosts of industry past, were alcoholics and down-and-outs.

Thornbank, as the child copes with the parents' problems, was suffering too. A lot of the redundancies from Graithnock had come here. But there were apparent differences. The same television programmes reached Thornbank, the schools had much the same problems, the hydrogen bomb had been heard of there too. But a stronger and continuing sense of identity remained. One reason was, perhaps, its size. It was a place where people vaguely felt they knew nearly everybody else. This absence of anonymity meant that in Thornbank they were often, paradoxically, more tolerant of nonconformism than people might have been in bigger places. Difference was likely to become eccentricity before it could develop anti-social tendencies.

There was in the small town, for example, a group of punks, working-class schismatics who had seceded from their parents' acceptance of middle-class conventions. Their changing hair colours, purples, greens and mauves, their earrings that were improvised from various objects, their clothes that looked as if they were acting in several plays at once, all of them bad, were not admired. But they were mainly confronted with a slightly embarrassed tolerance, like a horrendous case of acne. Of Big Andy, who led a local punk group called Animal Farm and whose Mohican haircut stood six-feet-three above the ground and seemed to change colour with his mood, it was often mentioned in mitigation that his Uncle Jimmy had been a terrible fancy dresser. Genes, the implication was, were not to be denied.

This communal sense of identity found its apotheosis in a few local people. Thornbank knew itself most strongly through them. They were as fixed as landmarks in the popular consciousness. If two expatriates from that little town had been talking and one of them mentioned the name of one of that handful of people, no further elaboration would have been necessary. They would have known themselves twinned. Those names were worn by Thornbank like an unofficial coat of arms. These were people to whom no civic monuments would ever be erected. They were too maverick for that. Part of their quality was precisely that they had never courted acceptance, refused to make a career of what they were. They were simply, and with an innocent kind of defiance, themselves.

There was Mary Barclay. She was in her seventies and fragile as bell metal. They called her Mary the Communist and although nearly everyone in the town thought Communism something historically discredited, a bit like thalidomide, the epithet as it applied to her carried no opprobrium. It wasn't that the term defined her so much as she qualified the term. She was Marx's witness for the defence in Thornbank. Her life had been an unsanctimonious expression of concern for others. While helping everybody she could, she had also helped herself without inhibition to what in life injured nobody else. She had lived with three men and married none. She had buried the one who died on her, decently, and been loving to her two daughters who, as far as anybody knew, had never reproached her. She was who she was and you could take it or leave it, but you would have been a fool to leave it.

There was Davie Dykes, known as Davie the Deaver, which meant if you listened long enough he would talk you deaf. But it was mainly good talk. He told elaborate and highly inventive lies. Each day he reconstructed his own genealogy. His ancestry was legion. At sixty, he still refused to be circumscribed by his circumstances. Here was just a route to anywhere.

There was Dan Scoular. His place in the local pantheon was more mysterious. He was young for such elevation, thirty-three. His most frequently commented on talent was a simple one. He could knock people unconscious very quickly, frequently with one punch. It wasn't easy to see why such a minimal ability and of such limited application should have earned him so much status. It was true that Thornbank, like a lot of small places which may feel themselves rendered insignificant by the much-publicised wonders of the bigger world, had a legendising affection for anything local that was in any way remarkable. There were those who kept a Thornbank version of *The Guinness Book of Records*: the heaviest child that had been born here, the fastest runner in the town, the man who had been arrested most for breach of the peace. But that hardly explained that converging ambience of something achieved and possibilities to come in which Dan Scoular moved for them.

Their name for him was, perhaps, a clue. They called him 'the big man'. It was an expression used of other men in the town, of course. But if the words were used out of any explanatory context, they meant Dan Scoular. Though he was six-feet-one, the implications were more than physical. They meant stature in some less definable sense. They had to do with his being, they suspected, in some way more inviolate than themselves, more autonomously himself. They had to do, perhaps most importantly, with the generosity and ease with which they felt he inhabited what was special about himself, his refusal to abuse a gift or turn it unfairly to his own advantage. For he could be quietly kind.

Yet the image the people of Thornbank had of him was false. They had mythologised his past and falsified his present. They had made him over into something that they wanted him to be. 'He's never picked on anybody in his life,' was a remark so often made in Thornbank in relation to Dan Scoular that it had acquired a seeming immutability, like a rubric carved on a plinth. It was a lie. It conveniently excised from public recollection a few years of his youth when his prodigious capacity for aggression had functioned on his whim and no casual encounter in a pub or at a dance was safe from its explosive arbitrariness.

'He's never looked at another woman,' the oral history said. Perhaps they should have asked his wife Betty, an attractive and spirited woman, about that.

'He's his own man, that one,' was a refrain that no one contradicted. But it was more an appearance than a fact. Dan Scoular didn't know who he was. He felt daily that people were giving him back a sense of him that in no way matched what was going on. His statue didn't fit.

But what they needed him to be they had partly accustomed him to pretend to be. He meant something in the life of

Thornbank and he tried to live inside that meaning as best he could, like a somnambulist pacing out someone else's dream. They looked to him to confirm that things were more or less all right. If he was as he had been, living along among them, coping quietly, things couldn't be that bad. Like the Mount Parish Church clock, he was a familiar fixture by which they checked how things were going. Like that notoriously erratic timepiece, he was misleading. Thornbank was in no better state than Graithnock. It was just less aware of its condition. Dan Scoular was becoming desperately aware of his.

Failing marriages are haunted. They have lost the will for mastery of the present and the future looms as re-enactment of the past. Every day is full of the ghosts of other days, most of them emitting unassuaged rancour at small and large betrayals. New possibilities drown in their lamentations.

That Sunday Betty had wakened first. She heard the voices of the boys downstairs, beginning the statutory quarrel. The sound pulled at her mind like a tether: did you imagine your thoughts could wander off for a moment by themselves? She wondered briefly if their noise had wakened her or if they had been waiting poised like demonic actors, cued into automatic conflict by her consciousness. She rose and put on her housecoat, careful not to waken Dan. It wasn't something done out of consideration but because it postponed the time when they would have to talk. That was the first small, renewed betrayal, confirmation of where they had come. It was a message in code, delivered to him though he was asleep. He would understand it when he woke.

As she crossed to find her slippers under the dressing-table, the noise downstairs subsided to a civilised murmur and she paused, having lost her motive for getting out of bed. She knelt in front of the mirror, picked up the hairbrush and made a couple of passes at her hair. She noticed herself in the glass and stopped. She was aware of the dishevelled heap of Dan's body on the bed, reflected from behind her. It was perhaps his humped image beside her face which triggered the memory.

'And I'd also like to thank my own parents. Apart from the obvious trick they pulled in bringing me about. Although I have it on very good authority that Mrs Davidson isn't too sure that's how it happened. She still thinks I fell off the back of a lorry.' (There was the kind of laughter people laugh at public events, as if a joke were a charity auction and they want to be seen to be bidding.) 'But apart from that. I'd like to thank my parents for what they did as soon as they realised Betty and me were getting married. They stopped taking any money from me for my keep. It's helped us a lot. They decided we needed all the money we could get to set up our own house. We'd both like to thank them for that. Mind you, I think they were beginning to get panicky towards the end there. I think they thought we were gonny have a seven-year engagement. Ah mean. I think they feel they're not so much losing a son. They're losing a liability. For the past year or so, if we'd been a Red Indian family . . .' (titters greeting amazing concept) '. . . where they've got funny names like Running Bear and Running Water. The only appropriate one for me would've been Running Sore.' (Total surrender to helpless mirth, corpulent uncles having cardiac arrests and aunties squawking like parakeets getting plucked alive.) 'Anyway, my wife and I . . .' (Stamping of feet, whistling, applause.)

It had been something like that. That was how Betty remembered it. Apart from having been there at the time (although she sometimes wondered if it was really herself who had been there), she had, the day before, found the piece of paper on which Dan had made the notes for his speech. She had remembered how much he had wanted to get that speech right, his nervous determination. He knew her parents' disapproval of him and the superciliousness of some of her aunts and uncles. He had felt like the champion of his 'side', not about to let them down, ready to demonstrate that he could string a few words together. He had made the best speech of the wedding and then almost undone his success by quarrelling in the lavatory with one of her cousins, who had expressed amazement at how well Dan had spoken. She heard later from an outraged uncle that Dan's immediate response had been, 'I'm not amazed at your amazement. The next time you get anything right'll be your first.'

Betty had been looking for the insurance policy for the house contents the day before when she had come across that folded, scuffed and fading piece of paper. She had opened it out carelessly and it had hit her like a jack-in-the-box with a knife. She had read it slowly, her stomach feeling slightly mushy with guilt, for in the words she sensed a confident assertion that was like a contract they had both failed to keep. She had remembered the moment when those words were said.

She remembered that moment now, as she knelt at her dressing-table mirror: 'My wife and I . . .' Staring at herself, she saw that other face, as if her past were a helpless spirit hovering over her present. In retrospect, the brocade wedding-dress and veil seemed somehow preposterous, a grotesquely ornamental, weird costume for a part nobody knew how to play. They gave you a few lines of ritual dialogue that came from God knows what lexicon of antiquated male prejudice and the rest of your life was endless improvisation, entirely up to the two of you.

She saw Dan standing making his speech, confidently belying his nervousness, herself sitting in demure white, the audience looking on, seeing what they wanted to see. As she remembered it, they both seemed to her, in a simple and not very dramatic way, sacrificial. She remembered a joke she had heard somewhere about married people, comparing them to swimmers in freezing water, shouting, 'Come on in. The water's great.' 'My wife and I . . .' It didn't seem to her to be imagination that she could remember a slightly derisive tone to some of the applause.

Watching her face without make-up, she remembered an expression that had fascinated her as a girl. She had always applied it to herself in the third person, making herself in her mind into the woman she imagined she might become. 'She put on her face.' The statement now seemed to her utterly apposite, an ambition that had closed around her like a trap. She put on her face. The face she had remembered in its veil was somehow lost, hadn't merely changed.

These days she built an alternative in front of her mirror, created a role as self-consciously as an actress might with stage make-up: the wife. In some way that threatened the convincingness of her performance, it wasn't truly her. Staring at herself, she vaguely felt that the accretions of experience she saw there weren't an expression of her at all. They were a denial of some basic potential in her. Perhaps what we see in

23

older people, she thought, are the complex stances and tics they have developed in response to the reactions to their original selves – not them so much as the camouflage they have had to become.

'Leave it alone!' Raymond shouted. 'Or you're gettin' battered.'

As Betty straightened up, she heard a knee crack like a reminder of human frailty, a warning that she had better try to realise herself before it was too late. But the awareness was smothered at birth. She put on her slippers and they might as well have been bindings for her feet, so much they hobbled her to the day's limitations. By the time she reached the bottom of the stairs, she had become 'the mother'.

Raymond and young Danny were quarrelling over the pack of cards. Her arrival encouraged them to push their respective attitudes towards caricature. Raymond became innocently preoccupied in laying out the cards, his monkish dedication astonished at her arrival. 'Oh, hello, Mum.' Danny's arms went out in outrage at the cruelty of man's ways. 'Mum!' She felt she couldn't face their trivial intensity at this time of the day. But Danny jumped up and danced before her eyes like a midge with messianic delusions ('Those who are not for me are against me').

'Mum! He's playin' patience!'

'Shurrup. So what?' Raymond said.

'Two canny play patience. Ya bam!'

'You said you didn't want to play.' Raymond was now using carefully formal English, showing his mother how calm he was, how full of rectitude.

'Ah said Ah didn't want to play whist. But there's other games.'

'That's right. Patience.'

'Ah said Ah would play rummy.'

'I'm not playin' rummy. You don't play right. You don't even know the rules. You make a run outa clubs and spades and everything. You're daft.'

Danny kicked away Raymond's line of cards and Raymond lunged to hit him and Betty screamed, 'Raymond! The two of you! Shut up! For God's sake, shut your mouths!' They both looked at her in a shocked way, as if they had just discovered that their mother was mad. Her own next remark made Betty think they might be right.

'What've you had to eat, the two of you?' she asked and couldn't herself see how that related to the problem.

'We had flakes,' Danny said in passing. 'Ye know what he did, Mum? He stopped playin' because Ah was winnin'. Ye did so!'

'Did not.'

'Did sot.'

'Not.'

'Sot.'

'Not, not, not.'

'Sot, sot, sot, sot, sot. Sot, sot. Sot, sot, sot –'

'Danny! Stop! Stop, Danny!'

In the silence she gathered up the cards and put them on the mantelpiece.

'Aw, Mum!' from Raymond.

She resentfully made them a breakfast of sausage and egg and toast, salving her rebellious conscience by making them lay the table. She tried not to let her affections take sides. But Raymond was so unfairly arrogant, playing his age advantage against Danny. He was thirteen against ten and he used those three years as a brutal birthright. His darkness of hair seemed to her for the moment sinister. Danny, still fair like herself, seemed an aggressed-on innocent, a small boy who sometimes gave the heart-wrenching impression that life was for him like jaywalking at Le Mans. She had a weakness for his passionate desire for justice, even when it was totally misguided.

While she fed them, she remembered an incident last year. She and Dan had been sitting in the house when Danny had rushed in from playing football in the street outside. His cheeks were florid from exertion and his eyes flamed with intensity.

'Dad! Dad!' he had been calling from the outside door.

He arrived in the room like the bearer of the news the world had been waiting for.

'Dad, Dad! Ah told the boys you would know the answer.'

Dan had glanced up from his paper.

'Twenty-two,' he said.

'Naw, naw. Listen, Dad. Andrew got hit in the face wi' the ball.'

Dan looked at her and rolled his eyes.

'Hit in the face wi' the ball!' Danny said.

'In the face,' Dan said. 'With the ball. Correct.'

'All right. He was goin' to tackle Michael. And Michael lashed it. He really thumped it. An' it hit Andrew right in the face. Full force.'

'Amazin',' Dan said.

'Naw. But listen, Dad. Is it a foul?'

Dan started to laugh.

'What d'ye mean?'

'Is it a foul?'

'How can it be a foul?'

'But it hit him right in the face!'

'Danny! It's not a foul. Because the ball hits somebody in the face. It's mebbe an accident. But it's not a foul.'

Betty remembered Danny's disappointment and then the hope that rekindled his eyes, the counsel for the defence who has found the incontrovertible point of law.

'But, Dad,' he said. 'Andrew's cryin'. He's really roarin'.'

While Dan explained that tears didn't make a foul, Betty thought she had glimpsed the core of Danny and remembered why she loved him so much. He believed that circumstances had to yield to feeling. He was such a lover that he couldn't understand why the deepest feeling didn't make the rules. As Danny trailed disconsolately back out the house to announce the bad news from the adult world, Betty felt a compassion for him that was out of all proportion to a football match.

It was perhaps that memory that determined how she would decide when Raymond picked up the cards from the mantelpiece as soon as he had finished eating. He was about to play patience again.

'Raymond,' she said. 'What are you doing?'

'Ah'm goin' to play at cards.'

'With Danny?'

'No way. Danny's a diddy.'

The venom of it annoyed her.

'No he's not,' she said. 'You want to play, Danny?'

'Uh-huh.' Danny put his last piece of toast in his mouth and crossed towards Raymond. Raymond threw the cards on to the floor. Danny painstakingly picked them up.

'Right, Raymond,' Betty said. 'You don't want to play with Danny, you don't want to play. But just make sure you leave him alone.'

She heard Dan coming downstairs as Raymond brushed past her. When she went into the kitchen, Dan was standing, wearing only a pair of old trousers and looking drowsily into a packet of cornflakes as if there was a message there he must decipher. His rumpled presence somehow provoked her and one of those familiar quarrels over nothing already hung in the air around them. The rules for such quarrels were that the cause of them should be irrelevant and that the venom they evoked should be out of all proportion. Raymond had exiled himself to the back green and she could hear him kicking a ball steadily against the wall of the house as if he was trying to tell her something. Danny was pretending to play with the cards that had caused the trouble but he had put the television on. Dan shook the cornflake packet and its contents rustled faintly. The sound made her grit her teeth.

'Oh-ho,' Dan said. 'No cornflakes.'

He said it gently enough but it was audible.

'There's some in it. I can hear them,' Betty said.

Dan pulled open the packet and held it towards her.

'If ye've got a microscope, Ah'll show ye them.'

'You normally take cornflakes for your supper?'

'It's ten past ten.'

'The money I'm getting, we're lucky we've got bread.'

He crushed the packet with unnecessary force and put it in the bin.

'Your period due?' he said.

It was the remark that rendered any mediating sanity powerless to intervene, the unfair reprisal that escalated the conflict. Until then she would have been herself inclined to admit that he was the offended party to begin with, but his spite had wakened to the possibilities quickly enough and she was content that the war was on, both sides wheeling out their weaponry.

They traversed some familiar ground, littered with the dead of old campaigns. Her contempt was loud for his need to relate any recriminations of hers to the menstrual cycle, as if having a womb precluded having a mind. He touched again on how she made a crisis out of every casual conversation, saw deliberate attacks in accidental gestures. The structure of the day was set, an expression of the complex of devious failures and abandoned possibilities and secret chambers of hurt where their lost hopes lived alone.

The fact that they weren't going anywhere that day seemed simple enough. But behind it lay a reminder that they had recently had to sell the second-hand car. Just staying in the house compounded her frustration at the way they had to live, his sense of how he was failing them. Lunch was communication through the boys.

When he took Raymond and Danny out the back to play with the ball in the afternoon, she sat indoors with her coffee, reading her own alternative text in the glossy magazine she leafed through. It was how she might have been living, somewhere among those advertisements. She wouldn't have minded that but the text between adverts depressed her, suggested that perhaps the price was too high. The bright preoccupied tone, so full of blind assurance, was like a more intellectual version of her mother set in type.

She thought about her mother. Were daughters condemned to fulfil their mothers' worst fears for them as punishment for disobedience? But then her mother's fears for her had been so chameleon that they would have been able to fit in with whatever habitat Betty had chosen, found a niche there and been ready to feed on any stray passing thoughts of hers, as now. Protectively, Betty reminded herself of her mother's desperately self-limiting philosophy, like a cage to keep her in. It was the cage she had kept herself in.

Her mother had known things with a certainty beyond the power of reason to refute. She had known that housework put off is housework doubled. She had known that you would see things differently when you were older. She had known that a girl shouldn't cheapen herself, steam irons never get the job done properly, once a Catholic always a Catholic, educate a girl you educate a family, some men only want the one thing, if she had her life to live again she would do it differently, you're only a virgin once, nobody needs to be out at two in

28

the morning, they should hang them, the truth never hurt anyone, marry in haste, repent at leisure and Dan Scoular wasn't good enough for her daughter.

She had also been a very good cook and baker and the house had always been tidy, very tidy, but Betty honestly couldn't remember when her mother had touched her spontaneously. She could recall her mother kissing her goodnight but that was a ritual, something she had decided you were supposed to do, not an unrehearsed act of affection. When she thought of her mother, and she had often tried so hard to do it justly, she thought of that voice like a barking dog forbidding the world to come near her. She thought of *One Thousand and One Nights* of clichés, of a Scheherazade whose frenetic variety of repetitions was not a postponement of death but of life, a charm against the dread of coming alive.

And her father had fallen in love with that ability. She thought of the way he used to raise his eyebrows and shrug, as if in conspiracy with Betty's outrage, but really – she had realised how many times since – in conspiracy with her mother. In return for those utterances neither of them could possibly believe, he was given his status, his small, imagined kingship of the house. Betty was, she had slowly and painfully come to realise, irrelevant here. A two-way charade was in progress. Nobody else knew the rules.

Dan Scoular had been an innocent intruder. She remembered them talking to her after his first time in the house, when he was gone. Quietness had been the first thing, her mother moving about and doing things only she could have imagined needed done, her father in soulful conclave with the gas-fire. They were talking to each other with silence and she was excluded, except insofar as she was meant to understand that she had somehow failed them. Their silence was hurt, deep shock which she was supposed to realise she was responsible for.

That night a lot of scattered misgivings about the way she and her parents lived had come together for her, and from them she had begun to make a kind of credo for herself. Her relationship with Dan had already given her an alternative sense of herself, an awareness of her own worth that contradicted her mother's dismissive criticisms, which ranged from

29

the way she dressed to her inability to cook. But the most painful forms those criticisms took were their trivial, momentary manifestations. It might be the way she had thrown down a magazine or the way she was sitting or a look she was supposed to have given. Her mother seemed capable of arranging endless ambushes in which Betty was taken by surprise and robbed of her self-esteem. Dan restored to her a more balanced sense of herself. His appreciation of her was like a constantly repeated present.

That night, after he had gone, that sense of herself remained with her. His absence had stayed stronger than their presence, had enabled her not to become a part of her parents' strange ritual but to maintain her own perspective on it and, with a quiet dismay, understand what was really happening. Her mother had eventually stopped fussing around and sat down across the fire from her father.

The atmosphere was one with which she was familiar. Sometimes, coming in from a night out, she had been invited into the lounge to sit with her parents and their friends. The invitation was usually extended with an elaborately insistent generosity, a privilege self-consciously granted.

They all sat around with their drinks, playing a game Betty had decided to call pass-the-bromide. The reek of complacency in the room was as strong as formaldehyde. She used to wonder if they changed their smiles daily with the flowers. If anything strange were mentioned as having happened, the shock of it was quickly neutered to surprise by common consent.

The only displays of strong emotion she had seen among them took a careful stylised form and seemed triggered by a pre-determined set of values. What was happening outside the immediate range of their own lives was disarmed, could provide no trigger for deep feeling. Things like the rates, the iniquity of conveyancing or the shabbiness of modern workmanship were rich in potential for long, heartfelt diatribes.

Once she had watched a neighbour come apart slowly and with dignity in her parents' lounge. She cried for several minutes, her mascara spiking the rims of her eyes. Betty's mother had gone across to comfort the woman. The others looked on in sympathy. It would have made a moving scene in a silent film. But Betty had heard the sound-track. The woman was crying because her teenage son had taken to wearing his hair long and his clothes were casually shabby. Everybody in the room except Betty seemed to understand instantly the grief he had caused his mother, to share in her sorrow at the wantonness with which life inflicts its sufferings. There were murmured condolences, remarks about 'no matter what you do for them' and 'he'll grow out of it'. Unfortunately, he had. Betty knew the boy, a fragile, earnest teenager, rebellious as a convention of kirk elders. She had been amazed by the scene: all those people huddled together for support against four inches of hair on a harmless boy. It was as if, unable to feel for things that mattered, they all colluded in exaggerated reactions to trivia, indulged without risk in a ceremony of feeling.

Dan Scoular was her parents' equivalent of long hair in their neighbour's life, the proof that trouble does eventually come to every door. In that family summit meeting it became clear that it wasn't who he was they had noticed but who he wasn't. He didn't have a very cultured accent. He wasn't at university. He had no prospects of becoming a professional man. Everything they said to her when he was gone was another door closed on the possibility of their seeing him as he was. Their talk was the noise of preconceptions sliding home like bolts: 'you're young yet', 'more fish in the sea than ever came out of it', 'marriage is more than physical', 'not what we thought you would finish with', 'manners maketh the man'. This last came from her mother because Dan had not cut his piece of cake into segments with his knife but had lifted it whole and bitten into it.

'Oh,' her mother had said as if a small, domestic crisis had arisen. She put on one of her favourite expressions of rehearsed surprise. 'I'm sorry. Didn't I give you a knife?'

'Aye, thanks,' Dan had said. 'But I never eat them.'

Betty had understood what had often troubled her about her parents' politeness: it was a form of rudeness. Her mother in that moment had used what she liked to regard as manners to make somebody feel uncomfortable. For her mother and father the manners had become the most important things, because that way they never needed to go beyond them, could make their lives a continuous ritual round of attitudes in which

31

any real feeling occurred like a short-circuit. The natural grace with which Dan had deflected an awkward moment into a joke was something they didn't appreciate.

Her parents, she had decided, deserved their friends. From that night on, her sense of them had hardened. She realised how her mother's pride in Betty's achievements at school had never seriously related to what they meant about Betty herself. It was something her mother could brag about, something to wear like a fancy feather in her hat. She recalled something her mother had said several times when her parents were having what passed for an argument, a monotonous reshuffling of stock responses. 'I did my duty by you, anyway.' She meant she had given him a child. Her daughter was an expression of duty. Her father was always appropriately humble before the resurrected spectre of that often referred to and agonising experience, a nightmare of sickness and contractions and bravely borne self-sacrifice beyond his capacity to imagine. Betty herself had been accused of her mother's pregnancy but had proved less susceptible to being intimidated by her birth than her father was.

Such memories were a farewell look at where she had been. From her reading she made up her own name for the place she was determined to leave: the lumpen-middle-class. If the dynamic of aristocratic life, she had thought, was the past (you inherited your status), that of middle-class life was the present, what you now materially possessed. For lineage, read money, the mechanical womb in which her parents had conceived her and from which they saw her own children coming. They seemed dead to the possibilities that lay beyond it.

That was one reason why, besides being in love with Dan Scoular, she had felt an intellectual identification with what she understood to be working-class life. The knowledge she had acquired of it through him made her want to be a part of it. From the first image she had had of him at a wedding to which she was taken by somebody else, she had wanted to know more about how he came to be the way he was, with a relaxed assurance and a smile that would have thawed a glacier. The company of his relatives she had found herself among welcomed her as if she belonged to a branch of

32

their family they were delighted to make contact with again.

That same openness was something he had brought to their continuing relationship. She had never quite become immune to the attractiveness of his vulnerability. She had never known a man who was so obviously without effective defences. He didn't hide behind any pretence of worldly wisdom. He seemed to have no sense of you that you were meant to be able to fit. He had met her with a kind of uninhibited innocence. It seemed to give them licence to find out together about themselves, and they did. Their previous involvements didn't cause any aggressions between them. Marriage happened as a natural consequence, or so it had felt at the time.

But somehow the daily proximity of marriage had eventually compromised their original feeling. She began to see less attractive implications in his easiness of manner. She sensed him struggling to come to terms with how many restrictions there were on her apparent acceptance of him as he was. In their coming to understand the small print of each other's nature, resentments grew.

The resentments were at first just the ghosts of things not done that haunt our lives in a gentle, house-trained way, the half-heard sough of chances missed, the memory of a relationship you allowed to starve to death through inattention, the place you might have been that stares reproachfully through the window of the place you are. But such resentments, born of the slow experience of how each choice must bury more potential than it fulfils, were always seeking incarnation. Then their tormentingness could be given shape, their slow corrosion be dynamic. In the shared closeness of a marriage, it was very easy to exorcise the growing awareness of the inevitable failures of the self to live near to its dreams into the nature of the other, to let the lost parts of yourself find malignant form in unearned antipathy to the other one's behaviour.

It had happened to them, not dramatically but in small, daily ways. But then habit commits its enormities quite casually, like a guard in an extermination camp looking forward to his tea. Each day Betty sensed something in herself she didn't like but couldn't prevent from happening. She knew that what presented themselves to her as random thoughts were taking careful note, like shabby spies compiling a dossier against him.

One reiterated secret accusation concerned his propensity for violence. She knew it was grossly exaggerated in Thornbank. He had said to her once, 'Thank God, one fight avoids ten years of scuffles.' He had confessed to her that he had never been in a fight without experiencing rejection symptoms of fear afterwards, a shivering withdrawal, a determination not to do the same again. She had seen that at first hand. Once he had struck her, one open-handed blow on the side of the head after – she admitted to herself afterwards – she had gone on at him for hours. His disgust at himself had been alarming, an almost tribal shame as of a native who has disturbed the graves of his ancestors. After her elaborate description of how far he fell short of being a man, she had stopped and begun to worry about his stillness. In the end, it had taken her two days to coax him like a small boy out of his self-contempt. He had promised her that it would never happen again, and it never had.

She believed she knew the truth of his reputation for violence. When he was young, it had been a gesture he knew how to make, which earned him an easy acceptance in the rough context he was born in, and it had remained something he could never believe in seriously. He had never hit the boys, even in a token way. Yet in the moments when her frustration with her own life left her with no charity for him, a voice in her that was like an echo of her mother would say he was a violent man.

The housing scheme they lived in, too, she would sometimes use against him. She liked their council house but she would keep handy in her mind her awareness of the haplessness of neighbours, the aimless family quarrels that they had two doors down, the way several people whom they knew organised their lives with all the precision of a road accident.

But all her accusations were subsumed under the one basic charge: he was wasting himself. He let days happen to him, that was all. Somehow, although less effectively and with increasing difficulty, he still provided a decent enough home, saw that she and the children lived more or less all right. But

34

he seemed to make that his only purpose, had a life but no sense of a career.

She had loved that in him when he was younger. But she sensed, around her, friends she had known at school constructing weatherproof lives for themselves against all the inclemencies of middle age and she and Dan still lived as if they didn't know the weather would change. He had no ambition. Under the constant abrasion of that thought, something she had always known about him, and had liked, turned septic and became a constant irritation. At school he had given up an academic course because it separated him from his friends. At one time she thought she had understood. He loved being out on the streets. He was big and strong and wanted to be in about life. There had been something in that she had admired. But it looked a lot less attractive to her now.

Part of the reason was a transferred guilt she felt about herself. When they got married, she had given up university. He had wanted her to go on but she had lost belief in what she was doing, felt she was dealing with hothouse concerns that would wither into irrelevance if you took them out into the open air. But though the action had been hers, it had turned with time into an accusation against him, as if she had given him herself and he had failed to justify the gift.

She knew the sense of betrayal was mutual. The openness between them had diminished and she sensed him believing the blame for that was originally hers. She knew he felt that no matter what he did now it would be misconstrued, that she attributed motives to his actions he had never imagined being there, so that he sometimes called her Mrs Freud. It must have felt to him that whatever small present he tried to give her, of a compliment or a generous remark, it was held cautiously to her ear and shaken, as if it might explode. He had once said to her in total frustration, 'Jesus Christ! Ah was tryin' to be nice. If a fucking gorilla gave you a banana, ye would take it. It might be a gorilla. But it's still a gift.'

These days she found herself wondering more and more what was wrong with the gift he had tried to give her. It wasn't that he had welshed on the giving. Perhaps it was connected to the fact that he had from the beginning seemed to her potentially more than himself, to be in some way a future (not a past and not a present) that had somehow never been fulfilled. There was a dream in her he had never realised. The irony that hurt her was that the dream was perhaps inseparable from him. But perhaps it wasn't. Lately, she had been thinking that maybe she had been too harsh to her own background. It wasn't that she was in any danger of agreeing with her mother. But perhaps there was another form of that kind of life that she could live. The offer had been made to her.

Automatically, she lifted her coffee cup and found that the remains of her coffee were cold. The noises from the back green returned to her awareness. Putting down the magazine her mind had long ago abandoned, she crossed to the window and looked out. Seeing him preoccupied in playing with the boys, she found it easy to admit how much she still felt for him. She saw his attractiveness fresh and in the wake of the thought some of the good memories surfaced.

She remembered him coming in one night when he had been given a rise in wages. They were renting a small flat, waiting for their name to come to the top of the council housing list. She had felt cumbersomely pregnant with who was to be Raymond. Dan came in, glowing like a new minting, and smiled and shuffled his shoulders gallously in that way that could still make her feel susceptible. The memory of him then was something she wouldn't lose.

'What's for the tea, Missus Wumman?' he had said.

'Fish.'

'Wrong.'

'How? It's fish.'

'No, it's not.'

He danced briefly in front of her.

'Ye know what it is? Ye want to know what it is? It's Steak Rossini. Or Sole Gouj-thingummy-jig. That's fish right enough, isn't it? Or a lot of other French names that Ah can't pronounce. It's anythin' ye fancy. Washed down with the wine of your choice. As long as it's not Asti Spumante. Ye can put yer fish in the midden, Missus.'

'What're you talking about?'

Crossing towards the tiger lily she had bought, he proceeded to festoon it with notes.

'We have here an interesting species. The flowering fiver plant. A variety of mint. Heh-heh.' He turned to her and smiled. 'Ah've got ma rise. We're worth a fortune.'

'That'll be right, Dan. We need to save the extra. For furniture. When we get the house.'

'That'll be right, Betty. Trust me. Ah'll sort that out when it comes. Tonight's just us. We're for a header into the bevvy, Missus. A wee bit of the knife and forkery in nice surroundings. Here, you been eatin' too much again?' He had one arm round her, stroking her stomach with the other. 'You've got a belly like a drum. Ye want to see about that.'

'The doctor says he knows what's doing it.'

'Right. Change into one of those tents you've got in the wardrobe. An' I'll hire a lorry to transport you to the restaurant of your dreams.' He put his head against her stomach. 'Okay in there? You fancy going out?'

He straightened up. She hadn't moved. He turned her face towards his and kissed her. He smiled and shook his head at her, as if she would never learn.

'Betty!' he said. 'Ye'll have to stop worryin' about money.'

'Dan!' she said. 'You'll need to start worrying about money.'

He winked at her.

'After the night. Okay?'

But she was still waiting. Daft bugger, she thought, and smiled to herself. He was a man who made memorable shapes out of moments but neglected to work them into a coherent structure. Maybe he was trying to make a moment like that just now. She watched his intense participation with the boys, as if through the fond expression of that trivial game he could somehow convey his love for them, square accounts in some way with the unease that presumably dogged his relationship with them, as it dogged hers like a creditor. Maybe he was right, she thought. As she watched him charge up and down the green, she could believe he would soon be feeling a sort of nostalgia for this moment in its passing, that he was performing his own obscure ceremony of lastingness by implanting the same shared memory in each of them. They would all perhaps remember this laughter and this happy exertion in the pale sunlight. The three-fold wrestling match that followed looked to her like rough, amateur faith-healing, Dan's attempt to cure small alienations by the laying on of hands. He looked up suddenly and noticed her and waved. She waved back.

But by the time he came in with the boys, they might as well have been waving goodbye. As the late afternoon decomposed into evening around them, they remained as distant from each other as they had been earlier in the day, again only meeting obliquely through the children (Betty re-establishing clear contact with Raymond over the meal) until Dan eventually stood up and stretched and, as his body relaxed, her body tightened, as if they functioned by mutual contradiction. As he went across to take his jerkin from the back of a chair, she felt beginning one of those exchanges of small utterances that mean so much, phrases packed with years, expressions of the microchip technology of married speech.

'Ah, well,' he said.

Her understanding of what he had said was roughly that she knew where he was going, he knew that she knew where he was going since it was where he usually went at this time, that he would prefer not to have any expressions of amazed surprise and he would like to get out the door just once without complications.

'Your homework checked, Raymond?' she said.

She was reminding him that they were supposed to be a family, that there were other responsibilities in life besides following your own pleasures to the exclusion of everybody else and that she didn't see why everything should be left to her.

'Aye, love. We've checked it,' he said, conveying that he was refusing to get riled and she was wrong to think he would neglect his duties as a father. Putting on his jerkin was a reminder that he was going out anyway, no matter what she said, and wouldn't it be better to let it happen pleasantly.

'Where are you going?'

It wasn't a question, since they both knew the answer. It was an invitation to feel guilt.

'Ah thought Ah'd nip out and have a look at Indo-China.'

'You going to the pub?'

He nodded.

'You can't think of anything else to do?'

'Well, you couldn't last night. Ah don't remember you gritting yer teeth with those vodkas.'

'But last night wasn't enough for you?'

'Look, Betty. It's Sunday night.'

'It's Sunday night for everybody else as well.'

They went on like that for a short time, exchanging ritual and opaque unpleasantries, not connecting with each other so much as remeasuring the distance between them. She knew she would remember and examine things he had said, open up a small remark like a portmanteau and find it full of old significances that had curdled in her. As he went out, she didn't know how much longer she could bear to watch him let circumstances take charge of him, erode him. She knew from a thousand conversations the reality of his intelligence but she despaired that he would ever apply it constructively to the terms of his own life. How often they had tried to talk towards an understanding of what was happening to them and it had been like trying to talk a tapeworm out through your mouth, never to find the head. He seemed to her to live his life so carelessly that everywhere he walked he was walking into an ambush. She was tired of shouting warnings.

The sky looked different here to Eddie Foley. There was so much of it. Getting out of the car, he felt nearer to the presence of the wind than he did in the city. It seemed to touch him more directly, make him more aware of it. He stood in the car park and stared at the bulk of the Red Lion. It was a strange building with an odd, turreted part at the back of it. There was a big, dark outhouse, the purpose of which he wondered about.

He breathed in deeply and, finding himself put down here outside his routine, remembered being younger. There had been a time in his early twenties when he and a group of friends used to look for out-of-the-way places like this. One of them could get the use of a car. They had all finally admitted to one another how amazing women were and it felt like a shared secret. Weekends were for them what an unexplored coast might have been to a Viking. They piled into the car and went 'somewhere' and talked among themselves and talked to girls and drank and the password of their group was 'we'll see what happens'. He wished he were coming here now on those terms. He wanted just to go into the place and have a drink and see what happened. He wished they hadn't a purpose in coming. But Matt Mason didn't seem to have noticed the place as itself, looking up at the lighted window that faced out into the car park.

'Move the car up to opposite the window.'

Eddie climbed back into the car, drove it towards the lighted window and then backed against the opposite wall of the car park so that the Mercedes faced towards the window. He shut off the engine and doused the lights. Lighting a cigarette, he studied the other two through the windscreen.

He saw Billy Fleming watch Matt Mason attentively, like a trained retriever waiting for the signal. Seeing Billy's preoccupation silenced by the windscreen and framed in it, as if through the lens of a microscope, Eddie thought what a strange thing he was – an expert in impersonal violence. He felt no compunction about contemplating Billy so coldly. Billy wasn't his friend. He wasn't anybody's friend, as far as Eddie knew. If Matt Mason had given Billy his instructions and nodded him towards the car, he would have come for Eddie as readily as anyone else. It was how he made his living, being an extension of Matt Mason's will.

He did it well. Eddie had several times been astonished by the agility of that hugeness. But the results of that dexterity had made Eddie look away. He remembered one man whose face looked as if it had been hit by a small truck. Could you talk about doing anything well the purpose of which was so bad?

Eddie would have felt contempt for him except that he was honest enough to admit to himself that he couldn't afford it. His own position wasn't so much different. He might spare a thought for the man who imagined he was just coming out for a quiet pint, but that was as useful as flowers on the grave.

Eddie might like to believe that he still had a conscience but the main effect of it at the moment was to make him glad he couldn't hear what was being said. It meant he didn't have to worry about it too much. He just sat, smoking his cigarette and knowing his place. He watched Matt Mason prepare what was going to happen. He looked like somebody setting a trap for a species he understands precisely.

2

The sign of the Red Lion had rebounded on itself a bit, like a statement to which subsequent circumstances have given an ironic significance. It seemed meant to be a lion rampant. But the projecting rod of metal to which the sign was fixed by two cleeks had buckled in some forgotten storm. The lion that had been rearing so proudly now looked as if it were in the process of lying down or even hiding, and exposure to rough weather appeared to have given it the mange.

That image of a defiant posture being beaten down was appropriate. The place still called itself a hotel, although the only two rooms that were kept in readiness stood nearly every night in stillness, ghostly with clean white bed-linen, shrines to the unknown traveller. The small dining-room was seldom used, since pub lunches were the only meals ever in demand. The Red Lion scavenged a lean life from the takings of the public bar.

Like alcohol for a terminal alcoholic, the bar was both the means of the hotel's survival and the guarantee that it couldn't survive much longer. It seemed helplessly set in its ways, making no attempt to adapt itself to a changing situation. There were no fruit-machines, no space-invaders. There was a long wooden counter. There were some wooden tables and wooden chairs set out across a wide expanse of fraying carpet. There was, dominating a room that could feel as large as a church when empty, the big gantry like an organ for the evocation of pagan moods. Quite a few empty optics suggested that the range of evocation now possible was not what it had been.

It had its regulars but they were mainly upwards of their thirties and there weren't many women among them. Except for occasional freak nights when the pub was busy and briefly achieved a more complicated sense of itself the way a person might when on holiday, its procedures were of a pattern. The people who came here were, after all, devotees of a dying tradition. They believed in pubs as they had been in the past and they came here simply to drink and talk among friends, refresh small dreams and opinionate on matters of national importance. It was a talking shop where people used conversation the way South American peasants chew coca leaves, to keep out the cold.

Most of the men who drank in the Red Lion couldn't afford to drink much. Sometimes a pint took so long to go down you might have imagined each mouthful had to be chewed before it was swallowed. They had all known better times and were fearing worse. The room they stood in was proof of how bad things were. It was common talk that Alan Morrison's hold on the premises was shaky and every other week, as the property mouldered around him, another rumour of the brewers buying him out blew through it like a draught. The more uncertain his tenure grew to be, the more determinedly his regulars came. It was a small warmth in their lives and they were like men reluctant to abandon their places round a fire, though they know it's going out.

Alan Morrison shared their feeling. He was simply holding out as long as he could. He knew that his monthly accounts were an unanswerable argument, but buying the hotel twenty years ago, after years of careful saving, had never been primarily an act of commercial logic. It had been the fulfilment of a dream for him and, being a stubborn man, he simply refused to wake up, though these days it was taking more and more whisky to keep him like that. For a while, knowing how badly things were going and lacking sufficient belief in new ways to change, he had settled for being a pedant of his own condition, a theorist about why things were so bad.

At one time he had blamed the Miners' Welfare Club. Everybody wanted to be a capitalist, he said. When that closed down, he decided that television was the cause. People sat at home drinking out of cans, he said. That annoyed him for a while. Some evenings in the quietness of the pub, he would stand with an abstracted air, tuned out of whatever muffled conversation was taking place, as if listening for the chorus of beer cans hissing open in all the houses of the town. When the television set he installed in the bar didn't help, he retired further into his whisky for deeper contemplation of the problem.

The answer he came out with was an old man's frozen reflex to the changes in the world, not so much a rational process as a mental snarl, the rictus of an animal that has died trying to intimidate the trap which has caught it. He became a kind of King Lear with a hotel, dismissive of all the world except his clientele. The commercial failure of his hotel wasn't the reason for his baffled anger, merely its rostrum. His wife had died of cancer. His only son emigrated. His own heart was giving out. The state of his trade was just external confirmation, like an official letter from the fates.

His son became his scapegoat. Alan Morrison somehow managed to hallucinate a great inheritance for his son if he hadn't gone to Australia. If he had stayed, everything would have been all right. The reason for Alec's going became in his father's mind something that he had caused. From there it was but a short tirade to Alan's main theme, a sweeping dismissal of the young. They loved going to loud places. 'Noise isny meaning' was one of his darker utterances. They smoked strange cigarettes in groups. He would talk of the dangers of such practices while he was downing a double whisky. It was as if they, too, had emigrated, not geographically but socially, to other customs, to new attitudes, to more exotic pleasures.

Like his son, they never came regularly to his place, except for one. Vince Mabon was a student. 'Politics' was his cryptic answer to anyone in the bar who asked him what he was studying. He often said it with a cupping gesture of his hands that seemed to imply a casual encompassing of the world and all it might contain. Vince had a kind of deliberate intensity, a way of turning forensically into any question, even if you were asking him the time. No conversation seemed trivial with him. He always gave the impression of being on a mission of some sort. He didn't drink here so much as he came among them.

He was in the bar that Sunday. He had explained to nobody in particular that, as he had no lectures the next morning, he had managed to stay in Thornbank another night. The news was received without a display of fireworks. The only others present at the time, besides old Alan behind the bar, were the three domino players and Fast Frankie White.

The domino players were always looking for a fourth because

43

as purists they hated sleeping dominoes. With not all the dominoes in use, arguments frequently broke out among them, arguments that almost always came back to theatrical complaints about the impossibility of deploying the full complexity of their skills when not every domino was brought into play. They sounded like Grand Masters being asked to play without the queen. Tonight there seemed no possibility of their artistry being given full range. Alan was engaged in trying to get Vince Mabon to admit the folly of being young. Fast Frankie White was drinking with his customary self-consciousness, as if checking the camera-angles.

He was an outsider in his home town, Frankie White, and perhaps everywhere. Nobody was even sure where the nickname 'Fast' had come from, maybe from the publicity agent he carried around in his head. Most people in Thornbank knew that whatever he did it wasn't strictly legal. But since they knew of nobody he had harmed, except for breaking his mother's heart (and what son didn't?), they tolerated him. He might be able to sell the image he had made of himself elsewhere but they knew him too well to take him seriously. He was a performance and they let it happen, as long as it didn't interfere significantly with them. Tonight he had kept to himself, drinking his whisky with a nervous expectation, and seeming to listen with sophisticated amusement to Vince and Alan.

Vince's mushroom hairstyle was nodding heatedly at Alan and he had spilled some of his light beer on his UCLA tee-shirt. Alan was holding his whisky glass to the optic and shaking his head.

'Well, I wouldn't go, anyway,' Vince said. 'And that's for sure.'

'But they're payin' his way,' Alan said, and dropped a token bead of water in his glass. 'The whole trip won't cost him a penny.'

'Doesn't matter. Doesn't matter.'

'It's his son and his wife, for God's sake. Bert's got two grand-daughters out there he's never even seen.'

'His son could bring them over.'

'It's not like he's goin' to *stay* in South Africa. Ah could see the force of yer objections then. It's just a holiday.'

44

'He's still sanctioning an oppressive regime,' Vince said.

Alan emptied an ashtray that had nothing in it, wiped it with a cloth that made it slightly less clean and replaced it on the bar. He looked at his glass for advice.

'You ever been to Prestwick for the day?' he asked.

'What?'

'You ever been to Prestwick for the day?'

Vince looked round, appealing to a non-existent public. He smiled to himself since nobody else was available.

'I think that's what they call a non sequitur, Alan,' he said.

'That's maybe what you call it. Ah just call it a question. Fuckin' answer it.'

'Yes. Guilty. I've been to Prestwick for the day. A lot of times.'

'Well. Don't go again. It's a Tory council.'

Vince was contemptuous and Frankie White was laughing into his glass when Matt Mason and Billy Fleming walked in. Matt Mason came in first and Billy Fleming followed close, like a consort. Everybody else in the bar paid attention but not much. Strangers dropped in from time to time, on their way from somewhere to somewhere, but seldom stayed long.

'Yes, sir?' Alan said.

'A gin and tonic,' Matt Mason said, 'and a pint of heavy.'

A small, barely perceptible event occurred in the room. Sam MacKinlay, one of the domino players, lifted his pint and sipped it briefly with his pinky out. Amusement almost happened between the other two domino players but didn't quite manage to survive the look that Billy Fleming sent over like a sudden frost. Matt Mason, watching Alan put tonic in the gin and begin to pull the pint, added to the chill with his preoccupied stare. The occurrence had been fiercely concentrated, was over in a moment, but it was as if the others had been shown a capsule it would be dangerous to swallow. In case they had missed the significance of their experience, Matt Mason imprinted his voice on it quietly.

'This it?' he said.

Alan was confused. He looked at the gin with half of the bottle of tonic poured into it and the pint, which had a perfect head on it.

'A gin and tonic and a pint of heavy,' he said.

45

'You never heard of lemon?'

Alan bristled for a second, looked and understood what he was seeing.

'We're just out of lemon, sir.'

'Ice?'

'Ah'll get ye some.'

He did. Matt Mason paid and walked over to the table beside the window, with Billy Fleming following. On his way, he glanced briefly at Frankie White, who was watching him. Before sitting down, he looked out of the window.

'A ringside seat,' he said quietly to Billy Fleming as they sat down.

They didn't have long to wait. Dan Scoular came in. He brought a change of atmosphere with him. He tended to make other people feel enlarged through his presence, through his physical expansiveness to make expansiveness seem natural. He never intimidated. When he came in, you felt he was for sharing. Coming in this time, he was the occasion for talk about the rain, which hadn't happened. Frankie White joined in the conversation pleasantly. The room relaxed. The domino players rediscovered how involving dominoes were. Alan and Vince stalked each other again through separate labyrinths of preconception. Dan Scoular tried to drown his sadness in his pint.

The beer seemed to turn sour as it touched his lips. He felt at once as if coming to the pub had been a mistake, one of the many things he did these days without being sure why he did them. It was as if habit was keeping appointments at which the largest part of him didn't turn up. Frankie White's calling him 'big man' hadn't helped. Big man. The implied stature beyond the physical the words sought to bestow on him was an embarrassment. He remembered an expression his mother had used to cut him down to size when he was in his arrogant teens and impressed by the status he felt himself acquiring. 'Aye, ye're a big man but a wee coat fits ye.' She hadn't been wrong. His sense of his own worth at the moment could have been comfortably contained in a peanut-shell. But the people he came from kept stubbornly dressing him up in regal robes of reputation, not seeming to realise he had abdicated.

Wullie Mairshall was an example. Coming out of the house

46

tonight, with his sense of Betty's growing disregard for him making him feel guilty, Dan had been met by Wullie.

'Hullo. It's Dan the Man. How's the head man gettin' on?'

Wullie was obviously coming from where Dan was going. Jim Steele had been with him. Steelie had a carry-out of cans of beer and they were at that stage of drunkenness of taking hostages.

'Dan,' Wullie said. 'You come with us. We're goin' up tae see auld Mary Barclay. Discuss the state of the world. The world!' he had suddenly declared to the houses around him. 'Find out what happened. Where the working class went wrong. Was a day, Dan, men like you woulda been ten a penny. Now you stand alone. Steelie! He stands alone!'

'Alone!' Steelie confirmed and offered him a can from his carry-out with sombre dignity.

'No, thanks, Steelie. Ah'm just goin' for a drink. Take care, you two.'

But Wullie had gripped Dan's arm.

'Don't let us down, Dan,' Wullie said. 'You know what Ah mean. Eh? You know, Steelie.'

'Ah know. Don't let us down.'

'He won't let us down!' Wullie snarled at Steelie, as if it was a ridiculous idea Steelie had broached from nowhere. 'Big Dan won't let us down. Ye know what Ah mean, Dan. We all know. Steelie knows.' His arms gathered them into a conspiracy. 'We all know. We know.'

Steelie nodded. Wullie slapped his hands together like applause for their communal wisdom. Everybody seemed to know but him, Dan had thought. Yet his knowledge of Wullie Mairshall was a kind of sub-text to the ridiculousness of the conversation, a gloss that shed some meaning on its cryptic nature. Wullie Mairshall was a believer in the working-class past and how the present had failed it. He spoke of the thirties as if they were last week. In the pressure of those times he had been formed and it was in relation to what he had learned then that he judged everything else.

What he judged mainly was the present, and found it wanting. In his search for something to continue having faith in, for some residual sign that the quality of the past was not entirely lost, he had – for reasons that baffled the subject of

47

his choice – picked Dan. If he were honest with himself, Dan Scoular understood quite clearly the meaning of that drunken exchange outside his house, the nudges, winks and loaded phrases, secret as passwords. He was being reminded that he had been entrusted with the heritage of Wullie Mairshall's sense of working-class tradition and he must stay true to it. He had been given a commission.

But it was one he wasn't sure he believed in any more. And he felt that he wasn't the only deserter. Standing now in this pub, he felt alone. He knew most of these people he stood among. He liked them. But he no longer felt the sense of community he had once known with them. They had somehow grown apart. There was a time when he thought he could have gone into any pub like this in Scotland and sensed kinship, felt wrapped round him instantly the warmth of shared circumstances, of lives a central part of which was concern for how *you* were living. But he had lost his awareness of that. After his few years in the pits, he couldn't find it. He was never sure how far the failure was his and how far his observation was the truth.

But he had looked hard enough. He had worked as a general labourer, he had worked in the brickworks, on the roads, on the high pylons, he had worked Sullom Voe. And he had progressively seen himself merely as an individual who happened to be working in these places, someone 'on for himself' as they said. He remembered some of those journeys on the train down from Aberdeen. Men whose parents had had the same kind of lives as his own talked among themselves of what they were individually getting out of it, compared themselves rather condescendingly with mates who had been made redundant at the same time as themselves and hadn't done nearly as well. It was as if every man and his family were a private company. Once, thanks to a man he had made friends with in Fraserburgh, he had gone out to make some extra money on a boat that fished out of Mallaig. Even those fishermen, brave, and kind to him, had sounded like wealthier versions of the men on the train.

He had wondered often if he had all his life been pursuing the wrong dream, since it was supposed to be a shared dream and so few other people seemed to be having it. More and more, he understood Betty's dismay at him. Lately, he had been thinking he should look more to his own perhaps, make what he could for Betty and the boys and forget anything else. It seemed a way he might win Betty back, for he dreaded he was losing her. Maybe it was just his preoccupation with that dread that had made him wonder if it was something about Betty Wullie Mairshall had been hinting at before Dan left them.

Dan had walked away several yards when Wullie followed him, leaving Steelie swaying on the pavement like a slightly top-heavy potted plant. Wullie put his hand on Dan's arm and looked at him with maudlin affection. His words seemed surfacing from the bottom of a very deep pool.

'Dan. Ah'll need to see ye in private sometime. A quiet talk.'

'What is it, Wullie?'

Wullie's forefinger hovered in front of his own lips like an eyesight test.

'Personal, Dan. Very personal.'

'Ye can come to the house anytime, Wullie.'

'Not suitable, Dan. Anyway, Ah'm not a hundred per cent sure of ma information yet. Let's leave it the now. But remember. Ah've always got your interests at heart. Nobody takes liberties wi' you on the fly while Ah'm around.'

'Liberties? In what way, Wullie?'

'Dan. Let's leave it there. Enquiries will be made. Meantime, my lips are sealed. Ah'll be sure before Ah speak. And when Ah am, it'll be for your ears only.' He winked. 'Ah'm your man, Dan Scoular. Ah'm *your* man.'

The knowledge hadn't reassured Dan. As he nodded to Frankie White in acknowledgment of his second pint, Dan hoped Wullie's drunkenly decorous secrecy hadn't been about Betty. He didn't know how he could cope with hearing bad things about her. He tried to convince himself it would be about something a lot less important, perhaps that somebody had informed on him to the Inland Revenue for building a garden wall for a man in Blackbrae and not declaring the money he earned for it. It could be that. Wullie Mairshall, who was still only sixty-four but had taken early retirement with his redundancy money two years ago, did gardens in Blackbrae, for some of what Wullie called 'the big hooses', and Wullie always talked as much as he delved. He might have heard something.

He hoped, whatever it was, it didn't impinge too immediately on his family. Being so insecure about himself, he felt an awareness of vulnerability spread to Betty and his children. He feared the susceptibility of Betty to another man. He worried about how his sons were supposed to grow up decent among the shifting values that surrounded them, when he wasn't sure himself what he stood for any more. Sometimes just the sheer amount of undigested experience they were asked to deal with through watching television troubled him. It seemed to him that at their age his experience had come at him through a filter of shared, accepted values which they perhaps lacked, or which at least had more gaps. Their experience came at them more quickly and they rushed more quickly to meet it.

He remembered Raymond telling him last week about a dream he had had. Raymond was walking in a street alone when he saw a woman lying there. He had known, as you know in dreams without knowing how you know, that she was dead. She was dressed in a skirt and a blouse. 'Maybe like an office worker,' Raymond had said. He had knelt over her and noticed blood trickling from the side of her mouth. While he was studying her, he had heard a noise that frightened him. As he glanced up, a creature was running towards him, completely covered in hair. 'But it was a woman,' Raymond said. 'It was an animal. But I knew it was a woman.' He had tried to run away but she had trapped him against the wall. He had wakened with her about to sink her fanged teeth in his throat.

Dan had explained to Raymond that he thought the dream was just about growing up, about seeing women not as neutral adults but as something sexual. But what had reassured Raymond had troubled Dan. It had told him how much Raymond was growing up, the difficult places he was moving into, and it showed Dan his own time contracting. Whatever significant influence he was still to have on them, whatever coherent message his life was meant to convey, he had better find it quick. He thought of seeing Betty through the window today and knowing how much she meant to him. Whatever love was supposed to be, that was what he felt. But his love was somehow isolated in him, like a genie in a bottle. He had to find the means to release it, to show himself to them as he wanted to be.

He took a sip of his beer and decided that it wasn't helping. One of the strangers over at the window rose and went through to the lavatory. When Dan turned a little later to see what Frankie White was having, he discovered that Frankie had gone as well. Dan set him up a drink in his absence.

Matt Mason was still urinating by the time Frankie White came through. Frankie took the stall beside him. Matt Mason didn't look up. He seemed transfixed by the sight of his water.

'That's your man?'

'That's Dan Scoular.'

'Seems a bit lost in himself.'

'Ah told ye. He's got a lot of problems. Who hasn't around here these days?'

'Who's the gonk with the mouth like a megaphone?'

'Vince Mabon. He's a student.'

'Big man likes him, does he?'

'Dan likes most people. But, aye, he seems to like Vince.'

'Uh-huh. We can maybe arrange to see how much. The gonk'll do.'

'How d'ye mean?'

Matt Mason was finished, waved his penis as if it were a large and cumbersome object. He went across to wash his hands and found no soap. He was fastidiously annoyed. Frankie finished and didn't bother to wash his hands. He was too preoccupied.

'How do you mean?'

Matt Mason was rubbing his hands together under the water, which, after testing, he had realised wasn't hot. He tutted like an old maid. Finished, he made sure the tap was fully turned off and looked round for a towel. He noticed that it was a hot-air hand-dryer.

'Daft old bastard,' he muttered. 'One modern convenience in his place and it's a bummer.'

He hit the button angrily and felt the hot air play ineffectually on his hands.

'Whoever invented these,' he shouted above the noise of the machine, 'should definitely not get a Nobel Prize.'

Standing amid the smell of his own urine, Frankie White suddenly realised where they were. Like a bank robber who has had his pocket picked, he felt outraged. The feeling gave him the courage to shout at Matt Mason above the sound.

'No, no. Wait a minute. We don't need any wee tests. Ah've told you what the man can do. That's not what Ah thought the night was about.'

Matt Mason was turning his hands back and forward in the heat.

'Come on, Matt! We don't need this.'

Suddenly, the machine shut itself off. Frankie White cringed from the sound of his own voice. Matt Mason was rubbing the fingers of each hand on the palms, dissatisfied. Without warning, he leaned across and dried them on Frankie's jacket.

'I'm not a punter,' he said. 'I'm a bookie. Always check the odds.' He turned at the door. 'But it's okay. I've warned Billy it's a fair fight.'

He went back through to the bar. Frankie hung about for a moment until he admitted to himself that there was nothing he could do but follow. Going back to his whisky, he saw the scene begin to move under its own impetus, as if he had accidentally hit the start-button of a machine he didn't know how to stop. Matt Mason was nodding to Billy Fleming. Billy Fleming lifted his pint and began to finish it.

'We'll never get anywhere,' Vince Mabon was saying, 'through the parliamentary system. It's a set-up. The game's rigged. Look at the last time. They brainwashed the public with a lotta lies.'

Billy Fleming walked up to the bar.

'A pint of heavy,' he said.

Preoccupied, Alan reached for the empty glass and made to put the next pint in it.

'You not got two glasses, like?' Billy Fleming said.

'Sorry.'

Alan lifted a fresh glass and started to fill it.

'I'm tellin' ye, Alan. To hell with gradualism. It's revolution we need. Violence is the only way we'll go forward. Take the struggle into the streets.'

'You talk shite!'

The remark had the suddenness of a gun going off, leaving you wondering where it came from or if that was what you had heard at all. The confirmation that it had happened was the solidity of the silence that followed it.

'You hear me? You talka loada shite. Ah'm fed up listenin' to you.'

Vince shuffled uncomfortably like a man looking for the way down from a platform. When he spoke, his voice had lost its rhetorical tone.

'I've got my opinions.'

'Shurrup!'

The pint Alan had been filling foamed, forgotten, over the rim of the glass.

'Ah don't want to hear yer opinions,' Billy Fleming said. 'You believe in violence? Come out here an' Ah'll show ye violence.'

Vince spoke quietly.

'That's not the kind of –'

'Ah said shurrup! You're not payin' attention. Open yer mouth again and I'll put a pint-dish down it.'

The others in the room watched helplessly while Vince went as still as if a block of ice had formed round him. Alan turned off the beer tap.

'Hey!'

The word was out of Dan Scoular's mouth before he knew he was going to say it. Some basic feeling had expressed itself beyond his conscious control. The trouble taking place in the pub wasn't his and he would have preferred to have no part in it. But the injustice of the event was so blatant. His instincts had cast his vote for him. But nobody else voted with him or, if they did, the ballot was secret. He felt his isolation, and his head was left to work out how to follow where his heart had led.

The word had been quiet but it introduced a counter-pressure in the room, a careful groping for leverage. Billy Fleming turned slowly, almost luxuriously, towards where he felt the pressure coming from. He looked steadily at Dan Scoular.

'Yes,' he said. 'Can Ah help ye?'

'The boy's just talkin'.'

'Not any more he's not.'

They watched each other.

'An' if he does open his mouth, he'll get it.'

'You'll not touch the boy.'

'Are you his daddy?'

The pressure was balanced evenly between them and, deliberately, with very measured calculation, Billy Fleming tilted it in his favour.

'Well, you'll get it as well, if ye interfere.'

Dan Scoular smiled, realising Vince had been a decoy. The smile was camouflage he knew couldn't protect him much longer. He was angry with himself for having been so easily left with no options. He thought of something Betty had once said of him: 'When you walk into a room, the only attitude that seems to occur to you is, "What game do you play here? I bet I can play that as good as you." It never seems to occur to you to say, "I don't believe in that game. I think it's a rotten game. I'm not playing." Why do you think you have to accept the rules?' It looked as if he had done it again. But he was in the game now and all he could think of to do was try and play it with style.

'You want it badly, don't ye?' he said.

He walked towards the other man and, as Billy Fleming tensed in preparation, walked past him. Billy Fleming was momentarily uncertain, thinking he was being walked out on. He was glancing towards Matt Mason as he heard Dan Scoular speaking from the door, which was open.

'Alan doesny like fights in his pub,' he said and went out.

As Billy Fleming followed, Matt Mason stood and went to the window. The assurance of his action, as if he had declared himself the promoter of this fight, magnetised the still-stunned reactions of the others into imitation. Nobody followed the two men out. Frankie White crossed towards the window and the three domino players rose and moved hurriedly after him. Alan came tentatively out from the carapace of his bar, paused, turned back for his glass, perhaps thinking he might need its assistance to get as far as the window, and slowly joined them. Vince Mabon, not knowing what else to do, took his place there, too. They had become an audience.

At first all they could see were their images reflected in the curtainless window, a motley group portrait straining into the darkness to look at themselves. Then the headlights of a car came on. They saw Billy Fleming take off his jacket and lay it across the bonnet of the car. Dan Scoular kept on his light jerkin.

The figures flickered briefly in the headlights of the car and it was over, like a lantern-slide show that breaks down just as it's getting started. They were looking at an effect that didn't appear to have had any very clear cause. Billy Fleming's head hit the ground with a soundless and sickening jolt that some grimacing expulsions of breath in the bar provided the sound-track for. He lay with a peacefulness that suggested he had found his final resting place. A man came out of the car and Dan Scoular started to help him to lift Billy Fleming into the back seat. Billy Fleming had obviously regained consciousness before they got him there but he raised no objections to their assistance.

The realisation that he didn't appear to be too seriously hurt opened a valve on the tension of what they had just seen and humour blew out, a gush of relief at not having to go on confronting seriously the reality of violence.

'Ah'm glad Ah didny buy a ticket for that one,' Sam Mac-Kinlay said. 'Ah wish it had been on the telly. At least we could see a slow-motion replay.'

Nearly everybody laughed. Dan Scoular walked back in to a festive atmosphere that caught him unawares. He had been involved in that mood of nervous recuperation that had always followed a fight for him, a dazed sense of having had his self-control mugged by his own violence. Their smiling faces seemed to him contrived. They couldn't be feeling something as simple as their expressions showed. He felt like a man in quicksand with whom other people were leaning over to shake hands. Nobody had wanted the fight to happen and now everybody seemed delighted that it had. Even the man who had been with the one he hit was smiling.

'Right!' he was saying to Alan. 'Everybody gets a drink. Give everybody what they're having. And a gin and tonic for me.'

Frankie White was looking at him and saying, 'What did Ah tell ye? One good hit!'

'Come on,' the man said. 'Do it. And a double for yourself.'

The room was becoming a party and Dan Scoular was apparently the guest of honour. It seemed churlish not to attend. He shrugged.

'Ye not want to get yer big bodyguard a pint on a drip?' Sam MacKinlay shouted.

Everybody was laughing. Alan Morrison was hurrying about behind the bar as if the place was crowded.

'A few folk will be sorry that they weren't here the night,' he said.

Before Dan Scoular had cleared his head, he was sitting at a table with Frankie White and the other man.

'Dan,' Frankie White was saying. 'This gentleman is Matt Mason. Matt, you've seen who this is. Dan Scoular in person. A man with a demolition-ball at the end of each wrist.'

The talk of the others was like background music, all being played by special request for Dan Scoular. Matt Mason shook hands with him. The man who had been in the car came in and sat at their table. Matt Mason introduced him.

'Ah think Big Billy has a slight case of concussion,' Eddie Foley said. 'His head hit the ground with a terrible wallop.'

The domino players were shouting over.

'Thanks, mate.'

'Cheers!'

'All the best.'

Matt Mason gave them a regal wave.

'A lucky hit, you think?' he asked Eddie Foley teasingly.

Eddie Foley laughed.

'Came out a telescopic rifle, that punch. If that was lucky, beatin' the Light Brigade was a fluke. This man can go a bit.'

'He would have to against Cutty.'

'Wait a minute,' Dan Scoular said. He looked at Frankie White. 'What did you set me up for here?'

Matt Mason held up his hands.

'I can explain,' he said. 'You want to give me a minute?'

'Ah don't know.'

Dan Scoular was trying to work out what had happened to bring him here. He had said 'Hey!' and the word had been as mysterious in effect as 'Open Sesame'. His night had been transformed. The result was slightly dazzling but he didn't like being dazzled and beyond the surface laughter and brightness he had already glimpsed shadows that troubled him. Frankie White had been standing at the bar when Dan came in but he hadn't just been standing at the bar. Matt Mason had been sitting with the man Dan hit and now he hadn't even asked about him. It was as if the man had served the purpose he was brought for. He was expendable. Someone had been waiting in the car to switch on the lights. Dan had thought he had been getting involved in a spontaneous fight but it had only been a controlled experiment. In doing what he had thought was winning for himself and Vince Mabon, Dan had been winning, it seemed, for Matt Mason. It had been a fight Matt Mason couldn't lose. The rules were strange here.

'Dan,' Frankie White said. 'Just listen to the man a minute, will you? Please?'

Alan had brought the drinks across, rested a stepfatherly hand on Dan's shoulder as he put down his pint.

'That's how we used to breed them in these parts,' he said, staking an early claim to proprietorship of this evening's legend.

Dan sipped his pint and waited. Realising Alan had gone off without giving him anything, Eddie Foley passed a pound to Frankie White.

'Get us a whisky and a half pint, Frankie.'

Dan Scoular watched Frankie White's receding back with thoughtfulness.

'That was Billy Fleming you saw away there,' Matt Mason said.

'How is he?' Dan asked Eddie Foley.

'Beat,' Matt Mason said. 'You ever lost a fight?'

'Aye.'

'How many?'

'Just the one. But Ah haven't had too many.'

'Who was that?'

'Ma feyther.'

'Your father? What age were you?'

'Ah would be nineteen.'

'How did that come about?'

Dan Scoular looked at him, decided that whatever his reasons for asking were, he had no reasons for not telling.

'Ah was a cocky boy. Ah hit a man for no reason. Just because Ah felt like it. He didny want to fight. Ah broke his jaw. Ma feyther took me out the back door. An' hammered me.'

Matt Mason gave the event his expert consideration, offered the balm of his wisdom to the dead wound.

'Maybe you weren't trying. I mean, fighting your father. That's bound to put brakes on you.'

'Oh, Ah was tryin' all right. But Ah was in the wrong. That's a bad corner to come out of.'

'You superstitious?'

'What's that got to do wi' superstition? Ah walk under ladders an' everythin'.'

'I mean, having less chance if you're in the wrong?'

Frankie White had returned from the camaraderie at the bar. He put down Eddie Foley's two drinks. Eddie held out his hand and Frankie remembered the change. Dan Scoular watched the handing over of the silver. He took a sip of his pint.

'Look,' he said. 'Ah just believe in certain things. Like what ma feyther told me that day. If ye can't fight for the right reasons, keep yer hands in yer pockets.'

'And what are the right reasons?'

'Ah'm not always sure. But he seemed to be.'

Matt Mason held up his glass and paused before taking a drink. He might have been showing off his rings.

'You want to make some money?'

Dan Scoular looked slowly round the group at the table. His look separated himself from them, as if they were a conspiracy.

'What?' he said. 'Was that an interview for a job?'

'In a way.'

'But, mister, Ah didny apply.'

'All right. But I'm asking you. Do you want to make some money?'

'Who doesny want to make some money? But there's money and money.'

Matt Mason looked at Frankie White.

'Does he like talking in riddles?' he said and looked back at Dan. 'There's only one kind of money. The good stuff. Unless it's home-made. And this won't be. All right?'

'Ah just mean some money's dearer than others. Some just costs sweat. Some costs yer self-respect. What do Ah do for it?'

'You do what you're good at. You fight.'

'For money? You mean in a ring?'

Matt Mason was enjoying the revelation to come. He took

58

out a leather cigar-case and offered Dan Scoular a cigar. Dan shook his head. Eddie, who had taken out his cigarettes, didn't seem to notice Frankie White about to take one. He held out the packet to Dan Scoular.

'Ah don't smoke.'

'Ah told ye,' Frankie said.

But he missed the point. It wasn't a matter of checking on his information. It was improvised stage-business, self-taught management technique for controlling situations. Matt Mason's timing was a matter of instinct but what he used it to promote was a well-rehearsed performance. He lit Eddie's cigarette with his gold lighter and then his own cigar. He re-emerged looking at Dan from behind a slowly dissipating cloud of smoke, Merlin of the cigar.

'I'm arranging a bare-knuckle fight,' he said.

Dan Scoular looked across towards the others in the bar as if checking his location in normalcy. Having confirmed his fix on where he was, he looked back at these three as if they were somewhere else, maybe inhabiting their own fantasy or just trying to take the mickey out of him. Frankie White was nodding reassuringly.

'What for?' Dan said.

'It's a complicated story,' Matt Mason said. 'Frankie White'll tell you. If you agree to do it. If you don't, you won't have to know, will you?'

'Ye're kiddin'.'

'I stopped kidding when I came out of the pram.'

Dan took a sip of his pint. It seemed to feel strange in his mouth. The idea was so bizarre that he came at it tangentially.

'Ah've had a few scuffles,' he said. 'But they were always for a reason.'

'Money's not a reason?'

'A fight in the street's different.'

'What's different? You're doing the same thing, aren't you? It's man against man.'

'Naw. It's different. Ah've watched a lot of boxing on the telly. That's a different game. More complicated. Street fightin's just two things.'

'What would they be?'

'Suddenness. And meanin' it. Ye go fast. If ye can, ye go first. An' ye stop when it's over. That's all Ah can do.'

'Should be enough.'

'Anyway,' Eddie Foley said, 'that's not true, big man. Listen –'

Vince Mabon had come over to their table. Matt Mason looked up as if wherever he sat he was booking a private room and Vince hadn't knocked. Eddie Foley cut his sentence dead. It was less polite than talking on and ignoring Vince's presence would have been.

'Excuse me, Dan,' Vince Mabon said. 'Ah want to thank you for what you did there.'

'Any time, Vince. We've got to protect the nation's intellectuals.'

But the demon of sloganising that was in Vince had to climb on to even his gratitude like a soap-box.

'But I still don't agree with that kind of violence. That wasn't the kind of violence I was talking about.'

'Maybe,' Matt Mason said, 'he should've left you to explain that to Big Billy. In the dummy alphabet.'

Perhaps Vince was learning from humiliation but this second time around he found a response. With a slightly unsteady hand, he put his partly drunk pint on their table.

'I don't think I want your drink, mister,' he said. 'It doesn't taste right.'

Matt Mason looked as if he was going to get up. Dan took hold of Vince's arm with his left hand and held up his right, palm towards Mason.

'Okay, Vince,' he said. 'Cheers.'

He let go of Vince's arm and Vince walked straight out of the pub.

'He's only a boy,' Dan said.

'He's only a shitehead.'

'He's only a boy. You're maybe big where you come from, sir. But this is his pub.'

'His pub?' Matt Mason smiled. 'Does he own it? Mind you, who would want to? It's your pub when you own it. Not when you buy a couple of beers in it. I should know. I own more than one.'

'Matt,' Eddie Foley said. 'Anyway, we came for a reason.

Listen, Dan. As Ah wis sayin'. Ye're wrong about all it is that ye can do. Suddenness and meanin' it? Against Big Billy, Ah could be just as sudden and mean it more. And it wouldn't do me a lotta good. It would still be a short-cut to the blood bank. You've got somethin' special. Ah'm tellin' ye. Ah've seen a few. It's just that ye haven't explored it yet. And you're a mug if ye don't. A mug! It's a talent like anythin' else. Maybe the only one ye've got. It might amaze ye what ye can do with it. It might amaze ye the money it could get ye. You never considered that?'

He had, of course. He had wondered about how good he really was many times. It would have been strange if he hadn't. Whoever hasn't dreamt of uniqueness must have achieved it by that. Dan Scoular, when he was younger, had had his share of ridiculous dreams, those adolescent imaginings that thrive on impossibility till they overdose on it. But he had come quickly to understand how few his real choices were.

By the time his early physical prime was passing, he knew there was only one thing he was especially good at. He didn't pretend to himself that it was a talent that mattered much. But he didn't have intellectual contempt for it either. It was for him related to pride and some kind of integrity. Not the use of it but the sense of himself it gave him meant a kind of wholeness. He couldn't understand politics too well or carve out an impressive career or say things that reduced other people to silence. But he had something that was quietly and relaxedly his own.

Lately, it had felt like all he had. With his job gone and no prospect of another and his marriage baffled, he had been forced to look steadily at the dwindling possibilities in his life. Faced with the blankness of the future, he had taken to wondering about the past. He had wondered if he could have been a boxer, if that would have changed their lives and made things better.

Eddie Foley had, without knowing it, opened a door on Dan Scoular's small, pathetic cache of hope. He had put a light on there and said that it was maybe more than he had thought, that it might not be too late. They were now talking to a different man, had activated something in him, like accidentally giving a drink to an alcoholic on the wagon. It meant

61

so much to him that he didn't want to let them know.

'Ah don't think so,' he said. 'Ah need to mean it. Why would Ah fight another man without a reason?'

'You fought Billy fast enough,' Matt Mason said.

'He was claiming Vince, wasn't he?'

'So what?'

'So Ah know Vince. That woulda been a liberty. The only damage Vince could do ye would be give ye cauliflower ears with talkin'.'

'So imagine the man you're fighting insulted Vince. Shouldn't be hard. Most people would.'

Dan moved another way.

'Anyway, Ah'm thirty-three. What do Ah need with this?'

Matt Mason shrugged and took a sip of his drink, as if it might be the end of the interview.

'What ye workin' at just now?' Eddie Foley asked.

'Not at answerin' questions you know the answer to already.'

'How d'ye mean?'

'Ye don't have to enter for Mastermind to know that Frankie here put ye up to this. An' if he did, he would've told ye certain things. Like Ah'm idle.'

'For a man that's unemployed, ye've still got a taste for luxuries.'

'Ye mean what Ah think ye mean?'

'Ah mean it's a luxury to want to fight for a reason.'

'Ah would've thought it was a luxury tae dae anythin' else.'

But Dan was talking automatically, as if from a script he had learned a long time ago. Matt Mason leaned forward suddenly and took a wad of money from his inside pocket. He started carefully to count tenners on to the table. He stopped at twenty and put the rest of the money back in his pocket.

'Two hundred quid,' he said. 'Tax free. Just to train for two weeks. Where are *you* going to get a better offer?'

Dan Scoular looked at the money. It was fanned out on the table so that each separate note was at least partly visible.

'What would be the rules of this fight?'

'Bare knuckles. No feet, no butting, no weapons. A knock-down ends a round. You get thirty seconds' rest – to be back at the line. First man to fail to make it loses. Last man standing at the line's the winner.'

'Who made the rules?'

'That's not your business. You get paid for obeying them. You take it or leave it. They're just the rules.'

'When would this be?'

'Three weeks today. He's got his man. I've got to get mine in a hurry. Have I got him?'

Dan Scoular waited.

'Why me?' he said. 'Ah'm just a boy from the country. A man like you must know a lotta harder men than me.'

'Oh, I do,' Matt Mason said. 'Don't worry about it. I know men could take you out while you were still wondering if there was something wrong. But we need fresh blood for this one. Somebody who only knows how to fight fair. That way we won't get disqualified. There'll be people watching. We've got to make it look right.'

'Where would this fight be?'

'In a place. You don't worry about that. In a safe place.'

'But this isn't legal.'

Matt Mason overdid his expression of horror.

'Away you go. I'll have to fire that lawyer of mine. He's misled me again. Look, if I want a holy text, I'll go to a wayside pulpit. You're not being asked to pass judgment on the thing. Just to participate.'

Dan Scoular thoughtfully riffled the notes.

'Training?'

'You would train two weeks with Frankie. Down here in your own backyard. We would want you kept out of the way. You would be our secret weapon. Running. Eating right. Staying off that stuff.' He pointed at the beer in the bottom of Dan's glass. 'Just getting fit. The last week I'd get you up to Glasgow. Into a gym. You'd get another hundred quid for that.'

Dan Scoular was seeing three hundred pounds on the table.

'If that's for trainin', what would Ah get for fightin'?'

'That depends.'

'On what?'

'How you fight.'

'So what's the wee print?'

'Winners win money. Losers lose it. I'd be betting a lot of

money on you. You win, you get your percentage. Double what's on the table. You lose, you get your bus money out of Glasgow. As far as the city boundary. The Tinto Firs.'

'Ah don't fancy that bit.'

'Then don't.' Matt Mason was getting impatient. 'It's a freelance job. It doesn't have a pension scheme.'

He lifted the notes and held them up, halfway between the table and his pocket, his rings glinting above the money like a promise of what it could lead to.

'Money depreciates fast these days,' he said. 'Look. I've got things to do. Your first fight, big man, is with yourself. Can you win it? You've got thirty seconds – to come to the line.'

He was smiling at his own pun. He was so sure of things. Dan couldn't think at the moment of one certainty, except the feeling he had to use himself in some way for his family. He sensed that what he was being offered must separate him from where he had been. But perhaps he was already separated from there. He looked at Alan Morrison and the others in the bar. They hadn't exactly rallied round when he challenged Billy Fleming. Why should he worry about distancing himself from them? He saw no particular merit in his ability to fight. It had meant something important to his father, almost a kind of sacred trust that you shouldn't abuse. But if you had lost the way to think like that, if you didn't believe in the gift, why not make money out of it? It was at least putting it to a use. If he wasn't who Wullie Mairshall and others thought he was, why not be who he could be? How many chances was he going to get? And the offer was closing.

'Well,' he said. 'Looks like either the money goes in your pocket or me.'

3

Fast Frankie White was a person of great but misdirected
enthusiasms, the sort of man who, if he had been of a more
literary inclination, might have devoted two years of his life to
learning Spanish in order to read Dante in the original. As a
young man, he had been inexplicably to America and, though
the trip was so short that people meeting him in the street on
his return would ask him when he was going, the experience
was something he always carried around with him, a fragment
of fool's gold he believed would lead him to the real thing. For
the hurried vision of America he had glimpsed, the sense of
how quickly and surprisingly money could be made, had left
him with a kind of Klondyke mentality. Like a mad prospector
who has lost his map, he stumbled around his life, looking for
gold where there was none, following hunches that were hardly
more than superstitions.

His main belief was that the quickest way to money was
through crime. It was a fixation which had persisted in the
face of spectacular proof to the contrary. Frankie White had
been involved in handling stolen property, break-ins, loads
switched from lorries on dark nights, bank-card swindles, none
of it ever on a big scale, and if the money he had made were
set against the sentences he had served, a just society would
have felt that it owed him. If crime had been a company, he
could have gone on strike and won his case. Yet he had a kind
of status in his own world. A lot of policemen had a liking for
him because he had never been known to use violence in his
life. A lot of more successful criminals didn't mind his presence
on the fringes of their activities because he had never informed
on anyone else, no matter what kind of mess he was in himself.
A novice who had never achieved ordination, he remained a
sincere believer and was a worldly innocent. Excluded from
participation in the more serious acts of crime, he had in his
amateur way memorised its rituals and its forms. He knew a
lot of its tricks and many of its ways of speaking. In him these

were no more than imitative but he himself wasn't conscious of that. He meant them.

Clothes were a part of his identification with the image he had made for himself. He could always believe in himself more strongly when he felt he looked as he ought to. This meant that most of the time he dressed the way he believed a successful criminal should – in flashy suits. This morning the costume was different.

He studied himself in the dressing-table mirror of the upstairs room, turning to look over his shoulder, bending down to see how his legs were. The maroon track-suit was a good fit. He looked like a boxing trainer, all right. He jumped quietly and athletically downstairs, trying to make sure he didn't waken his mother. But she was already in the kitchen. She must have heard him moving around in his room, which meant that they were going to go through one of those occasions when they were like people who were appearing in two different plays at the same time. In his play the hero was a worldly-wise criminal who, as worldly-wise criminals will, loved his mother too much to let her know about the dark side of his life. In her play the hero was a basically good-hearted man who had gone wrong but was going to turn over a new leaf. Every time he had come out of prison, her belief in his role had increased.

She had the advantage of having set the scene. There was half a grapefruit, sugared, on the table beside a bowl of cornflakes and a jug of milk. She was making toast.

'Morning, Maw,' he said.

'Hullo, Son. You're up early. My, what ye dressed like that for?'

'Joggin',' he said. 'Got to get a bit fitter.'

'That's a good idea. Ye should do more of that.'

'Ah was talkin' to Dan Scoular in the pub last night. He's comin' out with me.'

'Has Dan not got a job yet, either?'

'Who has, Maw, these days?'

'That's true. Everybody has to bide their time with these things. The whole country's in a terrible state.'

He finished his grapefruit, put the rind in the waste-bin, ran hot water on the saucer, watching the pips go down the drain, and put the saucer on the draining-board. He started on his cornflakes.

'Aye,' she said. 'It's good that ye're keepin' yerself fit. Ye're nearly forty.'

'Ah'm all right. Ah just want to be righter.'

'Ye're nearly forty. That's when Sarah Haggerty's man died. Have ye seen her since ye were back in the town?'

'Saw her on Saturday,' he mumbled through his cornflakes. 'Two weans with her. They're gettin' up.'

'Oh, her weans are really off her hands now. She's got the bigger lassie, ye see. She's eighteen. An' very sensible. She's that fond of the young yins, too. Sarah's really a free agent noo.'

Frankie was busy finishing his cornflakes.

'Aye,' Mrs White said. 'We never ken the day or the hour. Like yer feyther, God rest him. Ye think ye'll stay a while this time, Son?'

'Ah'll be here for two weeks anyway, Maw. Then Ah've got to go up to Glasgow for a week or so. On business.'

'Ah must get that bedroom of mine redecorated. Ye miss Bert Haggerty for that. And never any mess wi' him. In and out and hardly a dent in yer purse. Funny the way he went. It's no' that he wisny looked after or not fed right. Not a better woman in the town than Sarah Haggerty. An' she's never taken up wi' another man. She's a loyal yin.'

Their two separate performances were not without poignancy in the way they played against each other. Frankie's style, as perhaps befitted his role, was more cinematic than theatrical, Hollywood-cryptic, a bit like Gary Cooper without the loquaciousness. He said so little and everything so obliquely partly because he specifically felt the need to minimise all information to his mother about his doings, because it would only worry her – possibly to death, he sometimes dreaded – and partly because he wasn't sure specifically what he felt, and didn't want to know. He was being laconic not only with her but with himself. His inscrutability was self-defence because he dreaded admitting to himself the potentially lacerating guilt his mother's presence evoked.

Mrs White's conversational technique was as highly stylised as a Japanese Noh play. Any verbal gesture might appear very arbitrary and sometimes virtually meaningless yet, to her son, each casual remark could evoke a history of meaning. Hers was a deep and abiding hurt refined by her way of life into bearable and graceful expressions of itself. Forty, for example, was an age of almost magical importance for her. It was then that Frankie's father, a terrible drinking man, had reformed himself into something like an ideal husband. Thereafter, his home was the most important thing in his life. She believed, she had to believe, that the same thing would happen with Frankie. The word was a charm in her mouth.

Sarah Haggerty was the girl Frankie had gone out with when he was young. Mrs White saw her as the most likely source of a cure for Frankie's instability. When she mentioned the state of the nation, she was forbidding him any excuse for committing crime. When she talked about having the bedroom decorated, she simultaneously gave him a blackmail note and reintroduced the saintly spirit of Sarah Haggerty.

Frankie chewed on his food like a rag that stopped him acknowledging the pain. Somewhere far inside himself he almost admitted, as he always almost admitted in the presence of his mother, what a renegade he was. He knew that his life affronted this house and what it stood for. Every time he came here, he half-hoped the pain would be less. It never was because his mother didn't seriously change. She had perhaps become slightly less tolerant and more cross-grained over the last few years but those were surface scratches. The substance of her hadn't altered and that was an awesome, benign endurance, a seemingly limitless capacity to forgive the world whatever it tried to do to her, an incompetence in self-pity. She stole nothing from life, neither materially nor emotionally. Daily, she bartered justly with her circumstances.

The self-contempt she always innocently threatened to bring out in Frankie, like an allergy to himself, was nearer the surface this morning anyway. Dan Scoular was the reason. Frankie was already trying not to feel guilt about the situation in which he had involved Dan. He wasn't sure that Dan could handle it. He remembered the expression on Dan's face when Frankie had given him the track-suit, as if Frankie was part of a plot which had already decided what Dan was going to do. Dan had taken it reluctantly, like a uniform for which he hadn't volunteered but been enlisted.

Frankie deliberately steered his thoughts between the twin guilts of big Dan and his mother. The compass he clutched tightly was that they didn't understand the way things were, the hardness of his life. He had to make a living any way he could.

As Frankie took his tea and toast, finishing the breakfast he hadn't wanted but couldn't commit the insult of refusing, she was still parading her delicate grief and he was still admitting almost nothing to her or himself.

When he came out, it still wasn't light. He got his sister Jessie's old bike out of the hut. He had checked it out before going to bed, blessed it with Three-in-One oil.

Cycling down through the darkened scheme, he found the exhilaration of the rushing wind act like a bellows on the enthusiasm his mother's talk had banked down almost to extinction. Possibilities flared up in his mind. This could put him right in with Matt Mason and that would mean some real money. He would have a way in to a lot of jobs, who knew how big. He might be really on his way. What he had to do was make sure that he kept big Dan to his contract. Matt had given him his instructions: tell the big man as little as possible, make him too knackered to ask. Work him hard. Matt Mason would be looking for a fit man in a fortnight.

Outside Dan Scoular's house, Fast Frankie swung off his bike and laid it against the hedge. The light was on in the living-room downstairs. He whistled once and saw the curtains part and close. He sat down on the kerbstone. The morning wind needled his cheeks. He heard the door open and stood up and took hold of the bike. But there was no sound of feet. Looking round, he saw that the light was off and the door was open but no one had appeared. Then he saw Dan's head come out and glance around.

'Anybody about?'

'Who ye expectin', Dan? The bogeyman?'

Dan Scoular came out on to the step and closed the front door very delicately, as if it was the fuse of a bomb. He glanced around again and tiptoed down the path. He stood shivering on the pavement.

'What's the problem, Dan?'

'Sh! Don't speak so loud.'

'What is it?' Frankie whispered. 'Ye feart the wife hears ye and doesny let ye out to play?'

Dan looked down at himself, dressed in the track-suit Frankie had given him.

'Ah feel such a diddy in this gear,' he said.

'All the joggers wear that. Okay. Are ye right?'

'Ah just don't want anybody tae see me.'

'Come on, Dan.'

'Can we not just walk till we're out the scheme?'

But Frankie was already on his bike and pushing off. Half-heartedly, in a kind of embarrassed lope, Dan Scoular joined him. Almost immediately he had stopped.

'Frankie!' he hissed. 'Who's that comin' up? Christ, it's auld Wullie Mairshall.'

'It doesny –' Frankie had started to say but Dan Scoular was off.

As Frankie looked round, he saw his charge disappear round the back of a house and start to go through the gardens. Frankie decided to pedal on and catch up with Dan when he re-emerged. As he came alongside Wullie Mairshall, he nodded and spoke.

'Fresh mornin', Wullie,' he called.

'That you, Frankie? Hold on a minute.'

Frankie stopped. Wullie was peering up towards where Dan had been.

'Ah could swear Ah saw some bastard goin' round the side of a hoose there. Did ye notice?'

'Not me, Wullie,' Frankie said. 'A trick of the light maybe.'

'No' wi' ma e'en, Frankie. The last thing to go wi' me will be ma eyes. Ah'll bet ye Ah can see through the coffin-lid. Ah saw somebody, Frankie. Ye for takin' a look wi' me? He looked like a big yin.'

'There's nobody, Wullie. Ah doubt ye've had too much to drink last night.'

As he finished speaking, there was a startlingly loud, deep barking, as if a big dog had a microphone held to its mouth. Muffled curses and scuffling noises were overwhelmed by the continuous barking.

'Aye, maybe ye're right, Frankie,' Wullie Mairshall said. 'But if Ah was drunk last night, there's a big dug been on the bevvy as well. Anyway, Ah don't think we'll have to worry. By the sound of things, big bastard's been turned into Kennomeat by noo. See ye, Frankie.'

In his nervousness Frankie forgot to say goodbye. He pedalled on as if he was part of a cortège and not sure that he wasn't in the hearse. If Dan had been torn in legs or hands or anywhere else for that matter, the fight was over before it had started and so was Frankie White's career in the big time, and maybe in any time at all. He heard a back door opening somewhere and a voice shouting oaths. He was already planning a trip to London when he saw Dan Scoular emerge back on to the road and keep on running. He seemed to be fit enough. Frankie had to pedal hard to catch up with him.

'Are you all right?' Frankie asked.

'Big, daft bloody dug!' Dan Scoular said and slowed to a walk.

Frankie came off his bike and walked beside him.

'Did it bite ye?'

'Not for the want of tryin'. Ah'm glad that chain held.'

'But it didny get ye?'

'Ah'll tell ye somethin'. Ah've learned some very fancy footwork already. Ah made Gentleman Jim Corbett look geriatric there. That was ma first bit of trainin'. Ah'm knackered already.' He *was* breathing deeply. 'See, that's somethin' nowadays. Ye noticed that? How many workin'-class folk have got hounds of the Baskerville? It's right. The place is lowpin wi' mad dugs. It's a sign of the times. They're all that feart from one another these days. They don't know where the next mugger's comin' from. It never used to be like that. Ah hate bad dugs. The bastards.'

'Right. Let's go,' Frankie said, having confirmed that no injuries threatened the big fight.

'Frankie, give us a chance. Ah left ma lungs back in that gairden.'

'Come on, come on. Ye'll be a lot harder pushed in three weeks. Work to be done.'

Frankie was on his bike and going. Dan had no option but to labour after him. He ran beyond the houses into a dawn that was at first just a little light spilled on the air, then seeping

71

imperceptibly till it was staining the sky into a marl of changing colours. Hedgerows rediscovered green and fields took shape. He found a rhythm and was trotting, not easily, through miles of morning. He was carefully asking his body questions and the answers were unsure but optimistic. He wasn't fit but he knew that the fitness was there, under its coating of rust, just needing the effort. He gave it a little just now but not too much.

Sometimes on the hills he would pass Frankie who would have to get off and walk. They passed each other with insulting comments. Once, from behind, he heard Frankie swearing. Looking back, he saw that the chain of the bike had come off and Frankie was struggling with it. Dan Scoular spun laughing on the road and carried on. He vaulted the gate below the hill of Farquhar's Farm, slithered up the slope and collapsed at the top. He could see the town from where he was. From here it looked like not a bad place to be. In the clarity that relaxation from exertion can give, he thought it was good here, good the way it was, himself aware of the presence of his strength and the town there waiting, a place where the people he loved were. It was good. Who needed complications? Then he heard Frankie White shouting, 'Dan!'

He saw him appear on the road below, pedalling with difficulty and looking around, confused. But he would find him. Dan didn't help, just waited till he was found. Frankie left his bike against the gate, climbed over and scrambled up the hill.

'Right! Up, big man,' he said.

Dan was puzzled.

'On yer feet. Phase Two of the training programme.'

Frankie was moving around with his oil-stained hands held out in front of him, palms towards Dan. Dan stood up and watched him.

'You try tae hit ma hands,' Frankie said. 'But only ma hands. You watch. Ah can move like a ghost. Don't worry. Ah'll let ma hands ride wi' the punches.'

Dan began at a reluctant shuffle but soon they were moving briskly around the flat top of the hill. Frankie was dodging and weaving and moving his hands about with bewildering speed and Dan Scoular was purpling the palms of them with hooks and jabs and crosses that seemed to pluck their force out of thin air, just happened, needing no time to build their whipping trajectories. They built up a desperate momentum until Frankie's hands got their own signals crossed and his right palm was against his own shoulder when Dan Scoular hit it. He went down so fast he did a backward roll down the hill. There was a moment of silence as he lay still. Then his voice came, very small and pretending to be calm.

'Fine. Ah was meanin' to take a break now anyway.' Then he groaned alarmingly. 'Ah just didny mean it to be ma hand.'

He rolled over on his back and Dan sat down beside him, laughing.

'Fast Frankie?' Dan said through his laughter. 'Trainin' for a fight? This has been some start. Ah nearly get etten alive wi' a dug. You canny even get a bike that goes right. Then Ah mistake ye for a punchbag. We better own up. We're Laurel an' Hardy at this game.'

They both lay back, looking up at the sky and laughing helplessly. The idea of it started to build between them.

'We could offer tae fight the Marx Brothers,' Frankie said.

'There's too many of them for us.'

'Ah'd be all right as long as there was no punchin' allowed.'

'Ah think we better tell Matt Mason we were only kiddin'.'

The mention of the name was like a lapse of taste in a comedy routine. It killed the laughter. Frankie White sat up and plucked a stalk of grass. He felt cold now that he had stopped sweating. Dan Scoular leaned on his elbow and looked back towards the town again.

'Who is this man, Frankie?' he said.

'Who?'

'The one Ah'm supposed to fight.'

'Ah've seen him about a bit. Ah don't know. Ah'd say he's about six feet. Bit heavier than you. Maybe fifteen stones. They say he's good. But he's gettin' on all right. Some reckon he's past it.' He slapped Dan on the leg. 'You'll take him, Dan. Don't worry. As long as ye're fit. And you'll be fit.'

'That's not what Ah asked ye, Frankie.'

'How?'

'Who *is* he?'

'He's Cutty Dawson.'

73

'But who's Cutty Dawson? What does he *do*? Does he have a family? What kinda man is he?'

'Christ, Dan. How would Ah know? What d'ye want to know that for? Ye're not gonny be his pen-pal. Ye're gonny batter the shite out 'im. The less ye know about him the better.'

'Ah just wonder what he's like.'

'Dan, listen. You're not getting paid to be a private detective. Don't ask. Just fight. Just as long as Cutty's handlers know his blood group. So that when they rush him tae hospital, there's no time wasted.'

They didn't feel so close any more. Frankie chewed his stalk of grass and stared down towards the road. He was grateful that it led away from Thornbank. He was here to earn some money. He didn't need complications.

Dan felt embarrassed again by their track-suits, a pretence of unified professionalism. They weren't engaged in preparation for the same event at all. Frankie was training him for Frankie, for the serving of a purpose in Frankie's life. Dan wasn't sure what he was training himself for but he would have to find out on his own.

Their previous laughter, which had seemed like camaraderie at the time, was in retrospect like the nervousness of strangers. It left a gloom on them. The cloud that went across the sun felt like a private arrangement.

There is an abandoned quarry near Thornbank, one of those mis-hewn, unfinished monuments to industry with which nature is left to improvise. It had at first grown grass and trees around its rim that attractively concealed the sheerness of its sides till you might unsuspectingly find yourself poised over a fifty-foot drop into a pool of black water, depth unknown. It is filled in now, but not before a few children had drunk the black water. Jack Ferguson, Dan's best friend at primary school, had been one of them. Every time Dan passed the place, Jack's death acknowledged him, seemed waiting for his own. Dan passed the quarry every day in training.

It was only one of many places on his route where ghosts of his childhood confronted, not reassuringly, the man he was trying to become. There was the park where he had played football as a boy through long, dishevelled games that could

reach exotic scores like 25–18 and where the numbers playing
could swell so much that sometimes, having the ball, you felt
as if you were trying to dribble through a city. He passed every
morning the tree where the rope had broken and catapulted
Andy Mills into a coma from which he emerged asking what
month it was. There was the small wood in which he and
Sadie McAvoy had explored each other through a series of
compulsively repeated evenings until they worked out how to
get it right and, in the first orgasm he had had in company,
he felt like a Catherine wheel going off and wondered where
the pieces of himself might land.

Memory feeding corrosively on the future and Dan living
still in the countryside where he had been born, he was running
every day through an intensifying awareness of his own tran-
sience, through an argument with his past he wasn't sure he
could resolve. Occasionally, his self-doubts referred themselves
to Frankie White in his need to bounce them off some surface,
no matter how hollow.

'You notice somethin'?' he said one day at the end of a run.
'You notice how much rubbish there is around?'

'Sorry?' Frankie was preoccupied with his own thoughts.

'The places we pass. People are dumpin' rubbish anywhere
these days.'

'It's not any different from it ever was, is it?'

'Oh, it is. It never used tae be like that. Just dumped at the
side of the road. As if they didny care much any more. This
place is different.'

'Maybe not. Maybe ye just notice it more because we're out
and about so much.'

'Naw. It's different.'

Frankie White shrugged and Dan Scoular didn't enlarge on
what he was trying to say. Those casual scatterings of litter
meant something to him he wouldn't have found it easy to
translate. They were like the place rejecting its sense of itself
and therefore his own sense of it as well. People said you
couldn't go back. More than that, it seemed to him, you
couldn't stay. He wondered if he had been trying to stay in a
place that was no longer there. The suspicion of its absence
made him question if it ever had been there. He remembered
Betty's disbelief in it early in their marriage.

75

A scene had stayed in his mind from their time in the rented flat. They had been sitting on the carpet in front of the fire. He was drinking from a can of beer. She was sipping coffee. It was one of those moments when a theme develops spontaneously out of random conversation. He had stumbled on her incredulity about his past and he had started to feed it scraps from his memory.

'Oh, come on,' became her refrain.

'Naw, it's true.'

'You don't expect me to believe that.'

'Cross ma heart an' hope for to die. Better still, Ah'll cross yours. It's more fun that way. There was another bloke. Sammy Ramsay. Stayed down the road from us. Know what he did one night? He had fags but no matches. Right? Desperate for a smoke. All the shops are shut. All the other houses in darkness. Know what Sammy does? True. Stands on a chair, holds his head up to the light wi' the fag in his mouth. Smashes the light bulb. Tryin' to get a light off the filament. That's gen. Pickin' Mazda out his heid for a fortnight, he was. The bold Sammy.'

'Uh-huh.'

'Then there was Freddie Taylor. Lookin' for eight draws on the treble chance. Got to seven. Waitin' for the eighth and a fortune. A home win. He fired the wireless out through the windae on to the front green. We were a passionate people.'

'I think you make them up.'

Now he wondered himself if he *had* made something up, not the substance of the incidents but the significance they had come to have for him. His former sense of his past seemed to him now about as incredible, as untrustworthy as it had to Betty. He found himself questioning the shared identity he had found there. But even as he questioned it, he was confronted daily with the stubbornness of place, the hauntingness of its familiar associations.

Passing every day the house where he had lived with his parents, he felt it most strongly. That small council cottage-type was his private museum of a past he seemed to understand less every day. He had been an only child, born when his mother and father were already in their thirties. That had at first made them even closer to him than they might have been,

76

for they were ready for a child, whetted with longing and bored with the unrestricted time they had, and they had made their lives around him. But when he came into his teens, things changed. It seemed they couldn't follow him, even in imagination, into the newness of his experience. They had conceived him to be an extension of their own lives, not a contradiction of them.

The first time it had become clear to all of them that he was becoming a stranger in the house was when he gave up his academic course at school. His parents were incredulous. They saw education as self-evidently the most important thing in his life, the culmination of their efforts on his behalf. For days they threatened, cajoled, bullied, and he refused. When the noise of argument subsided, something irrevocable had happened in their three-fold relationship. It was as if a betrayal had taken place.

He had lived with that awareness ever since, still did. His motivation at the time, he now knew, had been partly emotional and instinctive, but only partly. It may have been to some extent compounded simply with impatience. But there had also been in it a blurred groping towards rationality. It had been a serious choice, related to a growing distrust of the dream his parents had nurtured for so long. When he tried to look at their lives, he saw them as a kind of deferment, a belief in the future. They gave you the past like a burden to be carried forward and transformed into fulfilment in your own life, or perhaps simply passed on to your own children, made even heavier. He had always found that the mortification of the present in order to beatify the future was an obscene principle. He believed that the present was all anyone truly had. Also, he simply didn't accept that the principle worked.

His parents' lives had been a long and quiet self-sacrifice. For what? His father had worked in the pits all his life. The gradually improving conditions had done no more than compensate for the erosions of ageing, so that his father had never seemed to do more than hold his own. His mother's only ambitions had appeared to be for others. He saw their experience as an injustice in which they had acquiesced. His mind tried to reject it.

Yet every time he passed that house, the memory of it stayed doggedly in step with him for a long time after. Time and again, he fought his father in the back green. Time and again he lost. He could try to generate contempt or pity or anger at what his father had done to him that day but the memory stayed brute, refused to domesticate. He had seen something in his father's face, a hard grieving, that no subsequent thinking upon could quite make powerless. It was as if his father knew something that he must convey to him, a bleak knowledge to impart beyond the mind to assimilate, a law for the blood to learn.

That dark transaction, past rationality, haunted him still. What it meant, what it might have done to him, he couldn't know. Perhaps he would find out with Cutty Dawson. Preparing for that meeting, running, training, he sensed himself building a rational structure on a foundation that was mystery. He might hone his body to a single purpose towards Matt Mason's 'line' but what would arrive there was unknowably more. Seeing Wullie Mairshall from time to time as he ran and being careful to avoid him, Dan realised that what Wullie stood for, as well as many other things, would be waiting for him when the running stopped.

Eddie Foley was in the office himself when the phone rang. Lifting it, he thought he was plugged into several crossed lines. At least three people were shouting somewhere and a fourth voice was saying, 'Keep it down, will ye?' Eddie waited with the phone held slightly away from his ear. He was glancing at the daily paper on Matt Mason's desk when the voice got through with a clear 'Hullo?'

'Frankie White,' Eddie said.

'That you, Eddie?'

'The very same.'

'Look, I'm checkin' in to say everythin's fine here. No sweat. Okay?'

Phones brought out the Hollywood in Frankie. Perhaps it was because the person at the other end couldn't see him and therefore couldn't contradict the image he wanted to project. No doubt it would have been even better if the phone had been an old wall phone so that he could hold one part to his ear and lean urgently into the other part. His voice took on a slightly American tinge.

'So that's the message,' he said. 'Things are looking good. If you would just pass that on to Matt, Eddie. See you.'

'Hold on a minute, Frankie,' Eddie said. 'Ye might be seein' us quicker than ye think if ye don't wait to speak to Matt personally. He doesn't like second-hand information.'

'But there's really nothin' to tell, Eddie. It's all goin' smooth.'

'Well, let's keep it that way, Frankie. You just wait there. Matt's out in the shop. He may be a wee while coming. But Ah would wait if Ah was you. Even if it costs ye a few bob more. Could cost ye dearer if you don't.'

Eddie put the phone down on the desk and crossed to the window of one-way glass that looked down on to Matt Mason's betting shop. He saw Matt talking to the marker up on his elevated platform. A couple of other people looked as if they were waiting to talk to Matt. Eddie went down, picked his way among the punters and whispered in Matt Mason's ear. Matt nodded and went on talking. Eddie came back up into the office, closed the door, lifted the phone and said, 'He's comin',' put it back down and started to read the paper.

At the other end of the line, Frankie White was standing behind the bar of the Red Lion, looking suave and nodding to Davie Dykes across the room. He was wishing he didn't have to speak to Matt Mason because he didn't want his feeling about how good things were here interfered with. It was the fifth day of their training and Frankie would have enjoyed just going on like this.

The place was more alive than he had seen it in a long time. For a Friday lunch-time this had to be a record in recent years. Dan and he had been making a small impact in the town. A lot of people didn't know exactly what was going on, just vaguely knew Dan Scoular was training for some kind of fight but that had been enough to arouse their interest. Alan Morrison had offered an outbuilding as training quarters. It was a place Alan had gone out to look at from time to time, presumably converted stables, and sometimes under the inspirational promptings of the whisky it had metamorphosed in his imagination to a Bierkeller or a function room where flushed and well-fed dinner-dancers swirled to the sound of real music. But always it had reverted with his hangover to its bleak, grey self. Now, without too large an expenditure of capital – a home-made heavy bag hung from the ceiling, a couple of old chairs, some towels and a skipping rope – it had become a gymnasium. It was proving a sound investment, for it meant that Dan and his trainer were in the pub every day and that meant a lot of other people were as well. One of their rewards was that Frankie could use Alan's private phone.

Frankie was enjoying his status. It was perhaps the first time since his childhood that he had felt he really belonged in Thornbank. He saw more to the place than he had seen in it before. This was the closest he had ever come to finding an external set of circumstances that matched the vague blueprint he had of himself. He was doing something he felt to be slightly glamorous and slightly disreputable and it made him known and he was getting paid for it. If Matt Mason were just to keep the expenses coming, Frankie felt he could have settled for this, the early-morning runs, the supervised sweating sessions, the banter in the pub, him training Dan Scoular for ever for a fight that never happened. Wouldn't that have done?

He looked across at the man who had been responsible for this feeling. Dan Scoular was sitting drinking his orange juice and talking to Davie Dykes. Wullie Mairshall, who hadn't yet worked out the solution to the barking dog mystery, had wandered over to them. Even Davie's stories seemed to have found an extra thrust to their fantasy. Dan was laughing. He looked already as if he was sitting in a slightly brighter light than the others, and he would get fitter. He was beginning to enjoy the emergence of harder edges in himself. Frankie felt a slight pang when he looked at him. He was so open and happy sitting there, like a party to which everybody was invited. He knew so little about what he was involved in. Frankie wasn't sure he himself knew much more. Their temporary happiness didn't belong to them, it was rented.

'Yes,' the landlord said.

'Hullo, Matt. Frankie White here.'

'I didn't think it was the Duke of Edinburgh. Where you speaking from? Dial-a-riot?'

'Ah'm in the Red Lion. Well, Matt, things are going well. We're –'

'I hope that big man's not in there with you.'

'Dan's on the orange juice. Come on, Matt. He's behaving like a champion. He's three times fitter than he was when you saw him already.'

'But I don't want him sitting in there advertising. We're not selling tickets for this, you know. You sorted out the misgivings you said he was having?'

'He's all right, Matt. He's just such a decent big man. Ah mean, it's not the sort of thing he's done before. But that's one of the reasons for letting him be about here. Keeps his spirits up.'

'All right. Just so long as he doesn't interfere with any other kind of spirits. You let me know the first sip of beer, even, he takes. I know he's going to turn up. Even if it's in a coffin. But I want his head as right for the job as we can get it. I'm going to arrange something for him when he gets up here. Just to put him right in the mood, if he's wavering.'

'How do you mean, Matt?'

'I know what I mean. You don't have to. Just you work on your end of it. It's not just the body, you know. I think he's got it there. But I'm not so sure about his head. He tries to see round corners too much.'

'On that very subject, Matt. How about this? Ah let three of the boys from down here come up for the fight. What Ah think —'

'You're not on.'

'But, Matt. What that would —'

'Forget it. We're not running buses with "Thornbank Supporters Club" on them. What's wrong with you? All that country air must be addling your three brain cells. That won't happen.'

Frankie smiled to somebody in the bar.

'That it then?' Matt Mason said.

'That's it.' Frankie was thinking of something else to say when the line went dead.

'Cheers then, Matt,' he said loudly, laughing. 'Sure, sure. Ah'll keep in touch.'

He put down the phone.

'Sorry Ah took so long there, Alan,' he said. 'But he likes to know how the man's doin'. How much for that then?'

'Forget it, Frankie,' Alan said. His hand gestured towards

the busy bar. 'I think it's covered. We've even got some ladies in, the day. Civilisation at last.'

Frankie had noticed the women. He usually did. Since his teens, they had been noticing him. His looks were perhaps the gift that had stunted his growth, as gifts often do. Finding it so easy to be attractive to people when he was young, Frankie had never really matured beyond the belief that effort was a sign of innate inferiority. One of the women was Sarah Haggerty. Sarah, like Frankie's mother, like most women, activated subtle danger signals in him. He secretly felt them to be much more substantial than he was, capable of such exotic emotions as passion and commitment. He knew his way around their anatomies all right but his visits there tended to be fleeting and functional because he had felt hidden in those marvellous recesses of flesh enough warmth and intensity to shrivel his awareness of himself into an admission of how much he lacked those qualities. Women were the place where Frankie had come nearest to having to acknowledge the hollowness that filled his flashy suits. And since he was afraid of them, he had adopted the most popular and the most convenient camouflage. He had become a philanderer. He made sure that when he was with one woman, he was always en route to another one, in case, should he stay too long, he might discover less in himself than he wanted to find. With them, he talked a filibuster against the coming of that moment when he might confess a stricken silence and lay his head against a woman and admit, uncleverly, incomprehensibly, he loved her.

Of all women, Sarah Haggerty set that alarm system ringing loudest because, being younger then, he had come closer than at any time since to taking the chance of finding out what was really in him. She was the more banal but the more substantial truth of himself he had been in flight from for so long. She had been watching him on the phone with such honest interest that it wasn't immodest of him to suspect that she was here to see him. The realisation did two things, in rapid succession. It made him wonder if he hadn't been wrong, all those years ago. It made him afraid to be wondering such things. He put on his act like a visor and went over.

'Sarah, love of my life,' he said and kissed her hand.

The three women started laughing. The other two would be

about the same age as Sarah, therefore about the same age as he was himself. One of them wasn't bad. She was blonde and mildly plump, held an expression of coquetry to her face like a slightly battered fan. The other, he thought, was gone. Her overdone make-up was a promise so desperate it could have been a threat. She looked like a reheated meal. Sarah was still very good-looking, the only one he could have been serious about, so he made sure to pay attention to the blonde one. Sarah introduced them but he was so involved in his own routine he didn't catch the names.

'As always, it's great to see you,' he said, his eyes including the blonde woman.

'What's this you and Dan are up to?' Sarah asked. 'Your second childhood?'

She was indicating his track-suit.

'Quite the *contraire*,' Frankie said. He had always thought the occasional word of French made all the difference with women. They had to be very occasional. The only other two he felt he could use with confidence were '*amour*' and '*bon*'. 'This is very serious business. Work for men.'

'They tell me Dan Scoular's goin' to fight somebody,' the blonde woman said. The fierceness of her stare had no connection with the lightness of the remark, as if her eyes were dislocated from her mouth.

'There is a rumour to that effect.' Frankie smiled at them mysteriously. 'Ah've heard as much myself.'

'So what are you?' the reheated meal was saying. 'His manager or what?'

'His trainer, lovely.' The epithet was the toll his indifference paid. 'Ah'm just gettin' him fit. Givin' him a few wrinkles. Few tricks of the trade.'

'So where is this?' Sarah asked. 'You couldn't get us some tickets?'

'It's not that kind of fight, Sarah,' Frankie said. 'A strictly private affair. Ah would if Ah could. You know that, love. Tell you what. As compensation, Ah'll buy ye all a drink.'

He had done it smoothly, conveyed an impression without getting involved in serious business and then got out, neat as shinning down the back ronepipe as the husband arrived. He could imagine the interest he was leaving behind him.

83

On his way towards Dan's table, he was stopped by Sam MacKinlay. Frankie enjoyed the experience of people reaching out to touch him. It was as near as he would get to fans tearing off a piece of his clothes. Harry Naismith and Alistair Corstorphine, the other two domino players, were sitting with him. Frankie gave them his attention the more generously because he couldn't remember them ever wanting it before. He saw Sam as the only one of the three really worth the time, at least a quick mouth. Harry was a man lost in his fifties, who had hitched his life to Sam's to see if he might not manage some mileage yet. Alistair was a gentle mid-thirties man, still testing life with his toe.

'Frankie, what's the news?' Sam MacKinlay said.

'He doesn't fancy it, Sam.'

'That's the best ye can do?'

'Sam. You saw the man. What he says goes.'

'But it's only us three and maybe old Alan,' Sam said. 'We're not askin' to book the whole North Stand. Christ, ye could smuggle that lot in in yer pockets.'

'We'd love to see it, Frankie,' Alistair said.

'That's a fact,' Harry said.

Frankie stared past them thoughtfully, let them register how much he cared. He thought he could see a way to play Matt Mason right but it wouldn't be to his advantage to tell them that. He thought suspense might be good for them. He had a commodity to sell.

'Ah'll be honest, boys,' he said. 'Ah asked him there. He shat on it from a great height. "Forget it!" That's what he said. "We're not running buses." "You're not on." Those were his exact words. What can Ah say?'

Alistair put his hand to his head. Harry looked at Sam MacKinlay.

'Come on, Frankie,' Sam said. 'Don't give us that. You count a bit up in Glasgow. We're where you come from. Big Dan's Thornbank. So are we. And so are you. Us country boys have to stick thegither. What ye say?'

Frankie was shaking his head, wishing he could find a way to help them. He made to speak, hesitated.

'There's one possible way,' he said. 'Ach, naw. Let's forget it. He says no, boys.'

84

'Frankie!' Sam said. 'Just tell us the way. Come on. Ah knew you when you had vents at yer arse the tailor never made. So what's the way?'

'Well. There's going to be checkers at the gate. Right? Ah could bung them a few quid. Maybe that way, Ah could get ye in. But it means it would cost ye. Maybe at least forty for the four of ye. It's a liberty. Ah don't want to do that with ma mates. Ah think we should forget it.'

'Don't worry, Frankie,' Sam said.

He looked at the other two. The money at the moment was a myth among them but their three pairs of eyes agreed to make it somehow a reality. They sealed the agreement with smiles.

'You do that, Frankie,' Sam said.

'You sure? Ah hate to do this.'

'Ye're doin' us a favour. Don't you worry. We want to see the big man do his stuff. You mark us down for four.'

'Okay,' Frankie said reluctantly. 'Ah'll do ma best. It's not a guarantee, now. But, listen, Ah'll really be tryin' for youse boys.'

Frankie touched Sam's shoulder and walked away. Harry Naismith winked at Sam MacKinlay.

'He's all right, him, eh?' Alistair Corstorphine said.

'Aye, but it's really Sam we've got to thank,' Harry said. 'You put the pressure on there, Sam. So ye did. He was goin' to bomb us out.'

'Aye, so ye did,' Alistair said admiringly.

'Well, Ah would hope Ah know how to handle Frankie White by this time,' Sam MacKinlay said.

His two brief public performances had reinstated Frankie's sense of himself. Matt Mason's ominousness was receding like a threatened headache which hasn't materialised. But as he jauntily approached Dan Scoular's table, there was something in Dan's face that bothered him. He might have looked to other people just like a man enjoying himself but in the week of their training together Frankie had learned to read that face more thoroughly than most. Dan was a more thoughtful man than Frankie had at first imagined. It was just that he was seldom in any hurry to voice his thoughts. If you were observant enough, you might notice that his expressions were reacting to

85

the conversation like afterthoughts, the eyes still watching you but opaque, the smile a second too slow, and you would realise the machinery was working away on something else. What it might be making of it you could only imagine.

Frankie just hoped it wasn't trouble as he sat down at the table. The mood was light enough. Davie the Deaver was recounting how in his youth he had been involved in cutting down the trees of the Sahara ('the nights were that cold there') and had helped to make it a desert. He seemed genuinely to regret the carelessness of their actions and the devastating results. He pleaded the ignorance of the times. ('There was never as much talk about ecology then.') Knowing the rules. Wullie Mairshall was patiently raising rational objections to see how Davie would cope with them. It was acknowledged that there always had been a desert known as the Sahara but it had been much smaller ('about the size of Troon beach') until the arrival of the army and Davie Dykes.

Like mouth music before a battle, Davie and Wullie receded and left fighter and trainer remembering the nature of what was ahead. There were fewer people in the pub. Sarah and her friends sent over a drink but Dan said his orange juice was enough.

'Alan's done all right the day,' Frankie said. 'We should be on commission.'

'Folk keep wishin' me well,' Dan said. 'Ye would think Ah was fightin' for them.'

'Well, ye're from Thornbank.'

'But they don't know anythin' about it.'

'How d'ye mean?'

'They don't know what the fight's about.'

'They don't have to. They're supporting you.'

'Why? They don't know what Ah'm doin'.'

'Dan, come on.'

'They don't. Ah feel as if Ah'm connin' them. Because the truth is Ah don't know maself.'

Frankie White was aware of Matt Mason's voice on the phone like an earpiece to which he was permanently plugged in, being prompted.

'You're earning money, Dan. That's what ye're doin'. At a time when there's very little to earn, you've found a way.'

'Aye, but Ah'm not sure what the way is. Ah think it's time you told me all ye know about this, Frankie.'

'What Ah know? That wouldn't take long.'

'So fair enough.'

'Dan. Take ma advice. As the man says, the more you know the less the better. You're goin' into a bad place. Cutty Dawson? He's been around a bit. A lotta experience. You don't know what ye're goin' to find in there. Even about yerself. We all know you're good, Dan. But this isny a scuffle outside a pub. This is a serious matter. You're goin' to discover what's in you. This is new territory. You're goin' up the Amazon, Dan. You only take essentials to a place like that. Ye don't clutter yerself with stuff that's not goin' to help you. Extra luggage'll finish you. Ah'm tellin' ye. Ye think Cutty Dawson's worried about the ins and outs of it? He's got one thought: batter Dan Scoular down. You be the same. It's the only way.'

'Cutty Dawson must've improved since Monday. You fancied ma chances then.'

'Ah still do, Dan. But only if everything's right. And Ah'm tellin' ye the way to get it right. Will ye listen? Anyway, there's another thing. It's a bit late to worry. Ye took the man's money. He's fixed up the whole thing. If ye decided ye didny like the smell of it, what ye goin' to do?'

'Ah would decide.'

'Dan, you've decided! You took that two hundred quid in here, what d'ye think that was? Time to think? That was money. That was Matt Mason's money. It might as well've been his head stamped on the notes.'

'Ah could have second thoughts.'

Sarah Haggerty and her friends had risen to leave and they waved across. Frankie made a very small, brief gesture of waving back, feeling distant from them, like an unwilling passenger on a ship he felt pulling away from the cosy normalcy of their lives. He had just realised it was a mystery cruise.

He remembered why he had never felt fully at home among these people. They were so simple. How did they think the world worked? How had they managed to live so long and learn so little? There was no hope for them. Industry had fleeced them for generations and they still wondered what it was all about. Whatever happened to them, they shrugged and thought maybe tomorrow would be a good day. When did they call 'enough!'? His own mother. He remembered going with her one day to pay her rent. A woman who had been through more hard times than he wanted to think about, a woman who through it all had never treated another person beneath the high standards she modestly called 'dacency', and she got mixed up with the money and the clerk behind the counter, a weedy nyaff with pimples and an underfed moustache, was treating her with contempt. The most painful moment had been outside when his mother gently lectured Frankie for swearing. 'He was only doin' his job,' she said. They never learned. Now Dan Scoular was talking about 'second thoughts'. Frankie White's fears for himself made him speak without any of his customary attention to the image he was projecting.

'Dan,' he said sincerely. 'Ye don't get second thoughts with these people. Your second thought could be your last. You offend this man, he'll hide in yer coalhouse for a week just to get ye.'

They stared at each other in the first moment of mutual honesty they had achieved. Dan Scoular saw very clearly the other's fear, the self-protective need to get his message across: 'We're both in a place of danger, we pull together here or we both go down.' Frankie White saw Dan Scoular's eyes steady on him, stare into the facts, try to consider the possibilities. In the honesty of those eyes, unmuddied by any deliberate deceit, Frankie White thought he could see the thoughts surface, vivid as fish: the first was accusation but it didn't stay long; the second looked a lot more dangerous, the refusal yet to believe that there was nothing else to do but go through with this.

'Ah want tae know exactly what ye mean,' Dan said. 'Ye mean like killin'?'

Impaled on those eyes, Frankie White had no option but to be honest.

'Ah might mean that,' he said. 'Dan, Ah don't know. Ah tell ye the truth. It's a certainty Matt Mason has done that before. Ah mean, Ah couldn't take ye and show ye the body. But that just makes it more worrying, doesn't it? If Ah could, he wouldn't be here. But he is here. And that's our problem. Ah don't know. Maybe if you reneged, it wouldn't be as serious as that. But, oh, it would be serious. Very, very serious. Bad injuries at the least. Like, very bad. And maybe just the chance of terminal ones. A man like him, Dan. He can't afford anybody makin' him look silly. That's his version of the Wall Street crash. Suddenly, he's got nothin' in the bank. Suddenly, it's goin' to take three weeks of threats to get him a free packet of fags. Fear. That's his currency, Dan. It's as good a money as any. An' he's got plenty of his kinda currency, Ah'm tellin' ye. Like very plenty. Ah've seen him go into places and buy them with a look. Ye think the delicate conscience of some big, nice man from Thornbank is something he's goin' to decide he can afford to subsidise? Grow up, big Dan. Ye're playin' in the first division here. We're not usin' jackets for goalposts. Dan, you made a promise with your hand. Ye took two hundred quid. It's simple. Keep the promise or maybe die.'

Dan Scoular stared, not without a certain amount of fear, into what he had said. When he spoke, the smallness of what he had to say was an inverse measure of his innocence. Hearing him, Frankie liked him for it and was frustrated by it at the same time.

'Ye could've told me what ye were gettin' me into,' Dan Scoular said.

'Dan!' Frankie said. 'Ah thought Ah was gettin' ye into a fight. Just one more fight. Just what ye're good at. That's all Ah thought Ah was doin'. Ah should've known better. In this place. But Ah know Matt Mason's lookin' for a puncher. Ah think to maself, Ah know a real puncher. Dan, it seemed simple at the time. It was easy, Ah'm tellin' ye. Here's a fight. Here's a man who can fight. Let's put them together. And Ah'll admit Ah saw somethin' in it for me. But Ah saw somethin' in it for you as well. That was the beauty of it. Everythin' fitted. It really did. Everythin' fitted. Everybody was making somethin' out it. You as well. An' there could be more in this for you if ye won. Matt Mason's got a lot of power. Could change yer life. And all you're bein' asked to do is what ye're good at.'

'What are you good at, Frankie?' Dan Scoular said.

'Hey, Ah'm still lookin'.' Frankie, for a moment, was back defensively performing. 'That's something Ah'm not sure Ah've found yet.'

'When ye do find it, Frankie, don't practise it on me. If we get out this all right.'

They sat in their own thoughts.

'Frankie. So tell me. If it's as serious as you say, Ah better know everythin' there is tae know. Ah want tae know where Ah am here.'

Frankie felt again the ambivalence this place caused in him. He thought perhaps he shouldn't come back, perhaps he should make this his last trip except for coming in to see his mother and geting out as quickly as possible. It was too complicated coming here. He remembered Matt Mason's warning about telling Dan Scoular as little as possible. He remembered how much he liked Dan Scoular. In choosing to tell Dan as much as he knew of the truth, he honestly didn't know whether he was obeying Matt Mason in a subtle way, making out of the truth the ultimate expediency, deploying the only method he knew to make Dan's honesty conform, or whether he was reacting straight to Dan Scoular's demand, obeying his growing liking and respect for an undevious man.

'Okay, Dan,' he said. 'This is what Ah know. And it won't take up a lot of yer time. Matt Mason is a bookie. He's got pubs. As Ah've suggested to ye, he's done a couple of other things. Don't ask me what they were. But they were nasty. As nasty as you can imagine, Ah'll settle for that. Now there's another man. He's called Cam Colvin. He's more severe than Matt. Don't have any doubts about that, Dan. Most of us live in a world we don't know's there. Ah promise you. People die and they call it natural causes. Ah wish Ah could believe in natural causes. Dan, Ah think maybe we've lost the natural causes. They used to be there. See when ma mother dies. They can call it what they like. But she was killed. When it happens, she was killed. So what am I goin' to do? Ah'll go to the funeral and be a nice son. But Ah'll know that she went through what she didn't have to go through. Ah know that, Dan. It's how we live. Some of us pay for others. That's not fair.'

Frankie took another sip of the double whisky Sarah Haggerty had sent over. Dan Scoular didn't want him to drink any more just at the moment, needed him clear.

'Frankie,' he said. 'You were sayin'.'

Frankie swallowed the indulgence of his own sadness.

'Well, that's it, Dan,' he said. 'Matt Mason and Cam Colvin. Something has happened there, Ah honestly don't know what. But there's some kind of trouble. It's not our business. How could it be our business? We're boys from the country. Like you said. But they need us just now. And there's money there for the takin'. *Because* they need us. Let's take it, Dan. Let's you and me just take what we can get. While it's goin'. The way things are, it might not be there for ever. Come on, Dan. Let's you and me take it. And we can. We really can. You can take Cutty Dawson, Dan. Ah know you can.'

'What kinda trouble is that, Frankie?'

'Ah don't know.' Frankie was strangely drunk, more drunk than the drink should have made him. 'Ah told ye that, Dan. Ah really don't know. There's something happened between them. This is the way they're goin' to settle it. That's all Ah know. But we better turn up. Because. If we don't, Matt Mason's lost without a fight. And there has to be a fight. There has to be. If it isn't you and Cutty, Matt'll make it another one. Better fighting Cutty, Dan. That's an easier proposition.'

Dan Scoular finished his orange juice. He rose and went through to the lavatory. Frankie took his whisky and lifted the empty glasses and crossed with them to the bar. The only other person in the bar besides Alan was Wullie Mairshall, hovering without apparent purpose, and he followed Dan into the lavatory.

While he passed the time with Alan, Frankie wondered what effect his words had had on Dan. You couldn't be sure with that big man. In the face of what seemed the most obvious necessity, he seemed to retain a belief in choice, as if his will was something he would insist on taking with him to the edge of his own grave. Thinking such an uncomfortable and troublesome thought, Frankie began to be concerned about how long Dan was taking in the lavatory. Maybe he had climbed out of a window and was gone.

Frankie went across to the lavatory, the door of which Alan had wedged open, presumably in preparation for cleaning it or perhaps just to give his customers the hint that he was closing. Pausing in the doorway, Frankie heard the hot-air dryer shut itself off. The silence that followed was too deep, too long to be a natural pause.

'What did ye say his name was?' Dan Scoular's voice said.

The voice was strained, emerged with difficulty from a man caught in a thumbscrew of private pain. It made Frankie want to hold back. Wullie Mairshall's answer was muted, as if he too wanted to back off. Perhaps he was afraid the hurt he was causing might rebound on himself.

'Struthers. Gordon Struthers.'

'How d'ye know about this?'

'Ah don't absolutely know. Ah'm doin' gardens in Blackbrae. Ah hear things. There's a woman cleans to this fella's wife. Ah know her man. He says they saw Betty and this man in a pub in Graithnock. That's what he says.'

Frankie walked back to the bar. He didn't want to know any more. The pain in Dan's voice was his own problem. All Frankie hoped was that whatever was going on in him didn't interfere with his ability to fight. While he waited for Dan and Wullie to emerge, Frankie was only interested to gauge the effect their conversation had had on Dan's commitment to the fight. But Dan's face, as he came out, told Frankie nothing. Certainly, Alan seemed to notice no difference. He was just glad to be finished. He became polite on the strength of knowing they didn't want anything else to drink.

'Thank you, boys,' he said. 'So it's back to the grind? It'll all pay off, big Dan. Don't you worry. How's Betty, by the way?'

Betty's first reactions to the fact that Dan was going to take part in a bare-knuckle fight had been no more than a practising of reactions, a confused search for the response that could contain the strangeness of the event. When he told her, coming in from the pub that night with a track-suit in his hands, he had been still large-eyed with the surprise of it. 'Ah just said "Hey!"', he said. 'And all this happens.'

She had first felt disbelief. He had gone out from a situation that was all too familiar, the two of them bleakly sending each other messages like dead letters, and he came back in with a strange new possibility in his hands. The maroon track-suit had lain on the settee where he had dropped it, mysterious with unforeseeable implications.

Disbelief moved towards a kind of envy of the energy he had

92

found. He was walking up and down the room as if trying to see beyond its walls towards the horizons he had only just realised might be there. The assumption that, wherever he was going, she would be happy to go along made her angry. The anger taught her one thing she was sure she felt – abhorrence of what he was preparing to do.

It seemed to her primitive that two men should agree to try to beat each other senseless, and especially in the furtherance of some quarrel that belonged to neither. Her contempt tried to persuade him to give the money back. But she couldn't refute him when he said how much they needed it and she knew from the desperation with which he wanted her to accept it that the two hundred pounds meant more than money to him. He laid most of it on the table when she refused to take it. It lay like a bet he was placing with himself, a gamble in which she wasn't sure if he himself knew what it was he hoped to gain.

It was then that what she thought was her true reaction crystallised. It was a cold relief, an admission of sterility where she had vainly been hoping for growth. There was no hope if he could go through with this. He was letting others buy him for their purposes even though, from the little information he could give, he had no understanding of what those purposes were. He was selling his life in a market.

She made it clear to him that she would have nothing to do with the fight. If it happened, she wouldn't be there. In the meantime, she would provide him with meals and a laundry service. The money she took as the children's commission on the sale of their father. And she felt within herself that a limit had perhaps at last been put on their marriage, a point of ultimatum reached.

Yet a strange thing happened. Suspecting the imminence of her separation from Dan, she began to see her relationship with Gordon Struthers with a colder clarity. Now that her relationship with Gordon was threatening to become real, she wondered how real it could be.

Sitting in the lounge bar where they had taken to meeting, she thought, the first time after Dan had told her about the fight, that the place itself seemed hardly real. Its carefully contrived, wall-lighted cosiness shut out the rainy night so effectively that it might have been the only place there was. The piped music was like double glazing. Conversations murmured privately.

Feeling the fragile hold these moments with Gordon had on the structure of her life, she wondered how deep their roots went. She had met him at a party. It had been a dire occasion, as she found so many parties were. She and Dan had been invited by Elspeth Murchie, a friend whom she had known at school and with whom she had never lost touch, just meaningful contact. At that time things were already so fraught between Dan and her that the house sometimes felt no more than a terminus where their separate days merely happened to end. They had prepared for the party in the way that was usual for that time, with a quarrel.

Dan didn't want to go. What was the point of it? They could have a fight in their own house. They didn't have to sell tickets for it. They hardly knew anybody who was going to be there. Hardly knew anybody? Elspeth Murchie had been at school with her. Barney Finnegan, the wino, had been at school with Dan but that didn't mean they had to go out and have a bevvy with him in his favourite bus-shelter. Elspeth Murchie was her *friend*. Betty hadn't bothered to add that the thing she remembered most vividly about Elspeth was her habit of cutting off model labels from old garments and sewing them on to clothes she had bought in a chain store. Betty wanted to go out, anywhere, even to Elspeth's.

Almost as soon as they arrived at the semi-detached sandstone house, which Elspeth's accountant husband had wittily named Hades and which was lit like a bonfire, Betty wasn't so sure. Their quarrel had made them late and Elspeth and John, her husband, seemed almost heartbroken that they had missed so much riotous fun already. Large drinks, like passports to pleasure, were put in their hands and they were ushered into a room where a laughing competition appeared to be in progress. The restless ebb and flow of people in pursuit of joy separated them at once.

'You must meet Bill,' Elspeth Murchie said. 'He's a lady-killer. But nice with it. Just watch he doesn't charm you out of your pants. This is Betty.'

'Hi,' Bill said, and it was the highlight of her conversation with him. Within five minutes Betty had decided that if Bill was a lady-killer he must be carrying a knife. While he kept his smile trained on her remorselessly like a laser beam – what was she supposed to do, crumble? – he started to tell her about the last time he had been on the ski-slopes at Gstaad. She was still wondering how they got there when she managed to escape, but not to safety.

She found herself with Ralph and Mary Brierley. They seemed to be a joint sales team. What they were selling was the story of their amazingly successful marriage. They had worked out a routine. What they did was they asked you about yourself, creating the cunning impression that they were interested. But really they were playing a private game, a sort of materialistic conkers. They were eliciting facts from you that they could top. If you said you had come in the car, they would ask what make, and then run over it with their BMW, closely followed by their Saab. Betty found herself nonplussed. They were obviously used to and expected certain reactions but she didn't know what they were supposed to be. Trade names – BMW, Everest, Moulinex – occurred in their talk with the frequency of conjunctions. It was like listening to a quick-fire vaudeville act in a foreign language.

The feeling of foreignness continued. Every time Elspeth reclaimed her from one conversation to subject her to another, she used words like 'charming' and 'fascinating', 'so funny' and 'interesting', until Betty, meeting the people the words were applied to, wondered if she had ever known what they meant. She began to cringe from the laughter that rang around her like cracked tubular bells. She felt trapped in a nightmare mannequin parade of egos. The offhand way Elspeth referred to Dan in introducing her to people made Betty wonder if she was being encouraged to see what she was missing in not having a husband like one of these men. She had never regretted not moving among these people and that night confirmed her earlier decision. She felt closer to Dan for having been separated from him by this hubbub. A few times she had tried to catch his attention, thinking they should leave soon. But he was pursuing his own mood with the whisky as a guide. Once when she had seen him coming back in with a refilled glass, he had mouthed at her, not pleasantly, 'Anaesthetic.' And then it was already too late.

95

She sensed before she was fully aware of the raised voice that it was coming from Dan.

'Crap!' he was saying. 'How can you say that? The people you'd be sorry for would be the white settlers? What they've put into South Africa? They've exploited it for generations.'

The incident flared briefly. Two of the three men Dan was arguing with turned round and smiled knowingly at some of the other guests while Dan ranted on.

'You call that compassion? Writing off ninety-odd per cent of the population. Fuck off!'

Betty saw what he was doing. In his antipathy to the whole event he had moled into himself with the whisky until he found the bedrock where he could make his stand. If it hadn't been South Africa, something else would have served. He was addressing this place, telling it what he thought of it, as wild and out of context as Savonarola at a cocktail party. She felt a familiar feeling in relation to him, emotional agreement locked with rational despair. She had never doubted his intelligence and she had never stopped doubting how he applied it. All he was doing for these people was providing the cabaret, being the party's dancing bear.

It was at that moment that the party died for her as a public event and became a private conversation. For she met Gordon. She had since wondered how far their almost immediate and effortless intimacy had been conditioned by her abdication of concern for Dan, her decision that she was alone in an unbearable place. It had been odd. She was spoken to by a stranger she had noticed a couple of times as she had been towed round by Elspeth and within minutes the gentle grin and the thoughtful eyes felt familiar to her. All she had observed about him before was that, sitting down, he looked like a big man and when he stood up he was barely medium height. ('Long torso, short legs,' he had later explained. 'I just missed being Toulouse-Lautrec.')

Their initial rapport came from a mutual rejection of the party. They had been cast up on the same desert island of mood, appeared to be its only inhabitants. As they talked, she felt that Gordon was providing an articulate gloss on the attitude Dan had tried to express with such uncontrolled vehemence that he had only succeeded in hurting himself, giving the others an excuse not to take him seriously. Gordon dismembered the pretensions of the party delicately and while he was doing it, the irony of his responses to others who spoke to them became a conspiracy between Betty and himself. They were a subversive group of two within the event.

That conversation between them had never stopped. Their discontent with the party became their shared discontent with their lives, as if this party were an intensification of what was wrong more generally and in experiencing it together they had clarified things for themselves. Their failing marriages provided them with matching despairs and the sharing of the despair was the beginning of trying to find a way out of it.

They had been meeting surreptitiously ever since, mainly in this lounge bar in Graithnock. Gordon wanted that they should both quit their marriages and live together. Since Dan had told her about the fight, Betty had been trying to move nearer to the acceptance of Gordon's suggestion. But she had misgivings. Listening to Gordon talk in the atmosphere of the bar, she found him convincing. But she wasn't sure how convincing he would have sounded elsewhere. The very secrecy which gave their talk its intensity made her wonder how far that intensity would transfer into the open. Perhaps their strength came from opposition. Take that away and how much would survive? Something else occurred to her.

'That was the worst phase,' Gordon was saying quietly. 'That had to be the worst. I couldn't believe what was happening. Everything I did was wrong. I was breathing in and out at the wrong time. Know what I did? What I used to do. I used to write whole conversations down. Just to prove to myself that was what had been said. To convince myself that I wasn't going mad.'

Betty was aware how much they talked to each other like that. She didn't feel dismissive of what Gordon was saying. She knew the feeling. She had talked like that often enough herself. She could see how open to mockery what Gordon was saying might be ('My wife doesn't understand me') but she understood the original pain there could be in living in a cliché, the horror you could have of being trapped for life inside another person's apparently total incomprehension.

What worried her was the uncertainty whether what they

97

were experiencing had more to do with group therapy than love. She didn't know what love was supposed to be but she couldn't doubt that it was there and that it mattered. She believed that part of it must have to do with a desire for mutual revelation, a wanting to know each other to the bone. Yet she felt that she and Gordon, for all their endless conversations, didn't come near to doing that. Gordon, she realised with surprise, remained a rather shadowy person to her, as she must be to him. They were an exchange of pasts, tentative promises for a future. Their present was a ghost in both their lives. And those pasts were carefully edited editions.

Even their love-making had been almost formal, like a convention they had followed. She wasn't sure whose choice that had been. Certainly she was wary of making it merely physical. She was aware of the way some men kept their genitals and their private lives at separate addresses and she wanted no part of that. Since she had always been determined to hold making love as an integral part of her life, she had perhaps not given herself to it fully.

But she sometimes wished that Gordon had simply come at her with passion so that happening, sheer physical occurrence, had stranded both of them beyond the viable range of their own doubts. This way, she felt that Gordon was offering her a contract. He analysed convincingly the unsatisfactoriness of the way they lived. He presented a logical solution to that dilemma. But it was as if their lives existed in the abstract. He had worked out financially how they could manage to realise a new situation for themselves but he gave no hint of the passion, the living reality by which it would be habitable. She often felt less like a lover than a co-opted member of a committee.

Sitting holding hands with Gordon in their lounge bar, she knew she was waiting for something to happen, for time to infiltrate the sureness of Gordon's theory with event – discovery of their secret, Dan's withdrawal from the fight, something. She was waiting for time, but not much time, to make her clearer to herself.

The Sunday he was due to go to Glasgow, Dan had decided to leave from the Red Lion. He and Frankie White were to be picked up by Eddie Foley – Dan didn't want Eddie Foley to come to the house. One reason was a protective instinct he didn't examine too carefully, a decision of the heart that the people he was dealing with shouldn't know where his family lived. Another reason was to deflect as far as possible Betty's disapproval of what he was doing.

When Frankie White came round for him after lunch, he found an atmosphere so alien he thought maybe he should have brought his passport. Dan let him in, greeting him quietly. Betty was in the kitchen. Frankie could hear her moving dishes around mysteriously but she didn't appear. Raymond and Danny hovered around their father and sometimes one of them would go across and fuss with the leather grip that was packed and zipped and waiting on the floor.

'Ye think ye'll win him, Dad?' Danny asked.

'We'll see, son, we'll see.'

Frankie, standing uncertainly in the middle of the floor, looked a question at Dan.

'They found out at the school,' Dan murmured. 'Somebody was nice enough to tell them.'

Frankie knew Dan had agreed with Betty that the boys shouldn't know what he was involved in. Dan had understood her desire not to have them think of their father in that way, had shared the desire. Frankie thought that was perhaps why she was in the kitchen, disowning the event. Her absence was an awkwardness in the room. The boys were obviously excited but their high spirits were baffled by the adult mood that surrounded them, like children at a funeral. They looked at their father a lot. They exchanged glances with each other, making grimaces of mute hysteria. They took turns at lifting the grip, testing its weight. When they asked him questions, where would he be fighting, was the other man a big man, would there be a crowd, the questions were quietly furtive. Dan's responses were muted too. He seemed to feel the need to touch them a lot, aimlessly ruffling their hair or giving one of them a slow-motion punch on the arm. At last he went across and put on his jerkin.

'Well,' he said and looked at Frankie.

'Ah'll get you outside, Dan,' Frankie said. 'Ah'll be porter. Ma stuff's up there already.'

99

But before he could reach the grip the boys were there, taking a strap each to carry it between them, and he followed them out. Dan went through to the kitchen.

Betty was standing in the middle of the kitchen floor, staring out of the window. She spoke as soon as he came in, still looking out.

'Do you have to do this?'

'I took the man's money, Bette.' The form of the name was a plea.

'What if we could give him it back?'

'We can't.'

'What if we could?'

'Bette. What's the point of talkin' like that?'

She turned and faced him.

'What's the point of talking at all?'

They looked at each other. It was a long way between them, too far to cross with words. There seemed no way to tell him what she thought she was planning to do. There seemed no way to tell her that he suspected what she was planning to do. Knowing nothing else but to admit the truth of his moment, he spoke, holding up his forefinger towards her.

'A cuddle?' he said. The jocularity of his expression struggled to overlay the pain of his face. 'Puts you under no obligation whatsoever. Oh, love, Ah need a cuddle.'

As they held each other, he spoke into her hair.

'Remember last night, love. Keep it in your head. Ah meant what Ah said. Just let me do this. Then we'll see.'

She held him very tightly. Her eyes were closed. It was easier to talk like that, without the possibility of seeing the confusions of a muddied past cloud the other's eyes.

'You,' she said. 'You, you. Well. Maybe. When you come back. Maybe.'

They kissed and he went out, leaving her looking out of the window. Frankie White was sparring with Raymond and Danny together on the front green. Dan hugged the boys and sent them back into the house. Somehow he didn't want them following him even part of the way. Dan picked up the grip, refusing Frankie's offer to carry it. Looking back several times, Dan saw the boys still waving frantically at the window. He thought he could see Betty standing behind them but he wasn't sure. He waved back until they were out of sight.

The walk to the Red Lion was a quiet one. Frankie felt Dan's thoughts were not for interrupting. Once a man working in his garden waved and shouted, 'Good luck, Dan!' Dan waved back.

The man's shout had been the herald of what was waiting for them in the Red Lion. The pub was full. A Sunday lunch-time was probably Alan Morrison's best few hours of trade in any week and today the Sunday regulars were augmented with well-wishers. The jogging figure of Dan Scoular had found its way into the awareness of a lot of people in the town during the past two weeks. Questions had been asked about him and the answers, though vague and often compensating for that vagueness with misinformation, hadn't lacked imagination. He was variously rumoured to be coming late to a career as a professional boxer, to be settling a grudge fight with a man from Sullom Voe, to be taking on all comers at a boxing-booth they were opening up in Glasgow.

Whatever he was doing, it was dramatic and he came from Thornbank. In the economic greyness of the times, his track-suited figure had moved romantically among them like the carried flame of one man's small rebellion. No one enquired too deeply into what he was rebelling against or for. He was doing something rather than rot in unemployment. So many of them knew and feared the internal, wasting effects of redundancy, of the slow, cumulative realisation that you didn't matter. It wasn't just the shortage of money. It was the constant daily rejection that surrounded you like an inimical air that was nevertheless all you had to breathe. It lodged its malignancies in you against your will. It gnawed at you in almost every thought, attacking your smallest ambition with the conviction that it wouldn't happen or, if it did, wouldn't make any difference. No wonder it overwhelmed some men so effectively that they lived thereafter until they died with an almost unmitigable deadness of mood, a total petrification of the will.

This man is different, Dan's doggedly running bulk had seemed to say. They admired the difference. They loved the spirit they believed had produced it. Few of them had watched him in his painful self-absorption without an igniting of the spirit in themselves, a smile of recognition for what they felt was a part of them, a piece of where they came from. He had, however briefly and however dubiously, rekindled in the town a small sense of itself. The presence of so many people here today looked like the evidence of that. The cheers and the stamping feet and the shouts as he came in felt like the proof.

Dan smiled with bewilderment and took the pint of orange juice that was waiting for him and looked a reprimand at Frankie White, who must have known what had been in store. Going through the back-slaps and the comments and the faces that wanted a bit of his attention, Dan couldn't resist the pleasure of the occasion but was wishing that he could. He was like a man with an ulcer drinking spirits. He knew both how good it felt and how bad it was going to feel. All this bonhomie he was accepting was later going to turn sour in him. For it didn't agree with his own sense of what he was doing. He was going to fight for his own strange reasons, reasons that were perhaps a rejection of his past among these people. He had no right to their good wishes. Like preliminary pangs of what he was going to suffer, two conversations spoiled the mood of the moment.

One was with Vince Mabon. Vince had been standing close to the bar, biding his time with that slightly complacent containment he often affected, as if he had an important message to deliver once all the nonsense subsided. Dan became aware of Vince behind him, talking into his ear, like the man who stood behind the victor in a Roman triumph.

'Dan,' he said.

And Dan turned round.

'Hullo, Vince. How are ye?'

'How are you? That's more to the point. You really going to do this?'

'Ah better now, Ah suppose, after all this carry-on.'

'Why?'

'Money for one thing.'

'You're being a mug. That's not the kind of fighting we should be doing.'

Perhaps because Vince was touching a sore place, perhaps because he seemed to have forgotten his own involvement in the start of this, Dan looked at him angrily and saw him through the clarity of his anger. He saw a student who at the same time boasted of smoking pot and despising the fashionable escapism of his society. He saw someone who returned among his own people offering theory and refused to let the often painful realities he found there compromise the theory for a second. He saw a boy who called 'be radical' from an armchair.

'Vince,' Dan said. 'You know what Ah don't need? Just at the moment. Your crappy theories. You can afford them, Vince. Because you're one of those people who're never goin' to be in any danger from their own ideas.'

But the exchange continued to trouble Dan, who couldn't pretend to himself that winning the verbal skirmish meant being right. His worries were added to by Wullie Mairshall.

Dan hadn't spoken to Wullie since their last conversation in the lavatory of the Red Lion. He had seen him a few times and always been glad of the distance between them. It wasn't that he confused the messenger with the bad news he had brought. It was more that Dan knew Wullie's watchfulness was prompting him. He wasn't a disinterested informant. He wanted something from him.

What Dan suspected Wullie wanted was a resurrection of the past. Wullie believed in working-class machismo, physical hardness as a kind of moral law. Adultery with the wife meant punishment from the husband, if not to the point of death then at least to prolonged hospitalisation. In his contempt for the laxity of modern life, Wullie was wishing – Dan would guess – for a sign of retribution, some Moses from the mountain who would re-engrave the old commandments on someone's body.

Dan sensed he might be Wullie's chosen man and, although he knew how far he was from Wullie's image of him, he dreaded the promptings. Since Wullie had told him of his suspicions about Betty, Dan had wandered a little wilderness of dementia. He hadn't confronted Betty, since there was nothing to confront her with, and he felt guilty at even having listened to Wullie. That husky, confiding voice was something he wished he had never heard. Yet he needed to hear it again. And when he did, the words went into his mind like poisoned darts.

'It looks as if Ah might have been right, big Dan,' he said. 'Seems a right bastard, this one.'

Dan was watching Davie Dykes and old Mary Barclay, who had been brought in a car to share the occasion. He didn't look at Wullie.

'Ah think you're wrong, Wullie. Let's leave it, eh?'

'Ah'm not wrong, Dan. Ah wish Ah was.'

'Not Betty,' Dan said. 'Not Betty.'

He said it quietly but vehemently, to the room, as if there might be others there who thought as Wullie did. The oppressiveness of the place was suddenly overwhelming. He wanted away from it, to leave the confusions it bred in him behind. Most of all he wanted away from Wullie's voice.

'Ah'm gettin' more on it.'

'Forget it, Ah said. Forget it.'

'Okay, Dan. You're the boss.'

Dan was pushing towards where Frankie White was standing, as if that would somehow bring departure nearer. But Wullie's voice found him one last time, leaving a mark on his mind that would bruise in the next few days.

'But Wednesday, Dan. Ah'll be sure by Wednesday. Ah'll be in here all night. If ye want to phone.'

Frankie was with the domino players. Alan Morrison had joined them. They were all very animated, discussing how they would get a car, since Alan had been advised to sell his Vauxhall after his last heart attack.

'We're comin' to see you, big man,' Sam MacKinlay said. 'Frankie's knocked it off. Got us in for free.'

Frankie smiled uncertainly. The euphoria here had affected him as well. Having convinced Matt Mason over the phone how important the presence of supporters might be for Dan, he had still been intending to take his commission from them. But the atmosphere in the pub made him feel for the moment this was where he belonged and he had decided to be honest with them. He could only hope his pockets didn't hurt him tomorrow.

Then Eddie Foley was there. While he had a quick drink, while they made their way through the crush, Dan kissing Mary Barclay, while most of the people in the bar crowded outside to see them off, through the waving and shouting, Dan held one thought to himself like a talisman – how Betty and he had been last night. He wanted her to remember, as if her thoughts could help him through what was ahead.

Betty remembered the night before but still wasn't sure what it meant. She wasn't certain she knew what anything meant any more. Her strongest objection to what he was doing was paradoxically what had made her more open to him again. It was the risk he was running. She dreaded what might happen to him in the fight. Once she had come to believe that he was going through with it, she couldn't withhold herself so effectively from him. No matter how unacceptable to her his intention was, he was doing it partly for her and Raymond and Danny. She also felt guilt that it might relate to a need to reinstate himself in her eyes, however misguided.

It was as if he was saying he wasn't finished yet, was trying to remind her of why she had fallen in love with him. He seemed dimly to sense a way simultaneously to reshape his future and reclaim his past. For the past few days she had felt him telling her in code that her support was essential to him but the nature of his pride had meant that he couldn't merely plead for it. By the showing of who and what he still was, he was trying to elicit it.

This oblique, taut second wooing was in the regained confidence of his presence, in his casual solicitousness, in an atmosphere of natural relaxation where Raymond and Danny had begun to realise that the minefield each day used to be had been temporarily defused. Reactions didn't have to go on tiptoe here. Betty understood that whatever worries Dan was having about what was ahead, he was determined not to bring them into the house. She felt herself responding to his plea for a truce but she didn't know how far she could come out past the entrenched entanglements of the past, her barbed confusions.

They became more accessible to each other in a fleeting, intermittent way as clumsy as courting. Then, before they were married, they had always been trying to find themselves alone. In a way, they were doing that again, though now the people who got in the way lived in themselves, those parts of them that had become estranged from each other. It was more difficult now.

Raymond and Danny helped by not knowing that they were

helping, suggested by their behaviour that they might still be a family. The Saturday night before Dan was due to leave for Glasgow, the boys' going to bed had been a series of exits and entrances, an impromptu skit of reluctance and fear of the dark that all of them enjoyed. When they had gone, Dan touched Betty in the passing and they saw themselves just as themselves and made love there in the living-room, sudden and slow, her hands with that touch he believed could stroke a bubble and not burst it, his voice low in the tender naming of parts. Lying together on the floor in front of the fire, Betty wondering vaguely if she had committed mental adultery, they were a tentative pact, trying to trust each other at least a little longer.

'You'll see,' he said. 'We'll make things good again, love.'

She knew that his certainty was a lie he hoped would come true. She understood that the love was in the hope.

4

Certain buildings have the capacity to impart awe from the interior. They give a sense of being consecrated places, devoted to a purpose which, whether you agree with it or not, forcibly impresses you with its intensity. Churches, of course, can be such buildings. Stock exchanges are, and so is a boxing gymnasium.

The gym at Ingram Street in Glasgow is like that. To see it still and empty may remind you of the small mysteries that move at the edge of our assumptions, the bafflements that haunt the commonplace. The ring that takes up so much of the small room seems such an arbitrary structure with its canvas floor and its taped ropes. Yet it dominates the dialectic of the room like an irrefutable premise, a bleak, simplistic statement the point of which is the abjuration of words. To duck under those ropes is to forswear equivocation or paraphrase, is to endorse brute fact.

The rest of the room is merely an antechamber to the ring. For those who want to go within the ropes, it offers a series of mystifying exercises by which they may believe in their fitness to go there. The heavy bag hangs like an inexhaustible source of power from which the arms may draw. The medicine balls wait to impart resistance to the body. The small punch ball, hung just above head height under its projecting wooden platform, promises to conjure speed and timing into the fists.

Along one wall there is a great gallery of photographs, so numerous and so casually stuck there that they overlap in places, since none of them is framed, and oblige the viewer to turn his head at different angles to see them properly. Some look like press photographs and others like snapshots taken by a drunken uncle on a dark night. They show faces and moments that cover a lot of years. There are handshakes and self-conscious groups and smiles fighting their way through the pain of recent bruises. There are the recognisably famous and those the mind almost remembers as having been Scottish champions and those whose anonymity evokes a different kind of identity, a memory of a face seen in a bus-station late at night or glimpsed in a dancehall. These are icons, reassurances to the faithful that out of pain comes glory.

If you wander in there off the streets – knowing where the insignificant door leads and mounting the shabby staircase – it will be like coming across the preoccupied activities of a fanatical sect. Your presence will not be remarkable. Nobody will resent you. There's nothing secret here. The matter-of-factness of it all may make you feel that you're the oddity and that this is simply what people do, the way it is. You may feel your own life rather flabbily pointless here where, under the encouraging stare of men with proprietary eyes, the young and the getting older pummel and strain and mortify their bodies. They are looking not just for muscles but for a way past the muscles to that place in themselves where they will find a hardness that defies all other hardness, forging themselves into weapons against one another.

Wandering in off his own streets, coming in out of a life where he had never applied such abilities as he had any other way than spontaneously, Dan Scoular was travelling a short distance geographically but a long way in experience. The assumptions here were foreign to him. Tommy Brogan was a strange guide.

'Come on, come on, come on, come on, come on, come on, come on,' he would say.

'If ye beat yerself, ye'll beat the other man.'

'There's stone in yer belly, find it.'

'It's no' me, it's Cutty Dawson makin' you suffer like this.'

'Come on, come on, come on, come on, come on, come on, come on.'

While he pushed Dan's body to places where, cornered, it turned and defied him in fusing stomach muscles and arms that quivered uncontrollably, Tommy Brogan didn't seem to notice, stared madly beyond at some vision only he could see. It had to be assumed that Matt Mason had hired him with the gym, three hours every day, from two to five. But his strange, one-dimensional presence, as if born of the one mad purpose, hardly seemed explicable by such an ordinary chain of circumstance. He had been in the gym the day that they arrived, haunting it like a discontented ghost. A rune in a desert, Matt Mason's introduction to him only told you that you didn't know what was being said: 'Tommy Brogan. You won't find two of him.' He was still in the gym every day Dan left at five. He was still in the gym each day Dan came back at two. Dan couldn't imagine him drinking a cup of tea or laughing at the television.

'Come on, come on, come on, come on, come on, come on, come on.'

While Dan pressed and punched and skipped, he had tormented visions of what a strange life must have shaped this man. He might have boxed himself but it was hard to tell if his leathery face had been marked by hands or not. He must have been about forty but was still very fit. His eyes stared out with a terrible bright stagnancy you felt nothing would ever trouble again. Clues to his feelings only came in an ambiguous code. When he threw Dan a towel, it could have been a sort of kindness. Staring out of the window to give Dan time to recover from his exertions, he could have been relaxing.

'It's him ye're hittin', hate the bastard, hate 'im.'

'Take yer body past yer body. Ye'll find that it's still there.'

'Too much is still not enough.'

In the moments of brief rest that had to punctuate even Tommy Brogan's progress to what he took for fitness, Dan sometimes tried to meet him in an ambience other than sweat. But whoever Tommy Brogan was, he wasn't for sharing. His answers took to questions the way a ferret takes to rabbits.

'You married, Tommy?'

'*Was* married. Once. Never again. She was tried and found wanton.'

Or, 'This all ye do? Training people, Ah mean?'

'A side-line.'

'What's yer main thing?'

'A semi-professional chastiser.'

Within two days Dan understood that their only point of contact was to be in physical effort, mainly his own. It was an unusual experience for him because he was a man for whom almost any meeting was a vestigial relationship. People normally responded to his openness. But Tommy Brogan neither liked him nor disliked him. He was a job of work. He would do the best he could with it and, beyond that, didn't care.

So, they must be alone together. In that room stale with the sweat of generations of men, like two people of different faiths worshipping in the same dilapidated chapel, they performed service and response in unison, and were apart. Tommy Brogan knew where Dan had to go. Dan went there and found what Tommy Brogan hadn't known was there, for Dan went there as himself. They worked the heavy bag, they worked the punch ball. Tommy Brogan battered Dan Scoular's stomach with the medicine ball and his stomach learned to absorb it without yielding much. Moving around the ring with the headguards and the gloves, they fought a stylised fight within a stylised fight. Tommy Brogan prodded, elicited, sought. Dan Scoular responded, chose, withheld. Sometimes, in the moments of tension their strange ballet created, Tommy Brogan would look for the bedrock of where Dan Scoular was. But it shifted in front of him.

'Come on, come on. Ye coulda hit me there.'

'Ah know, Ah know. Ah imagined doin' it.'

Or, 'Don't worry about me. Give it all ye've got.'

'Don't need to. Ah'm keepin' it for after.'

In the hardening body and quickening reflexes of Dan Scoular, they each saw different things. Tommy Brogan saw a machine being programmed. Dan felt a widening area of choice, a physical precision that could split a second into options. They were greater strangers than they had been before they met, by the time Matt Mason came on the third day.

He wasn't alone. Dan Scoular was noticing that he was never alone. He wore other people like armour. This time, besides Eddie Foley, there was a man Dan recognised from having seen his photograph in the papers. It was as well he did, because nobody introduced him. The man's name was Roddy Stewart. He was a well-known lawyer, defender in a few widely reported cases.

Dan had the fine gloves on and was punching the heavy bag. Tommy Brogan had opened the locked door at the sound of the knock, without taking his eyes off Dan, as if he had known that whoever was coming was coming. The three men came in and closed the door and the four of them stood watching Dan work. He was stripped to the waist with his track-suit trousers on and his body was sheened in sweat.

Matt Mason and Roddy Stewart were smoking cigars. They had the afterglow of a brandy-lunch on them. Their eyes were sternly appraising.

'Well, Roddy. What do you think?' Matt Mason said.

'Looks a bit tasty,' Roddy Stewart said. 'But a lot of people can look like that.'

'What says the man?' Matt Mason said.

He was speaking to Tommy Brogan.

'We'll see, we'll see,' Tommy Brogan said. 'He's got everything else. But has he got the thing? Ah know a boy in the SAS. He's got a sayin': Does he go for it? Ye'll only find that out on Sunday. Ah'll bring him the best he can be tae the line. Then we'll have tae wait an' find out, won't we? Right. Ye can rest now.'

Dan Scoular went on beating the heavy bag, counting up to twenty in his head before he stopped. He stood letting the pain in his arms subside. He had counted slowly.

'How are you feeling . . .' Roddy Stewart turned questioning towards Matt Mason.

'Dan,' Matt Mason said. 'Dan Scoular.'

'How are you feeling, Dan?'

'Ah feel all right.'

Dan Scoular peeled the gloves like an extra layer of skin from his sweating hands and walked about the room, cowled in his own exhaustion. He picked up a towel that stank with his sweat and tried to dry himself off. But his pores were still working, and beaded him again at once. He kept on walking.

'You think I should bet on you?' Roddy Stewart said.

'It's your moncy.'

'Well.' Roddy Stewart was talking to Matt Mason. 'The horse looks good. But the jockey seems to have doubts. I wonder what Cutty's saying.'

'Who cares?' Matt Mason said. 'I didn't buy the big man for his mouth. I don't expect him to talk Cutty out the game. The only thing his head needs to be able to do is take a punch. Not even a kick. This is going to be a fair fight.'

The others laughed, except for Tommy Brogan.

'Well, we'll see,' Roddy Stewart said. 'Tommy. There's something I have to talk to you about. I think it's a bit important.'

Roddy Stewart was looking at the wall. His expression was a customer looking for a waiter.

'Dan,' Matt Mason said. He said it gently, like the name of someone he cared about. He nodded approximately towards the wall where there were two doors, one into the dressing-room and one into what Dan had assumed was an office. 'You think you could give us a minute?'

Dan was nearer the door to the office. As he went in, he heard Roddy Stewart saying, 'I'll tell you what, Matt. I think that dinner tonight is an interesting idea.'

Dan pushed the door shut. He sat on the one chair in the place, a wooden one, and dabbed himself again. He spread the towel and draped it over his shoulders. As he sat excluded from the importance of their conversation, his body shivered as if in confirmation of the indignity his mind had registered. He recalled a moment from the past, one of those incidents which seem casual at the time but which the mind keeps like a found instrument by which to measure subsequent experience.

It was early evening in his parents' house. His father wasn't long home from his work and they were at their tea when the club-man came. The club-man's presence was never a comfortable one in their house. They paid him money weekly and in return they could buy clothes from the 'club' – the name had always seemed an odd one to Dan, suggesting a nice chumminess that belied the hard financial basis of the arrangement. His father resented that he worked as hard as he did and yet the only way they could afford the clothes they needed was to buy them 'a fuckin' button at a time'. His mother's pride was that everything they had was paid for. Forced by their circumstances to use the club, they had worked out, as they always did, the precise terms of their transaction with the demands of their own experience. They would never take anything from the club until they had almost fully paid the money it required to buy it. No matter how often Mr Burnley, the club-man, tried to talk them into taking the clothes first and paying them up afterwards, they never would.

It was how they made their circumstances submit to their pride.

That evening Mr Burnley had been talking in his usual, free-associating way, as if reluctant to leave. He no longer ever mentioned other houses he had been to, because, once when he had done that, trying to elicit a laugh out of something he had seen, Dan's mother had said, 'Other folk's business is other folk's business. It's not ours.' Mr Burnley was talking about the weather and how well his oldest son was doing at school and how quickly children outgrew their clothes. Dan and his father were still at the table. Dan's mother was standing beside Mr Burnley, waiting for him to give her back the book in which he had recorded her latest payment. As he gave her back the book, Mr Burnley reached across to the mantelpiece.

'I'll take a couple of your cigarettes,' he said. 'I've run out.'

He took three cigarettes. Putting two in his breast pocket, he lit one and threw the match in the fire. As he exhaled the smoke, Dan's father said the first thing he had said for a few minutes.

'See next week,' he said. 'You wait at the door. We'll bring the book out tae ye.'

'I beg your pardon?'

Dan's father was spreading a piece of bread.

'What do you mean, Mr Scoular?'

Dan's father looked at him.

'Just chap the door. We'll bring the book out.'

Mr Burnley looked at Dan's mother, who was embarrassed for him.

'Is it the cigarettes?' Mr Burnley was shaking his head tolerantly. His hand moved towards his breast pocket. 'If that's all it is –'

'Leave them where they are.' The quiet commandingness of the voice held the hand still in mid-air. 'Ye miss the point. Ye could have the packet if ye want. Why no'? Ah've given more to a blin' fiddler. But in people's houses, ye don't take. Ye ask. Ah wouldny smoke in a tramp's bothy unless Ah was sure it was all right with him.'

'Mr Scoular –'

'Cheerio.'

'Ah'll see ye tae the door, Mr Burnley,' Dan's mother said.

Shivering under his towel, Dan smiled wryly to himself. He had to admit he agreed with his parents about some things. He was glad they had passed on to him a sense of pride so finely calibrated that it could have registered a fly landing where it shouldn't. He had missed none of the insults the last few minutes had offhandedly given him: the arranged inspection about which everybody seemed to know except him, although he was the focus of it; the discussion of him as if he weren't there; Roddy Stewart's vagueness about who he was, as though he only mattered as a function; his withdrawal to the servants' quarters while they conducted serious business.

As he carefully quantified their insultingness, he could imagine his father's reaction to the fact that he had done nothing but accept the insults. He envisaged a facial expression of his father's, a grimace so familiar to Dan's memory that it was how he almost always remembered his father, his personal death-mask of him. It was how Dan's father had endured the preparedness of others to submit to treatment no one should submit to. He turned his face towards his own right shoulder and his eyes stared conspiratorially at nothing and his right cheek developed a moving lump as if he were chewing on a wad of disbelief that tasted bitter. Perhaps he had been communing with all the proud Scoulars he was convinced he came from. Dan confronted that expression in his memory and acknowledged its rightness for his father but also felt its irrelevance to where he was.

He had the same sense of pride as his father but it had had to develop even finer calibrations because it had to lead him through a more complicated, a more various experience. In a way, precisely because the terms he had to face were more harsh and more obvious, the pride of Dan's father had been a luxury, his only luxury and one Dan knew he himself couldn't quite afford.

His parents' poverty had been not spectacular but sheer. They ate and they managed to feed and clothe themselves and him. But beyond that, from the time that they were children, there had been just a cliff-edge. Nothing more for so long had been possible. Given the clarity of the terms by which they lived, their responses to those terms were equally clear. They knew precisely how little they had and since the area they had was so small, they could defend it totally without exhausting their moral resources. For someone to move into the narrow enclave of their lives was like moving into themselves. They knew the mental placement of everything that mattered to them. The minutest aggression was observed as soon as it occurred and action taken. They knew what they were fighting for and what they were fighting against and had drawn up their lines accordingly.

But Dan was aware of how much the conflict had changed for him. His parents had been engaged in a kind of trench-warfare with their circumstances. Do certain things, you were a traitor. Cross certain lines and die to them. They knew enemy action when they saw it. They were enlisted young and their experience formed them and they were never sub-sequently able to demobilise themselves. While the weaponry ranged against them became modernised, while the tactics of social exploitation developed unforeseen subtleties that out-manoeuvred their past principles completely, they stayed stub-bornly at their posts, though the battle had moved past them, and they died there, still clutching beliefs that their confused leadership had forgotten to countermand. And even their son, trained by his own experience in different methods, couldn't endorse their actions.

But too late, in retrospect and with them dead, he could appreciate. Sitting alone there, preparing for a strange fight of his own and one the implications of which he couldn't fully grasp, he thought perhaps he was nearer to understanding his father's dark rage against him in the back green. Maybe his father hadn't just been fighting him. Maybe he had been trying to fight all the changes he felt coming, the loss of crucial principles. Maybe he had tried to bar at least from his own house the fifth column of careless self-interest he felt infiltrating all around him.

Dan felt a liberating affection for his father. Poor, old, hard, honest bastard. Having lashed himself to his principles to survive, he couldn't be blamed for not being able to move, though the times did. Dan's love of his mother, never com-promised, came back to him. He wished he could speak to them now to reassure them that he wasn't lost entirely to the past they had believed in, that he hadn't quite forsaken what they stood for, that he, too, had his pride. It wouldn't have been an elaborate speech – they never were in his parents' house. It would have been something gruffly cryptic, in a code they would have understood, something like: 'Don't panic, Feyther. Mither, Ah'm still me.'

But he had to admit to himself that his pride, if it was still there, was in a funny place. His parents' pride had been like a medal they could wear, one they had earned. His own was something he felt was still with him but he couldn't have pointed to it. The explicitness of their experience had bestowed on them a kind of brute heroism. His experience had been different, still was. If their lives had been as clear-cut as trench-warfare, his was as confusing as espionage, a labyrinth of double-agents.

What did you trust these days? You couldn't vaguely trust the historical future in which his parents had believed. Part of it was already here and it was unrecognisable as what had been foretold. Better material conditions hadn't created solidarity but fragmentation. Working-class parvenus were at least as selfish as any other kind. You couldn't simply vote Labour and trust that Socialism would triumph. The innocence of his parents' early belief in the purity of Socialism couldn't be transplanted to the time that followed Socialism's exercising of power, however spasmodic. In power, Socialism had found it hard to recognise itself, had become neurotic with expediency, had forgotten that it had never merely been a policy but a policy growing from a faith founded in experience. Lose the faith that had been justly earned from the lives of generations of people and Socialism was merely words and words were infinitely flexible. You couldn't trust the modern generation of those who had formerly been the source at which Socialism had reaffirmed its faith. All around they were reaching private settlements with their society's materialism in terms that contained no clauses to safeguard others of their own who might be less fortunate.

If you were honest, you couldn't even trust yourself. He had often enough expressed his contempt for people he had known who, coming from his own background, had succeeded academically or in business and had turned their backs on where they came from. He had heard them at parties and in pubs preaching the worthlessness of their own heritage and he had despised them. But he also knew that you couldn't trust yourself not to be like them until you had been to a place where the temptations were real, where you too had the opportunity to make a purely private enterprise of your life and the rewards were sufficient to put such principles as you had to the test. He had never been to such a place.

He sometimes wondered if part of his motivation for giving up his academic course at school had been to avoid making the kind of choice for which he had blamed others. If so, perhaps that choice had found him out in any case. For what was he doing here, if not moving towards it? When his own situation had been bad enough, he hadn't taken long to conform to an arrangement that fitted no principles he had previously held.

He knew he was wise not to trust himself too much. That distrust helped to explain why he hadn't reacted to the insults of Matt Mason and the others. He was far out in himself, out of touch with his own instincts, and waiting to find out what he really thought and felt. He had set out on his own small voyage of self-discovery and he wouldn't predetermine his destination. He would suspect the glibness of his own habitual responses. He would put his pride in abeyance for the time being. He would wait and see where all this was leading, where he was going.

He listened for a moment to the muffled voices beyond the door but couldn't make out what they were saying. In his preoccupation he had lifted from the desk in front of him a pile of what looked like old advertising leaflets, of a dim blue cardboard that was stained and unevenly discoloured with age, stiff single sheets. He had been riffling them in his hands for minutes before he looked and became very still and slowly understood what they were. They had been lying among other papers and a couple of pencils and a few manila folders, as if someone had been clearing out the drawers of the desk.

Eddie McAvoy v. John Malloy (9 st 9 lbs). Mickey Macrae v. Andy Parvin (8 st 6 lbs). Bert Morrison v. Martin Shinoeth (8 st). Alec Corrigan v. Tony Bertelotti (12 st 7 lbs). John Wajda v. Iain McTavish (9 st 9 lbs). John McLintock v. Allan Devoy (11 st 6 lbs).

The names went on endlessly, it seemed to him, and no one today would have recognised one of them. The cards were boxing programmes from the Thirties. He read them avidly like some lost roll of honour, combatants in a war that had never officially been declared. Some had in brackets after the names odd, tantalising references: 'The Dancing Pole', 'The Man Your Sister Couldn't Take Home To Your Mother', 'The Mad Miner'.

Each fight had both the fighters' purses marked in pencil under their names. A common figure was five shillings. These must have been mainly scratch fights between men whose training had been the dole queue. There were several programmes in which a full bill of five fights was covered by fifty shillings in old money. Today's £2.50 would have bought a night's entertainment in which five men would box or batter another five into submission, or maybe the wiser ones would box a draw.

Dan found himself pondering impossible questions. What had those men been like? What had they felt towards one another in their circumstantially conditioned aggression? Out of what demolished tenements or lost miners' rows had they come? No answer was the loud reply, he thought, remembering a saying of his father's.

'He's still got a bit to go,' he suddenly heard Tommy Brogan saying.

Dan didn't know if the remark referred to him but he took it as doing so. What interested him as much as the distance he had to go was his recharging sense of the distance he was coming from. He studied the faded sheets painstakingly, aware of a kinship. He no longer minded the closed door. It occurred to him that doors exclude from both sides.

Frankie White had been demoted to chaperon. He and Dan had adjoining rooms in the Burleigh Hotel, a place where the floors were so uneven with age that Frankie said it gave a new meaning to the term 'listed building'. All the time Dan wasn't in the gym, he was supposed to be with Frankie. Apart from the early-morning training runs along Kelvin Walkway, their time together was amorphous. There was nowhere they had to go, nothing they must do. The first day in Dan's hotel room, Frankie had started to worry.

Boredom always worried Frankie. It was time unshaped by imagination. All Frankie had to know himself by was the ability of his small but persistent fantasy to triumph over the banal facts of his life. In such moments as these the facts reasserted themselves, obliterating like drifting sand the shaky structure he had been maintaining. This time the feeling gained strength from the depressing image of Dan Scoular stretched out on his bed staring at the wall and from the room itself.

Sitting in that room, Frankie decided that the word people so often used of hotel rooms, 'impersonal', didn't fit there. That was maybe true of new places where the rooms could seem just small architectures of assorted functions that reduced people to a series of processes. But in that old hotel room it was the proliferation of identities that was overwhelming. You could neither ignore those past presences nor imagine who they were and their meaninglessness seemed to talk to you of your own.

Dan Scoular's room whispered endlessly of people who were no one. The stains around the place were a muted hubbub of the past that couldn't be effectively silenced by the vaguely Arabian-looking woman Dan sometimes saw in the morning. He had tried to pass the time of day with her and she replied in what was presumably English, incantatory monosyllables that seemed to lack hard endings. He had wondered where she came from, what she was doing there. He wasn't even sure what she did in the room. Coming back into it after she had been there, he had noticed ritual gestures, the dried streak of a cloth-mark across the small, cobbled bedside table. One of the small squares of soap that looked made to fit the hand of a foetus might have been moved from one side of the washhand basin to the other. Perhaps she mainly just talked to the room in her strange language, telling the ghosts to keep their voices down.

Above the wooden bedhead there was a mark on the wall that looked like blood, a brown smear shaped not unlike Italy, with Sicily vanished. A drunken stumble, a quarrel, or maybe just a drink spilled? Along the edges of the bedside table were the black grooves of cigarette burns. They were numerous enough to suggest a casual attempt at furniture design or notches made to measure an endless boredom. Dan had soon learned to read those stains and scrapes and scratches like a secret map of where he was, a chart that led him unerringly to the same sense of his own smallness, with time passing and nothing achieved. Sometimes the feeling induced him to cross to the glass above the washhand basin, which didn't help much, for it was so dim and striated and freckled with age, it was like a mirror that has lost its memory and gives you back an uncertain image of yourself, as if it is confusing you with some of the other mysterious faces stored in its dull recesses.

Dan Scoular, lying back with his head resting thoughtfully on clasped hands, seemed able to endure the sense of futility that seeped from the walls of this place like nerve gas slowly numbing self-delusion. For Frankie White, it was unbearable. It told him too insistently who he wasn't. It also made him doubt if Dan Scoular was really what Frankie had taken him to be. Frankie began to wonder if big Dan, prostrate and still as a piece of fallen statuary, was the force Frankie, in his eagerness to make capital out of him with Matt Mason, had convinced himself he was. Sitting there with him in the shabby room that was like a locked compartment moving them inexorably towards an already fixed destination, Frankie was given to dreading what they would find when they got there. Maybe Dan simply wasn't up to it. Where Dan was going, Cutty Dawson had been before. He knew the terrain. It was asking a lot to expect Dan to wander in from a softer place and, with the experience that had taught him his slow smile, wrest submission from the clenching purpose Cutty's harder experience had made of him. And if he failed, if Dan came apart at the final asking, and deep questions would be put to him in there, the status Frankie bought with Dan Scoular would rebound on him like bad currency.

To escape the thought, Frankie had suggested they go out as much as they could and walk, see a bit of the city. Dan seemed happy enough to do that. He knew Glasgow as a place to visit occasionally or to pass through from Queen Street Station to Central Station or the Anderston Bus Station. But Frankie knew it as a place to live in. Dan let the other man's desperate chattiness play across the places they walked through but mostly without paying it much attention. Some of us, faced with the prospect of new experiences, like to send our own or other people's preconceptions ahead of us like couriers who will process the strangeness of things into the comfort of familiarity, however contrived. Dan Scoular wasn't like that. He let things happen to him, introduce themselves until he could work out his own sense of them.

Glasgow came at him with bewildering variety. The handsomeness surprised him. There were whole terraces of buildings he found beautiful, big solid acts of pride. There was more greenery than he had imagined, parks that grew expanses of sudden grass among the stonework. There were streets he wouldn't have thought anybody could bear to live in, most strikingly for him in the place Frankie called Possil, which he seemed to know well. There was an area they walked once, along the riverside, that depressed him with the size of its emptiness, like an abandoned warehouse.

There was an elusive but coherent unity he sensed behind the fragmentary impressions he took in, a feeling that identified Glasgow for him as distinct from other places he'd been in. To try to fix it for himself, he groped for a comparison. He knew Edinburgh slightly. He tried to lay his impression of one against the other, wondering where he felt the difference was. He had heard often enough of the supposed rivalries of the two places, familiar crutches for stand-up comedians, how Edinburgh was cold and Glasgow warmer, both in climate and people; how Edinburgh was snooty and Glasgow coarse. He didn't believe it. He had always liked both places and the people in them. But for him there was a difference, just as physical places, that had always made him feel more at home in Glasgow.

Walking with Frankie, he worked out without saying it what he thought this was. It went back to something he had felt when they had taught him Scottish history at school. He had been aware of no continuity in it, just a series of jumps from one dramatic figure to another, until the figures became English. It had been as if nobody wanted to try to link the gaps or find out what they meant. It was almost as if Scotland didn't have any history or, if it did, not many people knew what it was. And he realised suddenly that was where he felt he was when he was walking through Glasgow, in the truth of

Scottish history, the living reality of it. It seemed to him that of the few cities he had been in, it was the most serious one, the one that spoke to you most directly. It wasn't solemn. A lot of times as they walked, they had heard its laughter and its banter on the street. But the genuineness of that laughter was itself the clue, Dan thought. Those who had come to their own difficult understanding with reality were the best laughers. Perhaps that was why Frankie, strolling beside him, laughed like a rattle somebody else was turning.

That was the difference of the two cities for him. He liked being in Edinburgh but he could never take its beauty quite seriously. It was a monument to a false sense of Scotland. Glasgow bothered him in its own way, the way its handsomeness was pitted with harshness, but it seemed to say without pretence: this is where we've really been, this is where we are.

Where he was had a particular relevance for him at the moment. It was where Cutty Dawson had come from. The half-remarks he had managed to pick up about Cutty Dawson had troubled him and made him more than a little nervous. They were shadows that made it hard to judge the size of the substance that had cast them. All you could tell was that it seemed to be very formidable. He wanted to admit his fear enough to be able to deal with it but not enough to have it overwhelm him. He absorbed Glasgow like a background report on Cutty Dawson, trying to read the signs.

He had to admit they didn't look too promising. He saw in the place something he decided was simply true of cities but which hadn't occurred to him before. Cities perfected individual violence in a way that country places didn't. It wasn't just that the competition was greater. It was also because anonymity released violence, not just the anonymity of the victim, the sense that the other might be nobody in particular, but the anonymity of the perpetrator, the loss of inhibiting roots, of the importance of others' awareness of you and how they might react. Dan sensed that this could be a catchweights contest if Cutty Dawson had learned through his experience here how to free his violence fully. Dan knew himself from Thornbank and he didn't know how far that sense of a shared morality, however hypocritically or imperfectly shared, might put bindings on his arms when the chances came, if they came at all.

Fortunately for Frankie White's already fragile state of mind, Dan didn't mention any of this to him. They had their walks and came back to the room and Dan sat or lay on the bed, and Frankie could only talk, instead of whistling in their mutual dark, and wonder what was going on behind Dan's stare as it checked off the stains on the walls in a way Frankie thought would drive him mad.

Something Matt Mason had said came back again and again into Dan Scoular's mind. 'Your first fight, big man, is with yourself.' He was still having it. It seemed to him a bit like the few times he had gone abroad. It always felt to him as if he didn't really arrive until a few days after he got there, as if parts of his sense of himself remained missing for a time, like pieces of misdirected luggage. All you could do was wait for them to catch up. In this case, he hoped they all arrived by Sunday.

In the meantime, he was trying to sharpen his mind as well as his body towards the event. Everything he saw, he was trying to use. Frankie White might not know it, but those walks in the city and his patient absorption of this room, they too were a kind of training.

'He's an interesting man,' Roddy Stewart said. 'I must get you to meet him sometime, Matt.'

'He would bore you to death, Matt,' Alice Stewart said. 'Don't listen to him. Roddy just likes the idea of knowing somebody who's been on television. Because he's an actor. And his acting's as bad in real life as it is on television. He says "Hello" as if it was a major speech.'

'He's an interesting man. And he's a better actor than any of the parts he's had show. He's one of those actors who's never found a suitable vehicle for his talent, that's all.'

'What about a hearse?'

Roddy and Alice Stewart were doing their cabaret act. They were a couple who had refined their public married life into a series of engagements. At parties or on visits to friends, they didn't just turn up, they appeared together, like the Lunts. Their special style was smiling invective, apparently venomless mutual antipathy. What went on in the dressing-room, nobody knew.

'And he's so dumb,' Alice said. 'But I think narcissistic people always are. They haven't taken the time to think of anything but themselves.'

'Maybe it takes one to know one,' Roddy said.

'He is dumb. He is very possibly the dumbest man I've ever met.'

'You're as generous as ever,' Roddy said. 'If there's re-incarnation, Alice is coming back as something else – a human being.'

'You obviously haven't met Johnny Mallieson,' Billy Tate said. 'He was the unofficial world champion for being dumb.'

Billy Tate had been a famous Scottish footballer, one of the best inside-forwards the country had produced. He owned a pub now and, like a war veteran, his life since retirement had been anti-climactic and slightly aimless. He tended to live off talk of the past like a pension.

'You know what Johnny did once? We were on the plane goin' to Hungary. One of the boys sets it up with the stewardesses. You know those intercom telephones? Gets a stewardess to tell Johnny he's wanted on the phone. Johnny sprachles desperately to his feet and follows her to the phone. Sammy Simpson's at the other end of the plane. Says he's looking for a filler for the *Evening Times* diary column. The thoughts of Johnny Mallieson on how he thinks the game'll go. He's got Johnny talkin' there for a full ten minutes. Johnny comes back to his seat tryin' not to look too big-headed. But he can't resist it. Says, "How about that, boys? They're even phonin' me on the plane now." Ah mean, he had ten minutes to twig it. How do you phone an aeroplane? We laughed that much, it was like turbulence.'

The others at the table had threatened to rival that laughter. Dan Scoular recovered first.

'He was a real player, though,' he said. 'Nobody that ever saw him is goin' to forget him. He was just the best at what he did. Any game he wis in, Ah never felt like askin' for ma money back. He wis a sore-throat player, him.'

'That's true,' Billy Tate said.

'The only other one of us at this table that'll be remembered by as many people is yerself,' Dan said to Billy Tate.

'A sore-throat player?' Alice said.

'And you set yourself up as a judge of dumbness?' Roddy said.

'He made people so excited, they shouted till their throats were sore,' Billy Tate said.

The waiter was dispensing more coffee and Matt Mason enjoyed the conjunction of his discreet, slightly sniffy presence and their raucous company. It was a reminder of where he had come from, which made where he had arrived all the more remarkable. He sensed the waiter's discomfort and it pleased him. The large Rémy Martin in his hand glowed warmly, proof against anyone's disapproval.

He looked round at the motley band his money had assembled. In spite of the talent Billy Tate had found for himself and Dan Scoular and Frankie White, Margaret, Mason's wife, was still the best-looking woman at the table. She usually was. She dressed well, he thought. She undressed well, too, and that was as much as he asked of her. He had his two sons, Matt and Eric, by his first wife, Anne. Anne's death, just when he was beginning to make real money, had simplified his basic nature further and the last traces of his altruism had been buried with her. He paid for services rendered, that was all. It was the way he liked it. Margaret knew the rules and, in return for what she gave him, she had as much money as she needed and an easy life. His sons, who were at boarding school, were expected to repay the investment by what they made of their lives. Even tonight, he bought the meal and the drinks and the others performed, whether it was Frankie White and Billy Tate telling stories or Roddy and Alice doing their turn or the girls Billy had brought just looking decorative.

The only one who didn't fit was Dan Scoular, and that interested Matt Mason. He had been observing Dan throughout the evening. The big man had had one glass of red wine and, at Matt Mason's suggestion, had been on Perrier water the rest of the time. The other two women Billy Tate had brought didn't seem too pleased that it was Melanie who had been assigned to Dan. He was shining with health and his movements had the unblurred quality of the well trained, as if he moved in a less sluggish atmosphere than everybody else.

He reminded Matt Mason of somewhere he had once been

himself, a place of simple self-assurance where every day was a straight transaction with the world, before Mason had had to make a careful structure of his life, turn himself into an organisation. Mason felt closer to him than he did to anyone else at the table. Feeling the dynastic impulse that often comes with success, he was wondering if Dan Scoular might not be somebody he could bring into his organisation and train to be like himself. It wasn't a selfless thought. He saw in Dan Scoular a force he wanted to acquire for, functioning naturally on its own terms, it contradicted him, suggesting another way he might have been, an alternative life he might have had. If he could absorb it, make it his own, it would reaffirm him, be a renewal of himself, like a monkey-gland injection.

But it would be foolish to buy before testing the quality. The fight would decide for him. If Dan Scoular didn't collapse but hardened in the glaze, Mason would know what he was getting. The casual signs tonight had been good, he thought. He liked the way Dan had handled himself. Unlike Frankie White, he had held himself a little apart from proceedings. Matt Mason liked that. Dan seemed quietly preoccupied. Melanie (Mason wondered what woman's magazine had provided her with the name) was leaning towards him, her black hair swinging forward to blinker her from everybody at the table but him. Mason was about to tell her to keep that till after the fight when Dan rose and excused himself. Mason happened to glance at Frankie White, not meaning anything, and Frankie winked knowingly and followed Dan Scoular out. Matt Mason smiled to himself, feeling like someone who had nodded unconsciously in agreement with his own thoughts and found a waiter fussing round him attentively.

Frankie White had gone past the pay-phone before he realised that was where Dan Scoular was. Frankie carried on into the toilet and waited a suitable time there. When he came back out, he saw that Dan was still on the phone and he became interested in the paintings in the foyer. Frankie didn't know himself what purpose he was serving but he assumed his attentiveness would please Matt Mason. He felt the more keen to do that because of tonight.

It had been the kind of occasion that could feed Frankie's imagination for weeks. He had eaten expensive food and drunk expensive wine. He had been chatting casually on equal terms with Billy Tate. Sandra, the girl Billy had brought along for him, had promised to come back to his hotel room later, once he was sure that big Dan was safely in bed. The way a crust of bread could ravish an anchorite's palate, these scraps of what Frankie took to be the good life were enough to sustain his lonely vision of himself as a man of consequence and success.

He was still savouring his mood when he realised that Dan Scoular was standing beside him, staring at the big abstract painting Frankie had been using as a surface on which to project his thoughts. From the pain on Dan's face, Frankie wondered if the painting was expressing something he had missed. But the glibness of the thought gave way to worry and the worry evoked Frankie's reflex response to trouble: try to joke it away.

'What is it, d'you think?' he said, nodding at the painting.

Dan said nothing.

'Obvious, isn't it?' Frankie went on. 'What we have here is blue and red and black paint in a gilt frame. If you'd been to art-appreciation classes like me, ye'd know that.'

'Is this goin' to take much longer in here?' Dan asked as they walked back into the restaurant.

The fact that Dan wasn't enjoying the evening confirmed Frankie's belief that some kind of crisis was imminent. Dan had obviously been phoning Thornbank. Something was wrong. As they came back to the table, the worry Frankie felt was in proportion to the width of his smile.

By the evening of the following day, which was the Thursday before the fight, Frankie's smile had festered into a grimace. Dan Scoular didn't return from training. Frankie wondered if he had gone to training at all. Preoccupied with Sandra, who had returned to the hotel room after lunch-time, Frankie hadn't accompanied Dan to Ingram Street. Just before five he and Sandra had parted, vowing to make a career out of an idyll. Frankie hadn't wanted Dan to catch them together, in case he got ideas, and then began to wish Dan had. By six o'clock annoyance was moving towards panic. Frankie found himself walking from his own room into Dan's and back again, addressing windows and walls and faded carpet. 'Come on, big man! You must be kidding.' 'Don't do this to me.' 'If ye've blown this, big Dan, Ah'll fight ye maself.'

At half-past six Frankie went out and took a taxi to Ingram Street. The gymnasium was shut. Frankie was by this time not only talking to himself but arguing with himself, taking both sides of a complicated discussion. Part of him was saying Dan was in a pub. Another part was telling himself not to be ridiculous. But he looked in at several pubs around Ingram Street. He resented Dan for making him do that because, while he didn't find Dan Scoular in any of the pubs, he saw reflections of himself, the way you sometimes see yourself accidentally in a shop window as you pass and have dismissed the image out of hand before you realise it's you. Frankie spent a lot of his time alone in pubs, refurbishing his image of himself, and it was a little shocking to look in as a man preoccupied with the job he had to do and see other men doing what he recognised as one of his own favourite activities, and find it sad. For it was an hour that was too early for enjoyment. The men he saw on his quick tour were not there from choice but from compulsion. They were lingering at an oasis because a desert was ahead.

In one of the pubs a man made it clearer than Frankie wanted him to make it. It was the Muscular Arms, under new management and drastically altered from the last time Frankie had seen it, presumably on the principle that any change is improvement. The downstairs bar was now all green with white chairs and occasional plants, like a garden centre with a licence. Frankie had walked round the bar to make sure Dan Scoular wasn't there. He was on his way back out when the man spoke.

'What you drinking?' the man said.

'Sorry?' Frankie said.

'A drink,' the man said.

'Well, Ah was just lookin' for somebody –'

'A large whisky for my friend and one for me,' the man said.

He said it with a certain grandeur of manner, as if he was booking a private plane. The woman behind the bar, who would be in her fifties and looked as if her feet might be giving her trouble, responded in a way that suggested she was fed up with people booking private planes. The man didn't seem to notice. He nodded in agreement as if Frankie had spoken.

'Yes, indeed,' he said.

Frankie felt immediately obligated to the man because he had bought him a double whisky.

'How's it goin?' Frankie said.

'I am,' the man said and paused with the air of someone who has declared the incontrovertible, as the whiskies arrived. He paid for the drinks with a difficulty that implied the currency was foreign to him.

'I am,' the man said, 'possibly the most successful business-man you will ever meet. Everything I touch turns to gold. Pure gold.'

Frankie nodded.

'And yet. I'm looking for something more. "What is it?" you may ask.'

'Uh-huh,' Frankie said.

'I do not know. I'm telling you now. I do not know. How about that?'

'Well,' Frankie said.

'I am totally successful,' the man said. 'My wish is my command. And where am I going tonight? Tell me that. Where am I going tonight? But make no mistake about it. I am very successful.'

Frankie began to think that, free, the double whisky was still too dear. He signalled the bored woman over and ordered one more double whisky. When your mirror started to talk back to you, it was time to leave. The whisky arrived, Frankie paid, and placed it in front of the man.

'Yes, indeed,' the man said.

Frankie went out. The streets baffled him and he admitted it to himself. He went back to the hotel. There began a bad time. He wondered whether he should phone Matt Mason or not. But all this might pass without Matt Mason knowing anything about it. Frankie spent some hours with that dilemma, to tell or not. Then something occurred to him. He went into Dan's room and checked inside the old, scarred wardrobe. Dan's suit was gone. Frankie thought he began to understand. He phoned Dan's house in Thornbank. Someone who said she was the baby-sitter answered. Betty, she said, had gone out. Frankie was partly relieved. At least, he felt he understood what was happening. He hadn't been feeling relieved for very long when he was told he was wanted downstairs on the phone. It was, as he had feared, Matt Mason.

'Hullo, Frankie?'

'Yes, Matt!'

'How are things?'

'Couldn't be better. Big man's havin' a sleep. Gettin' fit for Saturday.'

'That's good. Any chance I could talk to him?'

'Well, Matt. He's sleepin'. Ye know what Ah mean? We don't want to break his sleep. Now, do we?'

'Well, Frankie. I think maybe we should.'

'Matt! Come on. He needs his sleep.'

'Uh-huh. Get him anyway, Frankie.'

Frankie put his hand over the mouthpiece and cursed Dan Scoular.

'What it is, Matt,' Frankie said. 'I didn't want to tell you this. The big man's been nervous, Ah gave him sleeping pills. A regimental band couldn't waken him. I'm sorry, Matt. But I had to make a decision. Ah thought it was better he had a sleep. Ah hope you don't mind me giving him those pills.'

'No, Frankie. I don't mind. But I think you should make them stronger.'

'How do you mean, Matt?'

'I mean, Frankie White, he's walking in his fucking sleep.'

'Sorry, Matt?'

'Not yet you're not. You don't know "sorry" yet. You've just failed the test. He's been seen.'

'He's been seen?'

Matt Mason said nothing. Frankie's mind fumbled for a role.

'Jesus. He must've – I'll go and –'

'So shut up. Spare us the vaudeville turn. You say another word, I'll come to the Burleigh and stand on your face. Sh! Just listen now. He's been seen. The word is he was leaving Glasgow, as well. So here's what you do. You find him. By hook, crook or any other way you can think of. But you will find that big man. And if you don't, decide which necropolis you want. So then you bring him to the gym tomorrow. Two o'clock sharp. Be waiting. Now just tell me one thing. Is that understood?'

'Yes, Matt.'

'All right. You've fucked it up. I hold you responsible. You're not going to put that right. Remember that. But you might put it less wrong by getting him there tomorrow for two o'clock.'

'He'll just be seeing his wife, Matt,' Frankie almost shouted suddenly. 'That's who he was phoning last night.'

The silence was like a noose round Frankie's throat. He had his hand over the mouthpiece, breathing uneasily.

'So you knew what was going on tonight? And you still want to talk shite. Worse and worse. I don't care if it's the Queen of Sheba. You blew it. Be happy you're still walking. And wonder how long. Now get your arse into gear.'

The phone went dead. Frankie put the receiver down and stood still, unable to move. For where was there that he could move to? What did Matt Mason expect him to do? Go to Thornbank and crash in on big Dan, pull him out by the scruff of the neck? Trapped between two forces he was afraid of, Frankie's only recourse was self-pity. He had gone to all this trouble to find a way for Dan to make money and this was the thanks he got. He had provided Matt Mason with the puncher he needed and now he was being threatened because of it. The injustice induced in Frankie a slight paranoia.

His condition wasn't helped when he saw the small night porter open the door with the complicated slowness of someone untying a knot and admit a policeman Frankie knew. Standing in the alcove where the phone was, Frankie stepped back into shadow. His teeth were clenched with the reflex guilt that caught him every time he saw a policeman. It was Jack Laidlaw, a detective with the Crime Squad. Had he heard about the fight? Was he coming to check on Frankie?

Frankie was anxiously rehearsing a story in his head when he noticed that Laidlaw looked drunk. He was followed into the hotel by the good-looking woman Frankie had seen on the desk. They spoke briefly with the night porter and started towards the old lift. Watching them, Frankie saw Laidlaw and the woman standing in the lift. He was muttering in a disgruntled, drunken way and she kissed him and said something in a low voice and he laughed. He had his arm round her as the metal grille of the lift closed and they ascended.

The small scene interested Frankie. He was sure that Laidlaw was married. He was thinking that the information might come in handy when common sense overtook the thought. What could he use it for? Blackmail? Blackmailing Laidlaw would be like trying to catch a bull with a butterfly net. Frankie contented himself with knowing that Laidlaw was in the hotel and, therefore, Frankie could make sure that neither he nor Dan was seen – that is, if Dan came back at all.

Back up in his room, Frankie frayed his already threadbare carpet some more. He had finally decided he had better get to Thornbank somehow, even if it was by taxi, when a sound made him stand very still, listening. He thought he had heard a light switched on next door. Waiting, he heard someone walking in Dan's room. He hurried out into the corridor and pushed open the door to Dan's room. Dan looked up from where he was sitting on the bed. He still had his jacket on. His shirt collar was open, the tie pulled away from it.

'You bastard!' Frankie greeted him. 'You've landed me right in it, haven't you. You've been seen, ya bastard. Matt Mason's been on the phone. They're probably bookin' me in at the cremmy right now. Where the fuck were you, anyway?'

'Leave it, Frankie,' Dan said.

'So Ah will. Ah'll leave it all right. Listen, you. Ma balls are an inch off the ham machine. That's what you did the night. Ye know who we're dealin' with here? This man fucking kills people!'

'Tomorrow, Frankie. Eh?'

'Tomorrow my arse! Where the hell *were* you?'

Dan looked up over the hand that had been covering his eyes.

'A far place. All right?'

'Don't play funny fuckers here. This is me. Remember? Ah went to the trouble to get you this fight. Ah put ma reputation on the line for you. Just to try an' make ye some money. Do ye a favour. An' this is the thanks Ah get? Listen –'

Dan stood up suddenly. Frankie realised he had been so angry that he hadn't properly noticed Dan since he came in. He was noticing him now all right. It occurred to Frankie that he hadn't seen Dan angry before. He was wishing he never had.

'You think stayin' in Thornbank cuts off the oxygen to the brain or somethin'? Ye did all this for me? You did it for you, Frankie. I was your pay-poke, that was all. Fair enough. But don't start tryin' to put it to music. You got me into this an' Ah'm workin' it out as Ah go along. Ah'll work it out for maself. You've done your bit. Promoter. Now take yer money an' shut yer face. Ah'll decide what Ah do. Your problems wi' Matt Mason are your problems wi' Matt Mason. Ah reckon you've earned them. Any problems I have wi' him, I'll work out for maself. Your help's not asked. Because the only person you want to help is you. Fair enough?'

Frankie had always been aware, since he had met him, of the raw force there was in Dan Scoular. But it had been chased with smiles, sheathed in an ease of manner. Frankie felt it bare and honed now, a hard edge he didn't want to push against. Something had been happening to big Dan. Perhaps the training was working. The realisation evoked contradictory feelings in Frankie. He felt a kind of thrill in the thought that Dan might have a good chance against Cutty Dawson after all. He felt a certain alarm because the force that was refining itself in Dan Scoular wasn't going to be easy to control. You couldn't assume its allegiances. It belonged to Dan. It might turn itself against any of them, and that could be bad news for Frankie.

'Fair enough, Dan,' he said. 'If that's the way you see it. But Ah'm supposed to take you to the gym tomorrow. All right?'

'That's all right.'

Dan sat back down on the bed.

'Matt Mason says we've got to get there before two. If we're not there for two, Dan, Ah better emigrate. Don't let me down.'

'Ah'll be there.'

'Oh. There's another thing. There's a polisman in the hotel the night. Ah saw him comin' in. Jack Laidlaw.'

Dan emerged briefly from his preoccupation.

'Ah know his brother,' Dan said. 'Scott. Lives in Graith-nock. He's a teacher. Nice fella.'

'Maybe, Dan. But Ah don't think we should have an Ayrshire reunion. Eh? Ah mean, try to make sure ye're not noticed tomorrow mornin'.'

'Aye. Ah see what ye mean.'

'Well.' Frankie stood at the door. 'See you tomorrow then. Don't stay up too late, big man. Sunday's close.'

'Sleep nice, Frankie.'

'Sure. The condemned man had a good night's sleep. Cheers.'

Promoter, Frankie thought as he lay in bed. Having the light on didn't help. The big, dingy flowers on the wallpaper palpitated before his eyes like a forest that was growing in on him. He was on the last glass from the bottle of whisky he and Sandra had been using. This afternoon seemed already a long way off, had turned into instant nostalgia.

He felt far away from everyone, especially Dan Scoular. There was more than a wall between them. Frankie thought of the force he had felt in Dan's presence and wondered about where it came from. It hadn't been to do with his size. It wasn't anything Dan had been deliberately projecting. Rather, Frankie thought, it came from the intensity of his preoccupation, the depth of his confusion. From the internal upheaval of such indecision as Frankie had thought he saw, decisions when they emerged were liable to be made of rock.

The threat of Matt Mason had made Frankie prepared to go in any direction to neutralise it. That threat hadn't even impinged seriously on Dan. To withstand a pressure as great as that meant you must have great pressures on you from inside. Frankie lived by an ability to transplant himself effortlessly from one situation to another but the roots of Dan's actions, he suspected, went very deep in him.

Frankie was haunted by the thought of Dan lying in the next room like the ghost of his past. Frankie had thought it was effectively buried. But irrelevant memories came back walking through his head of people he wished he felt more worthy of. They weren't necessarily particularly good people or impressive or noble but they had had a stubborn adherence to earned values that he sensed he lacked.

The image of old Jenny Brannigan bothered him particularly with its persistence. He had known her when she was younger and fond of a drink. But his mother had told him recently how she died. She was in her late seventies and blind and living alone. She had been asleep in her chair when her clothes caught fire. After beating out the flames herself, she had lain for a while. Then she had crawled through to her bedroom and changed every stitch of clothing, putting on fresh, because you didn't go to hospital unless everything on you was clean. She must have been peeling her skin off with the clothes. Then she had called for help and been taken to hospital, where she died a week later. One part of him could call her a silly old bugger. But the rest of him was awed. Even death she had met on her own terms.

Frankie just wanted Dan away from him. He sipped slowly at the glass, hoping sleep would come before he reached the bottom. Promoter. What worried him about the word was that he had maybe promoted one fight more than he had intended. He dreaded a clash between Matt Mason and Dan Scoular because he was bound to be somewhere between them when they collided.

But the next day began well enough for Frankie. He had noticed that before. Just when you thought the faceless forces that ran your life were going to foreclose, you found the lease extended and a bright day landed in your lap. Dan was up at his usual time and they did the run in weather sharp as a cold shower and relaxed, if that was the word, in their separate rooms and were at the gym at five to two.

Tommy Brogan let them in and Matt Mason and Eddie Foley were there. Frankie was looking for a clue to where he stood. Matt Mason's ignoring of him left him uncertain, but at least it might mean sentence was suspended. Matt shook his head at Dan Scoular the way a headmaster might at an unruly pupil he couldn't quite dislike.

'Well,' he said. 'Did you get it out of your system?'

Dan Scoular said nothing. He crossed and took off his jacket, hung it on a peg.

'I hope you didn't leave yourself in the bed.'

Dan turned and looked at him.

'Last night was personal,' he said. 'We won't talk about that.'

'It felt a bit personal to me as well,' Matt Mason said. 'Pains in the wallet always do. I'm paying you money.'

'Ah'm here.'

'Aye, but how much of you's here? I'm hiring you. All of you. Not what you decide to give me.'

'Naw,' Dan said. 'Maybe ye should get Mr Stewart to check the contract. Ye haven't understood it.'

'Either that or you haven't.'

The other three lounged in the sunlit silence. Eddie Foley examined the fingernails of his left hand. Tommy Brogan was whistling under his breath. Frankie was aware of sunshine seeming intrusive here among the paraphernalia he had always associated with night and smoky halls and unnatural light.

'Well,' Matt Mason said. 'We can talk any time. If there are things you don't want to talk about just now, let's not talk at all. Let's just see what you can do.'

He nodded to Tommy Brogan.

'Right, let's go,' Tommy Brogan said.

'Is it all right if Ah change?' Dan said.

When he came out of the dressing-room with only his track-suit trousers on and his trainer shoes, he stood in a different relationship to the others. Three of them had their street clothes on and the fourth was wearing a polo-neck. Dan looked more vulnerable, the one who must be tested. Matt Mason's nod had been the beginning of a ceremony the others were witnessing. Everybody in the room knew this wasn't just a training session but exactly what more it was perhaps varied in the thoughts of each.

For Tommy Brogan it might have been the chastisement of a sinner, repentance through mortification of the flesh. He seemed determined to find the place where Dan's physical arrogance might yield and acknowledge a limit. While the others watched, he justified the name Dan had suggested for him to Frankie White – the mad monk. Every effort Dan gave him, he demanded more.

Yet Frankie noted that a perverse pleasure happened in Tommy's eyes every time Dan Scoular refused to yield, every time he clenched harder on his determination and went on. It occurred to Frankie that he had perhaps been missing the point. Tommy's purpose wasn't to take Dan down a bit but the opposite. He was trying to tap Dan's sense of his own strength, to take him to the point where he would realise what force was in him and be able to use it against others. It was impressive to watch how Dan responded.

Eddie Foley, his eyes steady in appreciation, was nodding as if in agreement with Frankie. He was thinking of Sunday. They had a real event on their hands. Watching Dan, he saw him in the setting they had chosen for him – the rough cup of the field with the trees around it. Whoever was there, the effort they had made to get the place wouldn't be wasted. The mechanics of the whole event fascinated Eddie, gave him an aesthetic pleasure. Having long ago decided that it was fruitless, not to say unhealthy, to judge the terms by which he lived, he had settled for being as competent a fixer as he could be. The efficiency with which things were worked out pleased him the way a well-made machine, whether it was a car or a gun, would.

He was glad the farmer had finally agreed. The other fields they had looked at hadn't been right. This one was ideal – a small, natural arena hidden among farms, an uncultivatable remnant of the past that the developed, arable land hadn't managed to obliterate. You could have imagined primitive champions meeting there, to settle the meaning of things, with the tribe and their elders looking on.

He was glad Matt had offered the extra money to clinch it. For a moment, as they talked to the farmer in the middle of the cattle market, Eddie had thought he wasn't going to agree. He was a big, balding man with a moustache and one of those deceptively open faces that Eddie now associated with farmers. He wore his red cheeks and his crinkled forthright expression, which suggested he was used to looking into all kinds of weather, like make-up that was almost convincing. Ah, well, ye see, he was troubled by the fact that all this wasn't strictly legal. His misgivings got higher and higher until the money managed to clear them. Eddie would never again take farmers for simple people. He supposed that if you had won arguments with the earth there weren't a lot of other ones you were likely to lose.

That had been the second-last cog in the machine. The last one, with his jaw clamped like a vice to hold his will in place, was looking good. He had come a long way from a pub car park in Thornbank, and Eddie had played his part in it. He remembered with a smile something Matt Mason had said as they were leaving the cattle market with the venue fixed. Among the stench and the bellowing and the loud voices, Matt had slapped the haunch of a penned bull and said, 'If Dan Scoular comes on all right, we might get him to take on one of these.' They had laughed, but Cutty Dawson might be well within his range.

Matt Mason wasn't so sure. He was looking for something he still wasn't convinced he had seen. He remembered Roddy Stewart's comment when he had seen Dan Scoular for the first time in the gym: 'The horse looks good but the jockey seems to have doubts.' And he remembered Tommy Brogan's question on the same occasion: 'Does he go for it?' Well, did he? After the two weeks' general training and fifteen hours locked in with Tommy Brogan, Matt Mason still couldn't tell. Perhaps the answer could only come in 'no-man's-land', as the farmer had called it. But, being a bookmaker, he would have liked to feel he could calculate the odds here and now, especially since he understood more and more that he wasn't just gambling on a fight but on a way to control the future so that it would be a continuation of his past. He wanted Dan Scoular to prove something for him and so he watched him greedily, willing him to acknowledge that he would, through some secret sign that only Matt Mason himself would understand.

The nearest Mason had come to believing in such an indication had been when they were confronting each other before the training. Whatever the others had thought was happening, he had been pleased with Dan's refusal to back off. It was the stance from which Mason himself had started out.

But since then only one moment had given him the same hope. It had come at the end of a punishing series of exercises. Tommy had slammed the medicine ball at Dan until he was tired. He had left Dan punching the heavy bag until Matt Mason could feel the pain in his own arms. He had him doing stretching exercises on the floor, again and again. Suddenly, Dan Scoular's eyes, lit with a fierce incandescence, had raked everybody else in the room as he laboured. It was a vicious look, declared everybody else an enemy.

As it hit Frankie White, he glanced away. That look had

138

been like a sudden transformation of Dan Scoular before his eyes. Frankie had never seen that expression on Dan's face before – not when he had dealt with Billy Fleming, not in Alan Morrison's improvised gym, not last night when his anger had been ingoing, troubled. Frankie wondered what they had done to him. He felt like leaving, dissociating himself from the rest of what would happen. As Dan said, he had done his bit. He would have preferred to take his money now and just go.

While Tommy Brogan peeled off his singlet and put on boxing gloves, having told Dan he could take a couple of minutes' rest, and while nobody else spoke, Frankie found the gym oppressive with its smells of embrocation and resin and sweat, pungent as the incense he associated with the church services of his schooldays when he had had to endure explanations of the meaning of life he didn't want to believe. Just as he had felt nothing was as serious as they had made out then, so he couldn't accept that anything was as serious as this. He didn't want to come too near to seeing clearly what the way he lived involved for he could only cope with his life as a series of unexamined, vaguely romantic gestures. But he was obliged to stay as Tommy Brogan led him nearer to the raw centre of what he had helped to bring about.

'Right, big man,' he said. 'Enough of the kiddin'. Now the real stuff.'

They went into the ring. Frankie knew that Tommy fancied himself at that. He had good reason. They said of him that he had never lost a street fight in his life. Tommy was a physical freak, Frankie thought. He moved with a speed he should have lost years ago. Watching him, Frankie was wondering if there were people of such strong will that what they wanted badly enough they got. He remembered reading in a magazine about Gandhi and how he had believed later in his life that having sex took away the vital juices from a person. That fitted Tommy. Frankie could recall talking to him in a pub once and hearing him say, quite casually, something that had chilled Frankie to the bone. 'See me when Ah was young,' Tommy had said. 'Ah would always rather fight than fuck. Always.' He hadn't changed. His reason for being was to perfect a single gift, the ability to destroy another man physically. If he could have split his private atom, he would have made himself into a bomb.

Yet he was completely and obviously outclassed by Dan Scoular, a man who had never tried as hard as he had and who, within a week, had surpassed him. Frankie didn't believe it was merely a matter of age. There might be six or seven years in it but Tommy was a maniac for fitness, and today he had tried to sap Dan before taking him into the ring. Yet Dan made him miss by inches time and again and placed punches on him that he simultaneously pulled, like someone constructing diagrams for a book on boxing.

Frankie relaxed a little, seeing the Dan Scoular who was familiar to him. There was an element of the comic in the situation and Frankie felt comfortable with comedy. Eddie appreciated the grace of what Dan was doing. Matt Mason felt cheated. Dan wasn't showing himself. You couldn't tell what he was capable of.

Tommy Brogan, presumably aware of the impression he was failing to make, precipitated the exhibition into an event. He wrestled Dan roughly into a corner, held him with his left hand and hooked him on the jaw with his right. It was then Matt Mason found his sign, brief it was true, but brilliantly clear. In a blurred sequence of reflexes that Dan was as much a victim of as Tommy, Dan ducked away and, as Tommy turned to find him, spun him with a left into position and crossed his right precisely into the moving arc of Tommy's head. Tommy volleyed on to his back.

'Jesus!'

The word was pulled out of Eddie Foley's mouth in compelled admiration. Frankie found his misgivings about what he had done temporarily suppressed yet again by the realisation that he might have picked a winner. Matt Mason believed he had seen what he was waiting for. The way Dan had confronted him when he had come in at first could be faked, was a gesture not an action. But in there with Tommy he had shown, however briefly, the unfakable will to fight that ignites the reflexes under pressure. Then, in the very giving of the sign, Dan erased it.

He was across immediately, helping Tommy up. Tommy let himself be helped and then, as consciousness came back, he angrily shook Dan off. The others' awareness was still behind what was happening in the ring, trying to reconstruct the punch. It was like trying to remember where a flash of lightning has been that fuses as it happens.

'Ah'm sorry,' Dan said. 'That wasn't needed.'

'Don't worry about me,' Tommy said.

'Ah was worried about me,' Dan said.

'Save it, save it. Start worryin' when ye miss.'

It was an exchange in mutually incompatible idioms that translated into their opposites. Tommy offered a gruff admiration and Dan heard a rejection. Dan extended a concern and Tommy received an insult. Tommy was deeply offended. The offence wasn't in the blow but in the offer of help. The blow was what a man took from another man, the gentleness wasn't. Matt Mason shared Tommy's feeling of offence. He watched Dan bend out of the ring and Frankie White come forward to take off his gloves. Dan picked up his towel and sat down alone. Still unsure of what he had bought, Mason decided he had better use what he had been keeping in reserve to tilt the odds in his favour as far as he could. A discreetly applied stimulant might be in order.

'There's something I want to show you,' he said.

Dan blinked away his sweat, looking up at him. Matt Mason turned towards Frankie White and winked. To Frankie it felt like an amnesty. Mason turned back towards Dan.

'In the office here,' he said.

Dan rose and followed him. As Mason closed the office door, he was studying Dan's reaction to the fact that there was somebody there, somebody who had been there all the time. Benny Smith's appearance matched that unobtrusiveness. He had moved the chair into the corner of the room beside the window and had almost managed to merge with the wall. Dressed in jeans and jerkin, he was very thin and his eyes were red-rimmed. He didn't look at Dan but his eyes took in Matt Mason briefly and then concentrated on the floor.

'This is Smithy,' Mason said.

Dan nodded to the downturned head.

'Show him your arms, Smithy.'

The man struggled out of his jerkin and pulled up first one sleeve of his checked shirt and then the other. The skin was conspicuously punctured, the needle-marks most dramatic in the soft hollow where forearm and upper arm met.

'You know what that means?' Mason said to Dan.

Dan nodded.

'You wondering why I'm showing you this?'

Dan didn't answer.

'Smithy. Tell the man who supplies you with that shite.'

'Cam Colvin.'

'And who put you on it in the first place?'

'One of Cam's operators.'

'You ever tried to come off it?'

'I've tried.'

'You ever going to come off it, do you think?'

'Oh aye. When they bury me.'

'What age are you, Smithy?'

'Twenty-six.'

Mason liked the way Smithy had responded, as if his only function was to illustrate the points Mason was making. But Dan Scoular's face was still impassive. Mason went on deliberately to talk about Smithy as if he couldn't hear what was being said, was only for their inspection like a specimen floating in formaldehyde.

'And look at him. He looks older already than he will ever be. He'll just go on till there's nothing left of him to stick a needle into. You know what can happen with people like that at the end? They run out of places to jag. I've known them injecting themselves in the prick. Only place they could find a vein. There's a lot of Smithy around. And getting more every year. What's wrong, big man? You not like facing the truth?'

Dan turned as if he was going to go out. He swung back towards Matt Mason.

'That's a man ye're talkin' about. Not a tailor's dummy. He can hear ye.'

'Oh. You think I'm hurting his pride. Grow up. What pride? Why do you think he's here?'

Dan looked back at Smithy.

'He's here for money. He's earning money. Look.' He took two ten-pound notes from his pocket and handed them to Smithy. 'Put that in your veins, Smithy. Cheers!'

The man went out without a word.

'What else do you want me to do? I'm doing him a favour. The quicker he gets to an overdose, the better it'll be for everybody.'

He took out his cigar-case, selected one. Dan wasn't going to speak but Mason held up his hand with the lighter in it as if to forestall him.

'Before you start talking like a social worker, Dan. You can maybe afford pride but he can't. It never occur to you that people get to places where pride can't follow them? He's there. Your worries about talking like that in front of him. That's *your* pride you're talking about. He doesn't have any left to worry about. And he never will again. You know why I showed you that?'

He lit up his cigar.

'To make something clear to you. That's what you're fighting, Dan. Cutty Dawson works for Cam Colvin. And that's how Cam Colvin makes his money. That's where we live. So I've bent a few rules myself. Because there's no other way to work in this shit-heap. But never anything like that. Remember that on Sunday, Dan. You better have your shower before you get a chill. We want you fit for Cutty.'

When he followed Dan out a moment later he found him staring at the ring. Tomorrow was a rest day. This was the last time he would see it. Matt Mason looked at Dan Scoular looking at the ring and wondered what he was seeing there.

There is a pub in Graithnock called the Akimbo Arms where the lounge bar and the public bar, though separate, are linked by an arched doorway from one gantry to the other. It means the same bar-staff can serve both places and so, like a reversible raincoat, it is an economical way of presenting two images to the changing times.

The public bar is what the pub originally was, a place where men drank. But it is smaller now, having been rendered peripheral by the encroachments of the lounge, where men and women drink together on soft seats and under alcove wall-lights. Sometimes women go into the bar but not often. When they drink there, it is usually because there is someone they want to meet and, occasionally, for the making of a point or from a self-conscious decision to go slumming. But they never become regulars.

The connecting door between the two is most commonly used for access to the men's lavatory or the pay-phone, both of which are in the public bar. The old bar largely retains its identity as a shrine to a traditional Scottish sense of manhood, though attracting fewer devotees than formerly. The rituals haven't changed much but the punctilious practice of them is less fanatically adhered to. Swearing is no longer compulsory. Indeed, it is rare enough for some traditionalists to savour a fine, orotund obscenity when they hear it, like a memory of when the service was in Latin.

It was in the public bar Dan Scoular stood on the night Frankie White missed him in Glasgow. On the occasion of the meal with Matt Mason and the others he had found himself unable any longer to drown with talk the pain of the wound Wullie Mairshall had put in his mind. It was Wednesday. He had risen from the table and phoned the Red Lion. Wullie, like an anti-doctor always on call, had been ready with ointment to exacerbate the sore. His informants had supplied him with it: Thursday was the night. They would be going to a place called the Akimbo Arms. 'A daft name,' Wullie said, 'whatever it means.' Wullie was a thorough practitioner, he even provided directions on how to get there.

Not knowing there were two parts to the pub, Dan, screwed up to cope with whatever he would find, had blundered into the public bar. He found some men looking at him curiously. There were no women. As both an expression of relief and a cover for his embarrassment, he ordered a pint. He felt stupid standing here as a projection of Wullie Mairshall's imagination, dream of the working-class avenging angel. It was then he saw them.

Framed in the archway leading to the lounge, lit attractively by a wall-light, she sat, like an unholy icon. The image, once seen, was a brand on the eyeballs, blinding him for the moment to everything else. Irrevocability was the first pain he felt, a lifetime fact expressing itself in an instant. I'm here to stay, the moment told him. You remember me till you die. Countless invisible props to his sense of himself, masculine vanities so secure it must have been years since he checked them, attitudes he had hardly questioned, went up like tinder in one sudden flame. It was lurid in the light of it that he saw the other man's face and vaguely remembered him as someone he had seen at a party. But that was a long time ago. Could it have been going on as long as that? The tremors from his collapsing present ran back into his past. Not only did he not know where he was. He didn't know where he had been. Suspicion had become fact and fact became again suspicion.

Why then did he not move through to the lounge and confront them immediately? He was to wonder about that. That was what, if he had been asked to imagine the scene, he would have been sure would happen. It surely couldn't have been because he became aware of the barman lugubriously paging his attention with 'All right, sir?' The fact that he found himself automatically conducting the trivial business of paying couldn't have been enough to divert him from acting. It might have been connected with the disorientation from the centre of himself he had felt since going to Glasgow. It might have been partly because he knew what Wullie Mairshall expected him to do. It might have been because he sensed the situation was too important to be expressed in a single action.

All he knew for sure was that he stood there and, in the time it takes to deny a reflex, felt fall from him like protective clothing his complacent assumptions about himself. He had unconsciously rehearsed for such a moment innumerable times. Since adolescence, the gruff, ritual responses had been taught to him and his friends from anecdotes and in answer to the speculative catechism, 'What would you do if . . .?' 'I'd have him first. An' then we'd see.' 'They like lyin' thegither, they could have the same grave.' 'Kick baith their ribs in.'

His own life, with its early aggressions and apparent endorsement of hard values, had been an implied subscription to that automatically shared ethos. Now experiencing the reality of it, he had hesitated and he wondered how many others would have behaved as he had done in practice. Those hard threats he had so often heard uttered against the possibility of a wife's adultery seemed to him here less statements of what would certainly happen than charms to frighten such an event out of taking place.

He moved slightly down the bar, away from the possibility of being seen by them, and with the one small, lateral movement seemed to shuck the code he had thought was his, became not the master of that rough ethic's baying principles but their prey. He felt unmanned. He became for himself an impostor among these men of raucous certainties and instant responses. Their laughter excluded him.

'It's true,' one of them was saying. He was in his fifties, his face lit from within by the beer like a Hallowe'en lantern. Sitting down, he held the attention of several men at the bar who were turned towards him. He had the sonorous delivery of a man who was used to being listened to. 'Apart from churches, the auldest thing in this toon's Tammy Bruce. An' even he's condemned. Ye seen him lately? What? He's no' gonny last. A waste o' time for him to wind up his watch. Naw. Nearly every buildin' in this toon is since the Thirties. Think about it. That's a fact. They've ta'en our past away from us. A sign o' the times.'

They all went on to argue and compare buildings and evoke past people. Dan's thoughts were a personal descant on their public theme, elegiac with self-pity. What they were discussing as an abstraction he felt he was experiencing. He saw himself briefly as the victim not of personal circumstances but of something larger. These were the changes that were all around. He was just a part of them. This wouldn't have happened before. He thought vaguely of his parents' house and evoked in himself a misty ambience of warmth and brightness and stability. He managed to believe in the image for a moment, like one of those coloured pictures he had stared at as a child, wishing he could go there, where flowers of different seasons bloomed together and wormless apples grew and no hen-shit clogged the tails of fluffy chickens. But now, as then, reality blocked his way, this time in the shape of a memory he never welcomed.

After his father died, he had gone round as often as he could, or as often as he told himself he could, to see his mother. Her life was contracting then to a narrowing circle of daily trivia and that in itself was painful to look on at, for her generosity of nature began to atrophy with disuse. Small, uncharacteristic bitternesses tared her speech and her mouth seemed often tasting aloes. Then one day she changed in the passing his sense of his own boyhood.

146

They had been talking about someone who lived locally and who was a little older than Dan. His habit of not giving his wife enough money was mentioned. Dan was laughing at the man's reputation for meanness.

'About as bad as yer feyther,' his mother suddenly said.

'What?' Dan thought she was joking.

'About as bad as yer feyther. A penny rolled a long, long way wi' him.'

'Come on, Mither. That was oor joke.'

'Was it? He woulda skinned a louse for the tallow. Ah think he was feart Ah would save up the bus fare tae Graithnock an' no' come back.'

The coldness of her voice chilled the air in the room. He stared at her in the twilight she would let turn almost to darkness before she pressed the switch, for the habits of a lifetime saw only financial waste in light that you weren't using to look at anything in particular. The fire was embers to which a few fresh nuggets tried to give the kiss of life. Perhaps it was what she had become herself she was accusing his father of. Perhaps the accusation was that he had made her so. Years of assumptive laughter went hollow for Dan.

Sitting with a stranger, he began to question her and she animated under his questions, almost shone eerily in the dusk with a truth she had found the occasion to tell and in the telling defined it for herself. She told him of slights so small you would have thought no memory could retain them. But hers had. There were embarrassments in shopping, masculine insensitivities, small things impossibly longed for – the terrible lifelong minutiae of unshared pain. There was the wish that she had the chance to do it again and the avowal that so many things would be different.

It wasn't the contradiction of his sense of their relationship that was shocking. It was the awareness of the host of denied selves that were dead in her and she mourned for still. As she talked, he caught glimpses of girls she almost was and women she had wanted to be. They came faintly from her dwindling body like an exorcism in the darkening room. In that moment the brutish inadequacy of his past appreciation of her shamed him.

He had always known her life a selfless giving, a bequest

from the living of everything she had. That moment was the codicil, not one that changed what was given but clarified the terms on which it was received. The proviso was the selfishness of others. The beneficiaries could only become beneficiaries through their own greedy indifference. Otherwise, how could they have accepted a gift so destructive of the donor?

Dan had seen a glimpsed truth not only of his mother's life that day but of whole generations of working-class women. From then on the praises he would hear given to those self-sacrificing many were to have a doubtful ring for him. It was justice that the true heroism of working-class life should be accorded to those women. But like all heroism it was a dubious commodity. That lost army of fraught, unglamorous women, with the coats they had to make last for years and the shoes inside which strips of cardboard, absorbing dampness, recorded the passage of hard times like the rings of a dead tree, had done unbelievable things. But they shouldn't have been asked to do them.

With a few pounds and some sticks of furniture, they had every day practised a very commonplace white magic. They had sewn comfort out of rags, brewed surprising satisfaction from unimpressive ingredients, calmed storms and taught decency in the face of the injustice their own lives suffered. But the cost of it had often been themselves. They were the ingredients of their own magic, last ounce of spirit, last shred of ambition, smallest fragment of dream. The wastage – the good minds starved, the talents denied, the potential distorted – was beyond computation. So when Dan was to hear afterwards a woman who had married well make a small shrine of her mother, or a man who had been successful praise his mother's sacrifice, he appreciated their feeling but thought it would have been better not to need to feel it. Those attitudes seemed to him like wreaths laid at the graves of the prematurely dead, ones on which the cards should read 'With fond misgivings' and 'Guiltily remembered'.

The guilt he had felt towards his mother extended now to include Betty. The looks through to the lounge he had continued to take had forced him to see the potential to be someone else that there was in her. He saw not only her attractiveness through the eyes of a stranger but her interestingness, realising afresh how much he didn't know about her. It was as if, having found the bay of a continent habitable, he hadn't explored the rest of it. He suspected it was mainly that honest admission which held him there. He didn't doubt his ability to go through and deal with the man. But, acknowledging how far Betty – by the very action of being here – had reminded him that she was incomprehensibly herself, he had doubts about the results of his going through the lounge.

He remembered, too, in seeing her, his own misgivings about their life together, his own longings for something other, his own times of unfaithfulness. He couldn't pretend that she had no right to be the same. The thought was a shared nakedness of doubt with her, a dismantling of his own machismo. Stripped of who he had thought he was, of Wullie Mairshall's moth-eaten robes of manhood, he felt the chilliness of honesty. He held balanced in himself two forces: a rage that could have demolished the furnishings of this pub and anybody who got in his way, especially Betty, and a certainty of how useless doing that would be. He knew simultaneously his strength and its pointlessness.

He understood how fragile he was and in the understanding, twinned in the same placenta, was his compassion for Betty's fragility, no matter what she did. One couldn't be born without the other. And in the realisation of his own rawness and that of others, he saw the flimsiness of the coverings sometimes made for it, the tatterdemalion beliefs, the certitudes any trivial accident could pierce. When he looked back into the lounge and saw that they were gone, it was like looking in a mirror and seeing no reflection.

Before he could stop himself, he had panicked, and gone through to check. Three girls on a night out assessed him calmly. He went out into the street. Two men were taking a prolonged farewell on the pavement. A car was refusing to start. There was only one person in it. Normalcy mocked him. Not knowing what else to do, he went back into the public bar and ordered another pint.

'John Logie Baird,' someone was saying. 'The inventor of television.'

'The steam engine. James Watt.'

'The phone.'

'Who was that?' somebody asked.

'The phone, does that no' ring a bell? An Alexander Graham Bell?'

'Alexander Fleming fae Darvel. Penicillin.'

'Sir Alexander Fleming.'

'Simpson. Chloroform.'

'Tar MacAdam.'

'Naw, but listen. Yese've all missed out the greatest Scotsman of them all.'

'Rabbie Burns!'

'The autodidact.'

Nobody else seemed to have heard of him.

'The self-taught man. That's Scotland's greatest tradition. There's men walkin' about these streets in boiler-suits wi' mair knowledge o' mair things than a lot o' professors have. Little wonder we've inventit an' discovered so mony things. We're intae everythin'. A very restless an' curious intelligence, the Scottish intelligence. Ask me any question.'

And he burst out laughing. With the obsessive desperation of the lost, Dan imagined a landmark in every casual observation. He had been listening to their talk as if he could deduce from it a fix on where he was. He had been thinking about how the Scots seemed to be curious about everything except themselves. The roster of names had come to him, like a surrogate identity, a list of aliases behind which it was possible to hide from the unexamined reality of your own experience. He understood the comfort of those familiar names. These talking men seemed to him like where he had been. He sensed them falling behind him like comfortable voices murmuring round a camp-fire while he moved on into a darkness disturbingly and unfamiliarly alive.

Like a brand aimlessly lifted from their fire, he took that one word: autodidact. His mind played with it. He was an autodidact who would be taking his official test on Sunday. But he was an autodidact of experience, and that was different from knowledge. Experience was an unlearning of certain kinds of knowledge, not a garnering but a stripping off.

He saw, perhaps because he had to in this moment of fearful vulnerability, a rough shape to his life. He had been preparing unselfconsciously for something like this. That instinctive boyhood decision to reject an academic course at school, that apparently casual turning away, had been a determined turning towards. He had chosen his own experience, undiluted, not filtered through the preconceptions of those who had gone before him. His parents had been wrong to see in his choice a rejection of his own intelligence. He had been choosing to develop his own intelligence, not as a career but as a way of life, something not compromised by its professional usefulness. What he had rejected was intellectuality, the force-feeding of intelligence in disjunction from personal experience.

From this distance that boy's determination seemed not a wilful silliness or a fear of taking on a hard challenge but an act of surprising self-confidence. For he had even then believed in the reality of his own intelligence, had no doubts that it was there. He hadn't felt the need to prove its existence to anyone else. Not much he had ever read had intimidated his mind, and he had read a lot. But he had always read in relation to his own life, using his intelligence to inform his experience, never to subvert it with unproven theory. Betty had often despaired of him. She said that he didn't use his intelligence or his reading to any purpose that affected his life significantly. But the purpose had been there, if opaque. Perhaps, he reflected ruefully, this moment was a fulfilment of it.

He stood at the bar and considered where all that ferreting among books, that patient coexistence with his own experience, that rejection of what he thought were false certainties, had brought him. If you had to come at experience without too many illusions about yourself, he seemed to be succeeding. He didn't know what his marriage was any more, he didn't know what he believed in, he wasn't sure who he was supposed to be. He felt he would be turning up on Sunday in a condition that would justify what Eddic said was the farmer's name for that patch of grass: 'no-man's-land'. He would be arriving as a body and not much else, so insubstantial he wondered if he would leave footprints.

But some reflexes of identity stayed with him, like the twitchings of a dying insect. He knew he had been waiting for time to pass. He looked at the clock above the bar and decided he had waited long enough. Betty and the man had left early. That had given Dan hope because it might mean she was concerned about the boys and didn't want to stay out too late. It might mean she was still as much their mother as she was whatever she was to the man. He wanted to check and hoped that she was home because he couldn't bear to face the images that would be running in his head all night like a blue movie if she wasn't. He crossed to the pay-phone and dialled. He had been phoning her from Glasgow every night. She would suspect nothing.

When Betty said 'Hullo', the meaning of the call was over. There was nothing they could seriously say to each other. They briefly told each other everything was all right, sentries guarding separate but adjoining states of loneliness, exchanging passwords. Putting down the phone, he submitted to the rest of the evening because there was nothing else he could think of to do.

He drank the rest of his pint and caught a bus to Glasgow and returned to the Burleigh Hotel and sat in his room and responded to Frankie White's remarks and lay in the darkness on his bed, through the wall from Frankie and far away from everyone, and wondered where he was to find enough will to clench a fist.

5

He wakened into a block of structured sunlight, no casual place but one imprisoning him in an experience he must confront. The unfamiliar room told him his loneliness. Time on his travelling alarm pointed at him like a gun: empty yourself and let's see what is there. The dull sounds in the hotel were too preoccupied to help him. He stirred his shoulders and arms and legs, probing for problems. There was none of the underwater sluggishness that sometimes held him on waking. His muscles responded instantly, gave him no excuse.

Necessity was waiting for him. But now, at this moment when he realised he must accept it, it seemed an invented necessity, not something he had discovered for himself. The happenings of the past three weeks, the money Matt Mason had given him, the companionship of Frankie White, the sessions with Tommy Brogan, all seemed an illusion of common purposes, a mirage of togetherness that dissipated leaving him only with himself, and in himself there was no discoverable reason for fighting Cutty Dawson. Who was Cutty Dawson?

The only way he could get himself out of bed towards what he would have to do was to imagine the reactions of the others if he didn't. He thought of the outrage, the contempt, the accusations of fear from Matt Mason and his friends, from the people who would be coming to watch, from Thornbank. Out of those thoughts he patiently constructed a ladder of shame by which to climb out of his disbelief in what was ahead.

Upright, he tried to conjure normalcy out of small actions. He took a long time washing himself at the basin. He brushed his teeth three times, as if Cutty Dawson and he were to meet for a smiling contest. Examining his rough chin in the deceiving mirror, he wondered about leaving it as it was. But he shaved because shaving was what he usually did. He did all of this very slowly and thoroughly because he was trying through the ceremony of habit to make the day real for him. It didn't work.

Instead of familiar objects giving him back himself, his strangeness imparted itself to them. Soap was a weird thing. How had they arrived at manufacturing that? The structure of a razor was outlandish. Everything oppressed him with its arbitrariness. What did all this have to do with him? He felt imprisoned in inventions of which he was one. He felt separate from his own life, as if seeing it for the unreal thing it was. The feeling persisted when Frankie White came in.

'Morning, morning, morning,' Frankie began briskly. 'We've got a good day for it.'

Dan nodded.

'You ready for the big breakfast?'

Frankie was reminding him of the arrangements Matt Mason had made. They were to meet in a hotel in the city centre. The fight was to begin at two o'clock and it had been decided that Dan should eat a big, late breakfast so that he would have digested the food properly by the time he met Cutty. Frankie kept talking as Dan finished dressing. He seemed to sense Dan's distance and was providing a running commentary of trivia as if to normalise things for him. But Dan was aware of how carefully Frankie was watching him. Frankie's caution isolated Dan further.

His isolation extended to the hotel where Eddie Foley took them. The big dining-room was empty except for themselves. They sat at a long table and were served by a waitress who stood well away from them unless she was signalled over to be asked for more toast or another pot of tea. It required some effort for Dan to eat the two well-done steaks that were put before him but he chewed his way through them determinedly, as if they were a substance with magical powers that would see him through what was ahead. Only Tommy Brogan, looking uncomfortable in this setting and perhaps in need of a purpose to hide behind, was checking on what Dan was eating.

Roddy Stewart was dividing his time between his meal and the *Observer*. Matt Mason, Eddie and Frankie were exchanging the sports pages of other papers. All strangers, Dan thought. He was a temporary adjunct to their lives, fuel for their own purposes. For Tommy Brogan, he was a test of his training skills, an experiment in how effectively Tommy could create a clone of himself within a week. For Matt Mason and Eddie Foley, he was an investment the point of which he didn't understand himself. For Frankie White, he was a wage. He couldn't be sure what he was for Roddy Stewart, perhaps a collector's item, like a primitive painting the worth of which would be decided today.

He was going there alone, Dan thought. No supporters would be going with him.

The car was a 1965 Hillman and seemed old for its years. It had been loaned to them for the day by Geordie Parker, who bought old cars less as a means of transport than as challenges to his engineering skills. He had cars the way a womaniser might have relationships, only holding on to them for as long as they offered scope for his orgiastic love of mechanical experimentation: 'Now if we put this bit here an' that bit there an' switched the cylinder-heads on her, that might be interesting.' Referring to any car by the feminine pronoun ('Ah handled 'er that rough, she blew a gasket'; 'Ye've got to double-declutch her or she'll give ye nothin''), his conversation could sound like an esoteric translation of the Kamasutra for garage mechanics.

Seeing them off in it, with Harry Naismith driving, Geordie made a small, formal speech, a bit like a Victorian father letting his daughter out without a chaperon.

'She doesn't do over fifty, Harry. It's not her style. She begins tae get the shakes. Soon as ye feel her doin' that, you ease up. Use her handbrake as little as possible. She's delicate there. An' when ye use it, gentle with her. Or the spring pops out an' ye'll have to throw bricks in front of the wheels to hold her. An' she's not keen on turnin' left. Ye'll find she won't keep the indicator there. As soon as ye let it go, it flicks back down. But you keep movin' it up an' down an' she'll be flashin' all right, though ye won't hear any o' that tickin' noise inside. By the way, she's champion for turning right. You'll be fine, boys. Just treat her nice an' ye'll find that she's a lady.'

Geordie's determined personalising of the car made more sense to Harry Naismith once he had started on the road. It felt less like driving than trying to please a crotchety old maid. Successive owners had attempted to remodel it to their own specifications, most notably changing what must once have been the back window of a shooting brake. It was now a hardboard hatchback, gone so spongy with weathering that to lean your hand on it was to leave your fingerprints for posterity. The back window had shrunk to a kind of Perspex porthole in the middle of the hardboard, and looking through it via the driver's mirror, you could just about work out whether it was day or night back there. More detailed information was hardly possible. Yet in spite of the efforts to reshape it, the car had retained a stubborn independence.

Not only did it not take kindly to going over fifty but when the needle stuttered nervously above forty a chill wind blew up the accelerator trouser leg in a very discouraging way. It also seemed to have a circulation problem and would cut out without warning when Harry was changing down, unless he coaxed it very carefully. Once, when they stopped to get cigarettes at a petrol station, they discovered that the back doors didn't open from the inside.

But such problems only added to the spirit of adventure that was among them. They were going to see something they had never seen before – a bare-knuckle fight – and they had more right to identify with one of the contestants than anybody else who would be there and it was a bright, crisp day and, in spite of or perhaps because of Frankie White's directions, they weren't sure of the way. That compound of circumstances acted upon their natural capacity for enjoying things like the elixir of youth. The car was full of boyish enthusiasm. The uncertainty of the car's progress was just the necessary element of mild hazard (Would they make it in time? Would they make it at all?) that made a journey out of what might have been merely a trip.

As they went, they spontaneously developed their roles in the drama of the situation. Alan Morrison was the world-weary traveller whom everything reminded of the past. He had been around all right but he was getting old and who knew how many such undertakings he had left in him? Sam MacKinlay was the leader of the expedition, not officious with it but never quite able to relax as much as the rest. He had to keep a careful eye on Harry Naismith, who was the driver who had once been good but who had been out of it for so long that his

rve was maybe gone. Alistair Corstorphine was the nervous
ewcomer and couldn't have played it any other way, with a
face that seemed only able to express varying degrees of
surprise. He got into character early on by telling Harry at a
side road that all was clear and they pulled out in front of a
bus. The blare of the horn heightened the atmosphere.

They even improvised their own plot lines. It wasn't long
before Sam and Harry had the quarrel. Sam, in the front
passenger seat, had been looking across meaningfully at Harry
several times. Sam would have liked to drive himself but he
had lost his licence eight months ago for what he called 'playing
at tig with both pavements on the front street'. He had been
driving a borrowed van. In the police station he had refused
to provide a sample of urine. When the police doctor arrived,
Sam had also been reluctant to submit to a blood test, claiming
he had only taken a pint and a half of lager. 'When did you
leave the pub, Mr MacKinlay?' the doctor had asked, looking
at him closely. 'Half-past eight,' Sam had said at once, deciding
that was a time early enough to suggest moderation. 'That's
interesting,' the doctor had said. 'It's only half-past seven just
now.' But the experience had in no way undermined his
confidence in his abilities as a driver.

'Harry,' he said. 'You heard Geordie. Take it easy with the
car. Ah've known people change religions wi' less bother than
you change gears.'

'Look,' Harry said. 'Who's drivin' the car?'

'Is that what ye're doin'?'

'At least Ah'm managin' to stay on one side of the road.'

'Don't give us that. Ah wis drunk at the time.'

'Aye. Well, see that sample of piss ye wouldn't give? It's
comin' out yer mouth.'

'At least Ah had an excuse that time. Ah've known people
pissed as a pub jaunt who could drive better than you. Ye'll
bugger the gears, man. We want to get there. The gears'll not
have a tooth to their name.'

'They might not be the only ones.'

'Well, stop at the first lay-by and we'll see.'

The tension in the car was real. Alistair, who had an
ignorance of cars that was almost nineteenth-century, could
think of nothing to say that might smooth things out. It was

Alan who intervened successfully with the offhand aplomb
an elder statesman whose talent in crisis stems from his havin
no inhibiting awareness of what is actually going on.

'I was in a car once,' he said, as if the rigid silence between
Harry and Sam were just a natural pause. 'Coming back from
Carlisle. An' one of the back wheels came off an' went past us
on the road. We pointed through the windscreen an' said,
"Oh, look. Whit's that?" Then we found out.'

His memory seemed to put their present situation in perspective. They weren't in a position as perilous as that. Also, he
had successfully evoked in Sam and Harry memories of fathers
and uncles who had had the same kind of relationship with
old cars as Geordie Parker did. The smell of oil in the car
helped. It was the distillation of a lot of working-class outings,
the smell of pleasures past. Travelling precariously in the old
Hillman, they felt themselves part of a tradition, as if they
were driving out of the past, a time when machines were less
of a status symbol and coexisted rather peremptorily with
people, and the repeated breakdowns tended less to arouse
self-righteous indignation in their owners than to leave them
in a state of puzzled respect for the wilfulness of the combustion
engine.

The four of them needed such a point of group identification
for they were all secretly feeling a certain amount of trepidation
about arriving, were experiencing the familiar sensation of
being country cousins. The car provided them with the best
way of coping with that feeling: a defiant declaration of it.
Arriving in a car like this was like coming in team colours.
They felt they were supporting what Dan stood for.

That feeling merged smoothly with the fact that they got
lost, which brought a nice, exciting edge to the end of their
journey. Time was running out and they couldn't find the
place and there was a real possibility that the fight would have
started before they had arrived, and nobody could tell how
near to the end of the fight the beginning might be. Harry was
being urged to put his foot down, regardless of what was
happening up his right trouser leg. Sam said if it was frost-
bitten and had to be amputated, they would all chip in to get
it mounted for above his fireplace, so that his grandchildren
would know of his heroism. The old car jolted them up and

down along the country roads, as if it couldn't quite remember what suspension was.

'Come on, Harry!' Sam was shouting. 'Knock the guts out the old bastard if ye have to.'

'Ah'm doin' that!'

'Do it some more.'

'Maybe if we stopped, we could hear the crowd shouting,' Alistair said.

His suggestion wasn't received with enthusiasm.

'Ask somebody,' Alan said. 'We've got to ask somebody.'

'Very good, Alan,' Sam said. 'You ask that coo there. An' Ah'll chat up a coupla rabbits. Who the hell are we gonny ask out here?'

'A farmer, ya daft bastard,' Alan said, losing his pub manner in the excitement.

That was what they did, accidentally. They had taken a turning Sam had said he was sure must be the road and they found themselves in a farmyard. A collie was circling the car and barking at them. None of them was keen to get out of the car and Sam, in his role as leader, leaned across and pressed the horn. It sounded like a lost sheep. The man who came out was balding, with a moustache. Sam wound down his window and found the winder come away in his hand.

'What d'ye want?' the man said. The dog started to bark again. 'Here!' The dog lay down and was quiet. 'What is it ye want?'

'We're looking for a fight,' Alistair called out excitedly from the back seat.

Sam grimaced.

'What he means is we've been invited to a bare-knuckle fight. To watch, like. We were told it was around here. Can ye help us?'

The man looked suspiciously at them and at the car. Whether from the appearance of the car or from Alistair's remark, he seemed convinced of their harmlessness. Two children had come out of the farmhouse into the yard and a woman stood in the doorway.

'Aye,' the man said. 'It's on ma land. Back doon the road there. There's a track to yer right. Brings ye tae the field.'

'Thanks, pal,' Sam said. 'Right, Harry.'

The man held up his hand.

'The only place ye can park is the house here. Round the back. It's a pound a head. Ah'll show ye.'

Harry drove slowly after him round the house and they came upon an acre of car-metal, gleaming multi-coloured in the pale sunshine.

'Jesus,' Sam said and called to the man, 'Ah don't know whit ye planted. But it's givin' ye a good crop.'

As they got out, Alistair and Alan having to wait until they were released by the other two, they were mesmerised by the money parked casually all around them. Geordie Parker's car looked as if it might be embarrassed, a feeling shared by Sam when he discovered on re-attaching the winder that it spun uselessly and he couldn't wind the window back up. He left the winder on the front seat and hoped it wasn't raining on the way back.

'An' Vince Mabon said it wouldny be worth comin' here,' Alistair said.

He looked in wonder at the cars and felt the importance of what was ahead. He had been the more hurt by Vince Mabon's dismissiveness of their journey, given in the incontrovertible tones of someone reading a prepared statement ('A meaningless event. The only possible result is no-contest'), because he hadn't been able, as he seldom was, to think of a reply. He felt he was looking at an effective answer now. A lot of important people must be here and surely that made the event itself important.

Alan was offering the man a pound note and the man was staring at it.

'A pound a head,' the man said.

'That's right,' Alan said.

'A pound a head. There's four of ye.'

'But there's only the one car.'

'A pound a head.'

'What if we'd come in a double-decker?' Sam said.

'A pound a head.'

Their silence was forming into a group vote for confrontation when the murmur of a small crowd came to them on the wind, the seductive sound of human expectation. They looked at one another and their eyes were a shared admission. Their common thought kindled every face to a smile. What did the money matter? He couldn't charge them more than their excitement was worth. The other three were searching for their pounds when Alan, catching the style of the moment, waved their efforts aside and gave the man three more single notes. As the man followed them round the edge of the farmhouse, he saw three of them begin to break into a run, but a hobbled run, as if they were trying to give the laggard Alan a tow from their enthusiasm. The man stood watching them, shaking his head. The two children drifted towards the running figures, magnetised by their eagerness.

'Here! You two!' the man said. 'Don't you go near there the day. Ah've warned ye alreadies. You play up here.'

'Is there somethin' ye're ashamed of down there, like?' the woman in the doorway said. She was younger than the man but her big, handsome face was already more worn than his.

'That's enough, Jessie. Ah've explained it tae ye.'

'Ye've explained it tae yerself. An' Ah hope ye're convinced.'

'The daftness of ither folk's no' ma problem.'

'Naw. But it's oor land.'

'Aye, an' that bit's makin' us money for the first time since we've had it.'

'Oan the Sabbath as well,' the woman said.

'You two!' the man said. 'Keep away from those cars.'

Alan caught up with the others at the gate where the narrow, rutted pathway ended. Beyond the gate two big men were standing. One was the man Dan Scoular had knocked out in the car park of the Red Lion. Alan assumed that the other man belonged to the rival camp. The men seemed reluctant to let them in until Frankie White came forward and said, 'It's all right. These are the boys from Thornbank. The official supporters' club. You should remember them, Billy.' Billy Fleming opened the gate quickly.

Alistair was effusive in his thanks to Frankie, who didn't bother to explain that he was glad to find a role for himself in the proceedings. He led them into the small, widening field towards the noise.

'How about this?' Frankie said. 'You don't see things like this too often in Thornbank, eh?'

The scene had a bright, heraldic simplicity. In the small

bowl of the field that was edged with a few trees, the crowd – not large, maybe a hundred – formed a rough, broken circle. The way they were all turned towards the centre and the muted expectancy among them and the green strangeness of the place created a frisson among the new arrivals, as if they had stumbled on the meeting of a secret sect. Alistair, romantic in proportion to his lack of experience, felt it most strongly. It was as if a ceremony were about to take place, a truth about to be revealed, and he was to share in it.

Drawing nearer and becoming a part of the crowd didn't dispel that first impression in him. For the others familiarity normalised the event. They had arrived at an exciting place among people who obviously had a lot of money and, with Geordie Parker's car safely out of sight, they could mingle and act as if they belonged here. Sam and Harry decided to move among the crowd, looking for good odds against the admission money Frankie White hadn't taken from them. Alan was a good audience for Frankie's proprietary running commentary on the occasion. But Alistair, wandering off himself, enlarged his awe on everything around him and found himself more and more mystified about where it was they had come to.

A woman in a red coat waved to someone. A group of four had a basket of food and were drinking from glasses. A man had his son sitting on his shoulders, a boy of about nine. There were people here Alistair recognised. He saw a face he knew from seeing it on television. After some thought, he identified the woman as an actress he had watched recently in a play about battered wives. There was a well-known footballer standing with his arm round a woman and on the other side of him was a team-mate. It gave Alistair an odd feeling to think how often he had talked about the player, discussed goals he had scored, and here he was standing beside him, just another member of the same crowd.

Then Alistair saw Dan. He was standing inside the edge of the circle of people, wearing only his track-suit trousers and trainer shoes. His body looked startlingly white. Alistair, having manoeuvred himself to the front of the crowd, looked across and saw the other man, stripped as well, looking huge and menacing. Alistair stared at Dan again and felt a sudden compassion for him. He remembered talking to Dan in the

Red Lion, seeing him in the streets of Thornbank. This man didn't look like Dan. He was bewildered and white and taut. His body looked to Alistair as tender as a piece of fruit peeled for consumption.

Alistair looked again at the people whose faces he had recognised. He thought of his mother watching the actress on television and being impressed by the emotion she had conveyed, the sense of the injustice of her life. He thought of the footballer and the number of people who looked on him as a hero. As he watched them, they were watching Dan, and he saw them not as solidities in themselves but as images that were the refraction of something else. Dan and the other man were that something else. In that moment the scene became sinister for Alistair.

He felt they had come to watch one of their own being used in a way they shouldn't have accepted. He didn't want Dan to fight and Dan, if Alistair could judge from the way he looked, didn't want to fight either. Alistair felt the moment out of the control of all of them. He thought that, instead of being here to watch, he and the others he had come with should be ranging themselves alongside Dan, ready to fight beside him. Impelled by the feeling beyond his usual timidity, he identified with Dan in the only way he could find. He shouted.

'Dan! Dan!'

Some people close to him started to laugh. He felt briefly embarrassed and then, in a moment of unusual boldness, shouted again.

'Dan!'

Dan was not to experience his fight with Cutty Dawson as something complete. What happened happened and he was part of it. The full reality of it was lost in its occurrence, like a prolonged explosion. It existed as a time he was only able to think about clearly once it was past and even then it was a kind of black hole in his life, something that only memory could come near to understanding and yet not too near or it vanished into the sheerness of unassimilable event.

It was the darkest experience of his life, the place where all the contradictions clashed, found free and rabid life beyond his ability to cage them in rational attitudes. He could only endure them. It was where ideas and beliefs and attitudes met too, in violent interaction. Doubts he had long thought tame went wild again and he was what they hunted. All that immediately survived their attack was the need for survival.

Yet, intractable as the experience was, thought had to come back to it to make it exist for him and let him keep his sense of his own continuity. So his fight was both what had happened and what his memory made of it, which was a strange amalgam of what he tried to remember and what his will put there.

He had heard in Alistair's voice just a sound, meaningless, like the other noises that came to him as dehumanised as the cries of seagulls quarrelling over food. Most of him was deferred. Friendship was a complication that didn't register here. He knew Matt Mason was talking to him but he didn't understand what was being said. He shivered slightly. Divested of his track-suit top, he seemed stripped to a sliver of himself, and felt himself oddly victimised by the others, still wrapped in the warm colours of their clothes. He wondered who they were. He was trying to impose on the amorphousness of what was happening his own sense of it. This was a fight coming up. But nothing he had done, none of the careful thought-processes through which he had led his mind, had prepared him for this. It was too various.

He had realised that he had seen Cutty Dawson before. He looked very powerful but was loose around the belly. Dan's mind recorded the fact like a filing-system. He had seen that face in newspapers some years ago. The beaten-down skin above the eyes was what he remembered. Cutty Dawson had been a heavyweight boxer. He had been Mike Dawson then. There was something Dan had read about him that he couldn't bring back to mind. That he knew Cutty Dawson was odder than confronting a stranger would have been. It seemed an elaborately incomprehensible contrivance that they should meet each other for the first time stripped to the waist across a patch of grass. He wondered if Matt Mason and Frankie White had avoided reminding him of who Cutty was in case they worried him with his reputation. Such practicality would have been irrelevant to an event as weird as this, a ridiculous pretence that the whole thing made sense.

This didn't make sense. An accident made sense. If you were in a car and you drove too fast or you were drunk or you hit black ice, the result made sense – injury or death. Those were understandable rules. They might not be fair but they were understandable. He found himself thinking that if the common enemy was death, what was the point of lesser fights? But he believed the thought was a weakness and he deliberately tried to turn away from it.

A bird volleyed past on the wind and he was aware of the size of the sky, could imagine the vast vaults of the day stretching around them and they were trapped in this small, dim preoccupation as under a shell. He knew he must concentrate and yet couldn't believe in what was about to happen. The expectant faces that ringed him were a conspiracy in which they all supported one another's conviction that they were in a real place to see a real event. He thought of the long runs on the roads around Thornbank and all he could remember of the purpose he had had was the beauty of the mornings. He could feel no anger against Cutty Dawson. This wasn't something that had ignited by accident between them, an incident fuelled by its own spontaneous intensity. He had as much reason for dancing with Cutty Dawson as for fighting him – more, given the brightness of the day. This was a meanness, a distortion of the possibilities.

Suddenly, fully realised and rank in his mind, like a weed he hadn't known had taken such firm root, was a memory of adolescence. He must have been seventeen and he was walking alone on a beach. An autumn sun was withering in the sky. It was just a cold afternoon with nowhere to be, when he had somehow mislaid his friends, and one of those teenage moods had rolled in like a fog and lost him in itself. He was nobody in particular. His sole substance seemed to be one walk on the shore. He had been improvising identities for himself as he went along. For a while he was a thrower of stones into the sea. Then he became a jumper on to clumps of seaweed, an artist of the popping sounds they made, searching with tireless ingenuity for the one true, ultimate, original and inimitable pop.

Then he found the rock-pool. It was oblong, barely a yard in length. At first, when he looked into it, he saw only himself thirsting after himself, like a variant of all those times he had stared for relentless minutes at his image in the glass of his bedroom, trying to discover who he was. But his shadow took the surface off the mirror and the pool became three-dimensional, a small water-chamber in which he soon saw creatures move. He didn't know whether they were insects or fish, fragile, almost-transparent entities that could have died of his forefinger. They sculled around in that little wave-worked aquarium, yards from the sea, darting menacingly at one another, having their own minute, self-absorbed war. The potential for gloom that follows adolescents around like a private, forty-piece band, ready to orchestrate passing depressions into despair, had found symphonic expression in him then. But now, standing with a light wind in his face, he felt an echo of that moment and it didn't seem something to be mocked. He thought maybe he had been looking in a mirror that day after all.

He would have liked these people to understand the strangeness of why he was here. It had nothing to do with Cutty Dawson. It was really about his wife, about the way his life hadn't been going right, about the fact that he had no job. And he had said 'Hey!' in a pub one night. It didn't make sense. He didn't understand it. He had always admired Cutty Dawson. He used to read about him in the papers and he had respected the way he took defeat. He had heard him interviewed on television once, after he had lost a fight. He had been very generous to his opponent. Dan remembered one thing that Cutty had said. 'Ah think maybe Ah taught the boy a coupla things. An' he learned them fast. Ah suppose everybody ye beat, ye take a bit of them with ye. Good luck to him.'

He didn't understand it. He didn't know where this field was. They had brought him in a car and unloaded him here. He didn't know who all these people were or what had made them come here. He wanted to believe his wife loved him again.

This wasn't right. Somebody else had arranged this. He and Cutty Dawson had nothing to fight about. Why were they fighting? He would have liked to talk to Cutty Dawson about his life. That would have been interesting. He must have had a strange life, to be a boxer and then be standing here. What had happened to him to bring him to this field?

Dan found himself being led towards Cutty Dawson as if no other possibility were present. Cutty Dawson seemed sure enough of the rightness of what was happening. He was flexing his massive shoulders and jerking his neck from side to side, his eyes never leaving Dan Scoular's face. He had a tattoo on his right forearm that looked like a sword with a snake curled round it. Cam Colvin, looking small and ordinary in a dark overcoat, and another man stood beside Cutty Dawson. Matt Mason and Tommy Brogan were with Dan. They all met where a length of thick rope had been stamped into the ground, held taut at either end by two small stakes.

Cutty Dawson was smiling and Dan saw a whole way of life in that smile, an unbendable conviction, a formed attitude. He saw his father in it, sensed behind it the weight of the past Dan himself had come from. It was as if he was confronting all the men he had worked with, all the men he had admired as a boy. Cutty Dawson's stance was an echo of theirs as Dan had seen them perform it at countless corners, the cocky tilt of the head, the shrug of the shoulders, all questions being irrelevant. Here they stood and they backed off from nothing.

Strangely, the smile didn't intimidate Dan, as it was meant to. Its intractability seemed to him at this moment a sign of weakness. Neither of them knew what was going to happen. Cutty Dawson was pre-deciding his response. His mind beginning to convert itself into an armoury, Dan found a memory and shaped it to a weapon. He remembered reading of a churchman being burnt for heresy who had said, 'If I flinch in the flames, believe not a word I have written.' Dan had always distrusted that statement. Human beings should flinch in flames. If they could distort the extremities of experience to that extent, what grotesqueness couldn't they impose on words and ideas? If Cutty Dawson had decided already that he knew where they were going, Dan might have a good chance against him, because he was lying to himself. He was nailing himself to his position. Dan, brimming with his own fear, knew the fluidity it gave him.

The referee had joined them. He was tall. His voice was hoarse and had a soft, hissing quality, like a lit fuse. He stated the rules in a matter-of-fact way, as if a rational tone of voice was a charm against the ugly ferocity of what was about to happen.

'Okay,' he said. 'Why waste words? We're no' here to talk. We all know the score here. It's the mitts only. Ye kick, butt, elbow, Ah'll decide how serious it is. If it's bad, ye're disqualified. Ye can write to yer MP, do whit ye like. Ye're disqualified. Ah'm neutral here.' He indicated Cam Colvin and Matt Mason. 'These two men have agreed ma judgment's final. It is. Ah'm warnin' the two of ye. If ye commit a foul Ah don't think is too serious. Like if ye try but don't connect right. Ah give the other man a free punch. Okay? If one of ye refuses that, Ah'll help the other one tae get intae ye. That's the story. A knock-down ends a round. Ye get thirty seconds to be back at the line. Ye don't make it, the fight's over.'

He held out his left hand, which contained a stop-watch.

'Ah'll be timing it exact. Ah call three times. "Ten seconds." "Twenty seconds." "Twenty-five seconds." Then Ah call, "Prepare." Then "Time!" If ye're not there by then, don't bother coming. Just hitch a lift out.'

He held out his right hand with a white handkerchief in it.

'When Ah drop this handkerchief, a round begins. Ye got all that? Ye've the three times called. Then it's "Prepare." Then "Time!" and the hanky falls. "Time!" and the hanky go at the same time. So ye can start on the word. Ah don't think it's advisable to be lookin' round for a hanky just at that meenit. Any questions?'

The arbitrary gibberish of the instructions had the effect on Dan not of rendering the event more coherent but of making it seem even more incomprehensible. The referee might have been lecturing on some abstruse theory of economics.

'Where's the nearest hospital to Thornbank?' Cam Colvin said.

'Mr Colvin!' the referee said. 'Remarks like that aren't allowed. Ah was askin' the boys a question. You an' Mr Mason here asked me tae referee this fight. That's what Ah'm gonny do. If ye're not pleased with me, ye can deal with me after. But don't try tae intimidate anybody durin' this fight. We've two big, healthy men here. Ready for a square go. That's what they're gonny have. Any questions, boys?'

Cutty Dawson and Dan Scoular stared at each other.

'Right! Back ye go.'

They retreated to the places where the fold-down canvas seats were and the plastic pails of water with sponges and the towels and the helpers who were strangers. Dan felt his place like a flimsy outpost, last camp of shared concern before he went out alone to explore parts of himself he had never ventured into. Out there where his wilderness was, the referee was standing and shouting, crazy as an anchorite the perfection of whose madness lies in the conviction that his ravings are rational.

'All right, everybody!' the referee shouted to the people gathered for their own strange reasons. 'Could we have order, please! Order! Order! Thank you. What we have here is a fight. To the finish. It will be a clean one. Ah'll see to that. A knock-down ends a round. Thirty seconds to get back to the line. Whoever stands alone at this line' – his legs were straddling it – 'When Ah call "Time!" an' drop this handkerchief –' he held it up – 'is the winner. No disputed verdicts. No points-system. One fight, one winner.'

He paused, perhaps to let the grandeur of the idea take root among them.

'Ah'll thank all of yese to hold your positions. Don't crowd in. We have people present who will deal with troublemakers. Trouble is *any* form of interference. Unless ye want to have an unofficial fight yerself – an' ye'll be starting at very long odds – do not, I repeat *not*, either hinder or help any of the two fighters. If ye so much as put yer hand on one of their elbows, that's a serious infringement of the rules. Punishable by punishment. The only people allowed to collect bodies are the corner-men. All right! Remember what ye've been told.'

He held his stop-watch high in the air.

'Ah'm now beginning the countdown to the contest.'

He made an expansive gesture of pressing the button.

'Beginning in thirty seconds from . . . Now!'

'Move a lot,' Matt Mason said.

The advice seemed preposterous to Dan at the time, like 'Try to win'. But it glanced off his mind without effect. He was hearing and seeing with an odd, aberrant clarity. He seemed to be aware of almost everything, of many fragments of the scene around him, and yet somewhere in him choices of what mattered were being made.

'Ten seconds!'

There was a woman with a marvellous face. Her cheeks were gently hollowed as if she were inhaling life with quiet intensity.

'Twenty seconds!'

He would rather have talked to her for half an hour than be doing what he was going to do.

'Twenty-five seconds!'

Yet presumably she wanted him to do this. Hands were pushing him forward. He walked towards the rope. Cutty Dawson was there already, smiling his shield of a smile. They stood within touching distance, awkwardly.

'Prepare! Time!'

Dan was aware of the handkerchief fluttering to the ground. Voices came at them as they circled each other, half-formed incantations that were meant to influence the outcome. Cutty rushed him suddenly, his arms pumping venom at him. Dan moved easily aside and threw a left that, meeting shoulder-bone, fused his own arm solid for a second. Cutty swung on to him at once, tested his stomach with a right, knuckled his head above the temple with a left.

From that first core of contact was spawned a complicated series of movements, a wild progression of punches and counter-punches, blocks, sidesteps and lunges, where chance and purpose fought each other in them. They had entered a labyrinth of possibilities down which they pursued each other, a place where the crowd's understanding couldn't follow them. The onlookers might catch fragments and force them into a shape but only the two men knew how lost they were, caught the sudden swerves of fortune, heard triumph in a grunt, panic in a whimper, convulsed in secret pain, saw fear down the tunnel of an iris.

Part of Dan still felt outside of the event. He was aware of the bystanders around them like a frieze, a clash of colours significantly brighter than he had noticed them to be before the fight. A face would suddenly detach itself in his vision with an etched clarity. Cutty's pale body was blotched where the first punches had hit him, faint, ugly roses. It was as if the tension in which he functioned was the generator that lit up everything around him, putting it under bright lights.

Even the tactical conclusions he was coming to were coldly clear, came to him like ways of approaching an abstract problem. He was struck by how much room there was. This was unlike any fight he had ever been in before, where it had all been about immediacy and speed and tightness of movement and where first advantage was usually final. This was less a battle than a war. It was like the difference he had felt between playing indoor football and playing on a full-sized pitch, where your skills needed to be harnessed to energy and fitness because big distances always stood between them and their realisation.

He was glad of the training he had done, even of Tommy Brogan's fanaticism. Cutty was heavier and slower and the covering of a lot of ground should cost him more than it would cost Dan. But his mind had barely assimilated that idea when a contradictory perception called it in question.

The ground was uneven, catching the foot every so often in a trap, so that fluidity of movement would freeze without warning and you were left for a second longer in a place your reflexes had already abandoned. Twice within a minute, because of the ground, Cutty had found him, once on the head, once on the body, with big punches he had already foreseen and arranged to avoid. The punches were less powerful than they might have been because Cutty, noticing Dan's evasion, had been redirecting them towards where their target should have been. Their glancing impact gave enough hurt to serve as a warning. This place was mined with risks for a fast mover.

But the first one the ground significantly helped was Dan. Trying to turn quickly in pursuit, Cutty found an unevenness that jarred his foot and left him standing square-on. Dan had hit him four times on the head before he went down.

The suddenness of it, the ease with which Cutty collapsed, drew an awed sound from the crowd, one of those reactions by which people create what has happened in preference to observing it. For a second of dazzled elation, Dan admitted the crowd's sense of what was taking place into his own. But it was like introducing a shaft of light into a cave. It hadn't clarified his vision, it had blinded him. Within a moment, Dan knew it was the imbalance that had put Cutty down more than the punches and that the very ease with which he fell had neutralised Dan's impact. Cutty was rising again at once. All that had happened was a chance for a rest.

Dan didn't sit down because he was surprised at how near to being tired he felt, and afraid to give in to the feeling. Matt Mason was saying something about 'a walkover' and Dan ignored him, since they didn't seem to be present at the same event.

In those desperately inhaled seconds, Dan took in knowledge with each breath. How trivial our skills are, he understood. We choose where we deploy our skills and project from that our own sense of ourselves. Then we believe it. How often did the professor dare to live outside his special subject, the politician live in the streets, the poet forego words? Dan, outside of that confrontation with his father, had never lost a fight in his life. Gifted with literally stunning reflexes, he had fabricated a fake sense of himself. A few minutes of different experience had disproved it. He wasn't who he was supposed to be. He'd better find out who he was.

He was glad he hadn't sat down because there would hardly have been time. The shortness of the rest time made him almost plead for more. He hadn't had long enough to settle his breathing before the referee was shouting, 'Prepare!' He decided he had better not get knocked unconscious or he would never make it back to the line where he now stood with Cutty smiling at him.

'Time!'

He heard someone shouting for him to finish it off and instead of encouraging him the shout angered him because its empty confidence diminished the reality of what was going on. They were still introducing themselves, finding their way past the surface gestures towards a real meeting between force and force at the centre of each. Cutty's strength seemed undiminished and he twice broke past Dan's attempts to parry him. Those were bad moments when Dan found himself struggling not to be overwhelmed. All he could do was try to keep moving and chip at Cutty's strength with a persistence that was already beginning to lose confidence in itself. It was like trying to chop down a tree without being able to hit it twice in the same place.

Cutty had started to talk in the wrestling clinches. 'Ye've no chance, son,' he was saying. 'No chance.' 'Make it easy for yerself.' 'Go down, stay down.' 'Now or later, same thing.'

A troubling realisation had entered Dan's understanding of the fight. Basic talent wasn't going to settle this. He had already brought to bear the skills that had always been enough for him before, the great natural reflexes that could take an opening almost before it was there or leave a thrown blow expended half an inch from his face, the instinctive correctness of punch that fed power every time up from the legs through the body's leverage. He had found out already that he was simply better at this than Cutty was now. But that wasn't going to be enough.

An accident might be enough, coupled with exhaustion. Whichever of them lost his legs first would probably lose everything because the rough ground was full of bad places for tiredness, and fatigue would kill the ability to make fast readjustments and it would be like trying to dance in quicksand. Even as he struggled to hold Cutty's body, greased with sweat, and, failing to throw Cutty off, threw himself off and staggered back, Dan was thinking that this fight would prove nothing that he believed in. They were both caught in it now, heading each other off into a happening it seemed to him they couldn't significantly settle, both obliged to wait till accident or unearned circumstance swatted one or the other down, while the shouts of the crowd refined the meaningless raw material of their contest into the meaning they chose. He sensed the people undulate around the progress of their conflict like protoplasm.

In a despondent panic, Dan poured himself on to Cutty. While his left hand buzzed distractingly around Cutty's head, he hit him three times on the left biceps and, as the arm wilted, chopped down on Cutty's jaw and deposited him on one knee. Cutty threw himself back up but the referee declared the end of a round.

Dan felt like walking on past Mason and Tommy Brogan but they fussed round him with the towel. Mason was complimenting him and Dan's head rejected the praise like counterfeit money. He was angry at everything, the way Tommy Brogan roughed his abraded cheek with the towel, the noise of the crowd like an appetite he was being forced to feed, the remorselessness of the referee's voice. He felt nobody could give him anything that he could take back in there. Mason and Tommy Brogan didn't know what was going on. He despised the crowd that needed their blood like a plasma-bank. He felt anger against Cutty for taking part in this.

He had hit Cutty the moment after the word 'Time!' was heard, and unloaded his banked rage in a cumulative fury of punches. Cutty stumbled back and fell.

Matt Mason interpreted the shouts for him. 'That was the turning-point, big man.' Dan was afraid he was right. Cutty had been on his feet again before his handlers could get to him. Dan felt more exhausted by his attack than Cutty seemed to be. He didn't know where he was supposed to go from here. That line was somewhere he never wanted to go back to. He had done as much as he could do. Wasn't that enough? He wanted to stay on this canvas seat for ever.

'Time!' was a command to go to a place he had never been before but Cutty seemed familiar with it.

Dan was listening for the voices of the crowd to lead him. They suggested, he imagined, that he was winning but he couldn't believe that from the inside. He wondered if they were still seeing the previous round.

Pain had found its way past the anaesthesia of tension and every punch seemed to bring the aches from all the earlier punches out in chorus. He felt as if he was discovering for the first time the reality of violence. He seemed pitted against a force that was just naturally greater than his. There are no fair fights, it occurred to him. He heard the voices draw on his spilled blood. As he began to founder, he knew something with certainty and yet knew that his knowledge was discredited because of where it came from, because it would be seen as the excuse of a loser. And he was losing, he was certain. He knew he was giving as much as Cutty, the same in his own terms, that what was being demonstrated here wasn't the superiority of one but the similarity of both, that they were expressing something jointly, not individually. The voices lied. What was there was as much as anybody could offer, was the same gift whoever made it. The voices lied, but he had accepted them and he was caught in them now.

He had to move back and he could find no further to go, in the field or in himself. He knew nothing but hurt coming at him. He thought every noise, every shout, the crowd, the whole day was attacking and the world was just vendettas against him. He hated them all. He hated them all and found there in the sheerness of his hate a hardness that defiantly didn't want to yield, clenched fist of his rage, marrow of his will. He found some small, last seed of himself still needing to flower. He must let it be fulfilled but he was stunned and stumbling. His feet groped along a maze of edges, trying to find footholds in air, until he stepped off suddenly into blackness.

Weights pressed against him at various parts and he felt himself tilt and plane awkwardly, find different angles in air. He couldn't tell himself upright or not, what position he held. The darkness was spiral. There was sound.

'Twenty seconds.'

'Twenty-five seconds.'

His mind held the voice like a rope to pull him out of the pit.

'Prepare.'

And he burst into dizzying light. The day was in pieces. Pressure was pushing his body out of shape towards somewhere. His knees couldn't hold. Ground bobbled, trees spun, the sky slowly turning.

'Time!'

He was moving. But he had surfaced again into pain, volleyed forces.

'Bedtime, son,' Cutty was saying.

'Only a matter of time.'

'No chance.'

The voice helped him. It was an assumption about what he was and he was determined not to allow that. Its glibness located the last of his anger. The anger came because he felt Cutty betraying both of them, aligning himself with the lie that was the crowd's sense of what had been happening. However this ended, Dan had fought honestly to the limits of himself. Nobody was going to take that from him. This fight wasn't over yet because he felt as if he had just discovered

175

what he was fighting. He knew that stony certainty, had heard it since childhood from so many other voices. It came from the same place as Cutty's smile, it was an echo of all those corner-standers who had peopled his boyhood. It was the voice that had spoken inside himself for years. And he knew now that he didn't agree with it. It spoke as if it knew the truth and it was hiding from the truth. It overruled those who couldn't meet the terms it demanded. In declaring its own strength it trampled on the weakness of others.

Trying to focus on the fragmentary images of Cutty that felt as if they were coming at him from every angle, Dan seemed to himself to be fighting all those working-class hardmen who had formed the pantheon of his youth, men who in thinking they defied the injustice of their lives had been acquiescing in it because they compounded the injustice by unloading their weakness on to someone else, making him carry it. Dan's past self was among them. So was his father on the back green. Like an argument Dan was still involved in, his father's voice came from somewhere: 'Whit is it you believe in, boay?' As he stumbled about the field, being flayed of his arrogance, he was looking for an answer.

He tried to rally against Cutty. He couldn't but as he felt himself stagger and fall again, even as he pitched sickeningly on to the ground with a jolt that threatened to bring his bones out through the skin, a part of his mind hung on to consciousness like a cliff-edge bush it wasn't sure would hold, and he was already struggling to rise when Matt Mason and Tommy Brogan found him and half-carried him to the canvas seat.

Their voices were talking to themselves. Dan sat staring at Cutty while the referee counted off the time and the sounds of the crowd were like translations of what was happening into different languages. Dan felt a terrible coldness spreading through his mind, an ice killing off everything but the most basic thought, the crudest life-forms. He was waiting to see what survived to take with him when he rose. Suddenly his own voice came to him from the past, something he had once said, he couldn't remember where. 'Living's the only game in town and it's fucking crooked.' Thinking that now, he felt the prodigious strength of despair. The whole thing was unbearable. To bear it, he wanted his wife and his family. He must have them. To have them, he must win.

'Time!'

As Cutty crowded him again at once, Dan's bleak decision that he must win stayed with him and the fixity of his will revealed to him at last the way he might do it. He heard, as if in a time-lock, Tommy Brogan saying something that mattered, as he sat on the canvas seat. His mind, while Cutty buffeted his body, was crouched patiently, waiting for the remark to come back. It was something Tommy Brogan had been saying since the beginning and Dan had been too tense to register it.

'His right eye. It's dead. That's what finished him wi' boxing.'

Dan understood suddenly what he had noticed throughout the fight. He hadn't missed Cutty with a left hand. Working on that, he began slowly to reassert himself and he knew what was going to happen. His will envisioned his victory and moved his body towards it.

He would do nothing but try to keep moving and hit Cutty there. Purpose gave him energy. He would make that dismissive voice stop talking, admit its weakness in silence. He would punch the bastard blind. He was galvanised with venom. He swung weight remorselessly from both shoulders into Cutty's eyes, drawing renewed strength from the juddering impact of his blows. He felt him go back and let himself be towed by the staggering bulk and, when the arms dropped, battered his face till he shuddered on to the ground.

Dan moved back and stood at the line, having held up his hand to warn off Matt Mason and Tommy Brogan. He wanted to waste no energy. He fed on the voices now. The line he stood at was some final marker of himself. He watched as they worked frantically on Cutty, throwing water on his face and standing him up and getting him to the line as time was called.

Dan stood and watched the handkerchief fall.

Cutty raised his hands by instinct. His beaten body sagged softly, looked unnatural, hardly like human flesh, more like a mollusc with its shell ripped off. His head moved, blind as a worm.

Dan felt only a rush of instinct, had tapped a force in himself that roared to fill his body, a dark greed of triumph that took him and Cutty to it like a chameleon's tongue. Dan looked down the maw of another man's exhaustion, saw a future. Cutty's weakness was a feast he wanted. His fists fed on it as if enough wasn't possible, wouldn't be satisfied till Cutty could give him no more, and he fell as hollow as rind, discarded waste of Dan Scoular's need.

The moment held its awe. Something was seen that held its watchers still, a black truth they had shared, a presence come that couldn't be denied, and seconds passed in utter silence while they endured its passing out of them. And in those seconds, just in seconds, banality came back to cover their naked awareness in the decency of facts.

A man was lying unconscious, the wind making a waving frond of his hair. His body lay in mud. The mud was all that was left of their intricacy and energy of movement, the infinite patterns that their feet had made, the courage of their efforts. Another man stood alone on the line. His face was cut and bleeding. He was leaning into the wind, eating chunks of the air.

Cutty was carried back to his canvas seat. Dan Scoular was alone at the line, crouched over the void his desperation had brought him to. The crowd was almost silent. Nobody approached him. He hung there wasted with effort, as dead to the meaning of what might have happened as Cutty Dawson was. Bleak emptiness was in his mind. The referee's voice was meaningless. A white handkerchief drifted to the ground aimlessly.

The cheering tugged him slowly erect, pulled him away from an unbearable place. His eyes, blind from the pit of where he had been, reached determinedly towards focus. People were waving and moving towards him. Faces bobbed like lights through the darkness, showing him the human ordinariness of this place where he was. The wind was the wind, the grass was the grass, Cutty Dawson was beaten. But glancing down at himself, Dan saw his own body blotched bizarrely as if he wore the map of a strange place.

And in seconds – it only took seconds – he was standing solidly inside himself again, letting the voices and faces tell him what had happened. This had been a hard fight but he was the winner. This hadn't been so bad. His smile answered the shouts of the crowd, so strongly, so clearly, it seemed as if no great distance had lain between them. He raised his right hand in the air, made a whinny of triumph.

The crowd broke towards him. He was their man, meant something they wanted to believe in. As he turned, Matt Mason was with him. He embraced Dan like a brother and they danced, hugging as if a lost member of the family had at last come home.

6

It was a long way back from where he had been. Images of the fight stayed with him like tendrils of vegetation clinging to a man who has nearly drowned: Cutty Dawson floundering before him, gaffed on his own exhaustion, a swell of biceps evoking a reek of sweat, a face from the crowd shouting up into air. These were what he was most strongly aware of while other things happened in a muffled way of which he was only half-conscious. Somewhere, he was being attended to, wrapped in the ministrations of other people. The first time he came fully to himself was in the water when, finding himself falling asleep, he snapped suddenly awake and it was as if he had come ashore in a strange land.

The walls were green. He felt the water and knew himself in a bath. The taps were gold-plated. There was a full-length mirror on the opposite wall, clouded with steam. In a tiled niche in the wall just above his head there was an array of shampoos and conditioners, talcum and deodorant. They looked for a moment like the mysterious paraphernalia of a strange civilisation, and then he was simply in a bathroom for which he felt a woman had been responsible. And he remembered Matt Mason's wife running a bath for him. She had put some kind of herbal bath in the water and he felt as if the aches in his body were being massaged. He was in their house in Bearsden.

Two bath-towels hung on the chromium towel-rail. He imagined the touch of them on his skin. The thought reattached him to time, a sense of the future. He saw his crumpled track-suit, underpants, socks and trainer shoes lying sloughed like a skin he was finished with. They were strange with a past he couldn't connect to this present.

Against the haunting pictures of the fight he tried to set his memory of what had come between then and now. It was like · trying to determine shape from touch alone. Disconnected sensations came back. He had been in a car. Margaret Mason's perfume ravished his senses again, first smell of land for a sailor long at sea. 'Jesus, was that a fight!' was being said by Eddie Foley. A man in a field was saying, 'Ah knew you at Sullom Voe.' The man was a stranger. Everything was a stranger.

Talking and laughter came to him. He tried to relate them to himself. Roddy Stewart and his wife had followed them to the house and others had arrived. Melanie (the name jarred his mind) had come in and kissed him to applause from the rest. He tried to realise that he was the cause of how happy they were. He saw the glass on the edge of the bath and took a sip of the whisky, replaced it. The ice floated thin on the surface. He had been here some time.

The door of the bathroom opened and he realised he had forgotten to bolt it. Melanie came in. He stared at her smile.

She had unpacked some clothes from the travelling bag. They were like clues to who he was supposed to be. She laid trousers, shirt and underpants over the towel-rail after putting one of the towels on top of the other. On the closed, wooden lid of the lavatory she put a pair of socks. She put his shoes on the floor. She did it all slowly and methodically, letting him watch her.

She had changed her clothes, presumably in preparation for the party. There was to be a party. It seemed a bizarre idea to him. She was wearing stiletto heels and a red velvet dress with a cheongsam-style slit at one side. As she bent over the towel-rail, the dress moulded itself to her and her cheeks were offered to him like some fabulous peach, exotic fruit of the country. Her black hair swung as she leant over and looked like a good place to hide. The ordinariness of her actions, the unselfconsciousness of glamour, struck him. What he saw was incidental to the naturalness of how she had come in, the casualness of her shared presence, as if she were telling him to relax into what was happening. There was nothing inaccessible about the luxury of the room, the opulence of her body. It was all within his reach.

She turned and watched him watching her. She crossed towards him and very gently touched his face.

'Your lovely bruises,' she said.

Her scent caught and held him like a fine-meshed net. She mouthed his abraded cheek delicately.

'I'll suck all the pain out later. All you'll have to do is rest. And I'll suck till you feel no pain.'

Her hand moved slowly across his wet chest and he felt his nipples stiffen.

'Mine feel the same,' she said.

Her hand moved lower, hovering, and he was embarrassed by the colour of the water, muddied from his body. The hand stroked his lower chest and then smoothly, with hardly a disturbance of the surface, went under the water.

'Oh,' she said.

She threw her hair back and caught it behind her head in her other hand and was moving her face nearer the water when they heard Roddy Stewart shouting.

'Melanie! What are you doing in there? You having a bath as well?'

There was laughter. She held him briefly and smiled at him, her eyes opaque.

'I'm putting my marker on you. For later.'

She rose and dried her hand on one of the towels. She lifted his dirty clothes and, looking at him, held them against her cheek.

'Your sweat's just become my favourite perfume,' she said.

When she went out, he lay still, waiting for the feeling in him to subside. He had accepted her attentions as if they were a rite of the unknown place where he found himself. He stood up and reached for a towel but the bathroom was too wide. He had to put one foot on the carpeted floor, grab the towel and step back. There were wet toe-prints on the bath-mat. They shouldn't take long to dry. As he was drying himself, standing in the bath, his body, foreign with bruises, was something he looked at with curiosity. He stepped out on to the towel and finished drying himself. Putting on his under-pants, he scrubbed at the bath with a soaped sponge till he got rid of the tide-mark his washing had left.

The familiar clothes brought him back to himself a little but, seeing the facial bruises against the blueness of the laundered shirt, he sensed again the unfamiliarity of where he had been. He knew it was still waiting to be understood. Watching the stranger in the mirror, he heard the others talking. He walked through and their voices, as if they knew what had happened, gave him an identity.

'The conquering hero.'

'Welcome back to civilisation.'

'Where's your drink?'

'The big man himself.'

Situation overtook self-doubt. He felt as if, by his walking into it, the room had bloomed on his presence. He remembered two occasions from his childhood with which this formed a trinity. One had been looking up from reading a book and seeing his mother sewing and his father fiddling with a broken watch. A last, fading patch of sunlight lay on the floor. The clock was talking quietly to itself. And he had known the rightness of his being here. He effortlessly belonged. The other was in his primary school. It was towards the end of a winter afternoon. The class were writing and the teacher suddenly put the lights on. He glanced up and was aware of everyone writing and himself among them and the teacher with her pink twin-set and the suspirations of his friends around him and he felt the physical joy of it.

It was what he felt now, as if his body had become a perfect fit. The French windows showed a lawn beyond them and against it the people in the room seemed as natural as flowers. He was aware of how attractive Matt Mason's wife was, smiling at him. There was no acquisitiveness in the awareness, just a gladness to be sharing her presence. Eddie Foley winked at him from the arm of the wide leather chair in which Melanie was sitting. The wink was an expression of instant friendship. Frankie White blew him a kiss and ruffled Sandra's hair.

'How you feeling?' Matt Mason said.

'Almost human again.'

'You should be feeling superhuman,' Frankie said.

'Let me get you another drink,' Melanie said.

The voices jingled in his ears like charms that were round his wrist. He could see the different-coloured drinks that were in the glasses as bright as jewels in the soft sunlight. Melanie gave him his own like a piece of gold and the others raised their drinks to him. He had joined them in drinking before he realised he was toasting himself. Roddy Stewart transformed his mistake by colluding in it.

'To us,' he said. 'The winners.'

They all laughed.

He withdrew from their feeling. He didn't know why. Something had happened in him that troubled his sense of what was going on. It wasn't a memory. It was an awareness of something he must remember. With his glass almost touching his mouth, he stood and was stubborn. There was something he wanted to know. He made the memory come. It came as panic, a wondering if he had spoken to Cutty Dawson after the fight. Then he remembered leaning over Cutty and Cutty gripping his arm but not looking up or rising from the canvas seat. 'You'll do,' Cutty had said. The generosity of it made him feel guilty, as if a drowning man had pushed him into the lifeboat. He owed his own sense of where he had been to whoever was there with him. These people hadn't been there. He was in foreign country. He didn't belong.

'Okay,' Matt Mason said. 'Let's drink these and get on our way. There's a party on. They're waiting for the guest of honour. Here, Dan. Your mates are going to be there. The boys from Thornbank. That boy Sam MacKinlay's a bit of a case, isn't he?'

Dan nodded and in the reflex response he found something, like an amnesiac having a flash of who he might be.

'Ah want to make a phone call,' Dan said.

'Just now?' Roddy Stewart said.

His expression suggested it was a strangely naive thing to want to do. The others smiled tolerantly.

'Sure he does,' Matt Mason said.

He took Dan out of the room and showed him into what he called his 'study'. He left the door ajar and Dan could still hear the murmur of voices as he dialled. Matt Mason put his hand on Dan's arm.

'I want to talk to you tonight,' he said. 'I've got a proposition for you. It means a lot more money than you made today.'

He patted Dan's arm affectionately and went out.

'Hello?'

The effect Betty's voice had on him took him by surprise. The ordinary human warmth and familiarity of it created complicated sensations in him. The voices from the other room and the sound of someone laughing were like a conspiracy from which Betty was excluded. He felt excluded from it, too, as well as from the place where Betty was.

'Hello?'

'It's all right, love,' he managed. 'It's not a heavy breather.'

'Dan.'

'Hello, Betty.'

There was a silence. He couldn't break it. The fight lay between him and where he had been and the difficulty of coming to terms with what had happened in the field was compounded by the difficulty of coming to terms with what had preceded it. He could see Betty sitting in the lounge bar with the man. He felt alien to everywhere, to this room with a large vase on the desk, to the background noise of television coming through the phone.

'What happened?'

He wished he knew.

'Ah won,' he said.

The words described his experience of it as adequately as the dates on a headstone describe a life.

'I'm glad you won, Dan. How are you?'

'Ah'm all right.'

'Are you badly hurt?'

'No, no. Some bruises.'

'Is the other man all right?'

'Aye, Ah think so. He seemed all right.'

'And you're sure you're all right?'

'Ah'm fine, Betty. Honest.'

There was another pause. He couldn't blame her.

'How's the kids?' he said quickly, and regretted it immediately, because he knew what she would do.

'They're fine, wait and I'll get them.'

'It's all –' but she was gone.

'Hello, Dad!'

'Dad!'

They were obviously wrestling for the phone.

'Did you win him, Dad?'

'Aye.'

'Great. What round did you knock him out in?'

185

The innocence of their pleasure reactivated the confused and ugly reality of the fight for him and made him feel he had perhaps fouled their lives. He experienced guilt. The effect of it was to make him determined to try to understand what had happened. He managed to get the boys to take 'chances each' on the phone, first Raymond, then Danny. He kept his answers to their questions minimal until he could get them talking about what they had been up to in his absence. It was news of home, a place he wasn't sure he knew how to get back to. When he asked to speak to their mother again, the phone whispered in his ear like a shell, suggesting a distance between him and them that mere transport couldn't cross.

'All right, Dan? When will you be down then?'

'Later tonight, Betty.'

He didn't tell her that he wasn't sure who would be arriving.

'All right, Dan. We'll see you then.'

'Okay, Betty.'

'Dan. I'm glad you're all right.'

'Aye.'

He put down the phone and looked round the room. The self-conscious deliberateness of the furnishings struck him. The room was an odd contrivance for the man who had arranged the fight. He must have sat among this civilised machinery and planned it all. Yet the brute nature of the fight was denied by this place. You couldn't sit here and know what truly happened. What happened? It had been Betty's question. It was his. He would have to answer it for himself.

But Matt Mason, looking in to check if Dan had finished using the phone, had found his own answers already. What had happened was a cause for celebration.

'Come on, come on, large Dan,' he said. 'Enjoyment's serious business. There's good fun going to waste while you're standing there.'

'Party' had been the word at Matt Mason's house as they all prepared to leave. Everyone used it with that vague expectation of the excitement it was going to produce, as if it was the chrysalis the everyday goes into hoping to emerge in iridescent colours. But Dan's feeling was more one of unfocused apprehension. He went with them in the spirit of an alien submitting to the strange customs of the natives. Although the party was ostensibly in his honour, it was Matt Mason's event and Dan arrived there like someone not sure he would get in.

Anyone standing outside the Black Chip disco and watching the ingredients arrive haphazardly over two or three hours of late afternoon and early evening might have wished that he had one of the small pink cards that guaranteed entry, or better still one of those faces so well known around Glasgow that they were an automatic coupon of admission. He would certainly have felt he needed something more substantial than cheek to brass his way past the three men on the door. Enchanted caves are guarded by dragons.

The guardians wore evening dress that suited them the way an apron suits a grizzly bear. Among themselves they spoke a language of sotto voce expletives but, taking tickets or welcoming a public face, they said 'Sir' and 'Madam' and 'Have a good evening'. The smiles they wore didn't fully conceal their true identity.

There were a few occasions when they had to refuse admission but these didn't involve taking the smile away from the face. The last was a man on his own. They saw him hesitate a little way off, his aimless walking waylaid by the music. He came uncertainly towards them and said, 'Deesco?' It took a moment for one of them to respond.

'I'm afraid not, sir.'

'How much?'

When they had managed to convey to him that admission was by invitation only (one of them shook hands with himself to indicate friendship), he wandered off to prospect further the tedium of a Scottish Sunday, not realising that he had made his own contribution to the party, like the cat mewing in the cold that makes the room seem warmer.

By that time the men on the door were themselves becoming curious about how far the event had taken shape. They had seen, as it were, the dismembered limbs arriving. They had noticed the promising clash of styles: the staid smartness of Matt Mason and Roddy Stewart and the self-conscious chic of their wives, clothes that were telling you something as sure as a sergeant's stripes; the vaguely camp gear of a couple of well-known footballers that seemed to say they were so butch they could afford to take chances; the harlequin parade of a lot of the young that suggested some of them bought themselves by the day at the Glasgow Barras; a blonde woman already lit up like a Christmas tree; four punters who looked as if they had stepped out of a time-machine, one with a Fair Isle pullover, another with what looked like your grandfather's waistcoat, all of them with determined enjoyment round their eyes like opera-glasses. It remained to see if the miracle of cohesion had taken place, if those separate parts had managed to join to a living whole. Chuck Walker suggested it first.

'Okay,' he said. 'This is like guardin' a cemetery. The worst that's gonny happen is a bird might shite on our heads. We'll take it in spells. Ah'll nip in first an' see what the story is. Should be some floatin' cuff in there. Youse two keep each other company. Okay? Back out in ten minutes.'

He was the smallest of the three but the most aimlessly violent. The other two agreed. Chuck Walker went in. Standing inside the inner door, he let his eyes circle the room with slow repetition. He could see a couple of women along with too many people to be with anyone in particular. The blonde woman was doing everything but open a stall. She had come alone but she didn't seem to want to leave that way. If she went on drinking the way she was – she was holding her glass to her mouth like one of those Spanish wine-skins – she might leave in the company of medical attendants. He wondered how she had got here. Matt Mason, like a lot of men of his kind, tended to be as formal as an undertaker. Maybe she had found a ticket on the street. There were possibilities here but it didn't look like too much of a party.

Chuck Walker was judging from a very specific viewpoint. He had been picking off strays from events like this for a while, women who had quarrelled with their boyfriends, had come looking for something that they couldn't find, drunk themselves deliberately past their own inhibitions. Many times, in the early hours of the morning, he had picked clean the bones of their hopes, taken from them what they were too lost or too weak not to give, in the back of a car or a dark street or once – he wore the memory like his brightest feather – in a room in one of Glasgow's most expensive hotels. His was a specialist eye. When he watched an event like this, he saw only potential carrion, the stagger of hurt, the pain that wandered away from the centre of things into its own lonely desert. He was a scavenger, remorseless in the pursuit of his own nature. All he could taste was his purpose.

If the blonde woman could steady herself and not pass out, she might be usable. The other two were worth watching but it was too early to move. As he went back out, he noticed that the big puncher from somewhere was smiling. If he had spent the day with Cutty Dawson and could still feel like that, he had to be slightly special. If it ever came to it with him, Chuck Walker thought, better to let him walk out first and give him it on the back of the head with a five-giller. He looked simple enough to take it that way.

Dan was experiencing the party by proxy. He sensed a quickening mood around him, fragile and uncertain, but beginning to happen. There was a man studying a woman's mouth as she spoke. His eyes seemed to have achieved tunnel vision. He watched her lips with terrible concentration. He was nodding as if he knew what she was saying but his eyes were devoting themselves to the sheer movement of her mouth. He looked as dedicated as a Japanese artist who has found the flower he must paint all his life.

There was a woman laughing. She couldn't stop. The group she was with, two men and another woman, looked at one another. One of the men put his arm around her, patted her back. She went on laughing, scattering her laughter like someone who wants to give away all of herself before it is too late. She was a klaxon announcing her own party. Dan wished he had been invited. He consoled himself with the thought that his friends seemed to be enjoying it.

Alistair Corstorphine had found the event amazing from the start. But then most things amazed him. He lived with his mother and drank too much, but always outside the house. He was so guiltily devoted to his mother that stepping out the door had the excitement of travelling abroad. Tonight was wilder than emigrating.

He had separated from Sam MacKinlay and Harry Naismith early on, to pursue his own compulsion. He had his quietly replenished drink as iron rations as he explored the strange out-there of other people's lives, and he kept a constant check on where Dan Scoular was, a regular chart-reading. Meantime, he was collecting specimens. There were some beauties.

'So they want to do me for police assault as well. A bloody liberty.'

The man who said it was surprisingly small. Alistair might have thought he could beat him himself. It just showed you you couldn't be too careful. The man to whom he had made the remark, big, with a mottled face, showed no response. He nodded and suggested they get another drink.

'No, we won't. You know what happened the last time I let you do that. I was sore for weeks.'

She was a delicate girl, pale, with wispy fair hair and eyes suggestive of tiredness, the purplish shadows moving out from the edge of her nose. The colour of one eye seemed possibly slightly paler than the other. The man was fat and balding. He had her against a pillar, leaning over her. He was whispering very quietly but Alistair heard him. 'Oh, I think we will,' the man was saying.

Alistair's hunt for exotica led him to find them in surprising places. Even the people he knew here seemed changed by their surroundings, as if they had taken on the more garish colours of the place. Sam MacKinlay had become a playboy for the night. He was moving around with two women in tow, ordering drinks for them and enjoying the way they laughed at nearly everything he said.

'I'm sorry I can't give you girls a run home in the car,' Alistair heard him saying at one point. 'But I've promised a few of the mates I'll get them back home. The fella who drives for me is over there.'

As Alistair moved away, he heard Sam describing Thornbank as a picturesque village. Alan Morrison came up and asked Alistair what he thought of the place. It was, Alan said as he looked round, giving him a few ideas. Considering the strobe lights and the mirrors and the fluted columns and the leather-upholstered bar, Alistair wondered what the ideas were. Alan told him.

'There's nothing like this around Thornbank. It's an untapped market. I wonder, I wonder. I've got that old stable building.'

Alistair had a confused vision of Mary Barclay discoing and Wullie Mairshall trying to read the *Socialist Weekly* in this light. He suspected they might be about as enthusiastic as Harry Naismith. Harry was revealing an unexpected streak of puritanism. There were two girls who were walking around checking that people were enjoying themselves. They wore low-cut, skimpy tunics, apparently supposed to be Grecian in design. Harry was outraged.

'The sowls!' he said to Alistair more than once. 'What would their mothers think if they saw them? They could get their death o' cold goin' about like that.'

Frankie White heard him, laughed and went about telling people what Harry had said. It was perhaps a way of distancing himself from the Thornbank men. He saw their entrenched parochialism as an indirect compliment to himself. They were the amazing disadvantages he had overcome.

For Frankie was feeling he had finally arrived. He was a figure in this company. Matt Mason had referred to him as 'my best scout'. Roddy Stewart had called him 'our man in Ayrshire'. Chuck Walker had said, 'Ah hear you picked a winner, Frankie.' Sandra treated him as if he were a celebrity. He had become quite proprietary about Dan Scoular within an hour, providing snippets of biographical detail ('The only man who ever beat him was his father', 'The only thing he's frightened of is dogs. That's true') and sometimes bringing strangers up to introduce them.

The introductions bewildered Dan further. It was as if the people were introducing him to himself. 'You're some man,' someone said. 'You really planned that fight to perfection,' another man said. A woman gave him a card with her phone number on it. 'Try not to make it too long,' she said. She winked and smiled at him, suggesting she knew exactly the kind of person he was. The room was full of a sense of him that he didn't agree with. He found himself taking note of their messages like a secretary who would pass them on if the person they were meant for turned up. He heard their voices as a refinement of the shouts of the crowd, confident assertions about what had happened that didn't match his experience of it from the inside. Matt Mason confirmed the unreality of it.

'I saw something today,' he said. 'I know what it means. You'll do. I've got a job for you.'

The possibility came to him as a threat. What the others had said was temporary, a mood of the moment. But if he accepted Matt Mason's offer, he had to accept the meaning of what had happened that it implied. But he still didn't know what had happened. To accept or reject that offer, he had to do it as himself, had to know what it meant.

Realising, from what had been said to him, that he was the centre of the party for the others, and that the centre of himself was such confusion, he saw the event as pretence. The identity they were trying to give him didn't relate to where he had been. It defied the past he had just come from. Having been washed up accidentally on their lives, he had been assigned the role they needed him to have. Precisely because they knew so little about him, he served their purpose. They could make him into what they wanted. They could dress him in their purposes and simplify him into an image. In parading him before themselves, they were parading their own beliefs. But they weren't beliefs he knew to be his.

He thought that at least he knew the meaning of the party. It meant renewal of what they wanted to believe through him. They weren't celebrating him, they were celebrating the surrogate means he had given them of reaffirming their own lives without responsibility to what was past. He hadn't created the reason for this party alone. Cutty Dawson had done that with him. These people were using Dan to obscure that truth. He thought he saw the spirit the party was trying to incarnate. It was the desire to happen without history, to escape through a loophole in time and find a new moment where maybe you could begin yourself afresh. It was a distortion of the reality of all of us to invent the reality of some of us. Realising that, Dan excluded himself from the exclusiveness of the party. Among them, he felt himself more with Cutty Dawson. Just as his will had created his victory, so now it unmade it.

Standing around like the skeleton at his own feast, he experienced a moment that entered his awareness like a messenger bringing news of himself. It happened on the edge of things, a voice hardly anyone heard. Dan was watching the blonde woman he had noticed earlier because she was so drunk. She was talking to the smallest of the three doormen. A man suddenly broke through the door beside them. Another of the doormen came in and caught the man's jacket. The man's face was like a reflection of Dan's mood – rejection of the room.

'Ya bastards!' he screamed.

The man was struggling to come all the way in. The doorman who was talking to the blonde moved away from her quickly. She stood looking vaguely around, trying to focus her drunkenness. The two doormen were wrestling with the man. People were talking among themselves. The music still played. Dan wasn't sure how much of what he took in was hearing and how much was lip-reading. But instinctively, he knew what the man shouted.

'Ma brother's blind, ya bastards! He's fuckin' blind! In the –' he shouted the name of a hospital Dan couldn't make out.

Then he was gone and the doors were swinging, erasing his presence. Dan went towards the doors quickly. He knew Frankie was following. Before Dan had reached the doors, the smallest doorman had come back through them.

'No problem,' he said to Dan.

Dan brushed past him and went outside. The second doorman was standing alone. But the third wasn't there. Dan walked to the left for about fifty yards. There was nobody there. By the time he came back to the door of the disco, the third doorman was back.

'Where's the man who came in?' Dan said.

'Ah walked him up the road a bit,' the third doorman said.

'You're sure?'

'Gospel, big man. He was all right.'

Dan went back inside. Frankie was there.

'Who was that?' Dan demanded.

'Davie Dawson. Cutty's brother,' Frankie said.

In the shipwreck of his senses since the fight, Dan knew there was someone left behind he had to go back for. He was aware of a lot of people looking at him. He thought how misguided they were. They hadn't seen the real event, only its reflection in their mirror for the evening. He saw the Thornbank men staring at him, alarmed. He was glad to trouble them. He felt he was being honest with them for the first time that night. They were, at last, staring past the pretence into the reality that lay behind the party.

'What hospital was that he mentioned?'

Frankie shrugged. Matt Mason had come over. Eddie Foley had followed him, as if attached by a leash.

'What's the problem, Dan?' Matt Mason said.

'Cutty Dawson's in hospital.'

'So?'

'Ah'm goin' to see him.'

'Why?'

'Because Ah put him there. That's why.'

'Relax. That's not part of the contract.'

'Pardon? What contract's that? You think you bought ma head as well as ma hands? Maybe you *should* fire that lawyer of yours. He's misled you, right enough.'

Chuck Walker had wandered over to join the group, perhaps sensing a problem. Dan pointed at him.

'You,' he said. 'Hireling. This isn't your business. Fuck off!'

Chuck Walker rode the remark as if it had been a punch. He contained himself and looked at Matt Mason. Matt Mason nodded. Chuck Walker went away.

'You seem upset,' Matt Mason said, tensely.

'The world's upset. You haven't noticed? Ah'm just reacting to it.'

'Come on. Don't give us your riddles. What is the problem?'

'Ah thought Ah told you,' he said carefully, as if he were teaching a child his ABC: 'Ah put a man in the hospital. Ah'm goin' to see him. Ah've got a contract with *me*. Or didn't you know? Goin' there is part of it.'

'And what about your guests?'

Dan glanced round the room and smiled.

'So where are they?' he said.

'They're here to see you.'

'Naw. They're here because you asked them. They don't know who Ah am. Ah'm the one that goes to the hospital to see Cutty Dawson.'

Matt Mason looked at Frankie. Frankie could find no reaction. All of the fears he had had about this arrangement had just walked in and said hullo. He shrugged. He was good at shrugging.

'Dan,' Matt Mason said. 'I would like to talk to you. I told you that.'

'So Ah'll come back. And we'll talk. Did you think Ah wouldn't? You owe me money.'

Matt Mason smiled. He was relaxed again.

'Now that I do understand,' he said. 'All right, all right. That's what you do. It's maybe good you should get this out of your system. Keys, Eddie.' Eddie Foley handed them over. Matt Mason passed them to Frankie. 'You take Dan, Frankie.' Matt Mason winked. 'Then bring him back here. Don't be too long.'

Dan noticed that Frankie didn't ask which hospital it was.

'How about this?' Frankie White was saying. He was enjoying driving the Mercedes. It helped him to forget his problems. 'You're sitting in the jackpot, big man. Feel the width. This is bigger than some of the houses the old folks used to live in. A week ago you were on Shanks's pony an' Ah was on a push-bike. Baby, look at us now. Funny old world, intit?'

He swung the car about with a confidence that suggested it was a tank and it was up to other drivers to keep out of its way. An oncoming car that had pulled out to pass a stationary bus honked him.

'Fade, ya bastard, fade,' Frankie said. 'The Germans are comin'.'

'How much did you drink in there?' Dan asked.

'How about that place? Wall-to-wall women. And they're all for you, Dan. Give or take the odd femm that could be very fatal. Like Margaret Mason. She's all right, eh? She's class, the big wumman. Imagine makin' it wi' her. She's probably got a built-in jacuzzi up there. An' that Black Chip is just starters for you, big man. You're a fully paid up member now.'

As if anxious to get full use of his toy before he had to return it to its owner, Frankie switched on the radio and the sound swelled to fill the car. Before Frankie had time to recognise the tune, Dan had reached across and switched it off. He didn't want distractions.

'Just drive,' he said.

Dan hadn't spoken again by the time Frankie had parked the car on the brow of the hill and they were walking down the incline into the hospital. Coming towards them was a group of people who had obviously just left the building. They were two women and two girls.

They seemed invisibly tethered together, moving along with a clumsy unity, the halting of the oldest woman pulling up the others haphazardly when they felt the tug of her stillness. Three of them were crying. Only the younger girl was silent, as if numbed by the shocking effect events were having on the others. As Dan and Frankie passed, the younger woman was cuddling the older woman and vaguely trying to gather the girls to her with her other arm. She was talking.

'Don't worry, Mother. He'll be all right. Ah know he will. He will, he will.'

What made the scene more painful for Dan was that the younger woman was crying more sorely than any of the others. Her face was crumpled and held to the side as if absorbing a blow and the tears sluiced helplessly down her cheeks. Her ritual comfort was offered blindly to the dusk and simultaneously denied by the hopelessness of her grief. She was like a failed priest dispensing a faith he could no longer share.

'Aye,' Frankie said to Dan sympathetically. 'It's always at somebody's door.'

He said it as if such grief were an inexplicable visitation, like a virus. Dan didn't feel that way. His guilt made the scene personal to him. He was like a pilot who, having bombed a place indiscriminately, walks its streets afterwards and wonders if every passing wound is part of his doing. These people might be Cutty Dawson's family. He saw them as Cutty's mother, his wife and his daughters. A feeling he had suppressed in himself just before the fight came back to him now, doubled through denial. He remembered thinking that if death was the common enemy, what was the point of lesser fights? If pain was finally inevitable, why inflict it unnecessarily on one another? The pain he had seen humbled him, made the rationalisations by which he had brought himself to the fight seem petty.

His sense of humility increased as he went into the hospital, as it always did in such places. A man who had so far avoided serious illness, he felt a familiar, vague guilt going into hospitals. It was almost as if all the people in here were paying his dues for him. Having no specific religion, it was probably the nearest feeling to church that he had. This was his church of latter-day saints where not through dogma but through the inevitable accidents of experience, people took upon themselves the extremities of our nature, the stigmata of cancered lung and exhausted heart and diseased brain. In an isolation as lonely as any monk's cell, they endured the last known realities of living and tried to stay human and allow the parade of normalcy to visit and pay its dubious respects. The first article of faith here was that every problem is a practical one.

The woman at the admissions desk was well versed in it. She looked up at them and then turned to the card she was filling in. 'Yes?' she said to the card. He asked for Cutty Dawson. Her eyes flickered for a moment like a computer that has been fed the wrong information. Then she traced the malfunction.

'There's no visiting just now.'

'Ah realise that,' Dan said. 'But Ah need to see him.'

'His family's just gone out.'

'Ah know,' Dan said. He had been right in identifying the people outside as his victims, and the thought masochistically increased his determination.

'He's resting,' the woman said tetchily.

'Ah know. But Ah've only just heard what's happened to him. Ah'm his brother.'

She frowned at him, her narrowing eyes staring him out of anonymity and into a category as neat as a medical card. She inventoried his bruises.

'Are you the brother he was fighting with?'

Dan caught the part he had to play.

'No,' he said.

'Are you sure? You look as if you could use a bed here yourself.'

'No. These' – his hand flicked towards his face – 'are about something else. Could Ah see him, please?'

'You must be some family. I hope you haven't been carrying on the feud. This really should be a matter for the police.'

'He's ma brother. Can Ah see him?'

She hesitated, reluctant to give up her moment of moral authority.

'He's in one of the side rooms in Ward Five. You can ask Sister there. She'll tell you whether you can get in or not.'

She gave them directions and they climbed stairs and passed wards where in the dim stillness rows of beds floated on their separate voyages. As they moved past the rooms leading to Ward Five, a woman whose air of authority declared her to be the Sister emerged from one of them.

'Excuse me,' she said. 'What are you doing here?'

Dan found his language making a concession to her formality.

'I'm looking for Mr Dawson,' Dan said. 'I'm his brother.'

'His family has already visited.'

'I know. But I was late. I need to see him, Sister.'

'He has to rest.'

'Sister. I won't stay long. But I need to see him.'

She contemplated him for a moment. He looked at her. Compassion came to her face, displacing her authoritarian manner with the ease of a familiar visitor. Dan liked her immediately, finding in her an antidote to all the bureaucratic creeps ensconced in labour exchanges and income tax offices and job centres.

'Wait here,' she said. 'I'll see if he's awake.'

She went into one of the rooms and they heard her muffled voice. She came back out and nodded.

'But only you,' she said to Dan.

'Absolutely, Sister,' Frankie said. The mode of address had undertones of Humphrey Bogart in Frankie's mouth. 'No problem. I'm just a friend of the family. More of a chauffeur here than anythin' else.'

'Listen,' she said to Dan. 'His head mustn't move. He has a retinal detachment. He's mildly sedated just now. Until we can confirm exactly how bad the injury is he stays absolutely still! You understand? And you haven't got long.'

She let Dan into the room and closed the door. Dan was disoriented at first. A night light glowed on the wall opposite, its dimness inducing in him a kind of awkward reverence. The figure on the bed intensified the feeling. The strangeness of its condition made him hesitant. It was so much itself, so deeply isolated in its separate entity that any word or gesture would have seemed an intrusion. Dan understood more fully than he ever had before the individuality of another person.

The man he had thought of as his opponent lay motionless, the white covers making of him a humped mystery. He was flat on the bed, without a pillow. He looked like a sacrificial offering.

'That you, Davie?'

Dan said nothing. The ordinariness of the voice coming from the mummified stillness took him aback. He was held suspended between the awesomeness of things and their banality.

'That you, Davie? You all right? What happened?'

Dan came to the bed and, not knowing anything to say, reached out clumsily and touched the right hand that lay on the counterpane and shook it.

'Who are you? Ah thought it was Davie.'

'Cutty. It's me. Dan Scoular.'

The hand Dan was holding in his froze and then withdrew, paused briefly an inch away and then closed firmly again on Dan's and shook it gently. Dan sensed the chasm of inner distance that inch had measured and the generosity of spirit it took to cross it.

'Ah thought it was Davie,' Cutty said. 'The nurse said it was ma brother.'

'Ah told her that. It was the only way Ah could get in.'

A smile almost came on Cutty's mouth, didn't survive.

'That's funny,' he said. 'Ah told them the fight had been with ma brother. Maybe they thought that's who ye were.'

'They did. Why did ye tell them that?'

'They were talkin' about the polis. Who needs that? Ah'm in enough bother. Wi'out puttin' the polis on to Cam Colvin an' Matt Mason. At least Ah'm still breathin'. Ye got a seat? Sit on the bed there.'

Sitting down, Dan was surprised at the measured practicality of Cutty's responses, not just in how he was solicitous that Dan should have a place to sit but in the way the enormity of what had happened to him was held in a vice of pragmatism.

199

Bad could still have been worse. This could be the way he was for life but he assessed it carefully.

'How did ye know Ah wis here?' he asked.

'Word gets around,' Dan said, not wanting to be too specific about what had happened to his brother.

'Oor Davie? What's happened to him?'

'Well, he came. Where we were.'

'The Black Chip. Naw. Ah told him. The daft bugger. So what's happened?'

'He's all right.'

'Tell me.'

'Well, he was shoutin' the odds a bit. No wonder.'

'Jesus Christ. Where does he think we live? Dodge City? Where is he?'

'He's all right.'

'What's happened?'

'He left walkin'. He's all right. He wis just ragin'. No wonder.'

'No wonder my arse. But maybe that's it out his system. He'll never learn. Two vodkas an' the pish goes over the brain.'

The stillness of his anger had been strange.

'So you're having a party?' he said.

'Well, aye.'

'Aye. Why would ye no'? Ah can remember some of those maself. Funny. Don't know how you felt. But they never worked too well for me after a fight. Remember winnin' the Scottish title. Christ, what's that? How many Scottish heavy-weights have there ever been? But it meant a lot to me at the time. It was somethin' Ah had been aimin' for. Well, we had a party after it. An' it went completely flat for me. Like ye couldny get anythin' tae match what ye thought ye had done.' For the first time since the fight, Dan felt his experience connect with someone else's. 'Still, Ah'd rather be havin' one o' those the night than be lyin' here.'

Dan heard movement in the corridor outside and, thinking they might be interrupted soon, cut across Cutty's remarks.

'Cutty,' he said. 'Ah'm sorry.'

Cutty's hand was up before Dan had finished speaking. His face looked almost prim, as if he hoped Dan wasn't going to commit a breach of etiquette.

'Naw,' he said. 'Naw, naw. That's the way it goes. Not your fault. Not anybody's fault.'

'But your eyes. What's the chances?'

'Not too clever. See, the right eye's a dead man, anyway. Has been for years. They told me at the time the left yin could go the same way. Warned me not to put it at risk. But Ah knew that, didn't Ah? So it was ma choice.'

'But why, Cutty?'

'Ah needed the money. Ye always need the money, don't ye?'

'Ye all right for money at least?'

Cutty smiled bitterly.

'Well, Ah almost was. Ah thought Ah had ye for a while there.'

'Ye did.'

'Aye, ye were goin'.'

'But ye still get yer money?'

Dan was remembering Matt Mason saying that winners win money, losers lose it.

'Ah owed Cam Colvin, didn't Ah? An' Mason took a right few quid off him.'

'Ye get nothin'?'

'That was the deal. Ah agreed to it.'

'But after what's happened?'

'What's happened is Ah got beat.'

'But ye could be blind. They reckon that, do they? Ah mean, can they tell at this stage?'

'They can tell so much. But Ah need to stay absolutely still for a day or that. Then they can confirm. An upper detachment, they call it. Whit Ah canny understand is it's the bottom o' ma e'e that's affected. Just greyness. Like the tide risin' up yer eyeball. Ah can just about keek over it. Ah'm terrified Ah waken up the morra an' Ah'm overheads wi' it.'

'Jesus Christ.'

Cutty's stillness seemed to Dan more than physical. It was as if his spirit was immobilised as well. 'That's the way it goes.' 'Not anybody's fault.' Something terrible and unnecessary had happened and even the victim of it acquiesced.

'Cutty. That was your family Ah saw outside there?'

'Coulda been. They just left.'

'Two women, two girls.'

'That would be them. That was ma mither, wi' Jean an' the lassies. Davie left earlier. But ye know that.'

'That's all the family ye've got?'

'Jean an' the lassies. Aye. Cathy and Maureen. They're fourteen an' twelve. Ah'd like to see them as women. But we'll have to wait and see. Still. They've got a good mither. She'll see them all right.'

Dan remembered sitting in that gloomy living-room with his mother and realising how much she had had to carry all her life. He saw those women outside as her descendants. Not only did they have to deal with the daily problems of living. They had to impart to it its true feeling as well, dignify it with their tears. By the passion of their pain they were offering some human measurement of what had happened to Cutty.

If those women were descended from his mother, he saw Cutty as his father's true heir, inheritor of a hard philosophy. He lay there, it seemed to Dan, having made a heroic statue of himself, sealed off from admitting the enormity of his own hurt. Dan felt admiration for Cutty and through him for his father and all those men he had felt he was fighting in that field, but he also felt the unadmitted pathos of them. In order to achieve that attitude of strength, much richness of feeling had to be foregone. The reality of their condition could not be admitted. It was as if true human responses to the mysteries of our experience became women's work and it was men's to predetermine themselves into an immutable stance.

The distinction between the two roles was false. They shared the same condition. The same fragility had to be admitted. Dan thought he began to understand for the first time what the fight meant. He hadn't won. Cutty had lost. His father had lost. All those self-defeatingly brave men of his boyhood had lost. Like their champion, Cutty had tried to deny the truth of his own situation, had agreed to the unfair odds, had tried to impose the strength of his will on impossible circumstances. Sitting with Cutty, Dan felt himself at a wake for a way of life, a brave philosophy which didn't work. In trying to prove that it did, Cutty had damaged himself, perhaps irreparably.

'So it was ma choice.' What kind of choice was that? They

hadn't been fighting each other. They had been using themselves as conduits for a quarrel that wasn't theirs.

'That fight, Cutty,' Dan said. 'What was it about?'

'Money.'

'Ye must know more than that. What was the quarrel between Matt Mason an' that Cam Colvin?'

'Hey. Ah'm a big, thick puncher. Or Ah was. Ma brains are in ma knuckles. How would Ah know?'

'Ye heard nothin' about the background to it? Ah canny believe that. Ye said ye owed Cam Colvin. That means ye must have been involved wi' him before this.'

'On the edges. Ye think these fellas advertise? They tell ye what to do, not why to do it. The less ye know the better. It's like insurance.'

'Is it true that Colvin's intae drugs?'

Cutty didn't answer at once, as if Dan was asking him to breach some code of manhood.

'Who told ye that?' Cutty asked.

'Matt Mason.'

'He should talk.'

'How d'ye mean?'

'Look. Ye've got yer wages. Ah think ye should go back to wherever it is an' let it go at that.'

'Matt Mason's talkin' about givin' me a job.'

'Oh.'

Cutty's lips pursed, trying to decide.

'Look, Ah don't like talkin' about this. But Ah'll tell ye what little Ah know. Aye, Colvin deals in drugs. Ye think Matt Mason doesny? It's where the money is, isn't it? What they call an expandin' market. Ah reckon they're both involved in it.'

'Matt Mason as well? So why were we fightin' the day?'

'Ah've heard different things.'

'Like what?'

'How many stories do ye want?'

'The one you believe.'

'Ah wouldn't know what to believe. But Ah can tell ye the most popular one. The rumour that's runnin' favourite. There's a man called Tony Freeman. Used tae be in Glesca. They reckon he's in Spain now. Round about Benidorm.

Marbella. That kinna area. But they reckon the money he's spendin' there isny his.'

'So?'

'Well, it's supposed to be somethin' to do wi' him. But the rumours fork out a bit from there. Take yer pick. But he diddled Matt Mason an' Cam Colvin in some way. They say he was supplyin' drugs an' made a dummy delivery to the two o' them. Wan theory is our fight wis settlin' two things. Who would compensate the other. An' who would attend to Freeman. But Ah don't know. Ah really don't.'

The little that Cutty knew gave Dan a fix on the dimensions of the ignorance of both of them. He had an image of the two of them in the centre of the field while the others watched without for a second seeing what was truly happening. Their efforts had been a decoy.

Even the fragments of his own experience of it he felt shifting painfully inside him, like pieces of shrapnel. The successive layers of pain he had gone through seemed meaningless. The triumph he had felt came back to mock him. The mutual ordeal to which they had subjected themselves, and which he had vaguely been thinking was a ferocious measuring of each other, was rigged. They had already been measured. In their crazy journey around the field the destination had been decided.

Thinking of it now, Dan felt their efforts take on an edge of irony. If there had been a commentary on their fight, he decided, it would have preceded their actions, determining them. They hadn't been controlling events. They were being controlled by them. The training for the fight, which he had thought he was doing around Thornbank and in the gym at Ingram Street, had taken place a long time before, for both of them. They had been conditioned over years in dead-end jobs and dole queues, picking the seams of empty pockets, learning to add up their individual bitterness and disillusionment and charge it against somebody as hapless as themselves. They had been well trained in futility.

And while they spent themselves against each other, cancelling out each other's force, neutralising the meaning of their joint experience, a parasitical significance had been feeding off them. A balance of power that they would never share in was affected, money of which they would only ever see a fraction shifted places, perhaps someone's life or death was being decided.

There couldn't be triumph in such a winning. Both fighters had lost. Only the promoters had won. He had no honour from it. The terms he had allowed himself to be judged in weren't his. In order to have honour, he had to introduce his own terms, but he didn't know how.

'You should have somethin' from this, Cutty,' he said. 'You should.'

'Maybe. But that's no' the way it works.'

'Why not?'

'Ask God that yin.'

'Ah think the responsibility's maybe nearer. Look. What we did wis illegal. We can put the hammer on them for your money. Or say we'll tell the polis.'

'That right?'

'That's right.'

'Oh aye.'

'We can have them where we want them.'

'The only place Ah want them is far away from me.'

'There's plenty of witnesses.'

'Talk sense. Who do ye think brought them there in the first place? Matt Mason an' Cam Colvin. Who's gonny turn their tongue on them?'

'You can still talk.'

'It might be tricky talkin' from a coffin.'

'Well, Ah can talk.'

'Listen, Dan Scoular. You're a country boy. Take yer money an' go back there. An' take yer mouth with ye. Ye don't play heroes wi' these men. They just kill ye. You maybe punched me blind. But Ah think Ah punched you daft. Forget it! This is me, whit's left o' me. An' that's you. An' those are the men in charge. Just concentrate on keepin' breathin'.'

'Cutty. Ah'm goin' tae stop them if they don't pay ye.'

'An' Ah'm gonny deny everything you say. Where'll that leave ye? Lookin' daft before ye're dead. All right? You leave it. Ah'm all right.'

It was as if they hadn't shared any common experience. Dan was to go back to Thornbank with his money and Cutty was to go back into his perhaps ruined life and that was it. Cam Colvin had lost money, Matt Mason had made money, and maybe a man in Spain would die. Thank you and separate bills, please.

'Cutty,' he said. 'What more can they do tae ye? Ye might be blind.'

'Maybe,' Cutty said. 'But ma family's not.'

Dan looked at him and sympathised but didn't agree. Cutty was offering both of them absolution. Dan didn't accept it. They were both guilty. It could have been Cutty's party tonight. That was Dan's forgiveness, if he had wanted it.

But he was guilty. So was Cutty, so was his father, so were his boyhood heroes. He saw their heroic stances as gestures of despair. They didn't believe there was anything else they could do. They chose a kind of stoical innocence and waited for others to improve their circumstances. For that to happen, they had to go on believing in innocence. Dan thought he understood at last, through his fight with Cutty, his fight with his father. It was his father's last stand against a possibility he couldn't admit. For if his own son were corruptible, what hope could he have of those who were supposed to be the liberators, the ones who would see that the conditions of his life were made more just? Despair needed false optimism to go on.

Dan had lost his. The argument he had been having with his father had clarified itself against Cutty. Assumption of your own innocence was guilt. He felt himself come into his patiently accrued experience as something earned. He would find how to spend it. He would spend it not just for himself, since others had helped him to earn it.

He remembered the darkness he had found in himself at the end of the fight. It had frightened him, that fierceness. He hadn't wanted to face it as part of himself. It had haunted him in the bath at Matt Mason's house. It had made him fear he might pollute his children. He saw the party as an attempt to celebrate the void he had found in himself. He wouldn't celebrate it. But he had to live with it.

He recalled looking down at his body after the fight and seeing the strange map of where he had been. He had explored himself and had discovered an anger to the bone he hadn't known was in him. Matt Mason obviously thought that made Dan the same as him. But it didn't. 'Whit is it you believe in, boay?'

He believed he had choice. He remembered his realisation, when he was training with Tommy Brogan, that you could split a second into options. No matter what the conditions, no matter what you discovered your nature to be, you still had choice. You couldn't choose what happened to you but you could choose what you did with it. You couldn't choose who you were but you could choose how to use who you were.

He looked at Cutty again and saw what he himself might become, as good as blind and just as helpless. He lay waiting for what would happen. What more was there for him to do? He hadn't only himself to think of. He had to protect his family. But Dan decided that the first thing he had to give his family was himself, as free as he could be. He couldn't accept the contract with events that Cutty and his father had agreed to. He had a clause of his own to insert. What the exact terms of it were he didn't yet know.

The door opened and the Sister looked in. She was holding something in her hands and kept the door open with her body. Her expression was a gentle reprimand to him for taking such advantage of her busyness. Dan nodded.

'Ah better go, Cutty,' he said.

'It was decent of ye to come in.'

'Ah'll hear how it goes with ye.'

'You take care of yerself.'

'Aye,' said Dan. 'Whatever that means.'

As he came out, Frankie rose from his chair in the corridor. 'Okay, Dan?'

'Terrible,' Dan said – then he winked, 'and okay.'

Frankie left it at that.

When Dan and Frankie came out of the car at the Black Chip, Dan smiled to see the Thornbank men straggling out. Their voices bobbed on the night air, swimmers going towards the open sea, innocent of what might be moving underneath the surface.

'What a night!'

'The day Thornbank came to town.'

'Better than winnin' the Junior Cup.'

Dan loved the generosity of their responses and saw its danger. These men had a worrying adaptability. They could cultivate pleasure anywhere. Put them on a battlefield and they would be grateful for every poppy that they found. They would improvise songs out of whatever was going on but they were a chorus that, often unable to see what was taking place, would chant a song of celebration as events dragged them down. He loved the tune but he had his own still-forming idea of what the words should be. They gave him the old ones.

'The man himself!'

'What a fight, what a night!'

'We're goin' to get them to put up a statue in Thornbank. The Dan Scoular memorial.'

Two blind men trying to gouge each other's eyes out, Dan thought. They were squeezing his arms and touching his back. They were honouring a cheque that, had he been only his past, was certain to bounce. But he would turn it into real currency.

'That Matt Mason knows how to lay it on, eh?' Sam Mac-Kinlay was saying. 'Some man, that.'

Dan looked at Sam's flushed face and added it to what was owed. Sam was the sort of guest who would have thanked the Borgias for a lovely meal.

'How's Cutty Dawson, Dan?'

The voice introduced the possibility of an alternative sense of things. Dan was grateful to Alistair, baffled listener into other people's lives.

'He might be blind,' Dan said.

Cutty was the guest they hadn't realised was at the party. They felt guilty at ignoring him. They all stood with the wind in their hair and realised it was cold. Feeling the sense of the night change around him, Frankie spoke like an MC trying to rally their mood.

'Come on, come on,' he said. 'It's not your fault, Dan. It was a fair fight.'

'Aye,' Dan said. 'If you weren't in it.'

The others murmured their penances.

'Pair sowl.'

208

'That's a bad break.'

'Hope he gets over it.'

'We'll see ye when ye get back down, Dan?' Alistair said. 'Ye don't want a lift just now?'

'No. Thanks, Alistair. Ah've a man to see.'

'Maybe just as well,' Sam said. 'We'll probably all be dead wi' frostbite when we get there. There's a windae we canny shut.'

'Maybe we should phone Geordie Parker,' Harry said. 'Find out the secret spell ye use tae get it shut. Everything else in the bloody car has a mind of its own.'

The levity was a rehearsal, not an achieved performance. As they walked away to find the car, debating where they had left it, Dan could imagine them having trouble finding their way home, but perhaps not as much as he might have.

Inside, the party was hectic. Dan realised that it was still carly, for some. Noise was round them like a plastic bubble. The doorman he had told to mind his own business seemed to be doing that. He was talking (confidentially) to two other men and he had his hand resting casually on the blonde woman's thigh. Eddie Foley was one of the other men. Tommy Brogan was standing alone at the bar.

'Dan.' Frankie appeared at his elbow, having been speaking to one of the other doormen. 'Matt an' the others are up at the house. We've got to go on up there.'

Dan felt as if he was seeing it for Cutty Dawson. It was, it seemed to him, like walking into a fancy restaurant straight from the slaughterhouse. Frankie was fidgeting.

'Dan,' he said. 'We're wastin' time.'

'Ah don't know,' Dan said. 'Sometimes the way yc go gives ye a better view of where ye're comin' to.'

7

It was the first time he had been aware of seeing the house. When they had brought him earlier today, the place had been just part of a continuing confusion of sensations, the clean smell of the hallway, the plushness of carpets, the soothing bath. Seeing it from the outside as Frankie turned the Mercedes riskily into the driveway, and gave himself a last thrill before he handed over the keys, Dan was struck by the size of the building.

It was a detached house set on a small prominence, having two gateways to it joined by a crescent of driveway that hemmed in a semi-circle of lawn with some trees. Built in grey sandstone, it belonged to a time before the aquarium school of modern architecture. Glass was used discreetly here. The downstairs bay windows were large but the overall size of the place made them seem modest. Upstairs, the solid base of the building began to be full of its own importance, turning whimsical. Several little turrets appeared, defying any purpose you could imagine. Crenellation ran along the roof-edge as if the house had begun to mistake itself for a castle.

The fortress-like impression made Dan realise suddenly that it was a building out of his childhood. It merged for him with some houses he had seen in and around Thornbank when he was small. Often enough, out playing or coming back from a walk in the country, he had stared at a house like that and wondered what it must be like inside. How many rooms would there be in a place like that? Would they have servants? What sort of people would live there? What would they talk about?

The vagueness of those other buildings, wrapped in mists of dreaming fancy and ignorance and incomprehension, had crystallised into this one. This was the house he had wondered about. He had been a long time getting here by a devious route but he had arrived. Mystery had an address.

As he got out of the car, he remembered the sitting-room where they had been drinking earlier and, thinking of the room and trying to work out its position in the house, he reckoned it must be an extension. The thought gave him a perspective different from the one he had had as a boy. Even these big solid houses that looked like immovable facts were changing and adapting subtly. They might still look from the front like statements that nothing could challenge but discreetly they were inserting extra clauses in the declaration they made, admitting qualifications. The realisation made them less awesome.

He was interested to be back here, having gone through the experience of the night. Knowing the little more he knew about Matt Mason, he was surprised how easy it was to walk in. Frankie rang the bell and pushed down the handle of the door and it opened. There was no guard, no grille, no Doberman. Perhaps Matt Mason's reputation was around it like a moat.

Matt Mason looked out from the sitting-room as Frankie closed the door, laying the car keys on the hall table, and he waved them into what Dan felt was the core of the evening. They went into the room and, while Matt Mason got them a drink, Dan saw who was there. It seemed to him as if the evening had been panned of all its dross and only the hard value remained. Cutty Dawson was stowed in hospital. The Thornbank men had gone home. The residue of the party was twitching itself to death in the Black Chip.

This was what the day had been about. Here was Matt Mason, whose money and power had controlled the events of the day. Here was Roddy Stewart, the mechanic who made sure the machinery of that power developed no hitches. Here were their women. Here were Melanie and Sandra, reward for the labourer, reward for the hirer. Matt Mason gave Dan and Frankie their drinks and they sat down.

Atmosphere redecorates a room, heightens certain features, mutes others. The spaciousness of earlier in the day, with the sunlight and the garden beyond, was gone. Dan was aware of the solidity of the furnishings, of how the chairs and the couch created alignments among them, made a group statuary that had a coherent meaning. The curtains weren't drawn across the French windows and their images were repeated out into the darkness, as if they were all there was.

Small whorls of reflective laughter from something Roddy

Stewart had been saying eddied around them. Dan realised how comfortably they had been absorbed into the room, as if they were already a natural part of it. Melanie's shoulder brushed his, familiar as a habit. Everybody was relaxed. The ease with which Matt Mason referred to Cutty Dawson conveyed that they were all confederates here.

'You saw him then, Dan?'

'Cutty? Aye.'

'How was he?'

'Not so good. They think he'll maybe finish blind.'

The words were like a draught through the cosiness of the room, a window blown open. Melanie put her hand on Dan's arm.

'It's not your fault, Dan. Don't blame yourself.'

'Of course it's not,' Margaret Mason said.

'Ah don't know,' Dan said. 'Ah was slightly involved at the time. Ah mean, Cutty didn't walk into a tree or anything.'

'You ran the same risk as he did,' Alice Stewart said.

'No' quite.'

'What do you mean?' It was Matt Mason, watching him and smiling. He gave the impression of being further back from the conversation than the others, letting it happen but monitoring it.

'Cutty's eyes were dicey before the fight started. He knew that. So did Tommy Brogan. He tipped me the wink. Did ye know yerself?'

'I'd heard things. But you hear a lot of things. What difference does it make?'

'Quite a lot to Cutty.'

'He should've thought of that. Was he complaining?'

'Naw. That's the most depressin' bit about it. He talks as if it wis an act of God.'

'Wasn't it?'

Dan looked across at him.

'If it was, Ah can give ye God's address.'

It was the kind of frontal remark that in another context Dan would have expected to be taken as a challenge. Said to Dan's father or to a man in the pubs he knew, it might have meant a physical confrontation. In this room it evoked laughter. Matt Mason led the procession, closely followed by

Roddy Stewart and the women, except Melanie. Frankie joined in, belatedly but enthusiastically – out of relief, Dan suspected.

'Well, I've been called many a thing,' Matt Mason said.

'Maybe I should be prostrate in your presence.' Roddy Stewart was miming his idea in sketch form.

'I should be keeping my head covered in bed,' Margaret said.

Dan felt the moment like a more complicated variant of his talk with Cutty Dawson. With Cutty, what he was trying to say hadn't been taken seriously either. But there the reaction had been closed, determined, could admit only one form of response because otherwise the complex content of what was happening would have been overwhelming. Here the reaction was open, relaxed. They played with the form of what he had said – Matt Mason as God – because they had pre-decided the ridiculousness of the content. They couldn't take seriously the fact that Cutty's blindness could in any way be traced back to this house. Their laughter wasn't malicious. In the way they looked at Dan and shook their heads, there was something like affection.

'Ah'll tell ye something even funnier,' Dan said.

'I don't know if I can take it,' Alice said.

'Cutty Dawson got nothin' from the fight.'

'What?' Melanie was interested.

'He got no money. The deal he had wi' Cam Colvin gives him nothin' because he lost.'

'I don't believe that,' Alice said.

'Maybe you've cleaned him out completely, Matt,' Roddy Stewart said.

'It's a hard life,' Matt Mason said.

They talked around it some more but Dan took little part in the conversation. He didn't see the point. He thought of how often, when he was younger, he had argued against the kind of isolation from others he felt in this room. But he sensed that if he did it here he would become no more than an entertainment. He felt his awkward difference from them, as if he spoke in a moral dialect strange to them, learned from his parents and his past. They would merely find it quaint, that idiom by which us and them desired to be the same.

What they seemed to be dealing with was a debating point

and what he had in his mind was the intractable image of Cutty Dawson lying on his bed. In this room that was inadmissible evidence. He felt an echo of this morning, breakfasting in the hotel before the fight. The others had seemed to know the nature of the event before it happened. He thought of the things they had said to him afterwards, telling him what he had done. Like their conversation, they pre-empted the reality of events. They were as much manipulated by Matt Mason as he had been.

'Anyway, I'm not cleaned out,' Matt Mason said. He winked at Dan. 'Margaret. You make sure the drink doesn't dry up?'

He stood up and looked at Dan, raised his eyebrows. Dan put down his drink and followed him out.

In the hall he opened the door of a room and put on the light. 'What do you think of this?'

It was a dining-room, wooden-floored and with a huge sideboard on which a hot-plate and metal serving dishes sat. A chandelier hung brilliantly from the ceiling. Dan studied it all and looked at Matt Mason. He was watching Dan expectantly. Dan nodded in a way he assumed was appreciative. Matt Mason put out the light and led him to another room. Dan recognised the study from which he had phoned Betty.

With the door closed, the room shut off the others' conversation. It was surprisingly still in here, as if it was lined with cork. If the house had seemed to Dan on arriving the centre of the night, this room was the core of the core. Very much Matt Mason's place, it was small and cluttered with objects in a way that intimidated sudden movement. The dominant feature was a big leather-topped desk with a cushioned wooden swivel-chair behind it and a deep leather chair in front of it. There was a painting of horses on the wall above the wooden chair and an abstract painting on the facing wall as you came in the door. On the desk were a heavily ornate silver box and a big vase, the glaze filamented with age. Dan had stared at that vase while he was phoning Betty and the boys and, confronting him now, it was a kind of accusation.

Mason opened a cabinet and took out a bottle and two crystal glasses. He poured two drinks, making a ritual of it. He kept one, gave one to Dan.

'Tequila Gold,' he said. 'To us.'

Dan sipped it carefully, felt its warmth. He was standing awkwardly like a guest who wasn't sure what he had been invited to.

'Sit down, Dan.'

The seat absorbed him in itself, was too comfortable, making him think he might need help to get back out of it. Mason sat behind his desk.

'I owe you money, Dan,' he said and smiled. 'But there's something else I want to talk to you about.'

He sipped his drink and seemed momentarily to have forgotten what it was he wanted to talk about.

'What do you think of the house?'

'Some house.'

'It's all right, isn't it? It'll do. For the moment, anyway. There's a lot of snobbery about here. Who cares? I've got as big a house as any of them. And it's paid for. But I think some of my neighbours don't think I should be here. A boy from the Gallowgate. You know the Gallowgate?'

'I've heard of it.'

Dan knew it was a district of Glasgow and not much more.

'It's not there now. Not the way it was. It's not just people that move away, Dan. Places move away. That was some place. Funny mixture. I remember a day. I would be twelve. Two mates and me had booked half an hour on a snooker table. Had scuffled two days to get the money. Ninepence. For half an hour's snooker. We were all keyed up for it. Like going on holiday. We set up the balls and broke. Two boys about nineteen said, "Right. We'll take it from there." They pushed us off the table and took over. We went outside. There was a man we knew standing there having a smoke. A wee man called Johnny Fagan. "What's the matter, boys?" he says. "Thought youse three were havin' a frame." We told him. Throws away his fag and went back in. Ten seconds later, a terrible noise. The two boys carried out. We played our game.'

In the silence and stillness of the room, the anecdote seemed to acquire a confessional significance. The moment reminded Dan of some of the early-hours drinking sessions he had been involved in when, with the rest of the world seeming to be asleep and reduced to a kind of abstraction, thoughts stumbled

215

upon and moments remembered became enlarged, as by some trick of mental acoustics, like a whisper in a cave. You were amazed at the importance of the small things you knew. Mason's brooding silence suggested the importance he was attaching to the story. He fingered the silver box on his desk thoughtfully.

'Johnny Fagan,' he said, with a kind of reverence. He seemed to be naming one of his spiritual fathers. 'He taught me a couple of things that my old man didn't. My old man. Drunk as a monkey most of the time. And spouting politics. He was useless. My mother kept us alive. I used to look at her and think this was her life. All she was ever going to get. And so it was. I helped her a wee bit before the end. But she died before I had made the real money.' His hand came away from the silver box and gestured at the room. 'If I'd brought her into this place, she'd probably have got down on her knees and started to clean it. Nah. She died trapped in what she had been. Harnessed to my old man's life. Social progress, Dan. Let all the lazy, gutless bastards hitch themselves up to the ones that get things done and get a free ride through their lives. The theories are maybe nice but that's how it works. Truth is, God's a hard case. He has to be, no? Look at the way he works. He doesn't hang about when he's foreclosing on lives. No redundancy payments there. Doesn't matter whether it's children or young men or pregnant mothers. When your contract's terminated, it's terminated. Try another universe.'

Dan remembered the moment in the fight when he had thought about something he had once said himself: 'Living's the only game in town and it's fucking crooked.'

It was a thought which had clarified for him what he had to do, which had helped to bring him through the fight. He couldn't now simply pretend it wasn't there. He had to follow where it appeared to lead. He didn't want the quiet, compelling voice to go on but it did.

'That's what I've got against all the fancy theories. They don't work. You're not changing the truth. You're just giving it a fancy shroud. It's still a fuck-up. The nice ideas don't fit us. How many do you know that died poor and tried it?'

The voice came at him like an echo of so many of his own thoughts. He was trying to believe it was a distorting echo.

But he thought of the men he used to work with at Sullom Voe – how quickly, making good money, they had distanced themselves from the men they had worked with before. Given a taste of their own limited financial success, it became a self-fulfilling addiction. Some of them would still talk of their parents' lives with a kind of wistful admiration for their belief in the solidarity of their class but there was almost a kind of condescension in that admiration, as if it had been similar to the touching beliefs children have in fairy tales. Also, their talk on those train journeys down from Aberdeen seemed to have no strong political focus. Among the talk of football and family and women and who had got a good deal on his car, politics might be mentioned, but never with the kind of righteous anger Dan had heard being voiced as a boy against the political principles that seemed to govern their lives. Where their fathers might have raged, these men shrugged. What else can you expect, they seemed to suggest. Dan had sometimes wondered if their music centres and their video machines and their foreign holidays were like hush money.

He had to admit that he had seen himself how demands for social equality could be used as a confidence trick. There were phases of history when it worked well. People could use it as a ticket of admission to the party that was going on at the time and, once they were inside, get on with the serious business of filling their faces and their pockets. Maybe those mates who had worried him on those train journeys had been brought by unemployment and the hard terms of their lives to the point he had only reached in the fight.

'You think I chose this, Dan? There is no choice. It's all there is.'

They sat in silence. Dan raised his glass to his mouth and put it back down without drinking. He didn't know why he had done that. Perhaps it was because he sensed himself at a point of utter equilibrium in his experience, where nothing trivial must tip the balance, not even one sip of tequila. Whatever he did now would define him for the rest of his life to himself. He knew where Mason was going and he didn't yet know how far he was prepared to follow him. He must wait very carefully and see. Mason had both hands on the vase, as if warming them at a fire.

217

'This house, Dan. I made this house. Oh, I didn't put the bricks together, right enough, but I made it all right. See that room I showed you? The dining-room? Know where I got the idea for that room? Mainly at the pictures. The idea for the floor I got out a colour supplement. But mainly it's from the pictures I saw when I was a wee snottery boy. I decided then I was going to have a house like them. If it was good enough for Ronald Colman, it was good enough for me. And I got it. Don't you worry. This vase.'

He lifted it gently and put it down on the desk in front of Dan.

'Lift that. Feel the weight.'

Dan did so.

'You're holding two thousand quid in your hands there.'

Dan put it back down immediately and Mason smiled. He moved the silver box across to Dan.

'Fifteen hundred pounds,' he said. 'Open it.'

Dan fiddled with the box and it wouldn't open. He felt beneath his hands the mysteriousness of old objects, their intimidatory history. The box didn't just baffle him, it made him feel stupid. Its carvings seemed as mystifying as the Rosetta Stone. He felt around him the strangeness of the house as if emanating from this centre, his incomprehension of the lives that had been lived here, the dignity of the place like an identity no changes made by Mason could erase. He felt as if both of them were interlopers.

'Careful,' Mason said. 'It's delicate.'

Dan's hands came away as if from an electric shock. Mason leaned across and touched something and the lid of the box eased itself slightly and soundlessly from the body. Mason nodded. Dan gently prised it open. Inside was a yellowed piece of paper. Dan glanced at Mason. Mason took out the paper tentatively and unfolded it carefully, passed it to Dan, who held it as if it might powder in his hands. It was a note in faded, fancy handwriting, undated, no address. 'Dear Mary Anne,' it said. 'The matter is decided. There shall be no further trouble from that source. Discretion, however, is still to be advised. Until soon. Francis.' Dan felt an eeriness in reading the words, as if he had heard whisperings from the grave. That long-irrelevant urgency seemed to put his own problems in a new perspective. Mason, putting the paper back in its box and closing the lid, appeared to catch his mood.

'Gives you a funny feeling, eh? That was in the box when I got it. I like that. I like to keep it there. It's like it tells you there's not much that changes. "Discretion, however, is still to be advised." True, Dan.'

He was still touching the box. They sat like conspirators, staring at it.

'You've made some money today, Dan,' Mason said. 'But that's nothing to what you could make. But to make the real stuff you've got to have a bit of iron in you. You've got that. I saw it today. Oh, I did.' He looked up directly at Dan. 'That's something I can use, Dan. I want you to come and work with me.'

Mason's hand came away from the box, gestured at the room.

'My sons,' Mason said. 'They'll be all right. With their elocution lessons. And their private school. Okay. But they're being trained to live a charade. I can see it in them already. Well, let them get on with it. But some of us have to handle the real world. Not many of us equipped to do that, Dan. I think you're one.'

They looked at each other and Dan was aware of the hunger in Mason's eyes, saw how important the making of this offer was to him.

'I'm not talking about being a puncher, Dan. I'm talking about learning from me. I'm talking about more money than you ever thought you would see. I think you should come in where the real work's done.'

Dan remembered times when he had thought he was comfortably off and realised how naive he had been to think that. There hadn't been a time in his life when more than a month or two separated him from being penniless. A week without work had always been enough to put him in financial bother. For the first time in his life, he saw security within his grasp. He thought of Betty. He felt that at the moment he needed every advantage in that area he could get.

'That party,' Dan said. 'Somebody told me ye were involved in drugs.'

Mason smiled.

'Who told you that?'

'Ah can't remember. Is it true?'

'Not really. Been around the edges, right enough. Dabbled. Not too successfully so far. You thinking about Friday? Smithy?'

Dan said nothing.

'Friday was Friday, Dan. This is Sunday. I said what I thought would help you at the time. Drugs. That's one of those words everybody gets hysterical about. Leaves the papers frothing at the mouth. Why? It's a commodity, isn't it? It's the coming market. People take it by choice, at least to begin with. Great thing about drugs is you've really got a captive market. It's a great commodity, isn't it? You don't even have to advertise. The consumer's breaking your door down to buy it off you. Talk about a seller's market.'

'Whit wis the fight about?'

'Just settling something.'

'Who would kill somebody?'

Mason studied him interestedly.

'You've been doing a bit of talking, Dan, eh? No. Just about who would settle something. Collect a bad debt. Cam Colvin's going to do that. Not my business any more. And definitely not yours. How he does it is how he does it. Well.'

Dan felt the impossibility of his understanding the exact ramifications, from where he sat, of the events he had been involved in. The only way to understand them fully would be to become more strongly part of them. Mason stood up. Dan joined him, awkwardly.

'I'll give you a wee while to think it over. But not too long. Times move on. So do opportunities. It's up to you to grab them.'

He pointed to the picture of horses behind his desk.

'You like the painting?'

'Aye, it's good.'

'"Jockeys sous la pluie." Jockeys in the rain. A man called Degas painted it. The real one's worth a fortune. Imagine that. You catch what it looks like, just horses and jockeys getting ready for a race in the rain. And it's worth a lot of money. Hm. But it's good. "Jockeys sous la pluie".'

He repeated the title like a magical formula. He gestured

Dan round to his side of the desk. He put his hand up to touch the painting and swung it on a hinge. Behind it was a wall safe. Dan felt as if he was back in the front row of the Saturday matinée. Mason looked at him and smiled. This was a ceremony, to be conducted slowly.

'Get it? Can you think of a better place for me to keep my money? The horses have always been the cover for where my money comes from.'

As Dan watched him make mystic passes with his fingers, unlocking the combination, he felt suddenly as if the safe were working Mason. He saw the way he stood before it, reaching towards it and wooing it with his fingers like an acolyte conjuring it to grant him access to its sanctum. The rapt, complacent concentration on his face was bestowed on him by its touch. The strangeness of the image distanced Dan from what was happening, made him an outsider to it. Like an unbeliever at a religious service, he felt the bizarreness of the rituals that had happened here, the weirdness of the assumptions that had underlain them. With the seductiveness of Mason's voice gone silent, Dan was left to the discomfort of his own thoughts, the need to decide what he believed.

As always, he didn't know. He had never deliberately formulated his thoughts or his beliefs into a system, always having sensed that to do that would be false. He had never imposed a coherent shape upon his life but instead had allowed his life to elicit its changing shape from events as they happened.

What was happening now would be proof of what he believed, not what his mind told him he believed. All he could do was abide the outcome of this event of which he was a part. He couldn't pre-empt the moment's force with any foreknowledge of how things ought to be. No moral precept surfaced in him to find firm footing where there was no solid ground and calm the doubts in him. You didn't define happenings, they defined you.

Matt Mason had taken money from the safe, began to count notes from a huge wad on to his desk.

'Like a wee, dark womb,' he said, smiling. 'That's where all the social possibilities are born, Dan.'

As he watched the money accumulate on the desk, Dan didn't know what he thought or felt. As if his very sense of himself were in thaw, impulses that were part thought, part feeling, broke off unevenly from one another and swirled, colliding in him. He needed the money. He wanted the money. Matt Mason had reconstructed his house from dead ideas. Dan thought of him touching the vase constantly, touching the metal box. It was as if he had needed to keep doing that to recharge his sense of himself. But those things had only a financial value to him. Only the price mattered and the price was a meaningless invention. Frankenstein's monster desperately re-plugging himself into dead generators. Dan wanted Betty to stay with him. What had happened to Cutty Dawson didn't need to happen. What difference could Dan make to anything anyway? The man Dan had seen with Betty had looked well-off. Dan had taken the same chances as Cutty. He wanted the money.

'Five hundred,' Mason said. 'A hundred for training with Tommy. Four for the fight.'

The money was in tens. It made a small, uneven pile on the desk.

'More than you bargained for, Dan, eh? Plus a wee bonus.'

Mason began to lay more money, note by note, on top of the pile. 'Hey!' Dan remembered saying in the Red Lion. Mason's story about the snooker could be seen as yielding a meaning different from the one Mason had given it. Johnny Fagan hadn't put himself at risk against the two men for his own sake. Cutty was to get nothing. Dan thought of giving the money to Betty.

'Seven hundred and fifty quid,' Matt Mason said.

Still holding the much larger wad of money in his left hand, he lifted the money from the desk with his right hand and formally presented it to Dan.

'If you're wise,' he said, 'you'll take it as a down payment on your future.'

Dan took the money, held it in his hand.

'What about Cutty?' he said.

He hadn't known he was going to say that. The words had happened and Dan was as surprised by them as Mason was. Why had he said it? Was he seriously trying to get money for Cutty? Were the words just a ritual for making himself feel better in taking it? If Mason gave him some money for Cutty, would that make it easier for him to accept Mason's offer?

'What about him?' Mason asked.

'He gets nothing?'

'He lost.'

'He was half o' the fight.'

'Not my half, he wasn't.'

'But you're the man that won the money.'

'That's right.'

'Ye could give him somethin'.'

'Aye. And I could give something to a blind beggar if I wanted.' He smiled. 'Unfortunate comparison. But I don't want to.'

'Ah think ye should, though.'

'That's interesting.'

They stood staring at each other. Mason was watching Dan expectantly, his eyebrows raised, his mouth slightly open. Dan knew in that moment that nothing he could say was going to change Mason's mind. Mason knew the way it had to be and for him the interest of what Dan was saying lay only in the amazingness of hearing someone who thought it could be otherwise. But Dan couldn't stop his mouth from talking. It was as if a part of him was still trying to redefine the terms on which one of them gave and one of them received the money, to haggle for a contract both of them could sign, to justify the fact that each of them stood there with shared money in his hand.

'He made you money,' Dan said.

Mason shook his head.

'He made you money,' Dan said. 'You made money from him.'

'I made money from me. I arranged it. I picked my man. I got him ready. I made the bet. So who made me money? Me. Cutty Dawson was just an incidental factor. Something I had to calculate for. And I got it right. The same way I got you right. If it hadn't been him, it would've been somebody else. If it hadn't been you, it would've been somebody else. This was between Cam Colvin and me. We're the ones who invested in it. We're the ones who say where the wages go.' He nodded at Dan's hand. 'I've paid you.'

'But Cutty helped tae make it happen.'

'Cutty did what he was told. Well, nearly. Except that he didn't win.'

'He should still get somethin'.'

Mason was getting impatient.

'So you've got money,' he said. 'You give him something.'

Dan hesitated briefly.

'All right,' he said. 'But then you match it?'

Mason's hand paused on its way back to the safe.

'What?'

'Look. Ah'll give Cutty what ye called the bonus.' Dan counted two hundred and fifty pounds out on the desk. He looked back at Mason. Mason's lips were pursed, as if he were trying not to smile. 'Two hundred and fifty pounds. You double it. Fair enough?'

'Sure,' Mason said. 'But that's all you want? You don't think I should pay him a pension? As well as a lump sum.'

Mason was smiling. He reached into the safe and left the rest of the money there. As his hand went to the door of the safe to push it shut, Dan knew this meant Cutty was locked out for good and that Dan himself was finally defined and from the confusion in him, instinctive as if some primitive sense of himself were calling out its name, came one word.

'No!' he said.

The word seemed to work his arm, and his hand, still clutching five hundred pounds, swung on the axis of his conviction, quenched Mason's smile. Mason fell, and his head made dull contact with the wooden back of his chair as he settled clumsily on the floor. He didn't move.

Dan listened to the silence – no one was coming – and stared into the darkness of the choice he had made, alive with unseen implications. But he had made it. The obliteration of a lot of vague possibilities clarified the real ones. Thought and action became fused, began to happen as one.

He stepped gingerly round Matt Mason, bent to check his breathing. He might have been peacefully asleep. Dan's hand paused at the mouth of the open safe. He couldn't see inside that small black hole. He found his hand reluctant to go inside, as though it might get bitten off. He had never stolen anything in his life. Even when his friends at school used to make the traditional group raids on Woolworth's, it was a rite of passage he had never engaged in. But he forced his hand into the darkness and groped there. He came out with something wrapped in plastic and took a second or two to realise it was a gun. He briefly imagined it pointed at himself. Holding the gun in his left hand, he stretched into the safe again and brought out the wad of money from which Mason had paid him. He replaced the gun. He quickly counted out twenty-five tenners on top of the money he had left on the desk and replaced the rest in the safe. He pushed the safe shut gently, hearing it click. He put the thousand pounds together and stuffed it into his pocket. He made sure Mason was still unconscious, came out of the room and closed the door very quietly.

He checked that the keys were still on the hall table and moved, almost at a run, towards the lounge. Clamping a smile on his face, he pushed the door open.

'Here, Frankie,' he said.

The faces that simultaneously turned in response seemed to him threatening, but he nodded to them and winked.

'Matt wants ye tae come through here wi' us for a minute.'

'Oh-ho,' Roddy Stewart said. 'Serious business being discussed.'

'When ye gotta go, ye gotta go,' Frankie said.

Sandra raised a mock protest.

'Don't worry, ladies,' Roddy Stewart said. 'I'll keep you entertained.'

'That's what's worrying me,' Frankie said as he came out.

Dan closed the door.

'So what's this? You two need to call in expert advice? I knew it would happen.'

'That's right, Frankie,' Dan said in a loud voice and grabbed his arm.

Frankie looked up at Dan in surprise. Dan put his finger over his mouth and walked past the door to Matt Mason's study. Seeing Frankie about to say something, Dan grimaced, shook his head and raised a clenched fist in an orgy of warning signals. The ludicrousness of it was enough to stun Frankie into silence. Still gripping Frankie's arm, Dan silently opened the cupboard in the hall where his travelling bag had been left. He lifted the bag out and eased the door shut with his foot. He let go of Frankie's arm long enough to open the outside-door and pushed Frankie firmly out on to the step. He lifted the car keys from the hall table. He stepped outside, put down his travelling bag and eased the door delicately shut.

The coolness of the night hit him with the realisation of what he had done, like an anaesthetic wearing off. Frankie was staring in horror at the closed door, acting out Dan's own feeling.

'Whit the fuck is this?'

'You're drivin',' Dan said.

In Frankie's eyes possibilities were trying to surface and drowning in disbelief.

'No way,' he said. 'Ye're on yer own, big man. Whit have ye done?'

Dan caught him and threw him against the car.

'Ah'm countin' ma chances in seconds, fucker,' Dan said.

He opened the driver's door and jabbed his forefinger at the seat.

'In! Now!'

Frankie was bundled in. Dan gave him the keys, eased the door closed and ran round the front of the car. He threw his travelling bag in the back seat as he got in.

'Drive quietly till ye're out the drive,' he said.

'Listen –'

Dan's hand was on the back of Frankie's neck. It felt like having his head caught in a clamp.

'Drive now or Ah'll break yer fuckin' neck.'

Frankie let the car murmur out on to the roadway.

'The hospital,' Dan said. 'As fast as ye can make it.'

As the car moved further away from the house, the silence was a widening separation. They sat in the same car but they felt like men travelling in different directions. The further they went, the more irrevocable became Dan's sense of what he had done. From the bright and sudden certainty of that moment in the house, he was moving into shadow, towards what felt to him at this moment like a future of doubts that would only end when he did. Frankie's head was making the opposite journey. Behind him was whatever had happened, which he didn't know about. All he knew was that it was something very bad and very dangerous and that the further they went away from it, the worse their destination was likely to be. He was trying to work out ways to make that destination safe. Whatever had taken place back at Matt's, there had to be some way to forestall its possible consequences for himself. But in order to do that, he had to know more about it.

'All right, Dan,' he said. 'So Ah'm drivin' ye. But at least tell me whit's happened. Whit did ye do in there?'

Dan seemed to be wondering himself.

'Ah knocked him out.'

'Jesus Christ! Oh, Jesus Christ! Have you went mad? Why? An' what's this we're doin'? You tryin' to steal his car now? This is Matt Mason ye're dealin' with.'

'You're here tae take the car back, Frankie. After ye run me tae the station.'

'Jesus Christ! Ah've to go back on ma own? Thanks very much. Why did ye have to involve me in this shite?'

'Ah know, Frankie,' Dan said. 'Ah just picked yer name out the hat.'

'Let's go back now, Dan.'

'Where to?'

'Listen. If we go back right now, there might still be a chance. Ye can say it was just like a fit or somethin'. Maybe even that ye're still a wee bit punchy from big Cutty. Somethin' like that.'

Frankie was wishing he could convince himself. That might have given him a better chance of persuading Dan.

'Ah'm goin' back tae see Cutty. Ah've got money for him.'

Frankie was so busy trying to follow through with his own specious reasoning that it took him a moment to hear what Dan had said. When it registered, he almost mounted the pavement.

'Money?'

Dan said nothing.

'What money, Dan? What money?'

'The money Ah took out the safe.'

Frankie was a robot for several seconds. When he spoke, he spoke quietly, in a flat voice.

'Ah'm drivin' a hearse, Dan,' he said.

He didn't want to know any more. He knew enough to know that Dan wouldn't be going back. Dan couldn't go back. I'm

227

right, Frankie thought, this is a hearse. The only thing Frankie could do now was to try to make sure that it only had one dead man in it. What Dan Scoular was dying of could be contagious.

Frankie glanced across at him staring through the windscreen. He felt as if he were already taking his farewell of that face which over the past weeks had seemed to him about as familiar as his own. He imagined it wouldn't find that slow, thoughtful smile many more times from now on. The wasted possibilities angered Frankie. He reflected on the ingratitude of Dan Scoular, the way in which he had so carelessly implicated Frankie in what he had done, the spectacular stupidity of his actions. Given time, there was a lot Frankie could have taught him. In three weeks he had opened up for himself the kind of opportunity Frankie had dreamed about most of his life. But Frankie said nothing. Words were wasted on a corpse.

Neither had spoken again when Frankie pulled up at the entrance to the hospital.

'Give me two minutes,' Dan said.

He got out of the car and stood for a minute on the hospital steps, separating his money into two bundles and putting each bundle in a different pocket. The reception desk was empty but he could hear movement in the office behind it. He moved quickly and quietly, knowing this time exactly where he was going. He reached the door of Cutty's room without being seen.

Cutty was lying with the night light on, just as Dan had left him. What else would he be doing? He sounded as if he might be asleep. Dan tiptoed across to the bed. He took the money from his right-hand pocket, neatly folded, and eased it into the palm of Cutty's hand. The hand made no response and Dan gently closed the fingers round the money.

'What?' Cutty said and was awake.

'Cutty. It's me. Dan Scoular.'

'Dan Scoular?'

'Dan Scoular.'

Cutty's hand stirred, feeling the notes.

'Whit's this?'

'We had a whip-roon' for ye, Cutty. That's for you.'

'For me, Dan? What is it?'

228

'Five hundred quid.'

'Where does this come fae?'

'It's whit ye earned, Cutty. You take it.'

Cutty's hand eventually closed on the money.

'Ah canny believe it,' he said.

'You hide it somewhere. Ye want me tae put it somewhere for ye?'

'Naw. Don't you worry. Ah'll hold it till the wife gets here.'

'Good luck, Cutty. Ah've got tae go.'

He pressed his arm and was at the door when Cutty's voice stopped him.

'Dan. You sure this is all right?'

'It is for the night. The morra's the morra.'

'Well, whatever happens about it. Thanks for doin' this.'

On the way downstairs Dan was stopped by a nurse who wanted to know what he was doing here.

'Don't worry, hen,' Dan said. 'Ah've already been chased. One o' the sisters saw me there an' gave me ma walkin' papers. Ah wis tryin' tae see somebody. Ah'm sorry.'

He moved too quickly to allow her professional indignation to regroup. He halted at the top of the steps outside and saw first that the car was gone and then that his travelling bag had been left on the bottom step. He was already running by the time he picked up the bag.

He remembered that they had passed a taxi-rank on the way to the hospital. There had been three taxis waiting. But he estimated that it was more than half a mile away. As he ran, he was watching any cars that were coming, very carefully. He was surprised at the freedom with which his body moved, at the clarity of his head, the decisiveness he felt in himself.

When he glanced back and saw a taxi coming with its 'for hire' sign lit, he ran into the middle of the road and flagged it down. It occurred to him that the quicker he got off the streets the better and that a taxi-rank was a place that they might watch. He was inside with his bag on the floor and the door shut before the driver had his handbrake on.

'How much tae take me tae Thornbank?' Dan said.

'Tae where?'

'Thornbank.'

'Thornliebank?'

'Naw. Thorn-bank.'

'Well, that depends.'

'On what?'

'Like where the hell it is, for starters. That could be south o' Manchester for all Ah know, by the way. Ye don't have tae take a boat, do ye?'

'Ye take the road tae Ayr. Ah can direct ye fae there.'

'Christ, ye're talkin' about somethin' there, son. Ye need the sherpa dogs for that yin. Yer name widny be Captain Oates, wid it? Ye see. Ye've a third on to the fare once ye go outside the city limits. An ye're well outside the limits wi' this yin. We could fa' off the edge o' the world here.'

'Look. If it's not on, just take me tae a taxi-rank. Like the one at Central Station.'

'Not on? Son, Outer Mongolia's on. That's what Ah'm here for. Ah'm just tryin' tae clarify the situation for ye, like. We're talkin' twenty-five tae thirty quid. Or we could be. Depends how far fae Ayr ye are.'

'That's fair enough.'

'Right ye are, ma son. You sit back an' enjoy the drive.'

The driver's attempts to keep a conversation going approached Dan's silence several times but could find no way past his monosyllabic responses. Action over for the moment, Dan was wondering how far he agreed with himself.

The image of his travelling bag sitting at the bottom of the steps came back to him. It seemed to convey to him what he had done, who he was. It fixed itself in his mind with a symbolic completeness, like a family crest. His sense of himself had no permanent residence. It would travel with him from day to day as long as he lived. Its luggage was light. There was no room there for the certainties his father had owned. Dan saw such certainties as dead weights.

He couldn't share his father's belief in the sureness of social improvement. All of his experience had made him doubt it. His discovery through the fight of what was in himself had confirmed these doubts. He couldn't imitate Cutty Dawson's stoic acceptance, the certainty of his faith in his own strength. Dan had learned the pointlessness of his strength. It had been his doubts that had enabled him to beat Cutty, his awareness of his own vulnerability that Betty had taught him. He couldn't obey Matt Mason's commandment. That would have been to pretend that his nature had only one reflex when it had many.

The fight which he had been regarding as some kind of arrival had become a new starting-point, one which presumed no particular future destination but which denied the arbitrariness of a past one. It hadn't said, 'This is where we'll go,' but simply, 'That is where we won't go.'

It had clarified his choices for him. Forced to go to the limits of himself, he had discovered a violence and a selfishness and a capacity to feed on others that he hadn't known the extent of before. He reflected that he had previously only found fragments of the awareness he now had, in dreams and when he did things in drink of which he wouldn't have thought himself capable.

Yet he was glad to know himself more fully. No matter how bad the news, it was of himself. He needed it. The fight with Cutty was a fight with himself and it would never be over, that second fight. Striking Matt Mason had proved that. Frightened as he was of what he had done, he couldn't wish to retract it. It was the gesture by which he insisted on a continuing choice. No one else was going to tell him what his experience meant. No matter what they did to his body, while his head worked he would decide what it meant to him.

They were beyond where Graithnock had been. The driver was asking for directions. It was a good question, Dan thought.

'Ye take left at the first roundabout. Then ye take yer first left off the dual carriageway.'

'Over an' out.'

He would come to Thornbank the back way, through Fardle Wood. That way, the driver wouldn't know where he was going. That was maybe crazy but so was his position. Paranoia was perhaps permissible just for tonight. When he told the driver to stop, they were on an empty road, with the wood a hill of darkness on their right.

'Here?'

'Here.'

The cab pulled into the side of the road. The driver put on the interior light. He did his calculations. He wanted twenty-five pounds. Dan gave him twenty-eight.

'Ye're a decent man, big yin.'

Dan noticed him studying his face for the first time. He hoped all the driver was taking note of were the bruises. Dan remembered someone saying at the party that he looked like a Red Indian. The driver looked as if he were trying to work out which tribe – maybe Hopi, being left here to go the rest of the way on foot.

'Ye sure this is where ye want off?'

'This is it.'

'It's just that it doesny look like anywhere.'

'Maybe no' to you.'

The driver stared back at him, suddenly smiled.

'Ah don't know whit ye're up to, big man,' he said. 'But Ah think Ah'm on your side.'

Dan winked.

'You're a sound judge,' he said. 'Cheers.'

'Cheerio. An' good luck tae ye.'

Dan slammed the door shut, crossed the road, climbed the fence and in fifty yards was wrapped in trees. He knew the wood but in the darkness it was unfamiliar. A lot of days of his boyhood had been spent in this place. It was as if he were back there. The place was liquid with darkness. Sounds happened with infinite suggestiveness around him. He sensed his way forward. Every step was a mystery. But he welcomed the strangeness, defined himself in relation to it. It was like rediscovering the excitement of boyhood. The strangeness of the place became the strangeness of himself. The unexplored possibilities around him became the unexplored possibilities within him. Here, Matt Mason's study contracted to the size of a stone.

'Fuck it!' he suddenly bellowed into the darkness. 'Ah'm who Ah'll be.' Don't make the headstone yet, he thought. And then he promised himself quietly, 'Betty! All Ah'm offering is me. You take it or leave it!'

He began to move through the darkness as if it were where he belonged. The bag swung in his hand weightless, just a part of himself.

8

The possible consequences followed him home over the next
few days. The aftermath of violence seized him like an ague,
bringing the nervous restlessness of a prolonged hangover. In
those moments of shivering rejection of a recent self, nothing
seemed trivial. Small problems magnified to overwhelming
proportions. An oppressive and focusless dread played on his
raw nerve-ends.

That was the time when Mr Hyde turns back into Doctor
Jekyll, obliging him to find accommodation in his daily life for
an enormity he isn't sure he can live with. Dan Scoular was
terrified by what he had done. He went through a time of
hallucinating Matt Mason's retribution in various forms. He
was walking in the street when a car pulled up beside him.
That was a recurring image in his mind, suddenly blocking
the progress of whatever he was trying to think about. It was
an image which spawned various extensions of itself like the
nodes of a proliferating cancer. Sometimes there were several
men in the car with harsh faces he didn't know but all of
them wearing expressions of intense malice towards him like
carvings. Sometimes only Matt Mason sat in the back seat of
the car. Sometimes the car was white and sometimes black.
Sometimes the street was dark, empty of everything except
what was to happen to him. Sometimes it was daylight and
the street was busy with people moving like sleepwalkers on
private errands that made them oblivious to him. Sometimes
the doors of the car burst open and the men came out and the
sensation he felt was of going under a stampede. Sometimes
the back window of the car slid down and a gun pointed out
and a galaxy of fiery light bloomed soundlessly from the
muzzle, scattering him into limitless space.

There were other images that happened without warning in
his mind, so sudden, so fully realised that he wondered if they
were remembered fragments of a dream. He knew he was
dreaming a lot but he couldn't remember the substance of the

233

dreams, perhaps because a part of him didn't want to face the content. Only he wakened so much, often several times in a night, with that fear that things were irreparably wrong, that there was no escape from where he was and where he was was a dangerous place.

The commonest of those sudden images was one of his own crumpled body. The background it lay against was vague. It could have been carpet or wooden floor or stone. He was looking down on it and he didn't know whether it was dead or just severely injured. But that wasn't the most frightening image. The most frightening images were ones he wouldn't allow to fulfil themselves in his thoughts. They remained fragmentary because his mind rejected them in panic, tore them as they occurred.

They were images of Betty and Raymond and young Danny injured. They were of blood and discoloured skin, head wounds, a pulped eye, a body twisted beyond the hope of being again what it had been. They were a terrible gallery he couldn't bear to enter, a room of his own mind that held the half-formed nightmare possibilities of what the world can make happen to the people we love. They were the last place of his fear and they turned him back towards trying to find a way to live where he found himself to be.

If he wasn't prepared to contemplate those things as imminent possibilities, he had to find a way to make them less likely. He must avoid the temptation to hide out in the house because that would be attracting the danger towards his family. If Matt Mason was determined to find him, he might get impatient of looking for him elsewhere. But if Dan was out and about, Matt Mason would presumably choose to deal with him outside. Dan would have to live with as few external signs of panic as possible and with the maximum vigilance possible. He must let the pattern of his life say one thing while he constantly reminded himself of the truth that was its secret. He must let himself be found and be constantly prepared for when he might be found. He must be vulnerable and strong.

In search of that strength, he forced himself to look honestly at what he had done, to think over its implications instead of cringing away from them. He had to admit to himself that the money he had given Cutty Dawson was a dubious gift. Apart from the fact that it was too little to be of much use to Cutty, Dan was in no way sure that he would be allowed to keep it. At least, whether it was taken back from him or not, he should be safe from violence. From Cutty's tone in the hospital, Dan could imagine him making efforts to have the money given back without his having been asked for it.

Yet that moment in the dimly lit room, when he had blindly given a gift that was blindly received, stayed with him as something he couldn't wish undone, one of the most necessary acts of his life. It was an acknowledgment of faith he had needed to find a way to make. The money, so trivial in itself, had been the only means to hand by which to express his belief. The water in a baptism is just water, the wafer in communion just a wafer. It was what he had taken on with the action that had mattered, where in the doing of it he had irrevocably placed himself.

That, he understood in thinking back to it, must have been one reason why he had done it. It locked him out of compromise, prevarication. He had defined his choices by turning towards what he truly believed and meeting whatever it involved. In the frightening tension of it was the truth of himself.

The clarity of the realisation burned away some of his past confusions like dross. The punch with which he had hit Matt Mason felt to him now like the last one he ever wanted to throw, the last and one true blow of his fight with Cutty Dawson, a paradox of violence terminating itself with violence, a voice speaking in him to say it didn't wish to speak. He saw the past violence he had offered other men like himself as self-inflicted wounds. If he had to fight again, he wanted it only to be against Matt Mason or whoever was hired by him. He was finished with skirmishes. He was enlisted in a war. He wanted to know who was on his side.

In a sense, they had started making love before the meal. Neither of them could have fixed the moment of its beginning, the time when the pleasure of being together and just sharing the same space, that marvellous rough alloy of looks and accidental brushings and unnecessary things said and thoughts shared without being spoken, began to refine itself into compulsion, to move towards the purity of lust. But by early that Wednesday evening, when Betty was making the meal and Dan was laying the table – while the boys watched television – they were already part of a ceremony being conducted in secret between them. Dan saw Betty reach upwards into a cupboard and her hips innocently achieved the angle of desire. She was aware of how his body seemed not just to be in the room but almost to fill it. Both felt a kindling of want in them.

The distances they had put between each other since Sunday had contracted. He had told her what he had done and the uncertainty of all he knew how to offer. In admitting about Gordon, she had stated no decision. She had refused to succumb merely because he was at risk. He had refused to woo her with false promises just because she held herself apart. Both were aware of lovers' blackmail and knew themselves in a place too serious for that. They knew how that black art could cripple truth of feeling. They had spoken to each other and listened to each other and they had waited. What happened would interpret. The thoughts were left to grow in acceptance or close in refusal. The risk was necessary, they knew. They were finding what they meant to each other. That wasn't a decision just for thought or voices.

That evening it was as though their bodies had begun to swim through those thoughts and fears and memories and hopes slowly towards each other. That was a complicated journey, full of treacherous eddies, sudden undercurrents. Past pain pulled against them, past happiness nudged them forward. But the fierceness of their secret, of the places they had taken each other, of the past admissions they had drawn from their own bodies, was gathering its compulsion and threatening to lay waste every other concern. While they moved around the banality of the kitchen, they were tentatively agreeing in coded looks and touches and feelings that each was where the other's passion was. Each might live without the other, they were discovering, but if they did, their lives, they believed, would always be less than they might have been. The feeling grew, vivid and wild, in the interstices of the ordinary things they did.

The meal was more than a meal. With remarks and glances and the passing of objects, they were reinforcing where they had been, putting a light in the window for where they might come from. It was a muted conjuration of the past, a sketch that gave the future putative shape. Small moments set up multiple echoes.

'Oor Danny says he wants to be a pilot,' Raymond said.

Danny sat staring calmly ahead, chewing.

'What kind of pilot?' Dan asked.

'A Spitfire pilot.'

Betty remembered the Second World War film that had been on television.

'Ye better get a leather hat then,' Dan said. 'Ye canny be a Spitfire pilot minus the leather hat.'

'You shouldn't be too busy, anyway,' Betty said.

'Aye.' Dan smiled at her. 'It's like the joke about wanting a job as a flag-day collector in Aberdeen.'

'Ah told him there aren't any Spitfires,' Raymond said smugly.

Dan looked at him.

'You ever travel on the Blackbrae bus?' Dan said.

'What?'

Betty laughed and nodded to Dan. She remembered telling him, a couple of years ago last Christmas, of an incident she had seen on the bus from Blackbrae. A woman and a child of about six had been chatting on the bus. The girl had been asking her mother if she was sure Santa Claus would come and how he was going to get into the house, since they didn't have a coal fire. Betty was aware of a small boy who might have been eight years old. He was sitting across from the mother and daughter, rocking backwards and forwards and clicking his fingers in rhythm to some tune that only he was hearing and he was listening intently to the conversation.

'But how will he know where we're stayin'? We didn't stay in this house last year.'

'Santa knows, love. Santa knows.'

'Will he come in the window?'

'He might. Santa's got his own way of doing things.'

They had all come off the bus at the same stop. Walking behind them, Betty saw the mother and daughter still engrossed in conversation and the small boy drawing level with them, timing his moment.

'Haw, hen,' he called as he passed them. 'There's nae fuckin' Santa!'

Then he was off at a run, laughing like a happy bacterium, to spread his disillusionment elsewhere.

'Ah can still be one if Ah want,' Danny said.

'Where? In a museum?'

'Dad!'

'Maybe not a Spitfire pilot, Danny,' Dan said. 'But ye could still be a pilot. Ye could be an airline pilot.'

'Ye've got to be clever to be that,' Raymond said. 'You don't like arithmetic. Ye would need to be good at arithmetic.'

'And what do you want to be, Ray?' Dan asked. 'A child murderer?'

Betty thought that she would never get tired of seeing Dan's face and, as they all went on to discuss bizarre ambitions with apparent seriousness, the conversation evoked a mood among them that couldn't have been explained by the specifics of what they said, no more than the effect of a piece of music could be explained by the notation. The boys projected the future as if it were located just across the room. Dan and Betty, less innocently certain about themselves, nevertheless caught the refraction of mutual possibilities and felt the regenerative force of the rooted past. On that feeling the certainty of what would happen this evening bloomed, like the first signs of possible new growth.

They would make love, were making love. By tone and movement and look, they were engaging in a kind of decorous and subtle foreplay. While experiencing the feeling, Betty was also trying to interpret it. She was aware how dangerous it would be for her to let happen something which she might want to renege on later. She didn't want to waken up and find that she had merely been trapped again by habit.

But that wasn't how she felt it would be. The sensation she had was not of familiarity but of renewed risk. She felt afresh the exciting unpredictability of their two presences. It was a feeling Gordon and she had never created between them. Perhaps that was why they hadn't tried to realise their relationship more fully. All the possibilities they had talked about were somehow anonymous, like package deals in a brochure. They could have been inhabited by any other two people as well as themselves. They were a shared abstraction, ideas of how a life might be. With some surprise she realised that the feeling she had just now was simply personal to her. It was an irrefutable part of herself, a compulsion that she might resist or try to manipulate but which she couldn't deny. Anything else was just a holiday, not quite to be taken seriously.

If this was what she meant by 'love', it didn't feel to her safe at all. It felt very dangerous. It had no form that she could trust in. It wasn't about being married to Dan. It was about their being together for just now. It wasn't form. It was content, waiting for form.

She understood that the risk of looking for that form was loss of self. At the furthest reaches of the intensity of commitment to the other lay the possibility of total betrayal. She thought some people emasculated their passion by calling comfort and withdrawal from doubt by the name of love. Whatever love was, she found it almost frighteningly various. It had many faces, all of them your own, and some of them were as terrifying as grotesque masks.

In the sexuality of Dan and herself, what love appeared to mean shifted bewilderingly. In the extremity of their love-making, she had sometimes been afraid of herself, had suspected 'love' of being a noble, ceremonial pretence that individuals conspired in with each other to contain, as with gossamer (the strength of which lay in believing in its strength), the utter rawness and promiscuity of their passion, a way of putting a face on the void, painting a mask on the darkness, the last socially habitable cliff-edge above the abyss of pure animality.

At such moments she depended on the tenderness that followed. That, too, was love – the iron rations of mutual concern they took with them on that most dangerous of journeys towards the truth of themselves, the cache at the last camp, the psychic strength of the other that eventually would be all that you could feed on.

You were taking so many chances. You were going beyond manners, self-censorship, deliberate projection of the 'good', conventional kindness, morality, your carefully structured sense of yourself. You were discovering yourself without cerebral protection. You were helplessly becoming who you were.

239

Knowing, throughout the evening, the intense exchange of selves towards which they were moving, feeling again the mysteriousness of her own body, Betty remembered the effect their early love-making had had on her. Before that, it had seemed to her in retrospect, her body had been like luggage. She felt now again the tremors of expectation, each pore coming alive. But as she moved towards the fulfilment of the feeling, she understood what she was leaving behind. The possibilities she had been imagining with Gordon would be erased for her. She couldn't release herself into what might happen unless she acknowledged that to herself. The force of what was coming would only yield itself to you if you yielded yourself to it, were prepared to be changed by it. She was prepared and when, with the children in bed, Dan raised his eyebrows in question, she nodded.

As he lay in bed, Dan heard her urinating and the sound excited him. He thought how even beyond the expressions of his love for her he had achieved there was an area that was still his secret, small moments too numerous to inventory to which his hoarded feelings attached themselves. There were movements she made and ways she looked that stirred him inexplicably. When she came into the bedroom, he was waiting for one of those moments. He knew the exact sequence in which she would undress and he watched her surface stage by stage out of her clothes until she was naked. She left the light on as she came into bed.

With their eyes closed, they became touch, a slow braille. They touched with skin, with hands, with mouths. They lost the sense of each other's body's contours and their own, felt themselves extend and drift, dissolving into each other. Coherent thought burnt to a smoke of sensation in which the gaudy images began. Sounds came, brute at first, evolving clumsily into words. The words became hyperboles, groping towards the feelings they tried to reach. They wanted to do more than one thing at a time. They made wild shapes of each other. They caught seen fragments of themselves: the savage eyes, the face a hewn intensity, the arching belly, the writhe of hips. They became lost in waves of feeling, the moiling of their own flesh, and clung to each other like an act of faith, a giving of fierce truth in trust, half-afraid that the other might pull back and leave them stranded there, naked, revealed. The force of what they had felt was only bearable by being shared, by nothing being done that both didn't want to do. And when they finally came together, they shuddered uncontrollably as if some spirit of each was trying to pass out of the body.

They lay still and held each other. There had been such a welter of tenderness and ferocity and caring and selfishness and submission and control that for a time it seemed that nothing had survived it. But they had had the courage to throw everything into the maelstrom and in the following calm that drifted them away from its whirling power, they found they had emerged with the human gifts of tenderness and passion and kindness cleanly theirs, earned on their bodies, not ingested like socially processed capsules. They had discovered them for themselves through the honesty of their experience. They hadn't learned them by rote in the abstract.

They faced each other and knew where they were. Nothing was certain. But they would try. They cuddled, which was their passion putting on its working clothes.

'Glad Ah picked this side of the bed,' Dan said.

'Why?'

'Because you're nearer the light. Gonny put it out?'

'You mean that's it?' Betty said.

They laughed.

The sound of her key in the lock was a whispered promise. He quickened into expectation and wanted to know what it was saying. When she came in, her face was heightened with the night air and her eyes, adjusting to the light, seemed startled by the room, the strange place where he was sitting. He caught a whiff of where she came from, spoor of an evening he would never know. He was jealous of her acquaintance with the night. She crossed and kissed him.

'I could use a coffee,' she said. 'You want one?'

'Aye. Why not, love?'

'The boys all right?'

'They're sleeping.'

She took off her coat and threw it on the couch and, as he heard her feet go up the stairs, the anger came. His rage was with her, with Gordon Struthers, with the innocence of the children, but mostly with himself. He should not have let her go. He should have done more than this. But he clung to the sound of her checking the children while the rage passed through him like a small hurricane, leaving him shaken. The sounds of her in the kitchen, the kettle being filled, the gas going on, cups finding their places in saucers, reminded him that he might not have them long. He wondered what she was thinking.

She was thinking that these sounds told her what she had done, and she was glad. She had given up an idea for a passion. She knew that the intensity she felt towards him was the greater for its foregoing of alternatives. She wanted to tell him so much and she made him coffee. Every smallest thing she did reaffirmed the passion of her choice. She hoped that somehow he might understand.

When she came back into the room, she loved the modesty of his uniqueness. He sat pursing his mouth into a thought. His blue eyes were vivid against the darkness of his hair. His face was a shape she wanted her future to have. He glanced at her and winked. The moment claimed her. Her heart rose in her like applause. She knew all the things he was balancing in himself and he did it with grace. His amazingness was utterly practical. She didn't know how to express what she felt. She gave him a cup of coffee. Returning the gorilla's banana, she thought, and knew they were a code no one else could crack.

'Thanks, love.'

He was grateful for the colour of her hair, those eyes so dark, they burned him. For he was glad he had made such provision as he could, taken the trips to Graithnock. He raised his coffee cup to toast her. They sat drinking together, haunted by the future. When she had finished her coffee, she came and knelt beside him.

'Forgive me,' she said.

His fingers were testing the texture of her hair, as if he had just discovered it.

'Only if you'll forgive me,' he said.

She partly knew and partly didn't know what he meant. The part she didn't know didn't matter, for his ignorance was as great as hers.

'Agreed.'

'Agreed.'

When they went upstairs, they made love and fell asleep and Betty woke suddenly, aware of Dan watching her in the dim light from outside. It was as if he had stared her awake.

'What?' she said.

He smiled and stroked her hair.

'What time is it?' she asked.

He said nothing. She turned her head round and peered at the digital alarm through her sleepiness. It was 2.28. They lay touching and stroking, and murmuring as if they were creating new words. Betty wanted to blindfold the alarm. She recalled a childhood desire of hers and felt it repeat itself in her now. It was to have a machine that could control the clock of public lives, put it back and let others go on sleeping until Dan and she had reached the limit of the moment, were ready to face them again. But she was thirty-two now and there was no such machine.

With the dressing-table mirror tilted up, he combed his hair carefully. The bruising on his face had almost gone. There was a slight yellowness around one eye. He didn't hear her coming in. She spoke from the doorway of the bedroom and when he glanced up he knew from her stillness that she had been watching him for some time.

'Where are you going?'

'Oh not again,' he said. He was smiling. 'Do we need this rigmarole every Sunday night?'

Her expression refused to join him in the joke. She stared at him and the fear in her eyes shamed his attempted flippancy. It was a fear he shared and their mutual acknowledgment of it estranged them from the room. What had been familiar became sinister. The bed looked cold and uninviting. The mobile of metal butterflies hanging from the ceiling found wind where there was none that they could feel and it span, clashing softly. The accoutrements on the dressing-table were an array of vanities.

The routine that had carried them through a week broke down in that moment and this was as far as it had brought them. They faced each other across a bleak admission. Dan

243

fingered some loose hairs from his comb in a pretence of normalcy. Neither of them was convinced.

'You can't go there,' Betty said.

'Come on, Betty. Where else would Ah go?'

'But why?'

'It's a thing Ah do. Ah haven't got much. Nobody's goin' to make me settle for less.'

She looked wildly round the room as if it was a trap.

'I wish we could go away from here.'

'Where would we go? The Bahamas? Nah, Betty. This is where we live. So do a lot of other good people. We should be trying to improve this place, not go elsewhere.'

'But this is the most likely night. If they're looking for you, this would be the night. And the pub would be the place. Not tonight, Dan. Wait even a week.'

'They're more likely to wait. Till things've died down a bit. Tonight's probably as safe as it's goin' tae get.'

'But what if they're there?'

'Then Ah better be as well. If they're there and Ah don't go. What d'you think they'll do? Leave it at that and go home? They would come here, Betty. Ah'm not havin' that. Not at any price. Ah'm goin'.'

'We could tell the police. I've been thinking about that. I think we should tell Scott Laidlaw.'

Dan winked at her.

'Ah already have. He's told his brother.'

'You told Scott?'

'Of course Ah did. Ah don't want to take any chances Ah don't have tae take. If Jack Laidlaw lets it be known discreetly that he's aware o' this, should be some kinda deterrent.'

'But did you tell him you took money?'

'Skated round that a bit. Ah mean, that's theft. But Ah don't think Matt Mason'll be keen tae file a complaint.'

The mention of the name broke through the numbness Betty had temporarily gained by talking about the practicalities of it. She heard the faint sounds of the television programme the boys were watching downstairs. She tried to think of something else to say but couldn't. The banal logic of Dan's reasons defeated her. Standing in the room, staring at her make-up accessories, hearing studio laughter from downstairs, she was horrified at the ordinariness of the terrible. Their lives were overhung by the will of others and the children were watching television and her husband was preparing to go out to the pub and any moment their right to the life they had could be foreclosed on. And who was to help them?

'It's going to be all right, Bette,' he said. 'Don't worry.'

'Dan. Who do you think you're speaking to? One of the children?'

'I just think it'll be all right.'

'Do you?'

She crossed towards the dressing-table, where her handbag was lying. She opened the bag and took out a folded form. It took Dan a few seconds to recognise the life insurance policy he had arranged during the week.

'Where did you get that?' he asked.

'Where you hid it.'

He had put it in the plastic bag where they kept such things, stored in a downstairs cupboard. Knowing that if anything happened to him she would have to look there, he had secreted it among a lot of other documents. While he was doing it, he had found the notes to his wedding speech, and the two of them held together in his hand, scribbled notes and precisely worded type, had been like a measure of the distance he had travelled since that time: from vague aspirations to a final contract, worked out in hard terms and offering no loopholes.

'Ah didn't hide it, Betty,' he said. 'Ah just put it in a safe place.'

'Was that all? I've had that in my handbag since yesterday, waiting for you to mention it first. Why didn't you tell me, Dan?'

'Ah would've done.'

'When? As a dramatic death-bed confession? Why did you do this?'

'Seemed like a good time to do it. Ah'm never goin' to be fitter, am Ah? That's the time tae let the medical men have a look at ye. An' Ah've got some money.'

'And you don't expect to live long?'

'Who doesn't?' He flexed his shoulders and winked at her but she didn't respond. 'Strong as a bull. But there's always the wee heart attacks an' runaway buses waitin' to have a go at ye. Betty. You've always been on at me to think of the future an' make some provision.'

He cuddled her and she put the piece of paper back in her handbag and they came downstairs. With the boys watching the television and Dan standing at the table with his jerkin on and discovering something in the paper that appeared to interest him and herself laying out some things for ironing, Betty felt there wasn't much more to be said. They both knew the fragility of where they were. They shared it beyond speech. It was their element. You didn't spend time discussing air, you just breathed it. This was normalcy, this preoccupation with small tasks in the face of possible death, this commitment to a marriage you weren't sure could last, this silent hysteria at the injustice of things. For Dan's sake, she tried to contain the panic that threatened her. But when he crossed and put his hands on the back of the boys' necks by way of cheerio and then made to go out, she followed him into the hall.

'Dan,' she said.

He turned and smiled at her.

'You've got two hours.'

His eyes widened.

'Sorry?'

'Two hours. All right?'

'Ye mean in the pub?'

'That's right.'

The smile enlarged.

'Ye kiddin,' Bette? What a hen peck ye're turnin' me into. Well, can Ah bring one of ma pals in to play when Ah come back?'

'I'm serious, Dan. You feel you've got to do this, all right. I'll accept it in a limited way. But if you're not back by that time, I'm going to get May in from next door and come up there myself.'

'All right, Bette. But Ah think you're just lookin' for an excuse for a bevvy.'

'Uh-huh.'

They laughed quietly and embraced. He felt her holding him tightly.

'It's got its advantages, this situation,' he said into her hair. 'Every time ye go to the pub ye say farewell as if ye were emigratin'. Ah like it fine.'

Outside, his last remark stayed with him. There was some truth in it. Everything felt heightened for him. He admitted to himself that he did think tonight was probably the most likely time. The awareness of his own danger gave everything around him a sharper edge, the way the threat of losing something intensifies your sense of its worth. Walking to the pub became a small experience. He appreciated the stillness of the evening, the lighted windows of the houses that colonised the darkness. At the same time, he was tense with the fear of what might be ahead.

Some stars were out. They gave perspective to the vastness of the sky, enlarged the night. He was reminded of the moment before the fight with Cutty, his awareness of how big the day was and how unnecessarily small their preoccupation was within it. He felt the same about where he was now.

But he accepted it. All experience was distorting lenses. What mattered was that, through maintaining the act of choice, you kept the freedom of your imagination to interpret the distortions. All anybody ultimately had the right to was their own vision. He had his, won from his own experience. He would abide the pain of his own findings.

He had chosen to live with the threat of Matt Mason's power and in the choice he had transformed that power. Matt Mason's power might be planning to determine the meaning of Dan Scoular's life, what significance it would have, perhaps even when it would end. But Dan Scoular was determining the significance of Matt Mason's power. By walking towards it, he put it in perspective. It wasn't master, it was servant to a truth it didn't realise, a truth Dan Scoular knew. It was Dan Scoular's sense of his own life given shape. The shape was already there and Matt Mason was deluding himself that he could make it different. So every day was a threat. Wasn't it always?

He thought of his father's life. His father, he thought, had taken this walk every day, with so many others. The only difference was in the awareness. He felt he was taking the walk for all of them again but this time with an understanding that was his gift to their baffled experience. He felt them with him. All that had happened between his walk here of a month ago and now was the truth. It lay in the tension between imposed experience and the vision that transformed it. That tension increased the nearer he came to the pub.

When he pushed open the door, the pub burst on his eyes, a sudden gift of colour and noise and smoke and warmth and danger. He was surprised how busy it was. Every table was occupied and there were several men at the bar. Voices greeted him and he tried to acknowledge them. By the time he reached the bar, a pint was waiting.

'This one's on me, Dan,' Alan said.

He was given his space. Drinking, he looked round in a way that was a habit with a new, heightened awareness concealed in it. All the faces seemed familiar, belonged there. The domino players had a fourth and at another table a second game was happening. He felt his tension tremor, settle for the moment. People at the bar to order a drink or on their way past to the lavatory would touch him or speak in the passing, congratulating him in a way that suggested they didn't just mean on winning a fight, or they would stop and talk for a time. Wullie Mairshall was one of them.

'Aye, Dan.'

'Wullie.'

'Well done, big man. Ma money was always on ye.'

'That was a chancy bet, Wullie. Ah was lucky tae get out alive, never mind win.'

'Nut at all, Dan. Ye were never in any danger.'

'Ah wish somebody had told me that.'

'That ither business, Dan?'

Dan looked at him and took a moment to know what he meant, as if the question were in an archaic language Dan could barely recognise. He saw Wullie staring out from his fixed position while everything around him was shifting and sliding. He was like a man still looking for landmarks in the open sea.

'Forget it, Wullie,' Dan said gently. 'Ah don't live there any more.'

'Ye mean you an' Betty –'

Dan shook his head and smiled.

248

'Betty an' me are fine. Ah mean all that other stuff's dead an' gone. You see you bury it. It's ma wife's business an' mine. All right?'

'Certainly, certainly. No offence . . .'

Dan saw Wullie's lips about to shape the familiar 'big man' and then abandon the sound. It was a mildly eerie feeling, like seeing your name erased from a commemorative tablet. As Wullie moved away, a worshipper who has found the shrine empty, Dan knew a just sense of himself in Wullie's disappointment. To be still Betty's man was a status greater than Wullie had wanted to bestow. He had never been who Wullie thought him to be. He was just glad to have discovered who he was, tense though that made him, coiling every time the pub door opened.

When it was Vince Mabon who came in, Dan watched him check the pub, still holding the door, and nod to someone outside. Frankie White followed him in. The presence of Frankie tautened Dan, as if he might be an outrunner. He had no substance in himself, Dan knew, but he suggested it, like the shadow of a hawk across a field.

Frankie was performing camaraderie as he came through the bar and Dan found it difficult to feel angry with him, even remembering his travelling bag sitting on the hospital steps, as if telling him he had been evicted from Frankie's life. You couldn't ask Frankie to stand by you. He was on the run from himself, had been all his life. Yet watching him improvise himself from person to person, Dan was moved by him. He was like a busker, earning his sense of himself from what other people could spare.

He came up and stood beside Dan while Vince Mabon stood on Dan's other side, as if they were putting him in brackets. Dan thought at first they were two strange people to be together and then thought perhaps they weren't, since one fed materially off people like himself and the other intellectually.

'Dan,' Frankie said. 'Can Ah buy ye a drink?'

'Thanks, Frankie. But Ah've got a pint.'

'A whisky then? After all, the fightin's over.'

'Is it? No thanks.'

Frankie seemed awkward for a moment, perhaps feeling the glibness of his mouth had said the wrong thing. He bought a whisky for himself and a pint for Vince Mabon.

'Dan. Ah'm sorry for leavin' ye like that. But Ah had no choice.'

'Forget it.'

Dan sipped at his pint.

'Ah mean that amounted to stealin' Matt Mason's car. An' then there was the money. Ah had tae get that car back. Ah had no choice.'

'It's all right. Ye just did whit ye do, Frankie.'

'As it was, Ah had tae make up a story.'

'Ah'm sure it was good. Ah hope Ah didn't disappoint ye by no' hangin' about the hospital till ye got back.'

'Ah didn't tell them that, Dan. Ah said Ah dropped ye in the town. Ah said ye told me you had Matt's permission.'

Dan felt the ambiguity of the moment, both the strangeness and the naturalness of their conversation held in balance. This was Frankie White, who came from Thornbank, often drank in here. This was a reminder of his possible death. This was a half-hearted friend, a half-hearted betrayer. This was the tension of threat alternating with the relaxation of ordinariness, like a prolonged experience of the moment when the whirr that stops the heart is just a bird rising suddenly from bushes. Dan felt the naturalness of danger, its ubiquity once you realised its nature.

'Does that mean they don't know Cutty got the money?'

'Don't know, Dan. Ah don't think so. Haven't heard too much. Ah mean, they're no' exactly invitin' me to join the inner circle. But as far as Ah know, they haven't looked near Cutty. He should be all right. One thing Ah *can* tell ye, Dan. They reckon his eyesight's goin' to be all right.'

'Huh. Where does that leave you, Dan?'

Vince Mabon had spoken for the first time. Dan looked at him.

'It leaves me where Ah'm standin', Vince.'

'But Cutty's going to be fine.'

'That's great. What else could it be?'

Frankie, with nostrils like a thoroughbred for changes in the atmosphere, intervened.

'What Vince means, Dan, is ye maybe feel ye jumped the gun a bit. Ah mean what ye did was spur o' the minute.'

'Ah know what Vince means, Frankie. He's no' that intellectual that Ah can't understand him. But do you know what Ah mean? Ah'm glad for Cutty. Ye think he's lettin' me down by gettin' his sight back? Ah didny just do it for Cutty. Ah did it for the two of us. It was maybe spur o' the minute. But it was good spur o' the minute. Ah'd been practisin' for it all ma life.'

Vince shook his head. Frankie seemed disappointed.

'Maybe Ah've wasted ma time comin' here,' Frankie said.

'It depends what ye came for, Frankie,' Dan said.

'To get you out.'

'Sorry?'

'Matt Mason's lookin' for ye, Dan. That's the word.'

'It would be, wouldn't it?'

'He's lookin' for ye.'

'He knows where Ah am.'

'It would be better if he didn't. Dan, it could be the night. Ah'm takin' a chance just bein' with you. But when Ah go out this pub, Ah'm havin' it away on ma toes. Like, well away. What about you?'

'What about me?'

'Dan. Don't ye understand what Ah'm tryin' to say?'

'Frankie, Ah don't think *you* understand what ye're tryin' to say. An' Ah don't think ye will. Ever. Where is it ye're goin'?'

'London!' Frankie said as if it was an incontrovertible argument.

'What good'll that do?'

'Ah'll be safe there. So would you. Ah know some people. Ah've got a few quid. Enough for the two of us. For a while at least. What d'ye say? Don't be a mug.'

Don't be a mug. Dan had often wondered about people's dread of being a mug, not getting it right, as if it was possible to get it right. He suspected that from the time Jack Ferguson had died in the quarry he had known you didn't get it right. If one person you loved could die, it couldn't be right. All you could do was try to get it wrong on your own terms; as honestly as you knew how. He thought of some of the times he had known people come together to lament a misguided life, a man on the drink or a woman who had thrown herself away. They were lamenting themselves by proxy, he had thought. For what did those who were sensible have that was so much better? Mortality was incurable, or didn't they know? Was it better to have a heart like a sewn purse and a life not so much spent as usured into death?

'Where's safe?' he said.

'London's safe! Ye comin'?'

'Ah live here, Frankie.'

'For how long?'

'Does anybody know that?'

Frankie took down his drink.

'Ah'm sorry if Ah helped to put ye in a bad place, Dan. But Ah'm doin' the best Ah can to put it right. Ah'm for London. Are ye comin'?'

'Cheerio, Frankie,' Dan said and, as Frankie's face went hurt and he turned away, 'Hey!'

Frankie turned back, tensed with the memory of that other time he had heard Dan say that. Dan smiled. For he meant the same thing now as he had meant then – give each of us the room to be ourselves – only now he knew what he meant.

'Ah'll miss you,' Dan said.

It was true, not just because he had come back from the dead in Dan Scoular's mind to offer him at least the chance to share in Frankie's demented life, such as it was, but because, as everybody did even in spite of themselves, he had helped Dan to a stronger sense of himself, and because he had never acted out of malice, only fear.

'Good luck wi' London.'

Frankie nodded and went out. Dan felt more vulnerable for his going. He missed him in that way, too. Frankie's changeability, once you had accustomed yourself to it, had its own value, in the way that the exact nature of a lie can give you an imaginative fix on the truth. Dan waited, checking the door by which Frankie had left, and then he checked the bar. A couple of people nodded into his wandering look. Everything was normal, even the way that Vince Mabon was shaking his head, as if the world would never get it right. Dan imagined Frankie telling Vince what had happened. He tried not to imagine Vince bringing his cosmic intelligence to bear upon the problem, solving it in seconds. But Vince didn't make it easy.

'You're a mug, Dan,' Vince said.

'So tell me what's new.'

'You've done it all wrong.'

'What is it wi' you two?' Dan said. 'Sentry duty? When one clocks off, the other clocks on?'

'You've done it all wrong.'

'How do ye do it right in this place? Ye do whit ye can. The best ye can.'

'You don't have the wider view, Dan.'

'Vince, who does?'

'Some do.'

'Very good then.'

'It's true. And the rest of us have to reach that higher consciousness.'

'Vince. There are people around have trouble readin' the *Daily Record*. Where do they figure in your Utopia? An' who told you you had "higher consciousness"? Whatever the fuck that is.'

'I didn't say I had it.'

'Then how do you know it's there?'

'Of course I know. You recognise it when you see it.'

'Any chance ye could attach yer mouth to yer brain? Ye judge everybody by what they do with what they've got an' how they cope with the circumstances they have. That's all. Ye're not goin' to ask an illiterate tae read a book. Ah think it's called context.'

'No, no. You're just compounding the problem. You did it wrong, Dan. You don't attack the individual. You attack the system.'

'The system. Where does it live? You got an address for it?'

'The individuals are irrelevant. Change the system, you'll change the individuals. It's the only way.'

Dan thought he wouldn't like to be discussing theory with Vince when the time came to confront Matt Mason.

'The future,' Vince said. 'See you and me, Dan, we don't matter much. Only what we can contribute to what's comin'.'

'Ye're a slander on life,' Dan said. He thought of himself and was generous enough not to exempt others from his condition. 'We're only even money tae have a future. You don't like people, Vince. You want to turn them intae ideas. Any future that has to sacrifice the present to get there isny worth goin' to. Don't save me a ticket.'

'Well, one thing I'm sure –'

'Anybody who's sure doesn't know, Vince.'

'That's pathetic, Dan.'

'So fair enough, Vince. Ah've got a lot on ma mind. Any chance ye could start yer revolution in the next street? An' if ye're gonny start it, could ye hurry up? Otherwise, Ah'm liable to miss it.'

Vince shrugged and took his pint across to check on one of the domino-tables. Dan watched Vince studying the dominoes as they were laid out, nodding to himself, as if he saw something in their partly accidental sequence that nobody else could see. That was Vince. He was nice enough but he lived inside his mind like an oxygen-tent. Everything had to submit to his conception of it, even the dominoes. It was as though ideas were his element, not air.

That would have been a nice place, inside an idea, but it wasn't a place to live. It was necessary to live where the idea and the fact collided. He was enjoying a pint and he was threatened with death. And he accepted Vince's term. He wasn't heroic, he was pathetic. Having chosen his place, he would struggle to live there as long as he could, by any means. He didn't want to die. Mortality was incurable. But given the space he had chosen, he would live with the disease as long as he could. If he had the chance, he wanted to die of old age. He was pathetic, but he believed in pathos. He believed in rheumy eyes and incontinence and hallucinations that the brisk middle-aged found quite distressing. He believed in the necessity of embarrassing those who think they know how life should be.

He was going to die. That was all. From the honesty of that admission the rest followed. If you didn't have control over your own life, you couldn't presume to have control over anyone else. If you did, you were cheating them of the reality that contained both of you. In the absolute fact of death was his morality.

Immorality lay in the refusal to share in the weakness of everyone, in the preparedness to pretend, for a day or a year or a lifetime, that you were different. It was self-deceit to pretend otherwise. You had to choose not to be victorious and to refuse to be defeated by anything smaller than death. That absolute humility implied a comparative arrogance. Matt Mason fell within the range of that arrogance. Dan Scoular was pathetic but he knew it. Matt Mason was pathetic but he didn't know it. Dan revelled in his pathos. It was his strength.

When Alistair Corstorphine came up to him and invited him to next year's Burns Supper in Liverpool, Dan accepted. Barney Farquharson, a local man, ran a hotel in Liverpool, and every year a busload of Thornbank men went down there for a Burns supper. Dan intended to be around to keep his promise.

But the thought that the future might not be his caused panic in him. Something Frankie White had said about Matt Mason came back and he knew he would live with it like a shadow: 'He would hide a week in yer coalhouse just to get ye.' Dan felt the proximity of Matt Mason. He was coming.

As the door of the pub swung, Dan clenched his hands and looked up quickly, knowing who it must be. It was Davie the Deaver. Dan lifted his glass to his mouth carefully, making sure his hand didn't shake, and took the last of his pint and glanced towards the domino players. Three of them winked like a chorus in slight disharmony.

'We'll get ye doon the road when ye're goin', Dan?' Harry Naismith said.

Dan smiled and nodded. In that moment he understood why the pub was so busy. The word was out from somewhere else, Frankie or Vince or Betty, as well as from Matt Mason. This wasn't a casual group of drinkers. It was an expression of solidarity. Looking around at their separate faces and postures, he sensed a disguised unity among them, an army in mufti. He thought that if somebody were to come to the door of the pub just now and summon him by name, a lot of these men would stand up in answer.

He thought of the moment outside the Black Chip disco. They knew more than their smiles and their clowning and their self-deprecation would readily admit. They were ready to share his pathos. He was glad to share theirs. The more who knew the truth, the more hope he had. Like them, he believed in the simple things he would try to do. If he could, he would watch his children grow up. He would be with Betty.

'Hey, Dan!' someone shouted. 'Ye goin' to stop laughin' so loud? Ah canny hear myself thinkin'.'

Some laughed and he was laughing too. He felt the joy of being here, whatever the terms. Tonight or tomorrow it might come. He wasn't unique in that. It was what his father had faced, and countless others. And when he spoke, his voice was an echo of the generations of people who had stood where he was standing.

'Ah'll have another pint when ye've time, Alan,' he said.